Triumph

PRAISE FOR HEATHER GRAHAM'S
BESTSELLING CIVIL WAR SAGA . . .

Glory

"A breathtaking story that encompasses every emotion, every human trial and triumph during a time of turbulence and change. Hurrah for Ms. Graham for bringing many little-known and fascinating historical events to life."   —*Romantic Times*

"Everyone who has read a Heather Graham Civil War novel knows they are in for a delightful reading experience. . . . *Glory* is another triumph for Ms. Graham."   —*Under the Covers Book Reviews*

"Compelling. . . . Graham sure does have a way with heroes."   —*The Romance Reader*

Surrender

"Refreshing, unique, classic. . . . Assured narratives, deft characterizations, and fast-moving plots are givens. Graham does it better than anyone!"
           —*Publishers Weekly*

"Wonderful characters . . . brilliant!"
           —Harriet Klausner for *Painted Rock Reviews*

continued on next page . . .

Drop Dead Gorgeous

Triumph

Heather Graham

A TOPAZ BOOK

To Donna Rausch
with lots of love, thanks, and
prayers for a beautiful lady.

SIGNET
Published by the Penguin Group
Penguin Putnam Inc., 375 Hudson Street, New York, New York 10014, U.S.A.
Penguin Books Ltd, 27 Wrights Lane, London W8 5TZ, England
Penguin Books Australia Ltd, Ringwood, Victoria, Australia
Penguin Books Canada Ltd, 10 Alcorn Avenue, Toronto, Ontario, Canada
M4V 3B2
Penguin Books (N.Z.) Ltd, 182–190 Wairau Road, Auckland 10, New Zealand

Penguin Books Ltd, Registered Offices: Harmondsworth, Middlesex, England

 REGISTERED TRADEMARK—MARCA REGISTRADA

Printed in the United States of America

PUBLISHER'S NOTE
This is a work of fiction. Names, characters, places, and incidents either
are the product of the author's imagination or are used fictitiously,
and any resemblance to actual persons, living or dead, business establish-
ments, events, or locales is entirely coincidental.

ISBN: 0-7394-0694-9

Triumph

Prologue

〜

Home Fires

Fall, 1864
The West Florida Coast, Near Tampa Bay

The sky was strange that night. Though dark, the lingering effects of a storm at dusk had left crimson streaks across the shadowy gray of the sky. A cloud passed over the moon, which seemed to glow with that strange red light. Tia McKenzie shivered, feeling an uneasy sense of fear and foreboding. Indeed, the color of the blood that stained a country torn apart seemed to touch the night, and the house that stood before her.

Ellington Manor had once been one of the finest examples of a large working plantation in the South. Once. Once the white-columned porches had borne fresh, snow-colored paint, and elegant ladies in their silk, satin, and velvet had swept up the stairs of the Greco-Federal home, had laughed, teased, danced, flirted, and prayed for the right Southern boy to come along.

Then had come the time when Southern troops had trained on the lawn, and Southern boys had given out their boastful battle cries, and in time, all those good Southern boys who had graced the steps along with the beautiful girls had been called forth to war. There they had fought, and there, by the tens of thousands, they had died.

Looking up at the now decaying, weed-covered facade of Ellington Manor, Tia felt a familiar pain sweep through her. She had come here often as a girl. She had danced here, laughed here, and imagined the world to come. Now the lawn was overgrown, the paint was gray and cracked and faded, the dense Florida foliage was encroaching, steps were broken, windows smashed, and spiders spun their webs where once youthful trysts had taken place. Old Captain Ellington had died early on at Manassas, and young Captain Ellington, who should have inherited the house, had died at Shiloh. Not even his bones had come back. Miss Liza Ellington had loved her family home and would have never let it come to this ruin, but she had gone forth to war as well, contracted measles while nursing boys at a camp outside Richmond, and died there. Her remains, at least, had come home, and lay beneath the marble angel in the family graveyard behind the main house.

Yet tonight, there was a small beacon of light within. Colonel Raymond Weir, Florida regulars, had come. Her friend, her countryman. Once upon a time, he had been a boy upon those steps, flirting with the girl that Tia had been. She had seen him since then, and she knew that he had lost none of his youthful ardor for her. Indeed, with time, his feelings had become something deeper, while she, herself, should have been in sympathy with his cause if not his intent—he meant to burn out a known Union sympathizer.

Yes, she should have understood. She should have shared his fury. Except that . . .

The Union sympathizer was her father.

Tia could hear the sounds of men and horses from the dilapidated outbuildings to the south of the main house. Weir's men were here, preparing to attack. Just as she had been warned. Five companies of them, ten to twenty men remaining alive within each of those companies. They were to ride out at Weir's command, eating the miles between here and Cimarron—her father's property, her home. The house was to be burned to the ground. Her father, should he survive the shelling, was to be given a mock trial and executed. While her mother . . . well, word was that Weir would turn a blind eye to whatever might become of the devoted wife of such a traitor. Raymond Weir was a Confederate officer taking military law into his own hands. This was what the war had become.

The soldiers had yet to see Tia; she had come alone. She had watched the house, biding her time. She was afraid tonight, afraid as she had never been before. In the last few years of the war, she had grown hardened and wary, but she had also learned courage—sometimes by accident. Tonight would be no accident. She had to stop Raymond, or at the least, delay him. Help would come, but only in time, because between her family and her state, life was divided. Her father was a Unionist, her brother Ian a Yankee hero. She and her other brother, Julian, a year younger than Ian, were ardent Rebs. Once she had believed in her cause with all the passion in her heart, but that was when the war had been fought on more decent ground, when honor had still meant something to men in both blue and gray.

She had left an urgent message for her Rebel brother to get hold of her Yankee brother, and she knew that help would arrive at her father's home. For a moment she breathed deeply, bitterly regretting that she could not call upon another Yank, but there was no help for it—he was fighting in the North—and if she'd possibly had the time to reach him, she wouldn't have known where to do so. It was only because Ian's wife had just had another baby that she dared to hope he had reached Florida, and would receive her message. So she'd come here herself. She had no choice. She had to buy time.

How? she asked herself for the thousandth time. How? All things *could* be done, she reminded herself. She had ridden from the camp alone, traveled nearly a hundred miles in just a few days—alone. How ironic, for her father would be furious; the men in her life would all be furious. But still—how could she waylay Raymond Weir?

Then the answer came back the same as it had each time she had asked herself.

Any way that she could. Tonight, she wasn't a Rebel. She'd done enough in the name of the great "Cause." Played dangerous games, begun by sheer chance perhaps, but perpetuated in the name of all that she had held dear—honor and freedom, and what few pathetic, battered lives she might save. And she had paid a strange, anguishing price for those efforts, swore she'd not ride out again . . . but tonight . . .

She couldn't back down. *Her father . . .*

Yet playing her very strange role in the war had been one thing. She had hurt no one except herself. While now . . .

What she planned was wrong. *She didn't want to do it . . .*

Stop. No time for morality, no time for thoughts of honor—or even promises given at another time when the world had seemed to spin too quickly. She couldn't stop the war. Nor could she help the fact that love must come before battle—she would die for her parents, for her brothers, for any member of her family. But she didn't intend to die here tonight.

No! Merely trade her heart and immortal soul for the lives of those she loved.

She was grimly aware of how it might all go. Weir would see her, of course. He had said that he would always do so. Perhaps he would allow her to plead and beg and flirt . . .

Then he would apologize, tell her that he was sorry, but her father was a traitor born and bred, to be hanged that very night if not shot down dead . . .

He would think himself the victor—he wouldn't know that she had bought the time she needed, all that she had come for that night. Her father employed a lot of men—black, white, Seminoles, Creeks, Germans, Irish, and more—in his defense. But Weir had made arrangements to meet up with another cavalry unit from the north of the state. Her father would fight, but his forces would be overwhelmed unless his Yankee son or some other soldiers—friend or supposed foe—brought reinforcements before the battle commenced.

Now. Time to move. To act.

Tia nudged her horse, moving quickly and quietly forward into the front yard. She rode straight to the steps that had once graced so many a lighthearted soiree. There, in a pool of light cast out from within, she slipped from her horse's back and started to the porch.

"Halt!" commanded a thick voice, and a slim picket stepped from the shadows to accost her. "Madame, what—"

"I need to see Colonel Weir, sir. You may tell him that Tia—"

"Why, Miss McKenzie!" the man gasped, recognizing her, his gaunt cheeks turning red. "Why, yes, Miss Tia, I'll tell him right away. It's Thackery, ma'am. I met you at General Roper's ball, soon after the battle of Olustee."

"Oh yes, good evening, sir." Thankfully, she did have a reputation as a devoted Rebel herself, despite her father's being a Unionist. But the way the man looked at her, with a gaze between guilt and pity, she knew he had to be wondering if she was aware of their purpose that night. She shouldn't have been, except that a soldier who had seen her own sacrifices had told her about the treacherous plan. The official government had long ago determined to leave her father be. His empathy for the Union was known, but he had chosen to practice a staunch neutrality throughout the war. Soldiers from both sides had, upon occasion, found a haven for a dying man there. Cimarron cattle had fed a number of Yanks, yes, but their cows had often fed the Confederacy as well. Tia dug her fingers into her palms. This was an act of judgment by a few men with power and troops, a depredation, one that must be stopped.

Thackery opened the front door to the house and started in. Tia followed him, despite the fact that he had surely wanted her to wait.

Raymond Weir was standing before the fireplace, hands clasped at his back. His uniform was threadbare, but very properly worn. He was tall, a formidable man with long blond locks, bright blue, seemingly all-seeing eyes, and a handsome face now richly darkened by the sun, despite his cavalry hat. He turned quickly at the sound of their entry, frowning as he saw her.

"Colonel, sir, Miss—"

"Tia!" Raymond exclaimed. Then he gazed sternly at Thackery. "Private, I haven't time tonight for visitors. Especially Miss McKenzie."

"Don't blame your soldier," Tia said quickly. "I followed him without permission."

"I can't see you now, Tia," he said gravely, and had the grace to flush. "I have business this evening. What are you doing here? I'd heard you were with Julian."

"I was heading home," she lied, meeting his eyes, "and I heard you were in the area." She hesitated. What was she going to do? "I felt I had to see you!" she declared passionately.

Raymond looked at her, then past her to his soldier. "You may leave us, Private Thackery."

"Are there orders, sir? For the men?"

"When the time is right, I'll give the orders, Private."

"Aye, sir!"

The private saluted sharply, then turned to exit the house. The heavy wooden front door closed behind him. Raymond stared at Tia. She held her ground, returning his stare. A log snapped on the fire. He lifted a hand toward a sideboard that held a crystal decanter.

"Tia . . ." he murmured softly, emotion naked in his voice. Then he cleared his throat. "We've nothing so fine as sherry to offer, Tia, but I imagine you've become accustomed to the coarser taste of a good Kentucky bourbon over the years?"

"Before the war, sir, I became familiar with Kentucky bourbon," she said and walked to the decanter, pouring out shots for both of them, the larger for him. She walked to him boldly then, offering the larger whiskey. He took it from her, studying her with longing—and suspicion. Once, he had courted her properly, flattered her to no end. She had flirted with him, entranced by his attention. He was a striking man, as impassioned about the South and their state as she had once been herself. She still loved her state, but she loved her father more. She had come to despise Weir.

"So," he said, not touching his whiskey, "why have you come?"

"Because . . . I heard you were here," she said, staying close. She had to hope that he hadn't heard rumors regarding her relationship with a certain Yankee. She had to keep Raymond here. Stall him. Play out this charade!

Oh, God. She was going to go to hell. And maybe quite soon—if Taylor were ever to discover what she was doing this night.

She didn't dare think about that now. Steady blue eyes were upon her. "As I said," Raymond reminded her, "I have business tonight, I'm afraid. Tell me—why have you come?"

This was it! The time to act, and act well, she warned herself. And so she lowered her head, fingering her glass of bourbon. "I have come because . . ." *Why?* "Because I have seen too much death. I thought my work with Julian was so important . . . but I . . ." She looked up, amazed that she had managed to bring a glistening of tears to her eyes. "I have realized that life, so precious, slips away too quickly. We can't be obliged to hold to the same restraints that might govern us were the world more fair. Time has new meaning, sir, as does life itself. I have come to regret my . . ."

Her voice trailed off. The whiskey was suddenly taken from her fingers, set upon the mantelpiece with his own empty glass. He held her hands tightly, staring into her eyes. "You regret your refusal to marry me? Can it be?"

She lowered her head again, nodding. *Yes, of course, that was it. They could have a marriage ceremony. That would take time!*

He lifted her chin. "I will still marry you, Tia. In a heartbeat. I have always thought you were the most beautiful, compelling creature in the world. Before the war, I was taken with your dreams, with your fierce desire to see the world, to know people and places. And since the war, I have seen your dedication, your devotion, your courage. I have always been in love with you, will always be in love with you. And yet . . ."

His voice trailed of. *And yet,* she thought, *you would*

hang my father, you bastard! Maybe he didn't realize that although she disagreed with her father, she had never been his enemy. Too many fathers, sons, brothers, and cousins had faced one another down with rifles and bayonets in this war. She loved her father. More than any cause, dream, or ideal.

"Tia . . . tonight, tonight I'm afraid I can't. Duty demands my time."

She touched his cheek gently with her fingertips, meeting his eyes. "Duty can wait. I've learned that war will go on—and so it can wait. You're right. I'm so sorry I refused you. It was a mistake. Marry me now, right now!" she urged him.

He shook his head sadly. "My troops ride without a priest or any manner of minister," he told her. "There is no one to marry us. I cannot tell you how very sorry I am, since you will come to your senses after this night and want no more to do with me again."

"Why would that be?" she asked softly, trying not to let him see how desperately she searched for another way to stall him.

He stared down at her, hesitating. He apparently believed that she didn't know the truth regarding his plans for the evening. It would never occur to him that what he planned was so wrong that he had been betrayed by a Southern soldier. "The things we must do in this war . . . we never know what the future will bring, do we?"

"It has been the war, the things I have done, the way I feel that I must serve until the end that have caused me to give up all hope of personal commitment," she told him. No, he didn't know the truth of her life either. Few men did. Those who knew had sworn themselves to secrecy. Anonymous in her deeds, she was a heroine. If the truth were known . . .

Taylor knew! she reminded herself. *And she had sworn to cease her part in the war. She had tried to do so. But now, now, here she was . . .*

"So you have loved me, too?" he queried with a hopeful doubt.

She forced a tender smile. "You are handsome, sir, a gallant cavalier of my own beliefs. What is there not to love? I thought that I had nothing to give until the war ended, but I've come to realize that so much is stolen from us, so many sweethearts will never know their lover's embrace . . ."

"My God, what a pity I have to leave!"

"No!"

She stopped, breathless, gritting her teeth very hard and looking at Raymond again. "Ray, I came tonight because I'm afraid of the future, afraid that I'll never experience life fully. I earnestly desire to take what . . . happiness I may before it is snatched from me."

He smiled, yet the sadness remained in his smile.

"I told you; I have to leave," he said with weary resolution. "The war—and death—beckon to me, even now."

"You mustn't leave me . . . not yet!" she insisted desperately.

"Yes, I must—"

"Not now, when we've both been so honest. When . . . death is always so near. You mustn't go, not when . . . not when I simply crave . . ."

"Yes?"

She opened her eyes wide upon his. She was losing him. She must do something. She couldn't . . . she had to. She spoke softly. "I want to know . . . love." The world seemed to spin.

"My God . . ." he breathed. Then he frowned. "Tia, do you know what you're saying?"

"Yes, as I know that you will ride out tonight, die for the Cause if you must, and I will then grow into a bitter old maid, without ever having tasted . . . life."

"My God . . ." he breathed again.

Then his lips were on hers and he crushed her to him. The strength of his hold, the ardor of his kiss were overwhelming. For a minute, she felt a rise of panic. Of revulsion. She could not do this. She wanted to scream. Then she reminded herself that any price, any despicable act must become her willing sin, for her father's life was at stake.

She drew herself from his arms, though, again alarmed at the strength within them. She looked toward the door, hesitating. There had to be a way to buy more time. "Isn't there a place more private?" she whispered.

"Yes. Upstairs, one bedroom has been swept, the bed remade with fresh linens found in a chest. I rested there earlier."

She nodded, slipped from his hold, and started for the stairs.

Just then, the front door burst open, and Private Thackery entered the parlor. Raymond stiffened, reminded of his quest that night. "Colonel, sir, the men grow restless. They—"

"I will be right with them," Raymond said with a sigh.

Silently, Tia swore to herself. She was losing him. She must not. Where she stood now, high against the wall of the stairway, only Raymond could see her. She loosened her long dark hair from the twist at her nape, her eyes meeting his. One by one, she began to unbutton the ceaseless closures on her bodice. She had done this too often, she thought a bit hysterically. She was becoming far too adept with buttons. She needed to slow down.

Ray was staring at her, then he looked from her back to his soldier. He was wavering. She almost had him.

"Sir!" Thackery said.

Thankfully, she had greatly reduced the amount of clothing she wore in the last years of privation. Ray started to turn away again. No. She slipped the bodice from her shoulders, her eyes riveted on his, and waited, bare-breasted, determined that he would not leave her.

Raymond looked back to Private Thackery.

"The time is not quite right. Thirty minutes; I will be with the men in thirty minutes. Tell them to be ready to ride at that time." *Thirty minutes! Would it be enough? If Ian had gotten her message, he would ride straight to Cimarron. He would have ridden across the state faster than she. Tia would delay the attack as long as she could.*

Private Thackery exited.

"Yes, by God, privacy. You, alone . . ." he said.

Tia continued up the steps, her heart slamming against her chest. A knife. She should have brought a knife. She could have executed him as he had intended to execute her father. But she didn't think that she could kill a man in cold blood. Not this way. If she were facing a man with a gun while she stood on her father's property, surely, she could shoot to kill. But murder, in this manner . . . It didn't matter anyway; she didn't have a knife.

"To the right," Raymond said. He was behind her, just inches away. She continued down the hallway, veering to the right as he had instructed.

She thought she heard a sound. Something. Movement in the house. Perhaps it was the whisper of the wind against the rattling, decaying old manse. Or perhaps she was at last losing her mind, fearing that God would strike her down for this act.

"The door there," Raymond said. Apparently, he had heard nothing. Her imagination.

She entered a room. Moonlight, still that strange, unearthly shade of red, filtered through the open drapes. Once, this room had belonged to the master here. A handsome mantel stood against the left wall. A large bed faced the windows with their fluttering, now tattered draperies.

"The bed is clean, the sheets are fresh, tended by my men," Raymond said softly.

"So you said," Tia whispered. And suddenly, she could do nothing but stand there, watching the eerie color of the night spill upon the room. She felt very cold. She started to shake, Oh God, of all the things that she had done, this was the worst.

"My love . . ." A whisper, and Raymond was behind her, swiftly. His hands moved upon her bare arms. He drew her against him. His lips touched her neck. She clenched down on her teeth, hating him. He shifted the fall of her hair, pressed his mouth to her shoulder. Then she felt his fingers on the tiny buttons that closed her skirt, felt it fall away, felt his fingers then entwine on the cord that held her pantalettes, and then they, too, had fallen, and the strange, bloodred dusting of moonbeams fell upon the length of her bare flesh. It had been all too easy for him. She needed more time!

"Come, my love . . ."

Come. Good God, how could she endure his touch when she had known another . . .

"Look at the moon!" she entreated, walking toward the window.

"Tia, the moon, like the war, will come again."

"It's a beautiful moon, yet shaded in red—"

"There's no time for talk."

His scabbard and sword were cast aside. His cavalry jacket and shirt were shed.

"I need another drink, Raymond. This is new to me."

"Madam," he said curtly, running his fingers through his hair. She had denied him too long in life, she realized. And now that she had offered him what he had so long wanted, he had no more patience. "I remind you— you invited me to this room. Shall I leave?"

"No! You mustn't leave!"

He lifted her, bore her down on the bed. He rose above her; his eyes met hers. Her heart hammered; she couldn't breathe, couldn't follow through with this. She was going to scream, to laugh, scream, beat against him . . .

"My love!" he said again, and kissed her fingertips.

"My—love," she whispered in return, but she choked on the words, fighting the tears that suddenly stung her eyes with a vengeance. She had to stop this; she could go no further. *My love! She had heard those words before. Spoken in another man's voice . . .*

"Oh, good God!"

The furious, mocking exclamation suddenly exploded from the shadows.

In another man's voice!

A deep-timbred voice, husky and mocking, suddenly thundered out of the red-coated darkness in the room. Not just another man's voice—*his* voice.

Yes, his. It couldn't be! She was losing her mind; she
had recalled that voice from memory, and brought with
her memory the flesh-and-blood appearance of the man.
Oh, God, her guilt had played havoc with her mind—he
couldn't possibly be here. But he was. And he had been
here, following them through the shadowed house!

Yes, he was here. She saw only a shadow then, hovering above her, but she knew it was him. She knew his
voice so well—knew it in laughter, taunting, as he
taunted now. She'd known it gentle upon rare occasions,
and sometimes, oh God, yes, sometimes she'd known it
in fury, as furious as it was now, as dangerous as the
portents of the bloodred color that danced upon the
moon.

She froze. Her blood seemed to congeal, colder than
ice. She felt Raymond atop her. Felt her own nakedness.
Taylor's deep voice struck her again like a whip.

"That's it—I've had it with this charade!" Taylor announced. And then she saw his towering form more
clearly, and she felt the fiery tension of his very presence. *Felt! Oh, God, she couldn't look his way!*

"What in the name of the Almighty?" Raymond demanded. "Taylor! You!" he spat out.

But the sound of steel could suddenly be heard in the
room, and in the eerie touch of moonlight, Tia saw a
flash of silver—and the touch of a sword at Raymond's
throat.

"Stop. Stop right now!" Tia cried. The sword rested
just at Raymond's jugular. Taylor's eyes remained riveted upon Tia as he gritted his teeth.

"Ah, good, I have your attention," Taylor said.

She should die right now, Tia thought.

Because certainly, *he* would kill her later.

She closed her eyes, praying that the night itself would
disappear. *He* was not supposed to be here; he was supposed to be in the North! Good God, if she'd imagined
he was near, she would have swallowed all pride and
thrown herself on his mercy, begging his assistance
rather than chancing this desperate game she now
played. She knew that he would have helped her father.

"I'm sorry," Taylor said, "but this charming little domestic adventure has gone quite far enough. Colonel Weir, if you will please rise carefully."

"Damn you, Taylor Douglas! You'll die for this. I swear it! How did you get in?" Weir demanded, rising, swallowing down his fury at the interruption—by a hated enemy.

"I entered by the door, Captain."

Thankfully, Tia thought, the scene was not as wretched as it might have been. Raymond Weir's trousers were still in place. But then again . . .

The point of Taylor's sword suddenly lay between Tia's breasts.

"Tia, get up. And for the love of God, get some clothing on. I grow weary of finding you naked everywhere I go—other than in our marital bed, of course."

"Marital bed!" Raymond repeated, stunned.

"Ah, poor fellow, you are indeed surprised. A fact that might spare your life, though I had thought of you before as something of an honorable man, just a fanatic. But yes, I did say marital bed. You hadn't heard? Though it grieves me deeply to admit, the lady is a liar and a fraud. She can marry no one for she is already married. She is wily, indeed, a vixen from the day we met. All for the Southern Cause, of course. She will play her games! But what of that great cause now, Tia?"

Humiliated, Tia braced herself against the fury behind the sarcasm in his words. *What would he do?* She'd sworn not to play the role she'd managed to make quite famous when they'd first met. Well, tonight, she had not ridden as the Lady Godiva. She'd tested his temper before. Never like this. But he *had* sent her home, sent her *away*. And he hadn't written, or even sent word.

And she'd had no choice in this!

So thinking, and finding refuge in anger herself, she caught the tip of his blade and cast the sword aside as she leapt from the bed. She wanted so desperately to find some dignity in this situation—difficult when she stumbled desperately in her search for all her clothing.

She could feel her husband watching her. She was amazed he hadn't simply killed her.

"Tia?" Raymond said, and the sudden streak of naked pain in his voice gave her so much pause that she had to remind herself that he had meant to kill her father. "You are *married* to him."

"Yes."

"But you came to me . . . tonight!" he rasped out, wanting to believe that she had desired him.

"You were going to attack Cimarron," she said, adding bitterly, "and kill my father."

Raymond shook his head. "Your father . . . no, Tia. I meant to seize the property, nothing more."

"That's not true! My father was to be killed—executed."

Yes, it was true. The truth of it was in Weir's eyes. He was, in his strange way, an honorable man, and found lying difficult. "I would have spared his life—for you!"

"How touching," Taylor interrupted, his voice a drawl that didn't hide his fury. "Tell me, Tia, was that explanation for him—or me?"

She moistened her lips to speak, but she was too hurt, angry, and ashamed to address Taylor. *I would have come to you!* she wanted to cry. *But I didn't know where you were, and there was no time! You must understand, my father's life is at risk . . .*

She couldn't explain. She lashed out instead. "Taylor, you're being a truly wretched bastard. You don't understand anything!" she screamed, her fingers trembling so hard she couldn't get her buttons fastened. Both men were staring at her.

She'd made a mistake with her bitter words, she quickly realized, for Raymond suddenly made a split second decision to defend her honor.

Her honor. It was laughable, for she had none left.

But Raymond made a dive for the sword he had so hastily discarded in his eagerness to be with her. He barely drew it from the sheath before the sound of crashing steel erupted in the night. Raymond's sword went flying across the room, and the tip of Taylor's blade was once again pressed to the Rebel's throat.

"Taylor!" Tia cried out, and at last dared look at her husband. "Don't . . . murder him. Please!"

No, she had never seen such anger, so barely controlled. They had met and clashed before, they had argued, indeed, the war had never burned more brightly than between them. But this . . . fury that now compelled him was such that she longed to shrink away, to run, to flee. Indeed, death itself would be far easier than facing what she must. He was tall, standing an even inch above Raymond, so filled with tension that the constriction of his muscles seemed evident even beneath the cut of his blue cavalry frockcoat. His eyes, a striking, curious hazel seemed to burn tonight with a red-gold fire as deadly as the haze about the moon. His features, very strongly and handsomely formed, were taut with his efforts to control the sheer fire of his anger.

She wanted so badly to cry out to him again. She had no words, but she wanted the anguish in her voice to convey what had been in her heart.

"Please, don't . . ." she said simply.

Those eyes rested upon her. Fire in the night.

Then Taylor gazed back at Raymond. "I've no intention of doing murder, sir. We are all forced to kill in battle, but I'll not be a cold-blooded murderer. I've yet to kill any man over a harlot, even if that harlot be my own wife."

Tia felt as if she'd been slapped, struck with an icy hand. And yet it was at that precise moment that she realized their situation. Good God! The yard was filled with soldiers! Rebel soldiers, enemies who could take Taylor down, *murder him,* without a thought!

"Call me what you will," she cried, "but your life is in danger here, and you fool, there is much more at stake! There are nearly a hundred men outside preparing to march on my father's house— "

"No, Tia, no longer," Taylor said, and his gaze focused upon her again. "The men below have been seized. Taken entirely by surprise. Quite a feat, if I do say so myself. Not a life lost, Colonel," he informed Raymond.

"So you'll not murder me. What then?" Raymond asked.

"I believe my men are coming for you now, if you would like to don your shirt and coat."

Raymond nodded, reaching for his shirt and frockcoat. The latter was barely slipped over his shoulders before two men appeared in the doorway. Yankee soldiers.

"To the ship, Colonel?" asked one of the men, a bearded, blond-headed fellow of perhaps twenty-five.

"Aye, Lieutenant Riley. Have Captain Maxwell take the lot of them north. Meet me with the horses below when the prisoners have been secured."

"Sir?" the lieutenant said politely to Raymond.

Raymond looked at Tia. He bowed deeply to her. She dared do nothing but look back. The perfect soldier, Raymond accepted the situation—and the metal restraints slipped on his wrists by his Yankee captors. They departed the room.

She remained dead still, waiting. She couldn't face Taylor. She wanted to cry out again, burst into tears, throw herself into his arms . . .

If he were to kill her, would anyone blame him? She had put his life in danger often enough, willingly at first—he was, after all, the enemy.

Or had been.

And he would never believe that she hadn't wanted to do what she'd done tonight, that the ties he had bound around her had been there, invisible but strong, a web he had woven that held her with far greater strength than the piece of paper that proclaimed them man and wife. She had fought him so often. Now, when she wanted peace, to pray for his forgiveness, he stared at her with no mercy.

But could that matter now? she asked herself. *She had prayed that Ian would come, her brother the enemy, with his Yankee troops, and he might have been the one to fight and save his inheritance. Ian hadn't come; Taylor*

*had, and he would make her father safe. Cimarron would
be saved. She had been willing to pay any price . . .*

And this, it seemed, was the price.

So she braced herself. Waiting, at least, for a blow to
fall. For him to touch her with some violence. She could
feel it in him, feel it in the air, the way he must long to
hurt her!

He came to her. Powerful hands gripped her shoulders, his fingers biting into her flesh. She met his eyes.
His arm moved, as if he would strike her with all the
force of his fury.

No blow fell. He pushed her from him. She closed her
eyes, shaking, looking for the right words to tell him that
she hadn't wanted to come here, that she would have
come to him . . .

She heard him turn from her, walk away, head for
the stairs.

She didn't know what foolhardy demon stirred her
then, but she found herself flying after him.

She caught him upon the stairs, stumbling to get ahead
of him, to force him to face her. And then she couldn't
speak, she stuttered, faltered, and tried again. "Taylor,
I—I—they said he meant to kill my father."

"Step aside, Tia," he said simply.

"Taylor, damn you! I had to come here, I had to do
what I could to stop him. Can't you see that, don't
you understand?"

He stood dead still then, staring at her with eyes still
seeming to burn with the red-gold blaze of the ghostly,
blood-haunted night. She had lost him, she thought. Lost
him. Just when she had begun to realize . . .

"I understand, *my love,* that you were ready, willing,
and able to sleep with another man. But then, Weir is a
good Southern soldier, is he not? A proper planter, a
fitting beau for the belle of Cimarron, indeed, someone
you have loved just a little for a very long time. How
convenient."

"No, I—"

"No?" His voice alone seemed to make her the most
despicable liar.

"Yes, you know that—*once* we were friends. But I . . ." She broke off, fighting the wave of tears that rushed to her eyes now. What was it? He was the enemy! And yet, staring into the gold steel of his eyes, feeling him there above her, knowing his anger, knowing how he leashed it now, knowing the scent of him . . . and remembering . . . the touch of his fingertips on her skin . . .

And she knew then, quite startlingly, clearly, despite the circumstance, just how very much she loved him. Had, for quite some time. Neither duty, debt, nor honor had given her pause tonight. It had been the way she felt about him, loved him, him, only him.

"Please!" she whispered.

He slowly arched a dark brow. And then he reached out, touching her cheek. "Please? Please what? Are you sorry, afraid? Or would you seduce me, too? Perhaps I'm not such easy prey, for I am, at least, familiar with the treasure offered, and I have played the game to a great price already. When I saw you tonight . . . do you know what I first intended to do? Throttle you, you may be thinking! Beat you black and blue. Well that, yes. Where pride and emotions are involved, men do think of violence. But I thought to do more. Clip your feathers, my love. Cut off those ebony locks and leave you shorn and costumeless, as it were—*naked* would not be the right word. But what if I were to sheer away these lustrous tresses? Would you still be about seducing men—friend and foe—to save your precious family and state? Not again, for until this war of ours is finished, I will have you hobbled—until your fate can be decided."

Hobbled . . . *imprisoned.* Did he really intend to make her a prisoner of war? He had threatened it before. It didn't seem to matter now. Too much had gone too far out of control.

"I—have seduced no one else. I . . ." She was again amazed that tears threatened to choke off her speech. "I'm not a harlot, Taylor!" she managed to whisper. Her eyes met his.

Then she gasped, startled and afraid, for he suddenly

reached out for her, drawing her into his arms. His lips were punishing as they crashed down upon hers, forcing her mouth apart, kissing her deeply, with passion, with anger . . . regret, perhaps, a tumultuous series of emotions that left her shaking, bruised . . . and longing for more. His fingers threaded into her hair, arching her neck. His palm cradled her cheek, fingertips stroked her throat and beyond, his touch then seeking more of her, tracing the form of her body beneath the thin cotton fabric of her bodice. She felt his fingers over her breast, his palm encompassing, thumb rubbing over her nipple, stroking, eliciting. A sweet weakness pervaded her. She wanted to fall against him, feel again a time she had known once at war . . . and let it become peace. She would have gladly given herself into his arms. She wished, prayed, that his anger would cause him to sweep her up, carry her back up the stairs to the scene of her almost-sin, and there, assert his right to be with her, punish her with a wild ravishment, remind her that she had sworn to be his, enemy or no . . .

Yet he pushed away from her. "Ah, Tia, what a pity! I'm not at all sure of your motives at the moment, but for once, when you are apparently ready to become a willing wife with no argument to give me, there remains too much at stake for me to take advantage of your remorse. There's a battle still to be waged."

She drew back, frowning. "A battle? But you've stopped Captain Weir from the war he would wage against my father."

"Tia, you little fool! Weir was only a half of it! There's a Major Hawkins with militia from the panhandle who will bear down upon Cimarron at any moment now. I don't know if Ian ever received word of this, or if Julian knows somehow. You apparently learned about it. But I may be the only help your father will have."

She stared at him, stunned. "Dear God! I'd forgotten there would be more troops. I've got to get home!" she cried, and she turned, running frantically down the remaining steps.

"No! Tia!"

She didn't make it to burst out into the night. She was caught.

By the long ebony flow of her hair. How ironic.

She cried out, but found herself whirled back inexorably into his arms. Meeting his eyes. Again, they were fire. Fire, and fury. His fingers bit into her as he held her. "You're going nowhere."

"My father—my home—"

"Your enemy will save them for you," he informed her bitterly.

"No, please, you have to let me ride with you. I beg of you, Taylor, in this, I swear, I—"

"Make me no more promises, Tia, for I am weary of you breaking them."

"But I swear—"

"This fight will be deadly, and I'll not have you seized by either side as a pawn in the battles to be waged."

"Please!" she begged, but even as she desperately entreated him, the front door burst open. She didn't turn. Her eyes locked with his. She heard soldiers, and knew his men had come—for her.

"Gentlemen, take my wife to the ship, please. They'll not be surprised to find another McKenzie prisoner at Old Capitol."

One of the soldiers cleared his throat politely. "Mrs. Douglas, if you will . . ."

She lowered her head, stepping away from Taylor's hold. He released her all too quickly.

She looked up at him again. "No!" she said softly. Then she cried out, "No!" and she turned, and did so with such speed and with so great an element of surprise that she was able to tear past the two Yankee soldiers who had come for her.

She raced down the steps. Those faded steps where ghostly couples had danced and laughed in days gone by.

She called out for her horse, and, thank God, Blaze, her blessed, wondrous mare, trotted in from the trees, just as Taylor burst out behind her.

She leapt upon her horse. Taylor wouldn't shoot her

down. And no one else could catch her. No one had such a mount. Except, of course . . .

Taylor himself.

"Home, girl, home!" she told Blaze, nudging the animal.

She lowered herself to her horse's haunches and sped into the night. She knew the trails. They were the paths of her youth.

Soon, the light of the house faded behind her. Only the bloodstained moon remained high above to illuminate the night.

The earth seemed to tremble; mud flew. She felt the great workings of the animal beneath her as they raced. And then she realized that she wasn't alone in the night, that *he* had come in pursuit, that he was almost upon her, with his men following behind.

"Please, God!" she prayed to the night. She had to get home. She had to see her mother, her father, Cimarron. "Please, God . . . !"

But God was not with her. Taylor was an expert horseman; he leapt from his own mount to hers, drawing in on the reins. She twisted on the mount, trying to fight him. Her efforts brought them both crashing down from the horse to the ground. She tried to rise, tried to fight again. He caught her flailing fists, pinned them to the ground, straddled her. Again she felt his eyes, and his fury, and still she gazed up at him desperately. "Please, Taylor, please, for the love of God . . ."

He stared down at her, gold fire in his eyes, and she was suddenly reminded that this was the way that they had met, on a night when a legend was born.

"Please, please!" she whispered. "Bring me home! Let me be there. Bring me home tonight. I'll stay by your side, obey your every command! I'll surrender, I'll cease to ride, I'll turn myself in to Old Capitol, I'll put a noose around my own neck, I swear it, Taylor, please, I'll—"

"Love, honor, and obey?" he demanded harshly, a tremor of some dark emotion in his voice.

And she realized that he, too, was thinking that this night was ironically similar to the one in which they had met. Was he wishing that he had never come across her in the woods?

He was suddenly on his feet, drawing her up. "You'll ride with me!" he told her harshly. "And go where I command, stay away from all fire! Blaze can follow on her own—she knows the way."

"Yes!" she promised, and she was amazed at first that he would show her this much mercy after what she had done, but realized then that if they didn't ride now, ride straight, ride hard, they would not reach her father's property in time.

As it was, they raced the horses almost to death. She rode before him, and yet twisted enough to estimate the strength of the troops following behind them. Sixty to eighty men. How many had come against Cimarron? Would Ian make it home? Would there be other help?

The night sky remained bathed in blood. Indeed, when they neared Cimarron, coming from the south below the river that would be one line of defense, the white plantation house itself was steeped in the blood.

And ahead! Far ahead, defenses had been erected against the river and men were already busy at the work of battle, shouting, taking places behind newly erected earthworks. She could hear her father shouting orders; she could see men running to obey. His workmen, and men in blue and . . .

Men in gray. *Both* of her brothers had made it here, she saw. Her heart was suddenly warmed. *Even in this horror, blood was thicker than water, friendship mattered, and a good man was a good man!*

Then she froze.

Tia saw her mother, her beautiful mother, still lithe and slim and golden blond, racing hard across the lawn with some all-important missive for her father. A foreboding filled her.

Someone, a defender at the rear of her father's house, called out, accosting Taylor's party as they approached the yard. "Halt, or be shot!"

"It's Colonel Douglas, here to defend with the McKenzies!" Taylor shouted, sliding down from his mount.

Beneath the bloodred sky, Tia could see soldiers loading a half-score of Enfield rifles onto a gunboat positioned on the river. Most of the men at Cimarron were behind the earthworks. Her mother was not. Tia jumped from Friar before Taylor realized her intent.

"Mother!" she shrieked, racing across the lawn.

"Tia!" she heard Taylor shout, his voice harsh with a desperate warning. "Tia!" she heard him shout again, and she knew he ran after her in pursuit. But she couldn't stop. Her mother was in danger. She had nearly reached Tara, who was still unaware of the soldiers taking aim at the earthworks.

Again, she saw the soldiers, heard the chain of command to fire . . .

She reached Tara, threw herself before her, trying to bring them both down.

"Tia!" her mother exclaimed, just before she heard the roar of the guns.

Fire tore into her.

In a field of crimson, she clung to her mother.

Then they were falling, falling . . . crashing to the earth together.

Dimly, she heard the cry that tore from Taylor's lips. She heard his shouts, the fire that emitted from his Colts in rapid succession. Then, he was beside her, on his knees, and she was staring into his eyes. Fire eyes, as gold as a blaze, eyes that had condemned her, held her, imprisoned her, and now . . .

She reached up to touch his cheek. His striking, powerful, ruggedly beautiful face was blurring before her. It seemed that her whole life began to flash before her eyes . . . no, not *her* life but the life that he had given her, filled with tempest, trouble, passion, fury . . . oh, yes, fury, but still life with a soul, with spirit, with love—

Their life . . .

Before the war had come here tonight, to Cimarron.

Chapter 1

〜

A House Divided

Winter, 1863
Eleven Months Earlier

"Tia! Tia! Miss Tia! There's someone coming!"

Tia McKenzie froze at the sound of alarm in Private Jemmy Johnson's voice as it filtered to her through the trees.

"Ma'am!" he whispered desperately. She heard him clear his throat. "I don't mean to interrupt your privacy, but . . ."

Here she was, totally vulnerable in a manner in which she had seldom been since the war had begun, and someone was coming.

"Miss Tia, I know you're . . . in an awkward state, but . . ."

Awkward? To say the least.

Ah, yes, "buck" naked, as the boys called such a state of complete undress. She had thought that they were deep enough inland to avoid the contact of any troops, indeed, any human inhabitants of the state, much less the movement of enemy troops.

These days, it was apparently no longer possible. New strategies were afoot. Right when they were most beleaguered by illness, malnutrition, and a lack of medical supplies, the enemy had chosen to make a new assault, hoping to cripple the most important war effort of the state—feeding an army.

She traveled with a pathetic, ragtag group herself. Three privates so green they were barely old enough to shave, and two sadly injured men, the latter being the

cause of her sudden determination that she had to strip
down to the buff to bathe away the encrusted dirt and
blood that had seemed to cling to her body with greater
vigor since they'd begun this hasty journey. The last action by the old camp along the river had left two youngsters—and they were no more than that, truly—with
minie ball injuries that were far too often fatal. Her
brother, Colonel Julian McKenzie, had performed the
surgery which had thus far saved their lives, but soon
after, they had broken camp. The fellows who could do
so pulled somewhat to the north while she and Julian
had determined to take these fellows on a southwest-
wardly trail which would bring them to an old Creek
camp, where they could seek shelter until the fellows
healed enough to return to the front. She'd been down
to one change of clothing—a sad state of affairs if she
were to look back—but now seemed the time for that
change. Indeed, she would be close to home once they
reached the Creek camp, and there might even be time
for the indulgence of returning to Cimarron, and throwing herself into the gentle care of her mother, father,
and other loved ones there—until she returned to the
field to resume assisting her brother.

"Miss Tia!"

Jemmy's voice came to her again. Ever more
desperate.

She had to think, to *unfreeze*!

Her horse stood by her side, but her clothing lay on
the opposite bank. She was soaking from head to toe,
though she hadn't yet had a chance to wash her hair,
which waved down her back and shoulders like a sweeping black cape.

The soldier would be in front of her any second.

"Stop where you are. Get the men, and—go!" she
ordered, her voice full of sudden authority.

"Go?"

"Yes, go! Get away quick. I'll follow."

"We can't leave you!" Jemmy said frantically.

She heard him moving along the pine-carpeted path
toward her. "Don't you dare come closer, young man!

Take our injured and move along. I know these trails
better than any one of you, so get moving. I'll see who
comes, and circle around to join you on the trail."

"But Miss Tia—"

"Damn you, listen to me. I gave you an order. Go!"

She had no rank, of course. She wasn't even in the
militia. But if truth be told, she possessed the simple
authority of all she had learned in years of helping to
patch wounded men back together again, of learning
when to strike and when to run. She'd been a very properly brought-up young woman when it all began, but
though privileged, she'd been the child of what she considered to be enlightened parents. Her education had
been thorough. She'd longed for more, for travel to far
distant lands, a chance to view the great pyramids of
Egypt, the castles in England, the palaces in France. Instead of those dreams, she'd spent years with men.
Young men, old men, handsome, gallant, rude, charming, educated. And when the war came, she'd met them
from every backwoods hole in the state. Rebs and Yankees. She'd seen them survive, and she'd seen them die.
She'd sewn them up, and she'd bathed them down. She
was far more familiar with male body parts than she'd
ever imagined . . .

So in truth, she reasoned suddenly, slightly amused
with the realization, she had some authority, much experience, but little modesty left.

"Miss Tia, someone is coming quickly now." Jemmy
was standing there. So much for the question of
modesty.

"Yes, I know, Jemmy. If you please . . . oh, never
mind."

She rose, still indecisive. It wasn't Jemmy's fault. He
was a boy, one who had lied regarding a few months to
a year to get himself into the service—he wasn't yet
eighteen, she was certain. Not that she was so ancient
herself, but as far as the war went, she was old, very old.

Now, of course, he was staring at her, stunned. Of
course. She was "buck" naked. But not really. She had
very long hair, ebony in color, thick and lustrous. It fell

over her shoulders, down her back—and her front—and blanketed the most strategic points of her form, she assured herself.

And so she stood on the trail, thus enwrapped, and stared at the now frozen, gaping Jemmy. "First, snap your jaw shut, soldier, this is war. As you said, someone is coming fast. It is likely to be the enemy. And we have injured. So go now—and I mean it! You get our men to safety, and Blaze and I will be right behind you, once we see the enemy, and what he is after—and draw him away from you, if need be."

Jemmy suddenly seemed to find his mind and senses. "No! You're a woman. We can't leave you. We can take on the enemy—"

"The hell you can!" she swore flatly. "My sex doesn't matter—can't matter!—now. I've been in this too long for such consideration. Longer than you, far longer than you. Listen to me! Would you kill our injured? Go."

"But—"

"Go! And don't you mention a word of this to anyone, Jemmy Johnson, or I'll shoot you down myself, do you hear? Take our injured down the Seminole trail. Move fast. I'll take Blaze along the eastern route, hopefully drawing any rider who would follow, and after I assess the enemy strength, I'll change course and meet up with you by nightfall."

"Yes, ma'am!"

To her relief and amusement, he saluted. She saluted back, then regretted the action—wondering just how much of her long, concealing hair she had readjusted so that it didn't quite conceal anymore. He tried to look into her eyes, but his gaze kept slipping. Then, as she had ordered, he turned and fled. She saw him and their little party of injured hurry along the trail, disappearing around the bend and slinking into the old Indian trail, just as she had ordered.

As soon as they were swallowed by the foliage, she started across the little tributary, thinking that she would regain her clothing, but she had barely taken a step when she realized that she could just hear the sound of hoofbeats against the soft earth and that someone was coming closer and closer. Blaze was on this side of the trickling little tributary of the river.

She would never manage to have both her horse and her clothing. The situation was desperate. Seconds were ticking away. She had to do something, make a decision.

Clothing . . . horse?

Clothing!

No! She had to make the right decision to protect the injured men who were in her care. What was a little *bareness* when death might be the alternative?

What in God's name had made her decide that today, of all days, she just really had to give herself a complete and thorough scrubbing?

Maybe the enemy would pause for water, and just go away.

Maybe he wouldn't be the enemy.

Just as that thought filled her mind, a rider came into view, a tall man on a tall horse. His face was hidden beneath the slant of his plumed, wide-brimmed hat, and his shoulders were encased in a *Union*-issue, cavalry frockcoat.

He was definitely the enemy, she thought, her heart sinking.

And he certainly wasn't hiding his identity as a Yank.

He was but one man. A lone rider. Tia felt a sense of relief, and even superiority—she knew this terrain as few men did. Her home was across the state, but she had learned her geography from her father and her uncle, whose Indian blood had led him in dozens of merry chases across the terrain throughout the long, treacherous, and deadly Seminole wars.

And yet . . .

Who was he? What was he doing? Not exactly a spy, for he was in full uniform. A scout? Yes, searching for troop movements, perhaps even looking for her own little pathetic band of injured and raw men who were, in truth, little more than children playing at being soldiers.

Just what would she do if he were to note that they had followed the old Indian trail.

He was a lone man . . .

But well armed. He had come with a sharpshooter's rifle tied across his saddle, a Spencer repeating rifle in a case below it, and a pair of six-shooting Colts holstered in the gun belt that rode his hips. Mean weapons. And something about the easy, agile, and assured way that he moved seemed to testify to his ability to use them.

The boys had already ridden on. If he followed them, there was no question in her mind—at least half of them would be dead.

Coming into the copse, the Federal cavalry scout paused. Felt the air, listened, surveyed the landscape. Hoof prints, near the water. Broken and bent branches. *Yes . . . someone was near.*

By dusk, the slender offshoot of the St. Johns was an exquisite place to be. Pines rose in green splendor, shading the little tributary, while shimmering rays of the dying sun broke through here and there to cast diamond sparkles upon the darkening water. A lone wading bird stalked the far side of the water, long-legged and graceful.

A crane. Tall, snow white except for its legs, it was the focal point of the glorious picture there. The bird was so still that if it weren't for the creature's coloring, it would have blended with the scene. Like any predator, however, this creature of ethereal beauty was sleek, cunning, and careful. It waited; it watched. Its stillness was so complete that it might indeed have been a painted picture that Taylor Douglas stared upon, a picture of serenity and peace.

The woman was much the same.

Yes! The woman.

Was she alone? Perhaps now . . .

But she hadn't been before! And so . . .

Though she was dead still, low and flattened against a pine, he saw her. *Or part of her. She was well concealed by the foliage. Still, strangely, he sized her up within his mind.*

Slim, graceful, striking, like the bird. Like the crane, she watched, and she waited.

And, he thought as well, like the crane, *she was a predator. No one watched and waited and calculated in such a manner without intending to strike.*

He dismounted from Friar, his bay horse, named for his deep brown color and long shaggy mane. He stretched in a leisurely manner, then hunkered down by the water, dousing his face, yet surreptitiously studying her there, across the water.

Yes, she watched.

She thought herself hidden, and indeed, he could see little of her, a long slender arm, a wealth of dark hair, a face as stunningly sculpted and delicate as that of the most elegant of belles. Her eyes were dark, large, hypnotic . . .

Pinned on him.

Ready for battle. To spring to pounce. She waited merely for the right moment . . .

Was she unaware that he had seen her? Most probably. His eyesight was exceptional. It was one of the gifts that made him an incredible marksman, as well as a good scout. And he knew this area as few other men did, just as he knew, indeed, that the Southern forces of Captain Dickinson—little Dixie—were in the near vicinity. He knew he was close to an encampment, and that he would find his prey.

And yet . . .

He had expected nothing like this. He couldn't help feeling a certain sorrow. *Had the Southern forces become so low, so pathetic, and so depleted that women were doing the work of the army? And so thinking, he couldn't help remembering back to the beginning of the war, when the reckless bravado and confidence of the men who would be soldiers had brought about the pointless tragedy that would scar his own life.*

No. This was different. This girl was here by no accident.

He threw more water on his face, adjusted his hat, and whistled for Friar to come to the water. Keeping low, his hat brim over his eyes, he surveyed the area around the little tributary. A number of roads here, different ways to go—different ways out. He rose slowly, seeing that beyond the obvious, there was a trail heading into what appeared to be thick foliage. It was as he stared at the trail that she suddenly made her presence known.

He'd thought himself a hardened soldier. But she stunned him, froze him in place.

She swept his breath away.

She was sheer audacity.

For suddenly, she stepped from her hideout among the pines in all her glory. Sheer, *naked* glory. A magnitude of splendor that wiped the mind clean, stealing into the senses, the fantasy of dreams. She was slim, compact, her form clad in nothing other than the superb blanket of her hair, falling down in rippling waves of pure ebony to cover her breasts, belly, and thighs in a manner that teased in the wickedest way . . .

"Good day, Yankee."

For a moment, he couldn't answer. He saw her smile.

"Madam," he said, his jaw tense but working.

"You're in a Rebel state."

"I am."

"So . . . I assume you're looking for rebellion, soldier?" she called in a taunting voice. "If so, then come this way."

To his amazement, she dashed off in a web of ebony grace, the stole of her hair flying about her in a cloud like a raven's wing, only to resettle as she sped along the pines to a trail just southward of their position. Still paralyzed with simple shock, he watched her.

Then he swore, bursting back to life.

Hurtling himself into his saddle, he urged Friar to take a wild plunge into the river. At its greatest depth, the water was only four feet, but there it rose in mighty showers and rushed back upon him in shimmering cascades.

By the time he had crossed the river, she'd mounted a large handsome horse—a far finer animal than he had seen in most of the South. And there, on the trail, she sat, a naked beauty cloaked in nothing but the black sable of her hair, staring his way. Her limbs were long, ivory, striking against the darkness of the horse's coat. Her face, though shadowed by that magnificent head of hair, again appeared young, striking . . .

And cunning.

She might have been startled, just at first, that he had so quickly crossed the water and found her upon the trail. But she gave that little thought, kneed her horse, and tore down the pine-carpeted trail.

Deeper and deeper she rode into the green darkness of the trails. Pines, oaks, webbed with ferns and mosses, created a rich canopy above them. She knew the trail, he thought. No one who didn't know the trail would ever dare ride its length so recklessly. Nor could they follow such a twisted course with such great speed for so long a time.

Only a fool would follow so recklessly! he thought.

And yet . . .

He followed. She was leading him astray, he knew. Tempting him from all his intent. Only a fool would follow, yet he was certain that, just as she would lead him away—she would lead him back again.

After twenty minutes of a heavy gallop in her pursuit, he came to a small bubbling brook. He was amazed that she had a horse with the speed and stamina to elude him so long. The Southern states had begun the war with the best horses—life in the South had been far more based upon the farm and the hunt than that in the North, and the majority of the best breeding stables had been in the South. But war had taken its toll on horses just as it had on humans—far too many of the Southern horses were little but flesh and bones.

Not to mention the horses that had been casualties of war, rotten carcasses next to their masters upon the killing fields of the fight.

He was lucky to have an exceptional mount himself. Friar was from Kentucky, a horse bred from specially chosen stock for both strength and speed. He still thought that he might have overtaken the woman if the trail hadn't been so narrow and treacherous. Perhaps it

was best to wait. Give her time to knot her own
noose . . .

She had just crossed the brook when he reached it.
Still, he reined in. It seemed a good time to hold off,
back away. To wait. And to watch. She wasn't without
sense, or was she? She would surely know that she had
to slow down her horse. To own such a creature, and to
ride it so well, she must be aware that she would kill
the animal if she raced it into the ground. But what did
he know of her? Maybe she would consider the act of
eluding him to be worth the life of the horse. Then
what? They were deep in the midst of nowhere, far between the habited lands of either coast. She would have
to care about the life of her horse.

Very soon, she would have to slow down, walk her
mount, allow it water.

He dismounted from his horse, and hunkered down by
the water. He drank, looked around. She had definitely
crossed the brook. He would wait, let her move on without being chased. She would see that he had stopped,
and perhaps believe that she had lost him, that his pursuit was finished.

Never.

He was determined.

*Why? She was a wanton little fool. Good God, didn't
she see the risks?*

He gave himself a shake, gritting his teeth, stiffening.
He hadn't felt this encompassing web of pain and bitterness enwrap him in a long time now. There had been a
goal in his life, a quest, and he had pursued it. The past
was over; he didn't know why this incident was forcing
him to recall events he had long since pressed to the
back of his mind—and soul.

It was the war.

Damn her . . .

He would pursue her because of the war.

Whatever she had led him away from, she would lead
him back to.

Chapter 2

Tia raced on after she was certain that her pursuer had given up the chase. But then she reined in, aware that she was riding Blaze into the ground. A cruel thing to do to such a fine, blessed animal! She patted the horse's neck. "Good girl! You are worth your weight in gold, you know? You can outrun almost anything on four legs, eh?"

She fell silent. Dusk was coming, and here she was, alone on an old Indian trail—stark naked. She felt chilled and very uncomfortable.

And unnerved.

She had never felt so alone. And yet, of course, she wanted to be alone. She needed to be alone. Totally alone.

Far, far away from . . . *him.*

Had she definitely lost her pursuer? She whirled around on her mount. He hadn't followed. She had probably lost him at the brook. So . . .

If she rode back on an even narrower, highly overgrown path, she could reach the brook by just moving a little to the south and west. If she had lost him at the water, she would emerge downstream of him, return to where she had been—and regain her clothing. Alone, she was moving so much more quickly than her party could possibly be going, she would have no problem catching up with them on the very path they had taken—once she was decent again.

"I know, you need water. So do I. Naturally, you need it more," she acknowledged, patting Blaze's neck again and urging her down the narrow path. She was careful all the while, feeling chilled and ridiculous. She was not accustomed to riding naked. The woods suddenly seemed to be filled with all manner of eyes.

She swore at herself, and gave her full attention to the trail. She looked up at the sky, hoping she had a few hours of light left. She couldn't begin to imagine being stuck out here, riding alone, naked on her horse— in the dark. "This has to be one of the insanest things I've done as yet, Blaze, though I admit, I had wanted adventures out of life. However, I had wanted to tour the pyramids of Egypt and the like, not the backwoods of my own home!"

As she had planned, she returned to the brook by way of the downstream trail. She dismounted quickly, drinking deeply from the fresh water, then leading the thirsting horse to drink as well. She looked around herself. Nothing . . . or no one. Just a brisk forty-five-minute trot and she could be back to her clothing, pretending that this wretched episode had never occurred.

Yet just as she was congratulating herself on being safe, she saw the huge brown horse with the long, thick mane—and the Yankee riding the animal. The rider had eschewed the trail all together—he came racing straight through the water, his speed uncanny, his body leaning low so that he was all but one with the animal.

She shrieked with surprise, tearing for Blaze, leaping up on her horse with a speed and agility born of sheer panic. She managed to seat herself on Blaze . . .

But that was all.

The huge brown horse was upon her.

As was its rider.

The man made the leap from horse to horse with the sure certainty of a circus performer. She screamed wildly, twisting in a vehement denial of what had happened, only to find his arms around her, the horse rearing, and the two of them plummeting to the ground.

She struck hard, but he struck harder, having somehow come around her as they had sailed to the earth to take the brunt of the fall. For seconds, she couldn't breathe, think, or shake herself from her state of pure surprise that she lived, yet lay on the ground. Then she realized the very serious—no, desperate!—nature of her predicament, and she tried to rise. His arm came around her. She jabbed an elbow into his rib, heard him grunt and groan. She tried again to jackknife to her feet, only to find him catching her, spinning her down again, and this time, straddling her, capturing her viciously flailing fists, and pinning them to her sides.

"All right, madam, who are you, and what is your game?" he demanded.

She drew in a ragged breath, staring up at the man, seeing him in truth for the first time. He was perhaps twenty-five to thirty years old, with striking hazel eyes that seemed to hold her with a greater force than the powerful hands that had pinned her wrists to the ground. His hair was dark, rich, and certainly askew at the moment, nearly as tangled as her own. His features were haunting . . . handsome features, a face well defined with clean lines, broad cheekbones, squared jaw, ample brow, and a dead straight nose. Yet the years had woven a tension into those features, and he might have been younger than he appeared. Fine lines teased around his eyes, and his mouth; she had never felt such a sheer force of will in a man. He seemed furious, and exceptionally contemptuous, as if her behavior were a personal assault and not the result of her stupidity. His hardened, rough-edged anger—along with the fact that she was in an entirely untenable position— brought back her own bravado. When all was lost and panic threatened, there was nothing left to do but keep fighting.

"Who the hell are you and what is your game, sir? Though you are no 'sir,' no gentleman, ah! But then again, you're a Yankee in a Southern state, are you not?"

"Who are *you*?" he repeated, snapping out the words.

Her name? Good God, she should die rather than give her name! What if he knew Ian? There were tens of thousands of troops, of course, but this fellow was cavalry, like her oldest brother. And he was in Florida, where Ian was sent often enough. And even if he didn't know Ian, Lord! He could give out her name and . . .

"Who do you think?" she spat out, bitter, furiously aware now that she *had* been caught—and far more than a little afraid, no matter how hard she fought to remain calm and seek any advantage for escape. "I'm Lady Godiva, of course."

That, at least, seemed to amuse him a bit. The smallest hint of a smile teased his lips.

"Then what, my dear lady, is your game?"

Her game . . .

She was pinned to the ground, stark naked, by a stranger. A young, powerful stranger with arms of steel and eyes that belonged to a cheetah. She was humiliatingly aware of the rough feel of his clothing against her bare flesh. Her hair . . . yes, her hair was still her cloak, yet it left so very much to be desired. Indeed, what was her game?

"No game, sir. You scared me, I ran . . . leaving my clothing, I'm afraid."

"What a liar you are!" he said smoothly, the gold cheetah eyes seeming to burn into her.

"I beg your pardon, but I am telling you the truth! Your arrival on the south side of the river kept me from my clothing—"

"And you just happened to be way out here, a good Southern lass, stripped bare and bathing in a little tributary far, far from the nearest civilization?"

"I was simply out riding, sir."

"From where?"

"From where? Well, from . . . um, my home, of course."

"And where is that?"

"Oh, well, I come from . . ."

"Yes?"

"I won't give away the location of my home to the enemy, sir. Suffice it to say that I live near, that I was out riding."

"No, you weren't."

She was alarmed to see that no argument on her part

would change him. Again, the seriousness and foolishness of her situation struck her, and she started to shake. He was all too aware of her distress as well, which naturally brought her temper rising again, even while her better senses warned her that she might well be in danger of both rape and murder, and there would be those wretches who might think she had brought about such a horror by her own wanton behavior.

"Sir, you are apparently an officer—"

"A Yankee, as you noted."

"As an officer of the Federal army, I charge you, sir, to rise, and to cease bringing such discomfort to a lady."

"A lady?"

"Yes! You must release me. Now!"

"Perhaps I'm not a Yankee officer."

"What?"

"I could be a deserter, with a stolen frockcoat. A man on the run from both Federal and Confederate law, a desperado, glad of any treasure to be found in the way of money, cash, goods, clothing—or human flesh."

She froze, staring at him, every inch of her flesh burning, terror seeming to wrap around her like the tentacles of an octopus. Somehow, she kept staring at him without blinking. And she told him, "Kill me then, and quickly, and steal what you will. My horse is all I have of value."

"Now, Madam Godiva, what man would want to kill you quickly, without enjoying the good sport to be had first?"

The deep crawl of his voice had a very serious edge, and yet staring at him, reading the harsh lines and character in his still striking face, she didn't believe that he was a deserter.

"Do what you will quickly, slowly, but threaten me no more!" she charged him, yet then she couldn't help but cry out, "Just exactly what is it you want?"

"I want to know your plan, Miss . . . er . . . Godiva. I mean, most obviously, you were trying to lure me away from something. What?"

"I don't know what you're talking about! And if you're an officer—"

"A might-be deserter," he reminded her.

"You are no deserter, you are a Yankee officer, and you must follow some rudimentary code of conduct. Yankees *are* accredited with atrocious manners, but this . . ."

"Bad manners? If I were to rape and murder you, madam, you would consider it nothing more than *bad manners*?"

"You are no cold-blooded murderer!" she cried. And perhaps, at last, something in her voice reached him. She heard the grating of his jaw, but something changed just slightly in his eyes, in the way he watched her. "If you would be a gentleman . . ."

"Oh, dear, Miss Godiva, I'm so very sorry," he said. He eased his hold on her wrists, then released them. Sitting back on his haunches without casting any great weight upon her, he crossed his arms over his chest. "If you think to shame me, you've come across the wrong man—at the wrong time. And in the wrong state of dress, I'm afraid. I do remember learning manners concerning the fairer sex, but in those classes, the ladies tended to have clothing on the bodies to whom one was to be so polite and correct."

"Would you please stop speaking to me in such a sarcastic manner? This is wretched and cruel, and obviously a terrible discomfort to me."

"Young woman!" he snapped, suddenly furious and leaning over her. "Have you lost your mind? Every day that the war lingers longer, there are more deserters roaming the woods and forests, more desperate men about, more men who wouldn't give a damn for the value of your life much less your virtue! Now who the hell are you and what the hell are you doing out here?"

She gritted her teeth, aware that he was right in many ways. She was frightened, as she had seldom been frightened in all her life.

"Yes!" she admitted. "Yes! I was trying to distract you! But you needn't fear—I kept you from no great troop movements, no desperately desired spy . . . just a few wounded men, seeking solace and healing!"

He stared at her for a very long time, then at last, he rose, and for a moment, her distress was greater, for without his frame to conceal her, she was all the more unclad. Yet as she awkwardly tried to rise and sweep her hair around her nakedness, he slipped his frockcoat from his shoulders, reached impatiently down to help her rise, and encompassed her in his coat. Her teeth were suddenly chattering.

"It's a Yankee garment!" she murmured, painfully aware that it was a laundered garment, with a hint of masculine aftershave about it, along with a faint scent of leather and tobacco, scents she associated with a time long ago, her father's drawing room, her brother after a day's hunt, so long ago.

"Do you want to give it back?" he asked, hands on hips.

Without his coat, he still cut a strong and imposing figure. His cotton shirt had somehow remained white, and the breadth of his shoulders seemed even more visible. His flesh was bronzed by the sun to a deep copper, and that, with the striking rise of his cheekbones, reminded her of someone she knew, but could not place.

She hugged the frockcoat to her. "No, I don't want to give the garment back. I thank you for the courtesy. But . . . now that you know I'm actually an innocent caught by circumstance, sir, you'll forgive me if I wish to part ways—"

"An innocent?" he inquired with dark skepticism.

"Yes, really! And I'm about to be on my way—"

"What?" he lashed out succinctly.

"I'm going," she said, then sighed with impatience. "I go my way, you go yours. You're a Yankee, I'm a Rebel, but since there's no one else here, just us, no real war about, it seems we should just go our separate ways."

"Lady Godiva! Not on your life!" he informed her.

She stared back at him, growing uneasy again. She lifted her chin. "I'm leaving," she informed him, turning about. But she didn't manage to leave.

"Take one step toward your horse, madam, and I'll

drag you down to the dirt again, and this time, I promise, I will not let you up."

He spoke quietly, with an almost pleasant warning, and yet, she was very afraid he meant exactly what he was saying.

She hesitated, spinning back to him.

"Then what is your intent?" she demanded.

"Well, first, we'll go back for your clothes. After all, I wouldn't want you thinking that Yankees *can't* be gentlemen."

"My clothing, good. That will be another honorable courtesy. And what then?"

"Then . . ." he said, his voice trailing.

"Yes!" she hissed. "Then—what then?"

"Then . . . we shall see," he said simply.

She turned to head for Blaze again, but then started as she felt his hand fall on her shoulder. "Oh no, my dear Lady Godiva," he told her.

She twisted around to meet his eyes, her own wide with innocence.

"You said that we were riding back. I was merely attempting to reach my horse—"

"You'll ride with me," he said, and turned her toward him, adjusting his way-too-big frockcoat over her shoulders. "I wouldn't want you tempted to run naked into the woods again. Alone."

"But—"

She never went further with her protest. His hands locked upon her waist and he set her upon his own mammoth gelding, slipped up behind her with the same uncanny agility she had seen before, and lifted the reins. She felt his chest at her back, his arms around her. Renewed anger and a wretched shaking seized hold of her at the same time. She didn't want to fight at the moment—or move. Movement only made things worse. She'd shared a greater intimacy with a stranger in a matter of minutes than she had known with any man in her life—father, brothers, and patients included.

"My horse—"

"She follows behind us," he assured her.

"There is no need to do this," she said, trying not to sound as if she pleaded too desperately. "I am no threat to you—"

"You are mistaken. You are a threat, to me—and to yourself. In fact, your intent is to be an incredible threat."

"But—"

"You were moving with soldiers, madam, weren't you? By your own admission," he reminded her.

"Yes, but—"

"You are bold enough to entice a soldier into the woods with a display of the . . . the barest beauty. Clever enough to try to lie your way out of any predicament. So I wonder, who are you? What other sacrifices do you make for your war department? Give me your name."

"I think not."

"I think so."

"Do you plan a Yankee torture?"

"I plan to have the truth."

"Then you explain yourself, and quit playing games. What do you intend to do once we have retrieved my clothing?"

"Why, remove you from the war. Take you into custody. Find out more about you. Perhaps in St. Augustine we'll discover that dozens of men have been lured to their doom by the wiles of the Lady Godiva."

"No!" she protested in horror. St. Augustine! She had kin throughout the city, some there permanently, some coming and going, her oldest brother being the worst of them. She would not, could not, be dragged to St. Augustine. Oh, God, Ian would . . .

She didn't even want to imagine what Ian would say and do. And her father would find out, and her mother . . .

"You have to let me go."

"No."

"But—"

"You will remain in my custody until I can give you over to the proper authorities, and that is that. You should thank me, you little fool! Keep up a lifestyle like this and you are sure to be ravaged if not slain. It's my fondest hope that your father is a good, stern Southern fellow who will quite simply find a good hickory stick and a wood shed and leave such an impression on your—dare we say bare?—flesh that you never think of such foolhardy behavior again."

She lowered her head slightly. Her father had one hell of a temper, for sure, but he had never raised a hand against any of them in anger. What would he do now? It wasn't his violence she feared. It was his disappointment. She adored him, had always adored him, as she did her mother. She'd been a normal child, she thought, angry and rebellious at times, but the last years had shown her time and time again that she'd been blessed, and she never, ever wanted to cause her parents harm. Or shame. They had all chosen their ways; they had even been encouraged to know their own hearts. Her father had never called anyone a traitor, though the name was thrown at him often enough because he refused to say that he had come to terms with secession.

"Don't you think you've chastised me quite enough for any father?"

"Not in the least."

"I did what I had to do."

"And I'm doing what I have to do."

"So I should be repentant—and grateful? Well, you bastard, I'm not sorry!" she proclaimed suddenly, tossing her hair back. "There were injured men who would not survive your dragging them to St. Augustine!"

"Oh, we'll find them," he assured her in such a way that she was chilled.

She shook her head again. This time, with her hair playing havoc beneath his nose, he sneezed.

"If you don't mind . . ." he began.

"I do mind! You must leave those men alone. They are just children, just boys, too young to be in the service, don't you see? But the state is so desperate, so many men are dead, rotting in Southern states that are actually far north of us! There is no militia left—" She broke off, realizing that she was telling a Yankee in just what horrible a condition the state's defenses were in. "Well, of course, troops will be sent back. There is an action that will surely go on to the north, there are so many troops, North and South accumulating . . . in that arena, of course, we have thousands of men—"

"Madam, neither of us is a fool."

"You must make no attempt on those boys! And you must leave me alone. I'll escape, you know, and if I have to, I'll kill you—"

"Thank you. I'll be forewarned. I believe we have now come back to where we began. In fact, I think that pile there might be your clothing."

Yes, they had come back to where they had begun. Where she had been such a fool, delighting in the feel of being really clean after so much blood and dirt . . .

There lay her clothing. Dried out over the log where she had laid it.

He leapt down from the horse, reaching up to her. With little choice, she accepted his arms. Yet, before he would lift her down, he asked her, "What is your real name, Godiva?" he asked her.

"Godiva—that is all!" she told him.

"I will find out."

"Will you? What is your name, sir? Tell me, so I can always remember the incredible rudeness of the invading Yanks," she demanded.

He grinned, but it seemed his teeth grit audibly for a number of seconds. "Ah, if you are Godiva, then call me Captor of Godiva, so it seems, madam. And I am no invader." He lifted her to the ground. "Madam, if you'll allow me . . ." he said, bowing with a polite flourish. Then he walked to the pile of clothing, bent over, and one by one began to retrieve her garments. His broad-shouldered back was to her. Pity she had nothing to throw against it! She thought again about running, but she had learned how quickly he could move. And she did want her clothing.

He turned at last, taking a few leisurely steps toward her. Impatiently, she strode forward, snatching her clothing from him. With it clutched in her hands, she demanded, "Do you mind?"

He grinned. "Yes, actually, I do. It's just a shade nerve-wracking to turn one's back on you. Just now, you considered an escape—but luckily for you, dear Godiva, you chose reason over stupidity."

"The gentlemanly thing to do—"

"That does not seem relevant here, does it, since you enticed me into the woods in something—shall we say—slightly less than a lady's apparel?"

She swung her back on him, dropped his frockcoat, and quickly dressed. Despite her bid for dignity, she tripped over her pantalettes. When she turned back to him, cheeks reddening, he was somewhat attempting to conceal an amused smile.

"What now, sir?" she demanded.

"I'll take my coat back." He came forward to retrieve it. He stared into her eyes, then reached to the ground for the coat she had dropped. Standing before her, he slipped the garment back over his shoulders. His eyes never left hers.

"And now?" she queried.

"We follow the path we should have taken."

She shook her head suddenly, with honest passion. "You don't want to find my injured lads. I swear to you that they are harmless—"

"We shall see."

"If you chase them, they will think they have to fight."

"Madam, I assure you—"

"Don't you see, they're young! They'll think they're honor-bound to die. All men seem to come into this wretched war thinking that they're obliged to die! Please . . . !"

She was startled to realize that she had reached out, touching his arm. She felt the hardness of his muscle beneath the fabric of his clothing. He was fit, rugged, in good shape. Not an officer whose men did his bidding while he sat back himself. His men . . .

He was here on his own. Did he command others? Or

had he gained his rank through his prowess with the weapons he carried?

She gazed at her hand where it rested on his arm. Met his eyes again. Snatched her hand away. She didn't want to touch him. She didn't want to think of him as being human, much less male, and a male in a healthy and rugged good condition which would make him all the more a very dangerous adversary.

She knew she was flushing as she stared at him.

"They don't need to die," she whispered. "Honestly. It would be like the murder of children."

"You can't begin to imagine how many children have died," he told her curtly.

"But . . ."

"I've no interest in causing further harm to your injured. Still, Godiva, you will come with me. And we will see this through. Together."

He turned around, heading toward the horses. Watching him, frustrated, furious, and more afraid than ever of his strength and determination, Tia remembered the small ladies' Smith and Wesson she carried in her skirt pocket.

With his back to her, she quickly dug in her pocket, reached for the weapon, curled her fingers around it, and pulled it out. She aimed it dead center on his spine.

"Sir!"

He swung around and paused when he saw the gun.

"Now—you will come with me. My prisoner." Feeling elated, she kept the gun level on his heart, but approached him, her eyes narrowed, her gait suddenly light. "Ever hear of Andersonville?" she asked quietly.

"Indeed, I have," he said coolly.

"Say your prayers, soldier," she told him, "for you will be going there."

"I think not," he told her.

"Why? I will shoot you, you know."

"Will you?"

"Do you doubt it?"

His narrowed gold eyes assessed her. "I don't know you well enough to know just what you will do. You do ride around the woods naked. Maybe you would shoot a man in cold blood."

"Don't tempt me!" she warned.

He stared at her for a long moment, then said, "It's growing late." He turned, starting for the horses.

"Stop, you fool! You are my prisoner. I am very capable with a gun. My marksmanship is excellent."

He ignored her. She gritted her teeth hard. She didn't want to shoot him. He was the enemy, of course, but he was a flesh-and-blood man. She couldn't just shoot him down, but he was simply walking away. "Stop, I mean it!"

Again, he ignored her.

She fired—intending to shoot into the dirt.

Except that . . . she didn't shoot at all.

He swung back around, slowly arching a brow. She stared from the gun to him, and back to the gun again.

"You didn't think I'd leave you with a loaded gun, did you?" he queried.

"But . . . how . . ." she began, and then she realized that he had quickly, subtly found the gun when he had gone to collect her clothing—when he had turned his back on her.

And now . . .

Now he thought that she had been ready to shoot him down in cold blood.

The color drained from her face as he stared at her.

She turned to run.

She went no more than ten feet before she found herself spinning, then crashing back down to the earth again. And he was straddling her, pinning her down. She couldn't breathe. She could only feel the heat from the fire in his eyes.

"Lady, trust me!" he said softly. "From here on out, *you* are *mine*."

Chapter 3

"Yours! Oh, no, you are mistaken," she promised him icily. "I'm not yours—or the Union's. I don't belong to any man or state or government. I'm not property—"

"As no woman—or man—should be," he interrupted quietly.

She caught her breath, well aware that he was suggesting she fought for what was called the "peculiar institution" of slavery.

She didn't owe him any explanations, nor could she possibly care what this stranger thought about her, her ideals, ethics, principles, or the reasons for any of her behaviors. And still, she found that she was defensively lashing out at him. "Kindly release me, sir. I don't belong to any man, and I don't own any men—or women or children. Neither do any members of my family."

"Who are you then? Where is your family? Tell me that, and I will gallantly help you to your feet."

She pursed her lips, staring at him stubbornly.

"I can wait."

She smiled icily. "Good. I can wait, too. I have no desire at all for you to try to behave 'gallantly' in any way, shape, or form."

"Fine. We'll both just wait."

To her horror, he stretched out beside her, an arm and a leg continuing to pin her to the ground. Infuriated, she started to struggle, only to find that she did nothing but edge more closely against his blue-clad frame.

And he watched her. Watched her with those large hazel eyes of his. Again, she felt a strange shivering sensation while meeting his gaze, as if she knew him, or should know something about him. And she grew desperate to free herself from the intimacy he forced.

"Catherine," she lied. "My name is Catherine—Moore."

That was all it took. He rose, offering a hand down to assist her with all the gallantry he had promised. She would have none of it, of course. Petty, childish, perhaps, but he could hang before she would accept the slightest assistance from him. She scrambled to her feet on her own, eyeing him warily all the while.

"And now?"

"Now we ride."

"My horse—"

"Will follow again."

She shook her head. "You're being unnecessarily cruel to a good horse, Yank. The added weight—"

"Your weight is nothing," he assured her dismissively, which made her want to draw up to her full height. Except that she was petite, which didn't seem at all fair. Her brothers were giants; even her mother was tall.

She wanted to be formidable.

"You're mistaken—" she began, but he interrupted her curtly.

"I will have your silence, madam!"

"I don't have to—"

"I can gag you."

She gritted her teeth again, standing with her arms folded firmly across her chest. "Be glad you did find the bullets in that gun, Yank. It doesn't take a wrestler to fire a lethal shot!"

"I stand forewarned. Now you shall stand silent," he said. He just looked at her and spoke with a low, almost pleasant tone. She had been threatened, really threatened, and she knew it. She lifted her hands, arching a brow, not willing to give him the last word, nor really willing to be silent.

And so she watched him.

Minutes later, she thought that the most distressing thing about being with the stranger—other than fearing for her life and future—was the uncanny way he seemed to have of *knowing* exactly where people had been, and where they had gone. He picked up on the trail taken by her party of green soldiers and injured men, though he barely glanced at the tracks in the pine-strewn trails, nor took time to study broken and bent foliage and trees. He quickly assessed the area, set her upon his horse again, and mounted behind her. Then they started riding. And despite the time he had taken pursuing her, capturing her, and returning to this spot along the river, she knew that they would overtake the others. Whether they did so before or after they reached the old abandoned Indian camp, she couldn't quite determine.

But they would find her little party of injured. That was a simple fact.

"You should just take me in," she told him suddenly. "I am the famed Godiva. I have led thousands of men to their deaths, I have caused ships to crash, I—along with General Lee perhaps, and blessed Stonewall, while he lived, and a few others—have almost single-handedly kept the Confederacy in the war. I have—"

"Graced many a stage, I imagine?" he queried dryly.

She bit her lip, lowering her eyes. Once upon a time, her mother had thought to find her livelihood on the stage. Long ago, before she had met and married her father. She certainly hadn't inherited her mother's golden coloring, but perhaps she did carry within her a certain talent for the dramatic—and as he had suggested, bald-faced lying.

"Take me in, I warn you. I am dangerous. If you wait for darkness, terrible things may happen. I'm not even human, really. I'm a shape-changer. I—"

"The cabin lies just ahead, and I imagine your men are within it," he said flatly.

"And what could you possibly want with my injured?" she queried.

"To see who they are," he told her.

"Green boys."

"Maybe, maybe not."

"But—"

"You've lied about everything."

"I'm not lying now!"

"But there's no way for me to tell that, is there—Catherine?"

The way he said the name was chilling. As if he knew she had lied even there.

"I warn you—given the opportunity, I will shoot you down before I'll let you injure a single one of those boys."

"If those boys are who and what you say, they are in no danger from me."

"And if they're not, you may be dead yourself in a matter of minutes!"

"I don't think so."

She didn't need to see his face to feel the strange hazel piercing of his eyes. She wondered again what it was that seemed so familiar about him, when she was sure she didn't know him. He reminded her of someone, and she couldn't quite place who, or why.

"Think about it—I could be leading you into a real trap," she warned quietly.

"I'm thinking, and I don't believe that you're leading me anywhere at the moment," he replied, his voice a very soft drawl. Then it struck her—he might be wearing a Yankee uniform, but he hailed from somewhere in the South.

She twisted around to accost him. "What kind of a traitor are you?"

"I'm true to my convictions, and that makes me an honest man. I wonder if there is any honesty in you whatsoever."

She turned again. The light had begun to fall. She might have lost her own way here, as familiar as she considered herself with the area. But he was right; they were almost upon the old Indian cabin in the woods.

"What do you think you're going to do? Barge in and shoot down a half-dozen men?" she inquired desperately. "Because, of course, they'll be forced to shoot at you if you come after them."

"Not if you keep them from doing so," he said.

"What? Why should I stop them?"

"Because you want them to live."

"The odds are—"

"That not one of your 'green' boys will get off a single shot before I mow them all down." It didn't sound as if he was bragging—merely stating a fact.

He reined to a halt along the trail right before the cove with the small cabin. It had been built and abandoned many years before, during the Seminole War, when the Florida Indians had built their homes with native pine before learning that they had to run so often and so fast that it made far more sense to build platform houses with nothing but thatch roofs—houses above the ground and the vermin in the swamps where they were finally forced.

Since those days, the cabin had been used often enough. Lovers had known it as a place to tryst; hunters and fishermen had found it a haven in the woods. It was known, however, only to the locals.

Or so she had thought.

"Well, Godiva?" he inquired.

"Let me down. I'll tell them not to fire. Except, if you think you can drag my wounded boys back to be seized for a wretched Yank camp—"

"All I want to do is see your wounded boys, Godiva."

That was difficult to believe. And the Yankee's Spencer repeating rifle didn't just look dangerous, it killed, "mowed" men down, just as he'd suggested.

"Let me down then."

This time, he dismounted from behind her. She braced herself to refuse any assistance to dismount from him.

She needn't have bothered. He didn't offer any assistance, and when she met his strange gold eyes as she dismounted on her own, she saw that he was fully aware she would have prided herself on her refusal of anything he offered. She felt let down—and furious.

"A hand might have been polite and proper."

"And you probably would have spit at it. Go, see to your men. Call one of them out and tell them to hold their fire."

She walked toward the cabin, tempted to run inside, take cover, and see that he was blasted. But she just didn't dare. Instinct warned her that this man meant business, and no cover would make her, or the boys, truly safe from his intent.

"Jemmy! Jemmy Johnson!" she called. "It's—" She nearly stated her name, then quickly caught herself. "It's me! Please, come out!"

The old, weather-beaten door to the cabin opened. Jemmy Johnson, Enfield in hand, stepped out warily. She was glad to see his caution, although it wasn't quite enough.

"Miss T—" he began carefully.

"Private!" she interrupted quickly. "The enemy is among us, but he has sworn to let us be if we are all that we say we are. Hold your fire. Command the others to hold their fire."

"But Miss T—"

"Jemmy, for your lives, and for the blessed love of God! Do as I say!" she pleaded. "Weapons down."

"Hell, Jemmy!" someone bellowed from within the cabin. "I ain't holding no weapon! I'm trying to keep Stuart here from bleeding to death!"

It might have been a lie; it might not. But the strange Yankee seemed to go by gut instinct as well. He went striding by Tia and straight into the cabin, his Colts secured to the gun belt at his waist, his Spencer held easily in his left hand.

Easily . . .

She was certain he could spin it around and fire in seconds flat.

She followed behind him quickly.

No lie had been spoken by Trev McCormack, the eighteen-year-old standing by Stuart Adair, one of the two patients. He had been laid atop a rough wooden workbench where Trev kept shifting to put more pressure on his friend's bleeding calf wound. Hadley Blake, the second wounded man, had passed out, and lay with his head supported by a saddle blanket in a corner of the dusky cabin. Gilly Shenley, one of the unwounded recruits, searched the cabin for a proper stick with which to form a tourniquet for Stuart's dangerously bleeding wound.

"Move, boys, let me see the source for that," the Yankee commanded. They stood dead still, staring at him.

"Move!" he snapped.

And they did.

Tia almost cried out as she watched him grip Stuart's calf and survey the damage. He stared at her. "Come on, Miss Godiva, you've surely had some medical training! Get some bandages ripped, a tourniquet going—"

"Can't find a sound stick—" Gilly complained.

"Break up that old broom over there. Come on, lad, a young thing like you can surely snap that pine bough!"

Gilly did as told. Tia quickly ripped up her hemline, glad that he meant to do his best to save Stuart's life, humiliated that he was telling them what to do. Hell yes, she knew her business, and if he hadn't steered her away from her boys, they wouldn't be in this predicament! She could have stopped the bleeding; she'd worked with her brother through the majority of the war, and she'd dare say she was as competent and efficient as most surgeons in the field.

Still, he was more efficient, she had to admit. Within seconds, a tourniquet had been fashioned, and the bleeding was slowing. A few seconds more, and it was coming to a halt. And he was telling them how to release it. She was glad she hadn't stopped him, or made any comments. What mattered here was not who did what, but that a man's life had been saved.

"Private Gilly, there, is that your name?" the Yankee asked.

"Private Gilly Shenley, sir!" said the boy, a straw blond with a sad little scraggle of chin whiskers. To Tia's sheer annoyance, he then saluted.

"I need you to go to the brook and bring me back a large quantity of the moss that forms on the stones there. We'll put some new stitching in here and get a poultice on the wound, and he should heal just fine."

"Yes, sir."

"Also, I need some wild mushrooms, the black-tipped ones. Do you know which ones I mean?"

"I can go," Tia said. "I know exactly what—"

"No, he'll go," the Yankee said, his eyes hard on her. "I'm assuming you can do excellent stitches?"

Her needles and a length of surgical thread—supplied to her by her cousin Jerome McKenzie, one of the few men still successfully running the blockade—were in her pocket. She withdrew them, then stared at her needle for a moment, well aware she had no matches left with which to burn the tip. Then she was startled as the Yank withdrew a box of matches from his pocket and lit one.

She held the tip of the needle in the flame to sterilize it, then threaded the needle, and proceeded very carefully to mend the tear ripped around the young man's wound during their forced flight.

She felt the Yankee watching her for a while, and when she was done, she looked up and saw the first light of approval in his hazel eyes.

"Perfect," he said.

"I've had experience," she told him dryly.

"You've been in Florida the whole war?"

"I have, and I assure you, we've had a constant flow of injuries and disease."

"I wasn't suggesting that your talents were wasted here. I was just thinking how appreciated they might have been during the really tragic battles when tens of thousands of men fell in a single day."

She shrugged. "I don't know what good I would have been elsewhere. I learned everything I know from . . ." She hesitated, not wanting to give herself away in any manner.

"She learned from her brother, the best surgeon in the field!" Trey McCormack provided.

Still watching her, the Yank slowly smiled. "The best surgeon in the field! And who might that be, Private?"

"Don't you tell him, Trey! I don't want this man knowing my name, and certainly not that of my brother. I don't want my brother—"

"Or yourself?" the Yank suggested, interrupting her.

"I don't want my brother jeopardized in any way!" she finished.

"But Miss Ti—"

"Trey!"

"Yes, ma'am."

The Yankee didn't force the point, but still she felt uneasy, aware that he was studying her, perhaps seeing more than she wanted him to see.

"What now?" she asked him.

"We wait for Gilly to get back with the poultice."

"I can make the poultice. I'm as familiar with the healing qualities of mosses and molds as most physicians."

"More so than most, I imagine," he said.

"Are you a physician yourself?"

He shook his head, hesitating slightly. She realized he had decided not to reveal too much about his own identity. "I have a witch doctor or two in my background."

"What?"

"Never mind. Like you, I've learned from experience."

Gilly came back in then, breathing hard, but carrying the moss and the mushrooms in his mess plate.

"They need to be mashed together . . ." the Yankee began.

"Truly, I do this well. Let me make the poultice," Tia said. "Gilly, you can help me. Bring them just outside. Bring your mess plate."

Gilly did as she had ordered. He knelt down by her side when she found a fallen log to use as a worktable.

"Gilly, don't turn around and look back as I talk to you, do you understand?"

"Don't turn around?"

"Gilly, we've got to take him by surprise somehow."

"Take him by surprise? But he hasn't come to hurt us."

"Gilly! He's a Yankee officer—he isn't coming through to applaud us on medical technique!"

"But Tia, he just saved Stuart's life."

"Yes, and I'm grateful for that, though if we hadn't been running, Stuart might not have ripped his previous stitches so badly! The point is, Gilly, we can't chance letting him leave, going for help, and bringing a score of men to take us in."

"A score of Yankees—"

"The state is riddled with them now, Gilly! They've decided that we are to be taken, that we are a danger. Troops are amassing to the north of the state, west of Jacksonville and St. Augustine. We know that they've decided on making a real movement against us here. Trust me, please, Gilly, if he leaves here, he might come back with plenty of reinforcements!"

"And how do we stop him?"

"By surprise, somehow by surprise!"

"Have you taken note of his weapons?"

"Yes, of course, and I'm sure he's adept at using them. We need to divert his attention, and you'll have to take him from the back. It will be our only chance."

"You want me to shoot a man in the back? I don't care if this is war, Miss Tia. That's cold-blooded murder. There are still such things as honor in this world, and if we survive the war, no matter who wins it, I'm still going to have to live with myself."

She stared at the very young man who seemed to know his own purpose so well. "I understand. I'm really not suggesting cold-blooded murder, though how our actions out in the field aren't murder, I don't know. You don't have to kill him. Taken by surprise, he can be knocked out. We can leave him hog-tied and immobile and we can move west again, hook up with Dixie's troops, and then, our wounded will have a far better chance of survival!"

"Leave him tied? There's varmints aplenty out here, Miss Tia."

"I'm sure he'll untie himself. I can only pray that it will take him time."

"But how will we divert him?"

"I don't know yet!" she admitted, exasperated. "Be ready for my signal. When you get the chance, warn Jemmy and Trey."

"Miss Tia, we can move Hadley now; but if we were

to try to move Stuart, I'm afraid the bleeding would start up again."

"Have we got any food on us?"

"What?"

"Food, Private, food. To eat!"

Gilly shook his head. "First you want me to shoot him down. Now you want to invite him to dinner, Miss Tia?"

She sighed, losing her patience. She was dealing with children here! Children already shot up in the defense of their native state, she reminded herself.

"I'm simply trying to buy time."

"We've spent a lot of time out here already," Gilly commented. "Is the poultice done?"

She looked down where she had been busy mashing mushrooms and moss together. It was amazing to see how mechanical her actions had become. The war had so inured her that she could function without thinking. She didn't know if that was good or bad.

Moss and mushrooms were now one pulpy mass, ready to be applied, and bandaged onto the wounded limb.

"Let's go in. And yes, we're inviting him to dinner. We're buying time."

Tia brought the poultice in; Gilly followed behind her. In the cabin, the Yankee was busy with Trey and Jemmy, seeing to the comfort and well-being of their other wounded man, Hadley Blake. The Yank had carried a small bottle of some kind of liquor in his frockcoat pocket. He was in the process of bathing Hadley's wound, this one in the lower arm.

Though he didn't turn around, Tia knew that he was instantly aware that they had returned. His eyes were fixed on the wound. "Your brother is one hell of a surgeon, all right—if he's the one who worked on this boy."

"He is."

"This arm should have been lost."

"He's excellent at saving limbs," she murmured, and she couldn't quite keep the pride from her voice.

The Yank stood. "The poultice?"

"Here."

"Go ahead. Tend to the other boy. I'm sure you know your business."

She stared at him, then walked on over to the work-table where Stuart lay, twitching restlessly now and then.

The boy was very young. Perhaps only fifteen or six-teen. The youngest of this sad little band, she thought, though he had certainly lied his way into the militia. She smoothed the hair back from his forehead. "Help me, Trey."

Trey came to her side.

"Think a splash of that whiskey would do well here?" she asked the Yank.

"Indeed." He stepped forward, bathing her fresh stit-chery. Stuart Adair groaned and twitched again. Al-ready, though, his face had more color.

Whiskey often seemed to be the best cleanser they had. Julian had commented that the wounds cleaned with whiskey often seemed to heal the best as well. She dabbed the wound dry, quickly and expertly applied the poultice, then bandaged the leg neatly.

"There's the remains of an old straw bed over there; let's get him on it," the Yank said.

With tremendous care, they moved the wounded boy. When both the injured lay in deep sleep, Trey asked, "Think they'll make it?"

"Half of it is in the spirit, boy," the Yank said. "Yes, I think they'll make it."

"How about joining us for some hardtack stew?" Gilly suggested. "Yank, you are most welcome to anything we've got."

"Well, you can melt down some hardtack with that clean brook water—I'll pick out the maggots. And maybe I can come up with something a bit better. Give me what's left of that broomstick, son."

Gilly found the broken broomstick and handed it to the Yank. He exited the cabin, not seeming to care that his back was to them. And yet it wasn't the right time to strike—Tia knew it. She shrugged to Trey, and fol-lowed him out.

The Yankee walked down to the brook. He stood curiously poised over the water.

"What the hel—sorry, Miss Tia. What on earth is he doing?" Jemmy demanded.

"I don't know . . ." Tia murmured, and she felt uncomfortable again, watching the Yank. As if she knew him. Or should understand something about him that she hadn't quite placed in her mind.

Suddenly, like lightning, he moved. When he straightened, he had a huge catfish dangling from the broomstick.

"Hell, yes!" Jemmy cried, delighted. "Oh, sorry, Miss Tia—"

"Quit apologizing for swearing!" she said with a sigh. "This is a war."

"Yes, ma'am, sorry, ma'am. I'll get the cooking fires a-burning!"

"Now, wait . . ." Tia began uneasily. She didn't want any gifts from the strange enemy.

But they weren't waiting. They hadn't really eaten in almost forty-eight hours, and they hadn't had a decent meal in months. A fire was quickly lit. Gilly was an expert at what was called hardtack stew, a meal made by boiling hardtack and adding in bacon grease—or real, smoked bacon, which the Yank had in his saddlebags, and in this case, the hardtack stew made a filling side dish for the main course of the very delicious, fresh fish. The Yankee stranger supplied coffee as well, and laced each cup with a sip of the whiskey. To Tia's alarm, by the time the moon had risen high in the night sky, the boys were looking up to the Yank as some kind of god.

Washing their utensils with Jemmy by the brook, she told him sternly, "He's still a Yank. He's dangerous, and you boys can't forget that."

"Yes, Miss Tia, but you said we needed to buy time. We've bought some time. Trey and Gilly are in the cabin now, getting some of the soft stew into Blake and Stuart. We're giving them the strength to run when the time comes, right?"

She nodded. That much was true.

"We'll also try to get them a night's sleep. It doesn't look as if the Yank's going anywhere yet. But don't go forgetting that he's the enemy."

"No, ma'am."

"In the morning . . ."

"Yes?"

"I'll get him to accompany me down to the brook somehow. You boys follow. I'll keep him occupied. Then you can come in and take him by surprise. You're going to have to move with speed and certainty. Can you do it?"

"I may be young, ma'am, but I know my duty."

"Good."

They returned to the camp.

The tall Yank alone remained by the fireside, standing with a tin camp cup in his hand while he watched the fire die down. He cut a very dashing figure in his handsomely fitted frockcoat, one booted foot set against a log, his head slightly bowed.

Again, she had the eerie feeling he knew the minute they drew near; his hearing was uncanny, as was his eyesight.

He turned to them as they reappeared. His eyes were the pure color of the blaze in the fire, and something about the way he looked at her was just as dangerous.

Jemmy paused with her by the Yank. "I'll go on in and see how our injured boys are doing, getting their nourishment down," Jemmy said.

"You do that, soldier," the Yank advised.

Jemmy left, a bit awkwardly.

And Tia found herself alone with the Yank once again. She felt his gaze as he assessed her with his fire-glowing eyes, a slight smile on his face. "Perhaps you should run in with your valiant, protecting army," he told her.

"Perhaps I should."

"Ah, but you think you should keep an eye on me."

"Perhaps."

"So why do you look like a bird about to take flight? Are you afraid of me, Godiva?"

"No."

"But your heart is beating a thousand times a second, so it seems. I know that look on your face, so wary . . ."

"You don't know me at all!"

"Every inch of you."

Her heart was indeed beating a thousand times a second. And still, she lifted her hair from her neck with a bored nonchalance. "I would appreciate it if you'd quit being so rude as to remind me of my most uncomfortable folly."

"I wouldn't remind you, if I were able to forget!" he said, still smiling, and she didn't know if he was in the least serious, or if he simply enjoyed his game of taunting her.

He indicated the log. "Sit, Godiva."

She stared at him uneasily. She should say good night—then run to the shelter of the cabin and the security of her boys.

He knew her hesitation, and smiled.

"Be reckless! Brave, bold, confident! Take the risk. Courage, Godiva! Indeed, I think you're going to need it."

"There is no risk in sitting with you!" she countered, but it was a lie, for suddenly . . .

She felt as if she were indeed in the greatest danger she had yet encountered.

Chapter 4

"Coffee with a shot of whiskey?" the Yank suggested. "I did make the offer earlier, though you refused me."

"Why, naturally, sir," she said, "I am quite careful with a stranger, when that stranger is an enemy."

"Ah, so speaks the Southern Belle!" he taunted.

"So speaks a war-weary, wary young woman, sir. Do you think you can make me drunk?"

"Drunk? You? From a single shot of whiskey?" She wasn't sure whether or not to be offended by the amusement in his eyes. "Not at all. I have a feeling that proper lady though you may be, you're quite familiar with whiskey and other spirits."

She ignored his tone then. "Fine. I'll have coffee with a good strong shot of whiskey. You're right—I am familiar with spirits."

He poured her coffee and added a generous dose of the whiskey. She accepted it, watching him.

"So . . . you're staying through the night?" she asked him.

"I am."

"What if you fall asleep, and we cut your throat?"

"You won't."

"Why not?"

"Because if I hear one of you near me—which I will— I'll put a bullet through flesh so fast there won't be time to scream."

She shivered at his tone, then huddled into herself, sipping her coffee, hoping that he hadn't seen her reaction.

But he was suddenly closer to her, hunkered down in front of her, his eyes searchingly on her own. "Did you intend to slit my throat, Godiva?" he inquired.

"No," she murmured uncomfortably.

She swallowed a huge sip of coffee, burned her mouth, and almost choked. She stared at him again, then shook her head. It was odd to have him so close again, and alarming to feel that she was coming to know him in some small way. Odd, the things she noticed, like the size of his hand, the rough texture of his palms, the length of his fingers, the neat, clean cut of his nails. She swallowed hard, wishing she did not feel so unnerved, and that she could find him to be a far more repulsive person. "Why are you staying here? Why haven't you moved on?"

He shrugged, still too close. "I have my reasons."

"We're just what I said we were, a small party of children. Injured children at that, as you can see. And very, very tired," she added, sighing.

"Then relax," he suggested. "Put your head back. Sit upon the ground there. Let the fire warm you. It is, in truth, a spectacular night. The air is cool, but the fire is warm. The stars remain beautiful in a clear, ebony sky. Rest."

"Rest?" she inquired. "With you? Lie down beside a rattler?"

He laughed easily. "Oh, Godiva! I think your fangs are probably far more dangerous than my own."

"But—"

"Had I meant to hurt you or molest you in any way, lady, I have certainly had my opportunities, don't you think?"

She lowered her lashes, flushing.

"Lie back on the saddle and blanket there." He rose, indicating the spot with a sweep of his arm. "The pines are soft beneath the blanket; the canopy of the sky is certainly a lovely one tonight."

Near the log, before the fire, he had laid out his saddle, saddle blanket, and army-issue bedroll. She was amazed to realize just how welcoming and comfortable it all looked.

But then, it had been a long day.

"You had intended that as your own bed," she said politely.

"Lady Godiva, it is yours."

"But—"

"Allow your enemy to be valiant."

She rose as well, meeting his eyes again as they stood before the fire.

"Fine, I will steal your bed. If—"

"If?" he interrupted her. "If I make no assumptions that your being in my bed means that, er, you wish to be in my bed. Trust me—I had no intention of doing so."

"Fine!" she said. She turned away from him, taking the few steps to the spot. Then, after she had stretched out, pulled his camp blanket around herself, and closed her eyes, she added a soft "Thank you."

"My pleasure, Godiva."

He didn't touch her, but he was near. She heard him sit down upon the log again, and though she didn't open her eyes, she knew that he kept his gaze upon the fire, and that he was thoughtful.

Would he tire? she wondered. Sleep soundly?

Soundly enough that they might surprise him in his sleep?

No. She was certain that assaulting him in the night would mean certain death. And not for him.

Yet would the morning be any better?

Perhaps, if she was any kind of seductress at all. If he had come to trust her at all . . .

She was so tired, yet surely, far too nervous to sleep. He was there, sitting beside her on the log. So close. His presence unlike any she had known before.

Strange, but that enemy presence lent a certain security to the night. She stretched like a cat, then eased more deeply into her makeshift bed, feeling a luxurious sense of comfort. The weather was so cool—a Florida winter, coming in earnest. The air seemed refreshingly sweet around. The bedroll was warm where she was cold, and the saddle and blanket did make a fine pillow. Half-awake and half-asleep, she slit her eyes, and she could see the fire as it flickered and danced in the night. She was exhausted. Indeed, she'd been so tired, and then so full of catfish, and then the coffee spiked with the whiskey . . .

The world fogged. She was still so keenly aware of him. And she strangely thought that he smelled good; he was bathed, shaven, smelling of soap and leather, clean and rugged. *Yet why did something about him seem familiar? Why did it seem she should know something, understand who he was, what he was . . .*

The answer eluded her. Her eyes closed further. She could dare to trust him tonight. So that she could betray him come morning.

It was easy to sleep, and yet later, she awoke, shivering.

The fire must have died.

She rose slightly and saw that he was up, stoking new life into the fire.

He heard her, sensed her, knew that she was awake.

"Cold?"

"No, not really."

"Yes, you are."

He came to her. With his unnerving agility, he was down and beside her before she even realized his intent. She started to move, to protest, but he set an arm around her firmly. "I mean you no harm, Godiva! Trust me, you hardheaded little wild thing. I'm only trying to warm you."

"I don't want the warmth of such an enemy."

"Didn't anyone ever tell you, Godiva, that we don't always get what we want?"

"No!"

"Then it's time someone did. Lie down, sleep."

She gritted her teeth. She hadn't quite realized the scope of his strength; the arm around her was like an iron clasp. She closed her eyes, protesting no more. She could hardly entice him to join her down by the stream in the morning and flirt with him so engagingly that he'd

forget his back if she fought being near him while they
slept.

It would just have to be a wretched night. One in
which she would never find any rest again.

But she did sleep. Comfortably, and very deeply. She
was amazed to feel the coming of the sun against her
cheeks, hear the chirping of birds.

The world, she thought, could be so strange. War everywhere. Men killing men. But the birds let out their calls
as usual, the sun rose each morning, winter came, and
the breeze was fresh. And it was possible to waken in
the morning and believe that there was no war . . .

Except that, when she awoke, he was there. Beside
her as he had been. She had twisted and turned and—
mortifying as it might be—she had used him. Used his
form for added warmth, curled into the curve of his
body, turned into it again. And now she looked his way.

She had slept beside the man, through the night, and
she didn't even know his name.

His eyes opened, hard on hers, and she realized that
he hadn't lied, that the softest whisper of sound, a bare
hint of movement, awoke him. She'd done nothing but
open her eyes, and she had awakened him.

Or had he already been awake?

She thought that was the case. He had awakened and
lain there without moving. Not to disturb her? Or to
study her. But there they lay, his eyes now on hers with
just inches between them, their bodies all but entwined.

She instantly pushed away, forgetting all thought of
seducing him into an entrapment. She awkwardly struggled to her feet, backed away from him, and turned,
fleeing toward the brook.

Her heart was hammering, lungs heaving. She felt hot
and cold, and hot again.

The water beckoned. Bubbling over the little rocks
midstream, powder blue, except for diamond-like crys-
tals that rode the surface, gifts of the sun.

At the brook, she fell to her knees. She splashed her
face, half-soaking her gown, and so she opened her bodice at the throat. The water was wonderful, so cleansing.

More and more. She scooped up big handfuls of the fresh, cold water, and dashed it against her face, her neck, her collarbone. She delved into her voluminous skirt pocket again and found what had become her most cherished possession—her horsehair toothbrush. It was wearing thin, but then again, this was war.

Fortunately, Christmas was near. And one of the blessings of being a civilian was that she could go home, and at Cimarron, her mother would give her a new toothbrush, maybe even understanding just how much such a small item meant.

"I've got baking powder," she heard.

She stiffened. He'd followed her. Already.

Were any of her men even awake yet? Would they arrive in time if she were to distract him here—now?

And then, that thought didn't really matter—she realized just what he had said.

Baking powder! A great luxury for cleaning teeth, now that she was so constantly on the road and on the run.

She jumped to her feet, spinning around to face him. He walked toward her, taking a leather satchel from his frockcoat and handing it to her. He remained amused, and yet he seemed to understand. She accepted the gift, knelt to the water again, and felt the delirious, sensual pleasure of really cleaning her teeth. She ran her tongue over and over them, delighting in the smooth feel.

When she rose and turned toward him, ready to thank him, she realized that Trey and Gilly were hovering near the rear of the pines. She lowered her eyes quickly, moistened her lips. Then she looked up at the Yank with a bright smile. She moved an inch closer to him. He still smelled like soap and leather, not at all repugnant. This was doable. She lay a hand against his frockcoat, aware that her bodice was opened to what she hoped was a temptingly low position. She looked up into his eyes. "Thank you. I'd thought you'd be the most horrible person in the world. A monster. But you've cared for men. You've looked after their health, their welfare. I don't know what you really want, why you're waiting, but . . ."

"Yes, but—go on."

He was challenging her. He didn't seem easily seduced in the least.

She bit her lip.

"But you're really not a monster."

"Can you be so certain? We are all different things to different people, aren't we? Maybe I am a monster."

"Well . . . I've talked to you now."

"Yes."

She offered what she hoped was a winning smile.

"Slept through the night with you."

He was watching her, but smiles and flirtatious talk didn't seem to create the smitten effect she had hoped for.

His hand curled over hers where it lay upon his chest. He was a towering man, gazing down at her. She drew his hand to her lips, pressed a soft kiss against it, led it to her breast. A fine hand, large, long-fingered, the palm calloused. He was a man who worked with those hands, and yet, they were still somehow quite fine. And when his hand lay against her flesh . . .

She was startled to find herself the one shaken by the contact. A lightning sizzle of heat seemed to flash through her. She was hot, cold, weak.

"I don't see you as a monster," she whispered.

"No?"

She shook her head slowly, then she rose on her toes, coming closer, closer, closer. She saw the fire in his eyes. His head lowered toward her own. She felt the pressure of his lips, and again the flash of fire, the touch of his tongue, and a feeling so hotly, damnably erotic . . .

Then suddenly she was spinning, forced around before him, and locked with her back against the wall of his chest as he pulled a Colt—and aimed it at Trey and Gilly, who had been rushing for him.

"Don't make me shoot," he warned with deadly quiet.

They both stood still, ashamed, looking at their feet, at one another, at him, at Tia.

"Don't shoot them!" she cried out. "They meant you no harm."

"No harm—other than a bullet in the back?" he suggested.

"No, that would be—"

"Foolish, since it might have killed you as well!" he said angrily. She felt his arm tighten around her waist.

"No, sir. We never intended to shoot you. That would be murder. We never intended that, sir," Gilly said.

Perhaps the Yankee believed him. "And Private, it wasn't exactly *your* plan, was it?" the Yank inquired.

Trey shifted uneasily. "No, sir."

"Go back to the cabin," the Yank advised.

They were green boys. They had been raised as gentlemen. They stared at Tia, afraid, awaiting her word.

"Go back to the cabin. I imagine I'll be joining you shortly," Tia said.

"We can't leave if you intend her harm," Gilly said. His Adam's apple was wiggling, but his words were admirably brave.

"On my word, gentlemen, the lady will remain unharmed."

"Go on back to the cabin," she murmured. It might be the only way the man would ever release her.

And at last, the two turned, as told. If they lived, she thought, they would be good men. She stood dead still, barely daring to breathe as they left.

Then suddenly, abruptly, and with a frightening force, the Yank spun her again in his arms. "Let's finish what we started."

"What?" she cried with alarm.

"We'll finish what we started. You were saying . . . I'm not a monster, my lips were on yours, my hand . . . fingers, they were in a delightful realm of exploration."

"No . . ."

She was certain that she'd said the word, that she'd voiced the protest. And yet . . .

Was she afraid? The word was so weak, a whisper on the air, nothing real, just a breath.

No, it was him, the relentless force with which he touched her . . .

She felt his lips again, his kiss, deep, hot, wet, seeming

to delve into her being and her soul. She set a hand against him, to push him away. She didn't know if he so much as felt her fight, if it meant anything to him, or if her intent was lost against the very power of his embrace. And she wasn't sure at all how it happened, but her bodice was opened completely, her breasts were bared, and his hands were upon them. She was backed against a tree, aware that as he kissed her—a searing, ravishing kiss, almost indecent in itself, seeming to consume both thought and honor—she was sliding to the cool ground. But he was with her. He was there to break her fall, to catch her, hold her, embrace her. The air was cool, but her flesh seemed ablaze. She must protest with a greater urgency, stop this madness raking her system, parting her lips, giving way to the force of his kiss, the heat of his passion. Dear God, where was this leading? Couldn't she put up a better fight. Oh God, not a better fight, just a fight at all . . .

Then suddenly, his lips broke from hers.

He stood. Towering there, he straddled her prone body from above, looking down at her. She met his eyes, confused, then aware of her half-naked state, flushed cheeks, damp, swollen lips. She jerked her bodice together, shimmied on her buttocks to a sitting position against the tree, staring at him. "What—" she gasped, moistening her lips, searching for words, "What—"

"What, indeed? I mean, you had been seducing me, right? Pretense, we both know that. So . . . were you supposed to be able to claim that you were callously ravished by a vicious Yank? Take my hand, get up. I have no intention of destroying the fragile flower of any *sweet, innocent* Southern woman."

She could hear just how sweet and innocent he considered her to be.

Her honor seemed as broken as the South.

"Oh, get away from me!" she cried, rising, the tree a fine bulwark behind her. "The men might have managed to take you this time."

He laughed. Very rudely. "Oh, Godiva, I don't think so! The men were gone, weren't they? They had refused to leave you without my word that I'd cause you no harm—"

"And you lied!"

"Never. You are not in the least harmed."

Oh, he was mistaken! Her pride and self-respect were damaged beyond redemption!

"Your conceit is unbearable! Get away from me. If you truly mean no harm—"

"I never meant harm, but you are dangerously over-zealous in your determination that you can outwit an enemy, and you certainly have and do intend great harm," he warned her. His voice was suddenly so angry that she bit into her lip, backing away. "You will find yourself caught in an awful backlash, you little fool. Setting out to hurt others may well be dangerous. You came upon me. You don't know who is out there, you truly don't know the full scope of what the war has created, and in your quest to destroy your enemy—"

"I'm not trying to destroy you—"

"Ah, there you have it! Fundamentally, we disagree. But damn you, you will listen to me. I'm trying to make you give a care for your own life and safety—"

"Hey, Yank!"

Tia was startled. If the Yank was, he gave no sign.

Still, she sprang hopefully to her feet. Reprieve.

It was Trey calling. Enfield in his hand, he was running through the pines, anxious to reach the brook. Breathlessly he called out, "Dixie's coming. Dickinson and his troops, sir. Fifty, sixty men, coming this way."

Dixie. Captain Jonathan Dickinson. He and his cavalry were often all that had defended the state of Florida. She'd been hoping to meet up with him.

And now . . .

The Yank had been looking for Dixie, as well, she thought, her heart thundering.

"Trey! You've given him Dixie's position, damn it!" she swore suddenly. "That's exactly why he has stayed with us, what he's been waiting for! He's been searching out Dixie's position, and we have led him to the very place!"

"No!" Trey protested. "No, that's not possible. He's been a decent human being to us. I've just given him a chance to leave!"

"Knowing Dixie's position!" Tia spat out. And it was true. He'd been out scouting for Dixie and his troops to begin with—he had just stumbled upon them. And they had given him the information he'd wanted.

"You needn't give your young soldier there any kind of a reprimand. I've known Captain Dixie to be in the area."

"You were looking for him."

"Maybe."

"And now you know exactly where he is."

He shrugged, and she wondered if he was even out to destroy Dixie—or if he had just come to make certain of the man's movements. Dixie was a small man—almost as small as she was herself. But he was a formidable soldier, and he'd kept the Yankees jumping many a time.

"Well, Godiva," the Yank said, "you've suggested that you want me gone. That I should leave, that you wanted to be quit of my presence. I think that time has come. And indeed, I feel assured for your personal safety— you're with your boys here, and soon enough you'll have the escort of larger forces."

"Are you insinuating that *you've* kept me safe in any way?" she inquired incredulously.

"Godiva, I'm sure you really don't understand all that's out there!"

"Enemies of my state, my *country,* are out there, that's all I know!" she informed him heatedly.

"I think I will be on my way," the Yankee said. He saluted Trey, who saluted in return. Then he startled Tia by drawing her to him with a frightening strength.

"A warning here," he said, and his voice grated. "A warning with true wishes that you survive the war with mind, body, and soul intact. Behave, Godiva, for yourself—and lest your good Southern parents discover their daughter's wanton ways!"

She lifted her chin. "Well, I just have to thank God you don't know them and that you will never darken their door!" she informed him. Oddly, her voice betrayed her—wavering just a hair.

"Ah! I've touched a nerve, have I? I'd quite begun to think that impossible. My, my, ravished in the woods—and she would have endured! A fine sacrifice for the great Southern Cause! Yet mention Mother and Father and . . . perhaps I do know them, my dear. Oh, Godiva! Do take care! You are far too reckless, and trust me, you never know just what wolves do lurk in the forest on the prowl for naked beauties!"

With a deep, mocking bow, he turned from her.

And disappeared into the pines.

Chapter 5

"Why, I'm telling you, sir, it's the truth, this is God's own free man, I swear it! And I promise you that I am a free woman myself, and have been since the day I was born!"

"Listen, darkee, ain't no person of color leaving here without a look over by the bounty hunters."

"I can't be detained! And neither can my brother, nor his wife here! He's one chance of a good job, and if I don't have him spruced up by tomorrow morning—"

"Get out of the line!" the white soldier shouted, his face turning red, the veins in his neck all bulging.

Curiously, Sydney found herself walking forward. She knew the voice of the woman talking. It was Sissy.

Sissy, with whom she had lived in Washington. A beautiful, extremely intelligent young black woman who had performed espionage for the Union. Who had worked with Jesse Halston, the man who was Sydney's—

Husband. Yes, and actually, Sydney was married to Jesse partially because of Sissy. Sissy had been privy to her moments on the night she'd been arrested, and so, in a roundabout way, she was partially responsible for the fact that Jesse had felt honor-bound to marry her—and get her out of Old Capitol.

Sydney, not sure at first what she was doing, excused herself, cutting through the line. She addressed the balding, sallow-faced officer in charge.

"What is the problem here, sir?"

She saw Sissy's eyes widen even as the officer stared at her, looking her up and down. Sissy knew that Sydney had gone to visit Brent, but perhaps she hadn't been expecting her back on the same day she was evidently returning home from some trip south herself.

A dangerous trip for a free black woman—especially one who had already been seized by slave hunters, and given over to a man with designs of becoming her master. A man responsible for the whip scars that littered Sissy's back.

"Ain't no darkees goin' by me, ma'am, and I don't care how prissy their language might be. Book learning!" He spat into the dirt.

"This darkee, sir, works for me," Sydney said imperiously.

"Does she, now?" the man demanded. "Thought you were a Southern woman, Miss McKenzie. You are Miss McKenzie, right? I seen you about a year ago, working down at the Chimborizo hospital then."

"Why, yes, I was there!" She smiled, grateful they'd hit common ground.

"Ain't no darkees getting by me, miss!" he insisted again.

She met Sissy's eyes and frowned, wondering what on earth had tempted Sissy to do something so stupid as to leave the safety of Washington.

"You don't understand. I give you my word that she is a free woman."

The soldier hesitated. "Maybe I ought to call my colonel in."

"Maybe you had best!" Sydney said. "My God! My eldest brother risks his life daily against the Union blockade to keep the South alive, and I have just come from seeing another brother who risks his life daily to save our soldiers! I have put my own life in peril again and again, sir, and you are trying to make my life difficult, denying me the right to leave my own country with my own servant?"

He cleared his throat.

"That, ma'am, is the point. You are attempting to return to Washington—a hotbed of illegal activity!"

"Call your superior, sir. Now! Or, I promise you, they will hear about this in the highest of government—and military—circles!"

That made the man pause. "Fine. You can take the darkee with the big mouth. Too bad she ain't somebody's slave—a good whomping might shut her up and show her her place! But the man and his wife stay."

Frowning, Sydney looked around Sissy at the tall, emaciated-looking black man and the thinner woman at his side. They looked forty, but probably weren't much more than twenty, she thought.

"Sissy—"

"Why ma'am, I told you my mommy died just outside Manassas, and that I was coming for Del here and his wife, Geraldine!" Sissy told her enthusiastically.

Sissy had told her no such thing. And she doubted that this man was Sissy's brother. But who was he. And what in God's name was Sissy doing?

Sissy suddenly let out an awful wail. "I can't leave my brother, Miss Sydney, ma'am. What with my momma newly dead and all—"

"Sir!" Sydney interrupted, "I'm telling you this woman is in my employ. I'll vouch for her and the others," she said firmly.

The soldier seemed indecisive. "There's word you married a Yank, ma'am."

"Word is true. But it hasn't changed who I am, or where I was born, sir. You said that you knew me. I helped hundreds of men in that hospital, sir."

"But you're going through the lines to return to your new husband in the Northern capital. Why should I take your word?"

Sydney knew she was capable of being extremely assertive when she chose. Partially because she had inherited her facial structure from her grandmother's family—she had strong, wide cheekbones, a dead straight nose, and wide eyes beneath a clear, defined brow. Yet her eyes, green as a forest, were from her mother, and it was from her mother as well that she had learned to be assertive and determined—and courteous, of course—all in one.

"You should take my word, sir, because I have offered it, and I promise you that I do not do so lightly."

"You have your papers?"

"Yes, of course, I have travel papers. I am on personal business, family business, and nothing more. My papers to leave the North were approved by General Magee, and my permission to return to the North was signed by General Longstreet just yesterday!"

"All right, then, ma'am, take your people and pass on through. I can't, however, promise you any safety from here on out. You're still some distance from the Yankee lines. But there ain't been much action of late."

"I know that, sir. Thank you for the warning. Sissy, come along now—with Del and Geraldine."

She squared her shoulders, lifted her chin, and walked on by. Slowly. An orderly from her brother's surgery remained with the crude wagon he had managed to allow her for transportation back to the North. Corporal Randall's skinny roan mare was tied to the rear of the wagon. When they reached Northern lines, he would leave her with the conveyance, and return to her brother's surgery outside Richmond.

She prayed that Sissy was walking along behind her—slowly. But she didn't turn back. She reached the wagon, and the young dark-haired man with the scraggly beard and blade of grass in his teeth. "Corporal Randall, we've company for the trip back."

Randall arched a brow.

"One of my servants, and her kin."

Randall looked over her shoulder, inspecting the three people following behind her. He spat out the blade of grass.

"You ain't bringing contraband slaves North, are you, Miss Sydney?"

"Heavens, no! May I remind you, I went to prison for my *Rebel* espionage."

"Just checking, ma'am. You do have a Yank husband now."

"Indeed, sir, I try not to condemn him for his loyalty, and I pray he will not condemn me for mine." She turned to Sissy and the thin pair who hovered just slightly behind her. "Up in the wagon, and let's go."

Sissy, her "brother," and his wife crawled up into the rear of the wagon. Sydney took a seat next to Corporal Randall, and he flicked the whip over the backs of the mules made available for her transport. Randall rode with his eyes straight ahead as they started out, then he turned to look at Sydney. "You do know these folks?"

She sighed. "Sissy has worked with my husband, Corporal. I met her through him. She became my servant because of her work with my husband. She was born a free woman, but Corporal, at one point she was seized as property and richly abused by her master." She stared at Randall. "It is possible, Corporal, to be a loyal Rebel, and deplore what monsters do to other human beings!"

Randall looked ahead again, a small smile playing on his features. "Miss Sydney, you don't need to go getting your dander up around me! I never did cotton to the idea of one man owning another. But then again, I never did cotton to the idea of the Federal government telling a *Virginian* what to do and what not to do. Still, I think we'd best get these mules moving, since folks are mighty touchy these days about all aspects of the war!"

Close to the enemy lines, Randall climbed down from the wagon and looked up at her. He shook his head with a sigh.

"I don't much like leaving you."

"I'm almost within Yankee lines."

"Well, that's just fine. As long as you meet up with Yankee troops. There's too many misfits in this war now, and you may meet up with men who have no loyalty in any direction."

"Deserters?"

"Deserters, drifters . . . trash. White and black. You take care now, you hear? Move fast. And get within those Yankee lines."

"Thank you, Corporal Randall. I promise you, I'll move with all speed."

"You do that for me," Randall said, untying his horse's lead from the rear of the wagon. He mounted his mare and came back around by the wagon, where Sydney had now taken up the reins. "God guard you," he said, saluting Sydney.

"And you." She smiled, saluting him in return. "Stay well!"

"I will! Wish you would have stayed with us, Miss Sydney!"

Maybe I should have done exactly that! she thought. She should have just stayed with Brent, assisting him in his surgery.

What had brought her back? The husband who'd had no desire to see her since the machinations of their marriage?

Christmas. It was nearly Christmas. She needed to be there, in case he came back. Only because he had done what seemed to be the honorable thing in marrying her, she felt she owed him at least the appearance of a home and a wife loyal to him, if not to his country.

Corporal Randall saluted again, called out to the mules, and when they had started up their journey again, he turned his mare, and left. When Sydney was certain they had ridden far apart down the long path, she turned around and called out sharply to Sissy where she sat in the rear of the wagon. "Come up here!"

Sissy, she had come to realize, could play any role. She had seemed as meek and mild as the most timid servant girl when they had met—but then, she'd been following Sydney around and spying on her spying activities! This small, beautiful, remarkable young black woman had a tempest and passion in her soul too often hidden by the thick, dark lashes that could conveniently sweep over her eyes when she didn't want her thoughts known. Now, she came forward as Sydney bid—carefully, lest the jerking gait of the mules send her crashing over the side of the wagon.

Taking a seat next to Sydney, Sissy informed her,

"You might have said 'please,' " and her tone was no less imperious than any Sydney had ever used herself.

"I might have, but I'm hardly in the mood!" Indeed, she cracked the whip over the backs of the poor mules with such a sharpness that the sound sent them bolting down the path. The wagon creaked and jolted; in the rear, the thin woman moaned, and Sydney gritted her teeth, irritated that Sissy could make her so foolishly angry.

"You've told me often enough that you know masters who are not only kind, but *polite* to their slaves."

"You're not my slave, you never have been, and you know darned well I never owned any slaves whatsoever. So don't play word games with me right now, Sissy, not when you might have risked my life back there."

"Your life was never in any danger," Sissy said.

"Oh yes, it was! Unless this really is your long lost brother—which I do not believe! So let's be honest and open here—are these escaped slaves? Have you forced me into a position of betraying my own country?"

Sissy turned on her. "Have you betrayed your own conscience?"

"My conscience, ethics, morals, heart, et cetera, are none of your business. You've used me, and we remain in danger."

"I didn't use you—you came forward to help me of your own free will."

"Yes! But I didn't know that you were trying to smuggle slaves out of the South! It's illegal."

"Only when you're in the South."

"We're still in the South!"

"Barely," Sissy assured her. Then she added quietly and desperately, "And I would have used you, yes! I am ready to use anyone, do anything, to help free people who are kept in bondage."

"Oh, my God."

"You've seen my back!" Sissy told her heatedly.

"Not every slave is viciously beaten."

"Look at those two!" Sissy implored her. "Do they

look as if they've been cherished and tenderly cared for?"

Sydney had to turn around—and admit that Sissy was right. The pair with her, overworked into an early old age, were stick-thin, sadly emaciated.

"You could see some real scars on his back!" Sissy said.

"Maybe he deserved them. Maybe he lied or cheated or—"

"Or tried to escape," Sissy said flatly.

"You're missing the point here. You have no right to make me a part of this!" Sydney insisted. "I am a Southerner—"

"You're Jesse's wife now."

"It doesn't change the fact that I think the North should let the South go!"

"Well, the North isn't going to let the South go."

Sydney shook her head. She was angry, unnerved, uncertain, and angrier still because she didn't want to be at all uncertain. *Yes, good God, these poor people most obviously and desperately need their freedom.* But she had gone to a Rebel camp, she'd been born a Floridian, and she had gone with her state, and there she was— *helping escaped slaves!* She shouldn't be doing it, it went against the laws of *her* country, the Confederate States of America, and yet . . .

She didn't believe in slavery, she had never believed in slavers, and she knew that her grandmother's people had often helped escaped slaves. There had even been large communities of escaped slaves who had taken on the Indian ways and become known as the Black Seminoles. The Indians, so constantly persecuted, had stubbornly resisted white efforts to find escaped slaves, often at the peril of their own lives.

And yet . . .

The persecution by the army had also been so rigorous that most Seminoles had readily embraced the Confederacy—the Union uniform was so very much hated by those who had managed to flee the mass migrations to the West.

It hadn't seemed to matter that many of the vicious men who had hounded the Indians had simply changed uniforms. To most Seminoles and other Indians in Florida, the Union uniform was a hated symbol, and so it would remain. Her father, her brothers were all Rebels. The irony of the contrasts in what they believed in and what they were fighting for suddenly seemed incredibly great.

"What you have done to me is a presumption on our friendship," Sydney began again angrily.

"Friendship? Was I your friend—or your servant?" Sissy demanded.

"Oh, my God! Here I am, risking my life, getting you through the Rebel lines, and you have the nerve to goad me. Let's see—were you my friend? Lord, no! You had me arrested!"

"I didn't have you arrested. I merely knew you were out to do some harm to Union troops, and I followed you, and listened—"

"And spied on me, and had me arrested."

"Jesse arrested you."

"Thanks to you."

"Well, then, he married you—and got you out of prison, right? So it all ended well for you, didn't it?"

"Oh, wonderfully! It was a forced marriage, and we hate one another—"

"He never hated you," Sissy interrupted. She looked at Sydney, her dark eyes serious and questing. "You hated him—because you thought he was betraying you by forcing you to remain here. Well, you were a fool. He let your brother go when it was against everything he believed. By forcing you to stay behind, he gave Jerome a better chance to escape. He kept you from danger. He arrested you because he had to. And I don't think you hate him at all. I think you're fighting a stupid war that you don't believe in yourself."

"And I don't care what you think!" Sydney flared.

"Sydney!" Sissy said suddenly, her face gray. "There's someone . . ."

Sydney fell silent, listening. There was a commotion

in the brush ahead. She felt the color drain from her own cheeks. She'd been arguing with Sissy out of anger—she hadn't thought that they might really be caught by Rebel troops.

Who was ahead?

A voice suddenly seemed to crack out of the air, as if God were speaking.

"Halt! In the name of God and the Union, halt!"

She reined in quickly, realizing that Corporal Randall had risked his own well-being, taking her as close to Yankee lines as he had. A soldier stepped onto the trail, rifle in his hand.

"Who are you and where are you going?"

"I have my papers right here, sir," Sydney said.

He came to the wagon, glanced over her travel pass, her and her company, and told her to move. "Farther up, you'll be asked out of the carriage, ma'am."

She thanked him and started down the road again.

Ahead was another stop. The road here was filled with soldiers. Tents and cooking fires were to one side of the road; a number of soldiers stood against trees nearby, drinking coffee, cleaning weapons, taking their leisure. Sydney crawled down from the wagon with her papers, nodding in return to the soldiers who acknowledged her presence. She felt their eyes watching her every step. She was unaccountably nervous leaving Sissy and her friends in the wagon. She'd left the South with these people. That should have been the hard part. She was tired now, with a blazing headache.

She handed the Union sergeant her papers. He stared at the papers, then he stared at her. He stared at her papers again, then peered into her face for the third time. She shifted from foot to foot and sighed with deep and obvious aggravation. "My papers, sir, are in perfect order."

"There's a McKenzie here in your name," the sergeant pointed out. "You kin to Colonel McKenzie?"

This was Union territory.

Which Colonel McKenzie? she was tempted to ask.

She knew that he was referring to her cousin, Ian, the

Union colonel. She was tempted to tell him that she was also related to Julian, her cousin and Ian's brother, but a Confederate colonel, and then there was another Colonel McKenzie, Colonel Brent McKenzie—her brother, the surgeon she had just gone to see. Then, of course, there was her other brother, naval Captain Jerome Mc-Kenzie, the one she had used when trying to leave the South—but mentioning his name to Federal forces often caused a severe reaction since he continued to run circles around the Union blockade.

Was she trying to make good use of renowned names here?

If so, naturally, there was still that other colonel she could mention . . . Colonel Jesse Halston, United States Cavalry, just like the one McKenzie relative she was ready to claim at the moment.

"I am a first cousin to Colonel Ian McKenzie, United States Cavalry," she said, but she knew by the man's sudden, snickering smile that he knew exactly who that made *her*. The McKenzie who had been instrumental in more than one prison escape from Old Capitol, the McKenzie who had helped break out her brother and a number of her countrymen dressed as a ladies singing group. She'd also helped her cousin escape by suggesting he slip into a coffin.

Yes, she was one of the McKenzies who had actually resided at Old Capitol for a while. Perhaps she could get into a friendly conversation here with this man and explain it all. Tell him how she had tended Jesse first in Virginia when he had been a wounded prisoner in the Confederate States of America. How much she had started to like him there, and how liking him had made her see more than ever that the war was a tragedy in which friends and brothers, fathers and sons, could walk out on a field any day, be ordered to fire—and shoot one another down.

But then Jesse had betrayed her, threatening to call out the guard should she attempt to leave the city with her brother Jerome.

Then came the part the guard would really like—there

she was, a good Rebel stuck in the heart of Washington. Before she knew it, she was passing information, and before she knew it, she was a Rebel spy. She hadn't come here with designs on espionage—she had really, truly just fallen right into it. Then, in a nutshell, Jesse— assisted by *Sissy,* who had ostensibly been living with her as a servant!—had learned what information she was to deliver, disguised himself to receive the information and prove her a spy, had her arrested, and seen her sent to Old Capitol. The man who had then been her downfall and total nemesis had come around at the urging of her cousin-in-law, Rhiannon McKenzie, Julian's wife. Because she'd asked Rhiannon for help—afraid that all her male kin would feel honor-bound to storm the Yankee citadel for her release. Rhiannon had gone to see Jesse. And Jesse had come to the prison—where she was incarcerated because he had tricked and betrayed her. There was only one way to get her out, and that was because of his own reputation as a heroic cavalry commander. He could marry her, and take responsibility for her future actions.

Would telling the man any of this help? No.

"Sergeant, you have no right to detain me in this manner," she told him firmly. "My papers are in perfect order."

"You went back behind Rebel lines, Miss McKenzie."

"*Mrs.* Halston," she hissed impatiently. It seemed ridiculous that he was giving her trouble—for once in her life, her motives had been strictly within the law. "And my husband has been out of the city—fighting. He was wounded, imprisoned, and wounded again—fighting for the Union, sir. But without him being here, I took the time I was left alone and went to see my brother. He is not a spy, nor engaged in any manner of undercover activity whatsoever—he is a surgeon. I hadn't seen him in a very, very long time. I left the city with permission from General McGee. But now I am back, because my husband is a Union soldier. This is his home, and this is where I will wait for him. Now I am weary, and I want to go home. Please let me pass!"

To her surprise, the man seemed to take a slight step back. "Mrs. Halston, you've got to realize that Washington, D.C., is a hotbed of snakes and spies. And with your known Rebel activities, I'm not sure it's such a good thing for you to be coming and going. Whether you are or aren't guilty of carrying information—"

"I am not carrying information!"

"Who are these people with you?" he demanded suddenly.

"What?"

"The Negroes?"

She straightened to her full height. Although the man naturally remained taller, she was aggravated enough to feel as tough as a little terrier. "This is a free woman who resides in Washington, and for your information, soldier, she has done the Union great favors upon many an occasion!"

He looked over at Sissy. "The Union—or other darkees?"

She stared at him, horrified and infuriated. "President Lincoln has taught us that the major issue we're fighting over is slavery! I can imagine being challenged in the South, but how dare you detain me here any longer regarding the Negroes in my company!"

"Look, Mrs. Halston, the city is teeming with refugees and darkees with no jobs and no place to go."

"This is Mr. Lincoln's city, and they will reside here. Let me pass now with these people, or so help me, sir, I will somehow see to it that you are very, very sorry for the difficulties you have caused me!"

The soldier suddenly looked as irritated and angry as she herself felt. "You should have never been let out of prison, Miz McKenzie, and that's a sad fact."

"But I have been let out!" she replied with soft vehemence, but as she turned away from him, he had a rejoinder for her.

"Leave it to a half-breed!"

She didn't know if he had meant for her to hear him or not. But it was the wrong night for him to come out with such fighting words.

She swung back around on him, catching his jaw with a sturdy slap that must have stung like the venom of a hundred bees.

"Quarter-breed soldier, and you can count on it. We just keep fighting and fighting, one way or the other. We are survivors!"

"Why . . ." the soldier began, incensed, his cheek reddening, his hand rising reflexively to touch the spot where she had struck him. "Why you—"

"Breed? Rebel? Just what would you like to call me?" she inquired. "Take care, sir, with what you do, since you must recall, you are dealing with someone carrying the blood of pure savages in her veins!"

She was startled by a sudden sound of applause. Swinging around, she saw that the group of Yankee soldiers standing by the trees had been watching her. They had kept their eyes on the entire altercation.

"Teach him his manners, ma'am!" a young soldier called out.

"And if he takes another step toward you, don't you worry none, we'll do some of the teaching for you!" another man said. He wore a sergeant's stripes on his arms as well, an older man, with rich gray whiskers, heavy jowls, and a round, muscled body. "Are you forgetting you're speaking to a lady, Sergeant?" he demanded sharply.

"The lady has been a Confederate spy!" the checkpoint sergeant argued.

"If we had to hang every lady in Washington who had lent a sympathetic ear to the South, we might be plumb out of ladies in the capital. As to Mrs. Halston, well, doesn't seem to me she's doing anything much against the Union now. Looks to me like she might be doing something for those poor people there in that wagon. There's been refugees by the hundreds piling into the city—I can't see what harm Mrs. Halston's bringing in two more can do to anyone."

"Why, she's Jesse's wife, is she?" a cavalryman asked. "Why, then, here's to you, ma'am. Jesse saw fit to marry the lady, and she seems like a fine, fierce beauty to me. To Jesse's wife!'' he declared.

The rest of the soldiers let out encouraging calls, clapped, and saluted her, appearing to be well entertained—and pleased with her show of courage. Flushing, she was tempted to bow, while at the same time, she wanted to run away. She'd been attacked for being a Southerner, then for trying to help blacks into the city— and then for her own Indian blood!

''Sergeant Walker!'' one of the men, an artillery colonel who had been leaning against an old oak, called out sharply, approaching the guard on duty. ''Let the lady pass!''

''Lady! But, sir—''

''Sergeant, let the lady pass!''

''But—''

''Now!''

Sydney met the colonel's eyes. He looked fifty—like the darkees, he was probably twenty years younger. His hair was stone gray. His eyes were as old as the hills. She managed a small smile to him in acknowledgment.

''Thank you, sir.''

He bowed low to her. ''Mrs. Halston, my pleasure.''

She hurried swiftly back to her wagon, crawling up to take the reins.

She felt incredibly weary—and confused. It didn't help that Sissy was staring at her with pride. ''My, my!'' Sissy said softly. ''It's a Rebel Yank!''

''I'm not a Rebel Yank!'' Sydney lashed out. ''Honestly, I wish you were my darkee! I'd skin your hide!'' she threatened.

Sissy broke into peals of laughter.

''You made me a conspirator in stealing contraband!'' Sydney charged her.

Sissy shook her head. ''No, Mrs. Halston, you just helped two human beings gain their freedom and their lives. I thank you with all my heart, and I know that God himself thanks you as well. Sydney, you were magnificent!''

Sydney shook her head. ''Sissy, I didn't want to be

magnificent! What I did was wrong, your tricking me was wrong—"

"The end defends the means, Sydney—Machiavelli."

"What is a slave doing reading Machiavelli?" Sydney asked.

"I was educated, Miss Sydney. Don't you see—it's all in the education."

Sydney shook her head, staring at Sissy. "Hundreds of people, thousands of people, have no education. Plantation slaves surely aren't all like you, Sissy! What will they do, how will they manage? This war will leave a world destroyed. Farms will be ruined, people will be homeless, and when this fighting is over, new fighting will begin. Life will be horrible."

"But freedom is the first step!"

"What is freedom if people starve?"

"Freedom is not feeling the crack of a whip on your back, Miss Sydney. It's knowing that your sons and daughters aren't going to be sold off to a master in another state who may or may not be a good man. Freedom, Sydney, think about it. You knew prison. Isn't freedom worth any cost?"

Sissy pleaded so eloquently.

Sydney shook her head slowly. "My God, Sissy, I don't know. I just don't know."

Sissy smiled. "I still say thank you! And when Jesse hears about this—"

"Oh, my God, don't you dare tell Jesse!"

"But—"

"No! I mean it. I swore I wouldn't be involved in any kind of espionage."

"But you just helped—"

"Sissy, you must understand! We were behind Rebel lines. We could have been arrested, killed!"

"You were determined and brave."

"Don't you dare tell Jesse! You promise me!"

Sissy reached out suddenly, touching a strand of Sydney's deep auburn hair. "Soldiers watch you and waylay you, Miss Sydney, because you are beautiful."

"For a quarter-breed," Sydney breathed through half-clenched teeth, and she was startled to realize the bitterness she had felt at the soldier's remark. She had seldom felt the stigma of prejudice; her grandmother might have been a Seminole, but her grandfather had been a McKenzie, and though her parents had chosen to live deep in the unsettled south of the state, she had attended dinners and balls at her uncle's house in Tampa, as well as those she'd been invited to throughout the state, and in her mother's native South Carolina as well. She was a child of privilege—very rich, no matter what her bloodlines. No man had ever dared taunt her, not with her brothers and cousins. And yet, sometimes, she had heard whispers when she entered a room. Heads turned toward her . . . men and women watched her, and sometimes they thought that it was such a pity that she should be "tainted" with Indian blood. She had never felt tainted—she had known nothing but love and pride from her grandmother's people. Before this war between the states, she had determined that she would never play a marriage game—she would far rather become a reclusive, but educated and intriguing, old maid. If and when she married, she would marry for love, and love alone, and if society happened to be against that love—and she had foolishly fallen for a man too weak to defy society—then she would surely fall out of love as quickly as she had fallen into it.

But then she had met Jesse, and he had found her background interesting, not tainted. He had fascinated, he had charmed . . . but he had been the enemy, and he had betrayed.

And still . . .

He had married her, and asked nothing of her. What came between them had nothing to do with color, race, or creed. It had simply been North and South.

"Miss Sydney, you silly *mostly* white child. It's because of all that you are that you're as stunning as you are!" Sissy said, shaking her head. "And yet . . ."

"And yet what?"

Sissy shrugged, but kept her eyes level on Sydney's. "Well, there are whites, you know, who consider a man or woman black, no matter how pale that black may be. Great-grandmother, great-great-grandfather . . . and you know, in your heart, *you know,* that there are lots and lots of slaves with the white blood of their masters running in their veins. But did you know, Miss Sydney, just how many whites consider an *Indjun* just as color tainted as a black man, and any amount of color tainting makes you just as colored."

"Sissy, you're not going to get beneath my skin and change me into a rabble-rousing fool like Harriet Beecher Stowe because I have Indian blood!"

Sissy shook her head again. "Sydney, I don't want to change you into anything. I just want you to realize that the world can be a hard, wicked place."

"I know that."

Sissy turned toward the road and the night. "Jesse is a real cavalier. He sees people." She turned to Sydney. "And he loves you."

"That's why he prefers the battlefield to coming home," Sydney murmured.

"I fell in love with a white man once," Sissy said quietly.

She was being baited, Sydney knew. But she couldn't help herself. "All right, Sissy. What happened."

"He lied and insisted he owned me, then he raped me, and we had a child."

"Sissy! I didn't know you had a baby—"

"I don't have a baby anymore. It was a healthy boy, but before he was born, my white 'owner' fell out of lust with me. He sold the baby."

"Sissy, I'm so sorry—"

"Don't be. You see, that's the world. He could lust for a Negroid woman, but certainly never, *never* marry her. Can you imagine, he *sold his own child*!"

"No, I cannot imagine," she said. "And yet, such things are true."

"Jesse *married* you. Just to help you, to keep your family safe, for God's sake!"

"I know that Sissy—"

"He'd be very, very proud of you tonight."

"Sissy, don't you even *think* about saying anything to Jesse. You don't understand the promise I made. You must swear not to say anything to him."

"But—"

"Swear!"

Sissy sighed. "I promise, *Mrs.* Halston. I promise."

"Good!" Sydney said firmly. She cracked the whip over the backs of the mules once again. They were close to home.

No, home was far, far away. Where it was warm. Where winter's frost never seeped into the bones . . .

And yet, she was suddenly anxious for her home away from home.

She wanted to crawl into darkness, away from everyone, and try to understand just what she was fighting for herself.

Chapter 6

Home.

Tia opened her eyes, not quite sure what had awakened her.

Sleeping was pure luxury. Her bed in her father's house was imported, her pillows were of goose down, her sheets were soft cotton, and in the coolness of the night, the quilt that covered her was warm and encompassing. Far different from the thin camp bed she had made her own at her brother's now constantly moving field hospital.

She knew that what they saw of the war was nowhere like what occurred in other places; the skirmishes they saw couldn't begin to be as severe as the fighting in the other areas. Casualty figures from battles fought across the South—and into Maryland and Pennsylvania—were staggering. Fifty thousand killed, wounded, missing, in a single day. Even seeing a battlefield so strewn could probably not even sink into the soul. Yet, no matter what the numbers, death was an individual thing, and she had watched men die, and each individual death had been a terrible thing. But others had lived, and that made the camp beds, the horrible food, the mosquitoes in summer and the damp cold in winter all bearable. She loved her brother; Julian was one of the best surgeons in the world, she was convinced. And from the beginning, she had wanted to come with him to his surgery. Her parents had never suggested that nursing in the wilds was not a suitable occupation for a lady—as had been the case with innumerable young women when the war had begun—but everyone in the household had teased her about the luxuries she would be leaving behind. She smiled, holding her pillow close to her chest. She had, indeed, shown them all. She might be an ivory-skinned "delicate little thing" to all appearances, but she had found her own inner strength serving in the field. She had gone from her down pillows to straw without a blink; she had bathed in cold springs—to tremendous ill effect, she might add!—she had stood by while wounded men had screamed in anguish, and she had never faltered or turned away when Julian had given his orders for help. She had stitched wounds, soaked up blood, cleaned out infected injuries—the stench of which had scarcely been bearable. She had done it all—forgoing all luxury, and maybe even proven something to herself. She had to admit, though, that at the beginning, it had been terrible. Far more terrible than she had ever imagined—and she had been sorely tempted to run home. She had never let it show.

It was so good to be home—there was nowhere in the world like Cimarron. The plantation sat upon the river coming in from Tampa Bay. Winter could become chilly, but never deadly cold, and on mornings such as this, the breeze just touched the chintz curtains by the latticed door to the balcony that surrounded the house. The rear of the house faced the river; to the front was the grand entrance; to the east lay the sloping lawn and, down from it, a thick pine forest filled with lush hammocks and fresh water springs. It was as if life went on forever here as it had before. And yet . . .

There were changes, of course. Most of her father's best horses were gone. Last night, though there was coffee in the house, they'd saved it and had a chicory brew after dinner. Candles were more carefully doled out; slivers of soap were collected to be molded again. Lying in bed, feeling the cool breeze slip through the latticed door, Tia felt her heart beat a little faster. Cimarron was strong. A little citadel unto itself. The house stood, the servants and workers remained, all was as it had been, except . . . the war was slowly coming here, too. There was no deprivation yet as there had been elsewhere. All

across the South, people had lost their homes to the
invading armies, they'd been robbed, their possessions
"confiscated." Refugees roamed the larger cities; invading armies sometimes stripped properties of all available
food and supplies, then burned homes and barns to the
ground. Some officers, North and South, tried to stop
the pillaging of their troops. Sometimes they were desperate to feed their men. No matter what the intent,
with hungry armies to be fed, the land was stripped. And
it was the women left behind, with the old and feeble,
with little children, who often paid the price of war. Tia
had heard it said that the war might have been over now
if it weren't for the patriotism of the women of the
South, of their determination to accept any hardship.
She wasn't so certain. It was one thing to be full and
warm and in good health and be patriotic; quite another
to be starving and homeless, with a dream left in the ashes.

It was especially good to come home now. Assisting
Julian, when their hospital had remained in one place,
had been one thing. She had felt strong, secure, and
confident in what she was doing. She had even felt very
mature—*old!*—as of late, with so many so very young
new recruits joining the militia. But with the renewed
interest recently shown the state by Yankee forces, situations were becoming very perilous. Julian had moved the
surgery. And she had taken the injured and eventually—
after being so rudely delayed—met up with Dixie's
troops. That wretched no-name man!

Dixie's men had delivered her safely home the previous afternoon. They'd been polite, courteous, and a pleasure to ride with. They were, she thought, the true
backbone of the state, especially when so many regular
troops were so constantly stripped from the state to go
north. After Christmas, she was determined, she would
join up with Julian again, wherever he was. His newly
acquired wife, Rhiannon, was an excellent assistant, but
she was expecting their first child any day now, and besides, any field hospital always needed whatever competent help could be had. But for now, home was good.

A place to repair the wounds done to her confidence, convictions, and sense of security by that awful man.

Tia clenched her teeth at the thought of him. While he hadn't brought the full force of the Yankees down on Dixie, he had seen to it that the Yankee troops and supply wagon Dixie had intended to take had been reinforced. The Rebels were forced not only to forgo their plans to confiscate desperately needed supplies, but to run as well, since the Yankee forces guarding the supplies were so many, and so well armed.

A twinge of uneasiness and guilt assailed her.

It might have been worse. Much worse. Except that . . .

According to rumor, some of the Yankee troops had been led astray. Led down the wrong path by a vision suddenly appearing in the woods. All of Dixie's troops had escaped and survived.

The vision in the woods had disappeared, so it seemed. They had told her all about it late in the night when they had rejoined her and the injured men at their rendezvous point fifteen miles westward, on the old Indian trail leading to Tampa.

There was a brief tapping at her door, then it swung open. "Good morning, dear!"

Her mother, Tara, came sweeping into the room. She was tall and elegant and very blond; in her mid-forties now, her hair was still her crowning glory, without a strand of gray among the gold. Her smile could still light up a room, Tia thought, grinning herself while burrowing more deeply into the covers. Her mother *looked* fragile, but she was all steel inside. No matter what her thoughts on a subject, she could temper her words. Jarrett McKenzie's determination to remain as neutral as he could in the war had been a difficult stand among his neighbors, but his wife supported him with total passion—and diplomacy. Each time one of her sons came home, she managed to keep the politics out of the matter of family love—quite a feat, since, throughout the country, some fathers and sons had sworn never to speak again for the stand taken by the other. Her nephews and nieces, ardent Rebels all, remained welcome in her home at any time. Injured soldiers, from either side, received the greatest care possible. Representatives from both armies came to Cimarron at times to negotiate various matters—prisoner exchanges, evacuations of newly occupied areas, surrenders, temporary truces.

Tara pulled open the draperies, allowing the sun to flood into the room.

"Mother, that's cruel," Tia groaned, sinking more deeply beneath the covers and casting an arm over her eyes to shade them from the sudden light.

"You've been sleeping nearly ten hours."

"But I'm home for Christmas!"

"And you chose to go to war with your brother," Tara reminded her. "You have no rank, no commission. No one pays you, and no one forces you to stay."

Tia sat up in the bed, staring at her mother, who had gone to throw open the latticed doors. The air that rushed in was cool. Tara seemed reflective, as if, looking out the widow, she saw the past, and not the coolness of the winter's day.

"You didn't stop me from going!" Tia reminded her, curious that her mother seemed so strange about the situation.

But Tara turned to her then and smiled. "You made a choice, and I admire the choice you made. You've helped your brother tremendously; God knows how many lives you may have helped to save. But I'm still glad you're home. Every time one of you leaves this house . . . well, I am afraid I'll never see you again. I hear the lists of the wounded and the dead, and . . ."

Tia jumped out of bed, running over to her mother, throwing her arms around her. "I'm certainly safe, Mother. And Julian is a surgeon—"

"A reckless one! Your father and I are neither deaf—nor stupid. We hear what goes on. And even when Julian does remain in his field hospitals, Ian is out there . . ."

Out there on the wrong side, Tia thought. But she didn't say anything. This was her father's house. And she adored her brother, no matter what his personal ethics decreed he must do.

"Oh, Mother, you mustn't worry."

"And the sun shouldn't rise," Tara murmured, pulling away slightly, studying her daughter's face. "You're too thin."

"Which is good, since I'm short."

"Not short, darling, petite."

"Short. What happened to me? This is a family of giants—even you're tall."

Tara sighed. "Petite, Tia, is just fine. But you're not short, really, your height is average at the least, and among other women, you might even be considered tall. You're only a bit smaller than I am—it's just that your brothers and your father are so very tall—"

"And bossy."

"—and therefore, you feel *short* in comparison."

"Is that all it is?"

"You really are just about my same size."

"Am I?"

"Just like me," Tara said.

Tia laughed. "I'm dark as night while you're pure sunshine."

"All right, so you have that fabulous head full of ebony hair, and indeed, your father's deep, dark, fathomless eyes! You are your father's daughter!" Tara said, smiling and hugging her tightly once again. "In most things!" she murmured, then pulled away. "Anyway, I'm glad you're home. And tonight, you will be your father's daughter in pure diplomacy, if you don't mind. I can't tell you how happy I am that you did come home for Christmas, what with the boys away and even Alaina and the babies staying in St. Augustine. It really isn't fair, you know, this war—it's not only destroying our country, our land, and—my God—an entire generation of young men, but I'm a grandmother, and I don't get to dote on my grandchildren, spoil them terribly, and hand them back. For that reason alone, I'm so happy I have my precious little daughter home—"

"Little! There you have it!" Tia said with a sigh.

"Sorry, dear, it's just a manner of speech. You are the baby, and always will be."

"Ah . . . be careful there, Mother! Aunt Teela thought Sydney was her baby, and then Mary made an appearance when everyone least expected it!"

"Well, that's true, but most likely your father and I are quite done, and that leaves you in the position of 'baby' and 'little.' "

"A baby old maid!" Tia sighed.

"Through your own choice," her mother said, somewhat sharply. Then she smiled. "But you're here and I'm so glad—"

"And you mentioned diplomacy. Why do I have to be diplomatic? Oh, Mother, don't tell me that Father has invited forlorn Yankee friends in the peninsula to come to Christmas dinner—"

"Your father would never do anything so foolhardy. This remains a state in rebellion, and the Yankees do not hold Tampa as they hold St. Augustine. Your father is a man of tremendous courage who does not lie about his views—but then, again, neither is he an idiot. He does not taunt the Rebel forces who control the state, and he respects the fact that the state did vote for secession."

"So what is going on?"

"Exchange negotiations."

"Exchange?"

"Some Florida militia boys have been taken by Northern troops, and some fresh young Yanks out of St. Augustine were seized trying to pillage a farmhouse west of the city. We're having some officers to dinner to make arrangements to exchange the boys for Christmas."

"What kind of officers?"

"*Kind* of officers?" Tara repeated. "Gentlemen, I imagine."

"Mother! *Which* officers? Union men? Confederates?"

"One of each, of course."

"Wonderful. The war will wind up being fought over the dinner table!" Tia said.

"There will be no fighting at the table."

"Is Ian coming?" Tia asked hopefully. "Is he going to be one of the Yankee officers?"

Tara shook her head. For a moment, Tia could see the strain in her mother's features, and yes, the war had aged even her. She never held her children back, and yet Tia saw briefly then the agony that she suffered, never knowing where they were.

"The last I heard, Ian was in Virginia again," she said. "When he is in the state, he is seldom able to come here. Alaina is praying to see him in St. Augustine sometime soon. He sent her a long letter, but God knows when he'll be in the state. Sometimes I pray he stays far away. It seems to me that people grow more bitter all the time, and there are plenty of fools and fanatics here who would gladly shoot a man in the back or hang him from the highest tree for his determination to fight for his own conscience."

"Ian is a remarkable survivor, Mother," she assured Tara. "He will come home when it's all over."

"Yes, of course. Well, I've a thousand things to do. And you needn't worry unduly. I'm acquainted with both officers coming here tonight. So are you."

"Oh? Who is coming?"

"Colonel Raymond Weir."

"Hm," Tia murmured. "Well, he is a pleasant gentleman."

"You should think so, dear. You used to flirt outrageously with him."

"He is attractive," Tia agreed. Tall, blond, handsome—a planter who loved his horses, his land, a good bourbon, and the smell of leather. Sometimes, he enjoyed one too many a good bourbon, but her friend Sally Anderson had told her once that all good Southern men were supposed to have a fondness for bourbon, and if it led them to start a few fights here and there, such was the substance of life. Men, in general, she thought, did tend to overindulge occasionally, but he was never rude or abusive to her when he drank; indeed, he tended to become more wistful. Then again, few men dared bother

her much—she had her father's watchful eye and that
of two powerful older brothers. If that wasn't enough,
she had her two male cousins to the south, reputed to
be somewhat "savage" because of their Indian blood.
Sometimes, she had felt a little too protected. Sometimes, as her mother had said, it had made her an outra-
geous flirt—she had dared anything.

But she had liked Raymond Weir, very much. And
she had loved the attention he paid her. Naturally, too—
before the war—it had been wonderfully flattering to
have the attention of a man so admired by many other
young women. She knew he had wanted to marry her.
She had always hesitated, flirting but keeping just a bit
of a distance between them. She'd had her dreams of
seeing the world, and though he was wonderfully handsome, smelled just fine, and seemed to have no dis-
gusting habits—such as chewing tobacco and having the
juice running through his beard, drinking beer and whiskey and passing gas all night, and the like—she was looking for something just a bit more before settling down
to plantation life. She wanted, at the least, a grand tour
of Europe. What she really wanted was to see the pyramids in Egypt, the lands of the Crusades, the Parthenon!
So she had held him at bay . . .

And the war had come.

"It will be nice to see Raymond again."

"And you will behave, of course?" Tara said sternly.

"Behave?"

"The poor man was madly in love with you at one
time, you know. So now you must behave. Don't tease
him mercilessly."

"Mother!"

"Tia, my darling, I pity the man who loves you. You
flirt, you tease, you become interested in a man, and if
it seems that he is becoming too interested in you, you
throw the poor fellow right over!"

"Mother!"

"It's true. But since Raymond is a Confederate with
the loudest Rebel yell in the war, and your father has

Unionist sympathies, I suggest you take great care not to create any arguments."

"I would never cause Father trouble!" she protested.

Tara smiled. "You've changed, my darling, with the war. Matured. With little choice, I'm afraid. Now you sometimes behave as if you're determined to become an eccentric spinster."

"Easy, when so many men are dead!"

"So many are dead," Tara agreed. "But you are young, Tia, and there will be men in your life. When you first began noticing the attention of our local swains, you changed your crushes even more quickly than President Lincoln changes generals! As soon as you had charmed them into being smitten, you brushed them off like so much dust on your boots."

"I did no such thing. I tried to be friendly and kind to everyone, but sometimes certain people would just take kindness too seriously."

"You are kind—and compassionate," Tara said softly, then grinned. "Just pure hell on those who would love you!"

"Pure hell? Mother, you told me a lady isn't to use such a word, much less in regard to her daughter—"

"I'm sorry, dear. You're so right. Speaking the truth can be such a burden!" Tara teased. "Anyway, be kind to Colonel Weir. But be careful."

"I did think about marrying him, you know," Tia admitted.

"He's a fine man," Tara said. There was something reserved in her tone.

"*Hm* . . . it sounds like there's a 'but' in there."

"I'm not sure if he's the right man for you."

"I'm not sure, either," Tia admitted. "But should I marry him just because you want me to be kind to him?"

"You should never marry for any reason but love," Tara said gravely.

Tia smiled, swirling around her bedroom and landing back on the bed, her fingers laced behind her head. "Mother, you are completely unorthodox! Most parents tell a daughter she must marry whom they say, and you encourage romantic notions!" She rolled across the bed again, looking curiously at her mother. "Strange, since I've heard you married my father on the spur of the moment, all to escape a rather dastardly villain, and that it had nothing at all to do with love."

Tara set her hands on her hips and inched up her chin. "You're an impudent girl, Miss Tia McKenzie. I adore your father and you know it."

"Ah, but love came!" Tia teased this time. "Naturally, since there is no finer man than my father."

Her mother stared at her for a long moment before saying softly, "A fine man, but you and Julian have disagreed with his teachings."

Tia sobered, sitting up Indian style, pulling her toes beneath her. "I don't disagree with him, Mother, but the state of Florida—"

"The state of Florida is full of fanatics who cry glory again and again. Like Colonel Weir. His passion for this 'cause' is so dedicated he sees nothing else—that is why I'm not at all sure he's the right man for you, whether he is still madly in love with you or not!"

"Really?" She and her mother were startled by a deep-voiced comment coming from the doorway. "I'm not sure if there is a right man out there for you, little sister. Mother, you're absolutely right! Pity the poor fellow who loves her! She is hell on men."

They both spun around. A man stood in the doorway. A Union soldier, yet very welcome in this Southern home. Tall, dark-haired, blue-eyed, filling the doorway with his presence.

"Ian!" Tara cried.

Tia followed suit, echoing her older brother's name. "Ian!"

As one, they rushed to the doorway. Tia stood back, letting her mother embrace her oldest son. Tara was shaking; there were tears in her eyes. She blinked them away quickly, looking him over carefully for any sign of injury as Tia took her turn, hurtling into his arms, hugging him tightly.

"Ian, how on earth . . ." Tara murmured.

"I came in by ship, Mother, south of here. We're holding some ground by the gulf. I was hoping to reach St. Augustine and Alaina and the children but—"

"Oh, my God, Ian, I want you to be with your wife and children, but please tell me you didn't come here just to leave immediately?"

He shook his head, blue eyes sparkling as they met his mother's. "If Alaina received my latest despatch, she should arrive before supper time tonight."

"What a Christmas gift! Two of my children home . . . and my grandchildren on the way!"

Ian looked over his mother's head to his sister. "Julian?" he queried. There was just the slightest trace of anxiety in his voice.

"Julian is well, but in the north of the state," Tia said quickly. Her brothers had met at times during the war. Never enough.

"I saw him after Gettysburg, but not since."

"He's very well; I left him just about a week ago. Rhiannon's baby is due soon." She hesitated a minute, remembering that as far as the war went, her brother was her enemy. "He had to break camp, change the position of his hospital, and he didn't want to travel with her any more than he had to right now, so . . ."

"So he won't be home for Christmas," Ian murmured.

"I'll have a grandchild, and I haven't even met his wife," Tara said.

"Don't worry, she's absolutely gorgeous," Tia said, and couldn't help adding, "for a Yankee, that is."

"A Florida Yankee," Ian reminded her.

She made a face at her brother, then remembered she hadn't really hugged him. "Oh, Ian!" she said, and threw herself at him. He caught her, embracing her, holding her very tightly for a minute, just as she held him. The family had always been close—they'd squabbled as children, but had immediately risen to one another's defense at the least provocation. The war made time shared between them all the more precious. Would they have been this very close if they hadn't seen that lives could be shattered in a split second with the explosive sound of gunfire or a cannon's charge? Yes, Tia thought. They had been taught the importance of their family; they had been lucky to grow in an environment ruled by parental love. They would have always cared, but they had seen so many people die that they had learned that each time they came together might be their last.

Grinning at Tia as he set her down, Ian said, "You will love Rhiannon, Mother, quite honestly. Naturally, she shares an intelligence as yet not realized by my young sibling here, but one with which you and Father are well versed."

Tia countered, "Ian, your own wife sees the intelligence of our belief in a loose confederation of states, in which decisions are made at far more local levels regarding the lives of those—"

"Children!" Tara chastised. "It's Christmas, and there will be no talk of war for Christmas."

"It's Christmas Eve," Tia corrected. "And there will be talk of war." She made a face at her brother. "We're hosting an exchange."

Ian nodded. "I know. There's to be a prisoner exchange."

"If you're aware of what's going on," Tia asked, "why are they risking another man in enemy territory when the negotiation is taking place in your father's own house?"

"These arrangements had been requested before I knew I was coming south—by a Southern colonel, I understand," Ian said. "Naturally, the situation proved provident for me—an added reason to be sent south."

"And what was the other reason?" Tia asked.

He stared at his sister for a long moment. She curled her fingers into her hands. Her brother was an exceptionally impressive man with his cool blue eyes, dark hair, and towering height. Every inch a colonel. And a Unionist. "The Northern armies are keeping General Lee moving, though he had hoped to go home for Christmas as well, I was told. I've had few nights in a bed since the Gettysburg campaign myself, but since other men are busy in the field, I've at last gained a reprieve. I'm grateful for the time given me. I can see my wife, my children, my mother . . . my sister."

She was sorry to feel suspicious—but she knew there was more reason to Ian's being there than time off for hours spent in the saddle. Many men had yet to make it home at all since the beginning of the war. Ian had probably been sent here because of the renewed conviction of the Northern powers that Florida needed to be stopped.

"Ian—" she murmured.

"I'm home for Christmas, and that is why I'm here," he said firmly. He looked at his mother. "Who is coming for these negotiations. Anyone I know?"

"Ray Weir and Taylor Douglas."

Ian shrugged. "Weir is all right. He'll bait me, but I'll be a perfect gentleman and ignore him, of course. And it will be a pleasure to see Taylor again."

"Who's Taylor?" Tia asked. The name seemed familiar.

"You don't remember him?" Ian asked curiously.

"No."

"He's our cousins' cousin," Ian said.

"We're our cousins' cousins," Tia protested.

"Other side. Uncle James's mother's sister's grandson. See the connection?" Ian asked. "We played as kids, but maybe you were too young to remember. Taylor was a class ahead of me at West Point."

"Another Yank?" she inquired tartly. She remembered now, not the man, but the fact that her cousins had talked about him often enough.

Ian arched a brow with a half-smile. "Since we know that good old Ray Weir is a righteous Rebel, then Taylor Douglas must be the Yank. We're having *negotiations,* dear sister. You need one party from each side of the question to negotiate."

"I'm merely mentioning that status quo," Tia said sweetly.

"My darlings, I'm so delighted to have you—and yet you're both giving me this ferocious headache," Tara said.

"No more talk of war, Mother, I promise,"

"Not until tonight, at any rate," Ian murmured. His eyes met his sister's, and he smiled, and she was suddenly just glad to see him, glad about Christmas, glad to be home—and blithely unaware of what the night would bring.

Cimarron.

Taylor Douglas came upon the house in the late afternoon. A slight fog lay upon the ground, just touched by the dying rays of the sun which had managed to stretch across the seasonally metallic sky. The house seemed to rise like a Greek-columned castle on a fairy-tale hill, though the best that could be said for any of the land was that it had a small roll—by Tampa Bay, there was nothing that could remotely be considered a hill. Still, the fog gave the house a strange magical cast, he thought, amazed at his own touch of whimsy. Magical indeed—it stood against the flood of passions that had ruled the foolish and the sane for so long now.

He had ridden by himself here, in full uniform. There had never been such a time when so many different companies of soldiers were roaming the state—Confederate and Federal—but it was equally true that a man could traverse miles without coming upon anyone who would care about the color of his uniform.

War was often for the rich—or those who had something to lose. Many small farmers in the state were totally uninterested. Life was always simply hand-to-mouth, and food would be sold to any man with money, especially if it was silver or gold.

Even in the South, people were becoming wary of Confederate currency.

If he had, however, run into Rebel troops, it wouldn't have mattered. His papers certified his right to be here. He'd been assigned to the state by his own government. He'd been requested for the negotiations by none other than his old West Point professor Robert E. Lee. There had been few men he had admired like Lee, and owing to his exceptional marksmanship, Taylor had piqued

Lee's interest. He had been a guest at Lee's beautiful home, while he had hosted the Lee family himself once at his father's Washington town house. He knew what it had cost Lee to leave the Union; the greatest Southern general of them all had been loath to break up the country. But he fought for the South, and though Taylor disagreed with his decision, he had to respect it, just as he prayed that Lee respected his decision to stay with the Union.

Taylor was glad to be leaving the main body of the war behind—at least for a time. He had a pleasant assignment for a change. Visiting a fine house, enjoying Christmas Eve dinner in the company of good people, and making arrangements for exchanges—a matter of life, rather than of battle, blood, and death.

He had been to Cimarron once, years and years ago, having come with James McKenzie, his mother's first cousin.

"Taylor!"

He was startled to hear himself suddenly and cheerfully hailed. Seeing the rider who raced across the long sloping lawn toward him, he grinned and waved in return with pleasure and surprise.

A moment later a handsome black stallion came to a perfect halt before him, and he found himself greeting Ian McKenzie, heir to this vast empire—should it, and he, survive the war.

"Ian!" he greeted his old friend. "By God, what are you doing here? Indeed, what am *I* doing here if you're here—now that's the real question!"

Ian dismounted from his horse, blue eyes alight as he approached Taylor, extending a hand in welcome. Taylor accepted it and leapt down from Friar, embracing the other man briefly, then drawing back with a grin. "Well, you look hale and hardy."

"Much to the chagrin of my brother, I believe," Ian said, smiling as well. "Before becoming his wife, my sister-in-law apparently mentioned that I was the 'stronger' looking of us two, which Julian took rather offensively. I'm afraid that our side is known to eat better, although I'm quite sure, were he able to make it home more often, my mother would see to it that none dared call him slim."

"Cimarron remains as impressive as always," Taylor said. "I'm sure he could become fat as a house himself were he able to remain. How are the rest of the McKenzies—have you any news? I'd heard that Sydney married Jesse Halston and was living in Washington, but I wasn't able to see her before I was sent here."

"Sydney is well; I saw Jesse after Gettysburg," Ian said gravely. "She'd been getting into a few fixes, helping the family out of Old Capitol, until she managed to find a place in prison herself. He's responsible for her now, and I'm assuming he'll be a good influence."

"Good—to our way of seeing the world," Taylor commented.

"Good as in safe," Ian said flatly.

"Safe is certainly good," Taylor said. "But what are you doing here? I wouldn't have needed to come if—"

"Well, then, I'm glad that no one, including me, knew that I might be able to make it here for the holiday," Ian said. "I promise you, there will be no hardship in spending Christmas with my family."

"I'd certainly not meant to imply such a thing. It's just that—"

"You'd asked not to be sent to the state, right?" Ian said.

"A request long granted, now denied," Taylor agreed. "I find it very difficult to be here."

Ian studied him. "For many reasons, I imagine," he said quietly. "Well, still, for the holiday, we're glad to have you here. My parents are delighted."

"They remember me?"

"My father forgets almost nothing, which can be quite a thorn in the side, since he can remind us all of transgressions many years gone by!"

"How does he manage with your brother a Rebel, and our mutual cousins casting their lots with the South?"

Ian hesitated just briefly, studying Taylor's face. "He watched his own brother battle an unrelenting army during the Indian wars—he has no quarrel with his brother, or his brother's children. As to Julian, he is glad that his younger son is a healer rather than a killer. And my sister—"

"She remains at home, with your parents? I must admit, I don't remember her. She was but a babe in arms, I think, when I came here with James. And I don't think she ventured to my mother's place with you when we were all children."

"Tia. She was just a toddler when you visited here with Uncle James all those years ago. She is home; you will meet her now. And thankfully, you will do so in my father's presence, for she seldom argues with him. In her heart she believes herself a Floridian first, rather than a Confederate, but certainly not a Unionist! She helps Julian with his injured, and so my parents believe her safe in his keeping, although I don't think they realize how often they might be parted. I worry about her frequently, but I do trust my brother to keep her well behind the lines."

"I haven't asked about your wife and children," Taylor said.

Ian's smile was very quick then. "They are here. They arrived just a few hours ago. In fact, I had just left Alaina sleeping and come out for a ride when I saw you emerge from the trail. My God, but it was good to see my wife—" He broke off abruptly, looking downward as if he inwardly cursed himself for his thoughtlessness.

"I'm sorry—"

"Don't be," Taylor interrupted quickly. "I would be a sorry fellow to despise others for their happiness. I shall be delighted to see Alaina. And your little ones. The boy is Sean, right?"

"Sean is now nearly three, and Ariana is almost two. They are pure mischief."

"Good for them."

"Come along to the house."

Taylor led Friar alongside Ian as they approached the rear of the house. At this time, it appeared that the docks by the river were quiet; all in fact, seemed quiet.

"How does your father manage here?" Taylor asked.

"Without the Florida Rebs burning him to the ground?" Ian asked.

"Frankly, yes."

"Well, he's acted as a go-between upon many an occasion. He hasn't involved himself in any espionage activity—in short, he's done nothing illegal."

"That hasn't always stopped either side from burning out those they consider to be traitors."

"Well, there's also the matter of his employees," Ian said.

Taylor grinned. "I knew I was being watched—before you appeared."

"By at least a good twelve men." Ian pointed to the loft of the barn far beyond the rear of the house, and to a guard tower along the river. "My father is like a nation unto himself. Throughout the years, he has gained the unquestioning loyalty of dozens of men. He has given work to outcasts, foreigners, blacks, Indians, Asians, and good white men of vision. The South would have to be able to spare a small army to take my father down; that time has not as yet come. I pray it never will. Then, again, to the Rebel forces, my father has bred one traitor—me. But my brother is known to save more lives than they can acquire in recruits these days, and my sister is wildfire and passion and adored by anyone who comes in contact with her—who would burn down the home that belongs to such ardent Rebels as well?"

"I imagine the danger remains."

"Always," Ian agreed. "Mark! Mark Espy, where are you, lad? My God, it's getting foggy tonight. Mark, come take our horses to the stables, will you, please? And show Colonel Douglas how well we care for our animals here!"

"Yes, sir!" A young, mixed-blood stableboy came running from the mist that had settled around the wide verandah that encircled the great plantation house. He grinned, taking Friar's reins from Taylor.

" 'Andsome fellow, sir!" the lad complimented.

"Thank you. Friar is his name; he'll be glad of a warm stall."

The boy grinned, leading the horses away. Even as he did so, the rear door of the house opened and banged. Two little urchins came running out into the mist, heedless of it, fast as cannon balls. They were followed by the whir of a woman, racing after them.

"Sean! Ariana! Don't you follow your brother when he's being bad, young lady! Your grandmother told you to stay in the house. Hey, you hellions! Ian, you wretch, you got the child you deserved—he doesn't listen to a thing. Ariana, you are a sweetheart, good girl. Stay here, on the porch—naturally you're an angel! Now you, come here, Sean, don't you disappear on me in this wretched fog!"

The voice was familiar.

She didn't seem aware of Taylor or Ian because she was so intent on tearing after the little boy who was squealing with wild pleasure as he raced outside, eluding her pursuit.

"Tia, it's all right. I'm here, I've got him," Ian said, scooping up the boy.

"What?" she cried, still running, apparently afraid she would lose the child.

Suddenly, the fog whirled and lifted.

She came flying through it, crying out as she saw a full-grown man in her path. She couldn't stop her impetus.

She plowed head-on into Taylor. He tried to catch her, lost his own balance, and fell backward to the ground.

He stared at her.

She stared at him.

Huge, thick-lashed dark eyes widened against the sculpted ivory pallor of her face.

He stared back, stunned.

She screamed, trying to rise.

He didn't let her. For a brief moment, his fingers vised around her arms. And he smiled grimly.

"Godiva!" he said softly.

Chapter 7

"Tia, it isn't the whole Federal army, coming to take your precious South," Tia heard her brother say. No, this was worse.

He was really there. The dreaded no-name Yank. He was on her lawn. Touching her again. He knew her. He knew Ian. He was here, at her father's house.

Oh, God . . .

She was staring down into his tawny eyes, eyes that seemed to glitter and narrow now like the devil's own. She could feel the force in his fingers, feel the length of him beneath her. She wanted to yell at God. What was this wretched irony?

Ian was reaching down to help them both. His son clung to his neck. Even as he leaned over, Taylor came quickly to his feet, drawing her up along with him. She was so shaken she couldn't stand. He steadied her; she shook him off.

"Tia!" Ian said sharply.

She closed her eyes, looking down, fighting to breathe. It was her father's house. There were to be negotiations here, discussions that would free Rebel prisoners.

Oh, good God, he could give her away! And he might share the "rumor" that "Godiva" had appeared again, disconcerting and confusing the Yankee troops when they should have been in hot pursuit of Dixie and his men.

"I—I—" she stuttered, teeth chattering, face surely as ashen as death.

"Tia, I don't believe you've ever met Colonel Taylor Douglas," Ian was saying sternly. "He is more than a guest; his grandmother is Uncle James's aunt. As I mentioned before, he is a cousin to our own cousins."

"No—no. We haven't met!" she said quickly. She stared at the wretched enemy who was now a guest in her own home. *He would give her away, certainly, and he would take pleasure in the disaster he would cause!*

"Miss McKenzie," he said, politely doffing his plumed cavalry hat and bowing. He rose, staring at her again. "Of course, we *have* met."

"I . . . I . . . I . . . no, we couldn't have. I would have remembered. I don't know many Yankees, I . . . I . . . I . . ."

He smiled politely, arching a brow as her voice trailed off. She had run out of words.

He shook his head. "How sad you don't remember!

"You have met?" Ian inquired. Her brother sounded very suspicious, Tia thought.

"No . . ." Tia protested.

"You were a babe-in-arms," Taylor said pleasantly, "so I can understand why you've no memory of my coming here."

She felt dizzy. Weak-kneed with relief. And yet by the way he was smiling at her . . .

He could still give her away.

Her jaw seemed locked. It was an effort to speak. "Welcome to Cimarron, Mr. Douglas. If you'll excuse me, I left Ariana on the porch. Sean McKenzie, come with me, and leave your father be with his guest. We'll go on in and find Gram, shall we?" She took Sean from his father. Her three-year-old nephew offered her a beautiful smile, curling his fingers into the length of her hair. "Auntie Tia, cookie, please!"

He was an angel now. Why not—he'd brought her running out straight into the arms of the very devil himself.

She spun around, hurrying toward the house with Sean in her arms. She could hear her brother and Taylor coming behind her. She found Ariana, big blue eyes wide as saucers, on the porch, waiting for her just as she'd been told. "Come, baby," she said, hiking up her niece as well. "Let's go upstairs to the nursery. Where I used to play. Have you been on the rocking horse yet? A friend of your great-uncle carved it for me when I was just as big as you are now, Ariana!"

Tia heard the men enter the house behind her; she heard her mother calling her name from her father's den. She pretended that she did not. She hurried up the stairs with her two charges in tow. On the second floor, she noted that her brother's door remained closed— Alaina, his wife, remained within. Alaina had arrived soon after Ian, and since the hours the two spent to- gether tended to be scarce, Tia had at that moment de- cided that she was going to give her older brother the best Christmas present she could—time alone. She'd ef- fused about how exhausted Alaina must be after having to cross the peninsula so carefully in the company of other civilians on their way to Tampa Bay. She'd swooped down on the children and told Alaina and her brother to get some rest. Of course, the last thing they wanted in one another's company was rest, and that was surely obvious to them all. Alaina and Ian had both been very grateful—her sister-in-law's smile had been well worth her effort. She even knew her little nephew and niece, since Julian's Rebel camp hospital in the pines hadn't been that far down the St. Johns River from the Yankee stronghold at St. Augustine, where Alaina lived as the war raged on. Most of the time, the children were good with her. Today, as she'd read to Ariana, Sean had grown bored—and escaped. And although there were others on the plantation who might have taken on the task of watching her brother's precocious toddlers, she had wanted to be with them. She adored them.

The nursery was at the far end of the hall. It was filled with cradles and cribs, books and toys, the blocks with which they had all played, the rag dolls which she herself had dragged around for years. The nursery hadn't changed. Her parents had always assumed that their chil- dren would grow, marry, and bring home their own chil- dren. The rocking horse sat in the center of the room.

"Sean, you haven't ridden this mighty steed as yet! Take a seat, my good man!"

Sean sat on the rocking horse. Ariana, apparently growing sleepy, curled into Tia's arms as she took a seat in one of the large rockers. She felt her own heart thundering against her chest as she tried to remain calm. *He was in her house. A guest. The no-name monster had a name and title now, and he was in her house, talking to her brother, and probably her father as well.*

"Charge!" Sean called from his rocking horse. "Charge!"

Ariana smiled angelically at Tia and closed her blue eyes. Tia kept rocking. The door to the nursery suddenly opened. She tensed.

"Tia?"

She exhaled with relief. It was Alaina, a golden blond with eyes to match, a Rebel in her heart as well, but a woman who had fought her own wars, had found her own peace, and lived—with a faith that would not fail her—for the day when the war would end.

"Tia, thank you so very much!" Alaina said, walking into the room. Tia drew a finger to her lips, indicating that Ariana slept in her arms.

Alaina nodded, coming to the baby and taking her from Tia. She hugged her daughter close to her, smiling at Tia above the baby's head. "I know I'm lucky. Some wives haven't seen their husbands since this madness began. My God, I live and breathe for the days when he can come back, but I live in terror as well, always afraid that . . ."

"That the next thing you'll hear is that there was a battle, and you cringe every time they read the list of the dead," Tia finished softly for her.

"I'm going to put her to bed in our room,." Alaina said. "I'll be right back for Sean!"

"Alaina, please, take your time."

"I can't take too much time. Raymond Weir and his attendant have arrived. Your father and mother are serving drinks in the den, and your mother wants us down as quickly as possible. Taylor is here, too."

Tia arched a brow. "You know Taylor as well?"

Alaina smiled. "Of course. He's a second cousin to Sydney, Jerome, and Brent. I grew up near them, you know that. He was with your Uncle James frequently enough. I can't believe the two of you never met!"

"We did."

"What?"

"When I was an infant," Tia said quickly. "So I've been told."

"He's been trying to stay out of the state; it's very difficult for him to be here."

"It should be," Tia muttered.

"It's difficult for Ian to be here as well," Alaina said.

"I know, and you know I love my brother—"

"Of course. Just—well, don't hate Taylor for being a Yankee. He really is an exceptional man. I had an awful crush on him when I was a child."

"Lovely," Tia said. Alaina didn't hear the sarcasm in her voice.

"I'm surprised you didn't meet him again. He was just ahead of Ian at West Point. They were both with General Magee when the war broke out, though assigned to different duty."

"How nice," Tia murmured. "He's kin to my own cousins, and friends with my brother."

"Yes, so this should all go very well. I mean, Ray Weir is representing the South, and Taylor is here for the North. Conversation should be smooth, the exchange pleasant—and Christmas peaceful for us all!" Alaina's smile was infectious; Tia smiled in return. After Alaina had left the room, Tia rose and walked over to the rocking horse, where Sean still played.

"Charge!" Sean called again, swinging an imaginary sword in the air. He smiled at Tia. "My father is a great cavalry officer!"

"Yes, he is," Tia agreed.

She turned around, aware that someone stood at the door to the nursery. She thought Alaina had come back, and then she was simply *afraid* that Taylor Douglas might be there. But it was Raymond Weir, tall, handsome, his blond hair long, curling around the collar of his gray uniform dress coat, his carriage very dashing.

"Raymond!" she said, relieved.

"Tia!" He swept off his hat and bowed, every inch a gentleman.

"Sir!" Sean said, and saluted sharply.

Raymond Weir looked at the child gravely before saluting in return. "Ian's boy?" he asked. She nodded, then smiled and whispered, "But far too young to be the enemy!"

Ray Weir smiled, but it was a slightly stiff smile, as though he didn't seem to have much sense of humor about the war itself. He stared at Tia then, his hat in his hand.

"No enemies here," he said softly. "My God, Tia, it's good to see you. You've been near me, and yet so far from me, for so long. I've been so anxious to see you. I know you've been with Julian through most of this; I almost craved an injury to come to see you."

"Desire no wounds on my behalf, I beg of you!" she said. "Survive this wretched war, Ray, if you would do me any favors."

"I would do anything for you," he replied.

She lowered her lashes, aware of the passion in his voice. If the war had come later . . . might she have been married to him? Or was her mother right—had she just been a horrible flirt totally unaware of what she wanted, or afraid to cast her fate beneath the power of any man? He was very good looking, charming.

And what would he think if he knew of her latest war efforts?

"It's so very good that you are here," she said. "Almost like old times. Before . . ."

"The war," he said.

She nodded.

"I admire your father's efforts here. It's a pity he doesn't see the true future of his state. He will, I believe, in time."

Her father's position had been exactly the same since

the very beginning. He was not going to change his mind.

"Perhaps we can forget out positions for a Christmas celebration tonight," she said.

Ray didn't answer; Alaina came sweeping back into the room at that moment for her son. "The baby is down. Sean, time for bed, my darling. Oh! Ray! How good it is to see you here alive and looking so very well!"

"Alaina! What a pleasure to see you as well."

"You were looking for a moment's rest and stumbled upon the nursery instead?" Alaina asked.

Half-laughing, Ray shook his head. "No." He inclined his head toward Tia. "Your mother most kindly showed me to a guest room. I'd heard a rumor bandied about downstairs that Tia was with the children, so I ventured here on my own."

"As long as you didn't come to the nursery looking for peace and quiet!" Alaina said.

"On the contrary. I was looking for something wild!" he said.

Alaina arched a brow, glancing at Tia. "Well, then. Sean, my love, let's go. Tia, your mother is anxious for you to come down."

"Then I will do so right away," Tia assured her.

Alaina departed with Sean. Tia walked to the door. Ray remained there, his eyes upon her gravely. "You've grown more beautiful with the years. I'd thought that impossible. You've matured. You've held my heart and haunted my dreams for years, you know."

"It's very sweet for you to say so, Ray."

He caught her hands, turned them over, kissed the palms. She met his eyes and was flattered, and also bemused by the strange stirrings she felt inside. She cared for him; she had always cared for him. He was handsome, dashing, reckless, and wild—the very pinnacle of Southern manhood. He would be right for her, and she felt . . .

Good. She needed a friend in the house tonight.

She smiled suddenly. "You're beautiful, too."

He laughed. "Thank you, ma'am. And I thank God for this chance to be at Cimarron—with you here as well!

"My mother . . ."

"Is anxious for you, yes." He stepped back, the perfect gentleman. He would want the perfect Southern bride, bred to proper behavior, courtesy, tact, discretion—and chastity—at all times. She felt a flush warming her face.

"Excuse me."

She fled from him, hurrying down the hallway, then down the length of the stairs. She walked quickly to her father's study. The door was open. She entered.

Her father was seated behind his desk, as dark, handsome, and impressive as ever. Her brother, her father's very image, stood by the side of the desk while pointing out some of her father's books to their guest—Taylor Douglas.

Her heart slammed against her chest as the men turned at her arrival. Douglas stood as tall as her brother, clad in a fresh white shirt and dress cavalry frockcoat. In the lamplight, she noted the thick, straight, raven darkness of his hair, the clear hazel of his eyes, and the cast of his cheekbones. She'd been blind, she thought. She had seen something familiar in him when they had met; she should have seen certain resemblances to her cousin Jerome, as in the very dark, straight hair that was a sure sign of his Indian blood.

She stared at him.

He stared at her.

Someone cleared his throat. She blinked.

Reeves, her father's very dignified valet, who had been at Cimarron as long as her family, was serving whiskey and sherry. He frowned at her, noting the way she stared at their guest, then arched a brow as she frowned back— but she reached properly for a sherry instead of the whiskey she suddenly craved.

"Tia, finally!" her father said, rising.

She swallowed the sherry quickly. "I'm sorry, Father. I'd not be late to this roomful of Yanks, except for the fact that I've dearly missed those little hellions my brother has bred. My time with them is precious as well!"

She noted her father's frown and instantly rued her flippancy. She swept on over to his side, kissing his cheek. "Ian, I do envy you your children."

"Naturally, they're my pride and joy," Ian said, "but you needn't envy them. You'll surely have your own."

"I may delight in being an old maid aunt!" she assured him, finishing her sherry.

"Do you remember Taylor Douglas, Tia?" Jarrett asked.

"No—I had not remembered him," she said, staring across the room at Taylor and wishing that he wouldn't look at her the way that he did, as if he knew her far too well. "But we have met now."

"Yes, we have met. And been formally introduced," Taylor said politely, his eyes remaining upon hers, his slight smile seeming always to be a threat. "Indeed, may I say, sir, that your daughter's warmth and charm have made me feel as if I've known her for quite some time."

"We welcome everyone at Cimarron, don't we, Father?" she said. Jarrett arched a brow at his daughter, and she knew that he was doubting her ability to be polite and charming to a Unionist guest. Turning to Reeves, she added, "I would love another sherry, Reeves. I taste nothing so sweet when I'm away."

"Yes," Taylor said agreeably. "The road is hard— *bare,* so frequently, of necessities."

She felt color flood her cheeks again, and she was delighted when Ray Weir made his appearance at her father's side.

"Ah, Ray, join us!" Jarrett said. "Please, come on in. Reeves, if you would, a whiskey for the colonel."

"Thank you, Jarrett," Ray said, accepting the drink offered to him. He lifted the glass. "To life!"

"To life!" all those in the room agreed, raising their glasses.

"Colonel Raymond Weir, Confederate States of

America . . . Colonel Taylor Douglas, United States of America," Jarrett said, formally introducing the two.

They assessed one another, both behaving with professional etiquette intact.

"Colonel," Ray said, nodding.

"Colonel," Taylor acknowledged.

"You are from here, sir?"

From hereabouts mainly, though I have spent some time away."

"It is my home, sir, with no time away," Ray said.

"So I understand," Taylor said.

"At this point, we should, perhaps, leave you gentlemen to your arrangements," Jarrett said. "Dinner will be at your leisure."

Several hours would pass before dinner. Apparently, there were a number of prisoners to be exchanged, but privates could only be exchanged for privates, corporals for corporals, lieutenants for lieutenants. Unless, of course, two privates should be bartered for a sergeant, or three sergeants for a major, or two privates and one sergeant for a lieutenant.

Reeves, coming and going from the den to refill whiskey glasses and offer cigars, assured the household that both men were adhering to a gentlemanly manner—when the discussions grew heated, they did so quietly. At seven-thirty, word came from the study that they had nearly solved their differences, and would be delighted to join the family for dinner at eight, should that be convenient.

Awaiting dinner on the verandah in the company of her family, Tia felt a sense of warmth and contentment unlike anything she had known for a very long time. Though their discussions could not help but include allusions to the war, it was not the war they discussed. Alaina talked of life in St. Augustine, and of Risa, Jerome's wife, with whom she lived. Risa had departed a few weeks earlier for the North—it had been some time since she had seen her father, the Union general Magee, and not having the least idea where her husband was at the moment, she had chosen the time to bring her son to see her father. Tia told her parents about Julian's wife, Rhiannon, and how she had really been the one to step in when Jerome had been seriously injured on one of his last forays. There were no arguments, only sincere conversation, and Tia, seated by her father on the steps on the porch, was glad simply to lean against the bulwark of his frame. If only . . .

Ray and Taylor appeared on the porch.

"Gentlemen, the matter is resolved?" Jarrett asked.

"Sir, it is," Ray assured him.

"And we offer our most sincere thanks for your hospitality," Taylor said. "As do the men who will be exchanged. It has been agreed as well that those men will no longer fight, but accept honorable discharge and return to private life."

Tia looked at Raymond Weir, certain that Taylor must have been mistaken in their agreement; the South could not afford to exchange men—and then not use them to fight.

But Raymond Weir stood listening, and making no correction to Taylor's words. Her father rose, announcing that they should adjourn into the dining room and enjoy the evening meal with thanks for the holiday— and the occasion.

With the children in bed, Alaina and Ian sat down next to one another at the large dining room table. Her father and mother were at opposite heads of the table while Tia found herself between Raymond and Taylor.

Passing biscuits.

Her father said grace, and then conversation at first revolved around the food, the house, the weather, and Christmas Eve.

Then, after the food had been served and Tara complimented, Raymond said, "Since we're looking to the Christmas season, I find it my duty as an officer and a gentlemen to make fair warning to you, Colonel Douglas, and to you as well, of course, Colonel McKenzie, to remove yourselves from this section of the state as soon as you are able, following the holiday. Sentiment is high against the enemy, and men captured after the transaction we've completed this evening are to be dealt with harshly."

Tia was aware of a piece of bread crumbling in the hands of Taylor Douglas, to her left. He did, however, maintain his poise. "I thank you for your warning."

"They are confiscating property as well, Colonel Douglas, so I've heard. Perhaps you should consider some quick sales. Such things have been done in the North, as you are aware. Robert E. Lee's wife's Arlington House was seized—the Union refused to accept payment of the taxes from anyone other than the owner, and that poor crippled lady, forced to flee, could not return."

"I'm afraid it was a very horrible act," Taylor agreed, looking across the table at Ian, who had given him some signal that they would maintain peace, no matter what. "Master Robert is a great man, and a great leader of men, and perhaps it is this very recognition by his friends in the North which makes it so difficult for them to accept the fact that he's their enemy."

"Ah, they will hate him more when he defeats the Union," Raymond said, shaking his head. "It's true, however, no offense meant, sirs, that traitors should be dealt with harshly. I might be interested in purchasing some of your property, Colonel Douglas."

"None is for sale."

"You risk a fortune."

"Not so great a fortune. I would make a gift of my property in the south of the peninsula to my second cousins, the James McKenzies, before selling it. And as to my home in Key West . . . the Union navy is firmly ensconced there. The property south of St. Augustine . . . well, at the moment, it is a no-man's-land. But I thank you for the offer."

"I have every reason to believe, Colonel Douglas, that European powers are ready to recognize the Confederacy as a sovereign state, and so will turn the tide of war."

"Again, sir, I say—I will wait."

"We run circles around you. Why, even our women drive your so-called soldiers to distraction, sir!"

"What women would that be?" Tara interrupted, her voice sweet but firm and she tried to dispel the growing argument.

"Why, madam, I've heard through good sources that we've a wild Rebel maid riding through the pines and leading the enemy astray. I heard this from Captain Dickinson's own men. They had been sent to seize a reinforced Yankee supply wagon, and were nearly run down by the number of soldiers suddenly put on duty, when a beautiful vixen, all in the bu—"

He broke off, staring from Tara to Alaina to Tia. He flushed.

"Yes?" Tara insisted.

"Well, she's a flame for justice, of course," Raymond said.

"But what were you about to say?" Tara insisted.

Tia concentrated on spearing a piece of fresh tomato. She felt her own face growing red. Felt tawny eyes upon her as Raymond continued to look for the right words.

"Well, they, er, they have a name for her."

"And that is?" Alaina insisted. "Please, Colonel Weir! You have two women with Rebel sympathies at the table, though we respect the beliefs of others around us—my husband and in-laws included, of course! Tell us about this vixen of virtue, or whatever she may be!"

Tia stared across the table at her sister-in-law. She wondered if there was a certain wistfulness to Alaina's question. She'd practiced serious espionage at the beginning of the war, and had she not been caught by her own husband, she might well have been executed. To the best of her knowledge, though male spies had suffered the ultimate penalty for their service to their countries, North and South, though it had been threatened, no woman had as yet been legally killed.

But Alaina was fascinated.

Raymond Weir looked across the table at Alaina. "Well, they call her 'Lady Godiva,' if that makes a proper explanation. Apparently, she shouted the name out at some point herself, and as it's so fitting, it seems to have stuck."

"Godiva—she rides around the countryside *naked*?" her father said, sounding angry and shocked.

Tia wanted to sink beneath the table.

"One would think that someone would stop a woman from such reckless and dangerous behavior," Ian said. "Maybe she doesn't realize how many men could be killed, thinking they owed it to her and all Southern honor to ride in her defense."

Alaina coughed suddenly, and the sound ended in a little squeak. Tia realized that her brother had squeezed his wife's hand beneath the table and that he was staring at her suspiciously.

She stared back, and though they were both trying to behave entirely circumspectly at the table, Tia could see that Alaina was furious that Ian would be suspicious.

From past history, maybe Ian had a right to his suspicions. But it was all so long ago. And of course, Alaina was entirely innocent.

"In all honesty, in many situations, the South has been quite desperate," Tara said. "Perhaps this woman was doing all she could to divert the soldiers, in order to save lives."

"But it's an interesting situation, isn't it?" Taylor Douglas said suddenly. His fingers rode over the rim of his wineglass and he stared down at it as he spoke. Then his eyes suddenly met Tia's. "To take soldiers by surprise at first might gain a few a reprieve. But few men, North or South, are entirely fools. I imagine the next time this Godiva appears, she could be in grave danger indeed, since men will know that she is out to do nothing but mislead them."

"It's amazing how stupid men can be at times!" Alaina announced.

"I'd not cast aspersions upon your gentle sex, Mrs. McKenzie, but one might say the same of women as well—since we do have this Rebel spy running around as naked as the day she was born."

"You seem to speak from experience!" Raymond said.

"Sir, were you diverted from some quest by this fair Rebel? Do you have knowledge of this vixen that I do not?"

Tia stared at Taylor, praying her face wasn't a dead giveaway. He hesitated.

She thought her heart would stop.

"I believe I saw her," he said gravely after a moment. "Yes, I admit to being a victim of the lady."

"Victim!" Tia muttered, then hastily bit her lip.

"Did you know her?" Alaina asked. "Did you know her—personally?"

He looked at Alaina. "Why would I know her?"

"Sir, you're from this state. Surely you attended some balls and barbecues, and would know if she was the daughter of a planter, a politician, or, say, a Florida botanist?" She stared hard at Ian, referring to her own father with the last.

Taylor Douglas smiled. "The child of no botanist I knew as a child. The lady I came across was definitely not at all blond."

"But she could have disguised herself, and acquired a wig," Ian suggested.

"No," Taylor said flatly. "I assure you, she was not blond. She did not wear a wig."

"How could you be so certain?" Alaina demanded, then her face flooded with crimson as she realized what his answer would have to be. "Oh!" she gasped in embarrassment.

"*Did* you know her, sir?" Raymond demanded harshly.

And again, Tia waited, her heart stopped, her lungs on fire. She couldn't bear it any longer. If he didn't answer, she'd scream and leap to her feet, and they'd all think she was crazy, and her father would know . . .

"I have been gone from the social arena of the state for quite some time. It is unlikely that I would have recognized the lady as the daughter of any one man," he said at last.

Tia felt as if she could pass out right into her plate. He wasn't going to betray her.

Not now anyway.

"Cigars and brandy, gentlemen?" Jarrett said. "It's such a balmy night, I thought we might enjoy our after-dinner drinks outside on the porch."

"As you wish, sir. Ladies . . ." Taylor rose, bowing to the women at the table, and followed his host out of the house.

"Ladies . . ." Ian echoed, rising, bowing politely, and following suit. Raymond Weir did the same.

"That went fairly well," Tara murmured. "No swords were drawn."

Tia didn't stay long in the salon with her mother and Alaina. Restless and needing to calm her nerves, she exited the house by the way of the back door and walked slowly around the verandah until she neared the front. She could hear the men speaking.

Eavesdropping, her mother had always warned her, was rude—and it often exposed one to things one would rather not hear about. The men were discussing Godiva—a topic she definitely did not want to hear about—but from the subdued tone of their conversation, it was clear that Taylor had not betrayed her secret.

Fortunately, their conversation did not last long. Tia heard Taylor thank her father for his hospitality, then she listened to footsteps entering the house, and muffled voices from within as the men met with her mother and thanked her as well for the evening.

Then after a few moments, she heard nothing more. She walked around the verandah, and was startled to find that Raymond Weir was still there, standing on the porch and looking out into the night.

"Tia," he said softly. She smiled, approaching him, yet wishing she did not feel so uneasy.

He inclined his head, his eyes pleasantly raking the length of her, his smile flatteringly appreciative.

"It's really good to have you here, Ray."

"If only this were a loyal household. How wonderful it would be, Tia, if your father would only realize that he must cast his fate with his state!"

"He loves the state, Ray, adores it."

"You, Tia, are all that is good in our life, in our state, in our being!"

She smiled. "Very poetic, for a solider, sir."

He reached out, taking her hands, drawing her to him. His hands covered hers. "Tia, marry me."

She didn't answer. How strange. She had joked about there being no men left to marry. He was the perfect mate. A rebel soldier, a brave man who led well and fought hard. Smart, handsome, passionate . . .

A man who might want a woman such as Godiva, but never marry her!

She was startled, but did not pull away, when he leaned down and pressed his mouth softly to hers. A kiss . . . she waited. For passion, for feeling . . .

What was she expecting? It wasn't as if she was experienced. And yet . . .

Yet she was. She'd felt a kiss before, filled with passion, boldness, a spark, a flame, a fire, a threat, a warning, and a promise . . .

Taylor. Taylor Douglas.

She pulled away from Raymond.

"I love you, Tia."

She shook her head. "Not . . . not now, Ray. The . . . the . . . war. My father, my own—well, I have my own duty within it."

"I love you," he repeated.

"And I . . ."

She what? She didn't know what she felt. Attraction? Disappointment? "Ray, when the war is over . . ."

"I can't wait for the war to be over."

"Maybe there will be another time."

"There will always be another time. I will take any time, Tia, that you give me. You, in any manner, in any way you wish."

He stepped back, bowed with a flourish, and headed back into the house. Tia walked out on the lawn. The fog had lifted. The night was beautiful. The curve of the moon was naked in the sky.

"Good night . . ." she murmured aloud.

"Good night, Godiva!" a voice replied.

She turned quickly, looking up—the voice had come from the upstairs balcony. There he was, Taylor Douglas. He had shed his frockcoat, and in the cool evening, he stood in only a white cotton shirt. It, and the dark tendrils of his hair, were being lifted slightly by the breeze.

"Don't say that!" she whispered furiously.

"Good night!" he repeated, and smiling, he turned and disappeared.

Cold.

Christmas Eve, and it was so damned cold.

Well, at the least, Brent McKenzie thought, hunkering down by the fire at the small house near the hospital he had taken for his quarters, his situation had changed somewhat.

He'd been called back to work on soldiers coming in from the battlefront.

There were so many of them.

Tonight, he wondered why he had wanted to be a doctor. From surely the strangest duty in the war—trying to help soldiers with syphilis and educate what seemed like an entire army of camp followers on how not to spread venereal disease—he was back helping men whose bodies had been shot, stabbed, sliced, and bombed to bits. Either way, it seemed a bitter detail. Even on Christmas eve, men were coming in, wounded in encounters beyond the city. Grant had been put in charge of the entire Union effort. He had made his own headquarters with the Army of the Potomac, and he'd ordered Meade to take Richmond. Lee's weary soldiers did their best to clock the army movements made by a man whose motto was that war should be as terrible as possible—that way it would end.

Brent was tired, he was worn out, and he was cold. He hadn't even gotten used to Christmas away from home. Christmas usually meant a crisp, cool day—but with the sun shining, his home surrounded by the blue of the sky and the sea and the green of the grass and the foliage. And flowers. His mother loved plants, herbs, and flowers. Teela always had flowers for Christmas. A wealth of them.

It was late. He'd been invited to dinner by a number of officers, but he'd had a boy come in with possible gangrene—and he'd refused to wait even a day to see the wounded young soldier, knowing how quickly infection could flourish. He'd taken the leg, something he had been very sorry to do. But while he was a good surgeon—a damned good surgeon who usually attempted every possible miracle to save a limb—he knew when to take a limb as well. The gangrene had been serious. He could only hope it hadn't spread through the boy's system.

Last Christmas, he reflected, he'd been far from home. Sydney had been with him. And actually, Sydney had been to see him not so long ago, but he had known, what seemed like a very long time ago now, when he'd treated Jesse Halston after the Union cavalry man had taken five bullets, that his sister had been falling in love with him. Sydney had gone to Washington to arrange for prisoner exchanges, wound up helping their brother escape instead—and marrying Jesse Halston. He was glad. He liked Halston, and he'd been glad to save his life. Now Sydney was back in Washington, waiting. Hopefully, Jesse Halston had enough rank and power to make it home for Christmas.

Hopefully, he wasn't lying dead on some forlorn battlefield.

Brent picked up the poker, stoked the fire, and reflected on the war. Strange. He'd hated being sent to deal with the prostitutes and the men with their sexual diseases. Giving lectures on the use of condoms. But after a while, he hadn't hated the duty so much. The prostitutes had been people, many of them warm, sad, caring, funny, wild individuals.

Face it, he told himself. He'd been forever changed by the experience. In many ways. He'd be forever haunted. Because of Mary.

He'd treated her father until he died. And, Brent reflected dryly, he had thought that the colonel's beautiful young daughter had been his mistress, and he'd made quite a fool out of himself, and an enemy out of her.

He jabbed the fire with a vengeance, wondering where she was tonight.

The flames flickered high and bright, blue and red. He set the poker down and warmed his hands before them. After a moment, he pulled off his military jacket, loosened his shirt, and walked over to the Queen Anne chair that sat on the hooked rug before the fire. An elegant cherry-wood occasional table by the chair carried a decanter of brandy. He poured himself a glass and spoke to the fire.

"Cheers, Doctor McKenzie. Merry Christmas."

He nearly threw his glass up when he received an answer.

"Yes, cheers. Merry Christmas, Doctor McKenzie."

The brandy sloshed as he leapt to his feet, spinning around to stare at the doorway to his bedroom. *She* was there. Mary. Either that, or the war had cost him his senses. His imagination had run riot. He was now stark, raving mad.

Her huge silver eyes were steady on his, her hair loosened around the snow-white robe that was all she wore.

"Mary!"

"Yes."

"What in God's name are you doing here?" he demanded, frowning fiercely.

She walked into the parlor before the fire. He thought that her hands were shaking but she reached down for the brandy decanter. "Do you mind? I thought I should help myself before you spilled it all."

He lifted a hand. "Go ahead," he murmured, still staring at her with astonishment. Yes, it was her; she was real. As stunning as a little snow queen in the white robe. She smelled of fresh soap and rose water; her hair, in the firelight, seemed as soft and sleek as sable. She seemed a pure assault on his senses. He had been exhausted; suddenly he was wide awake. He had been cold. Now his flesh seemed on fire, touched by lightning. *She isn't wearing a thing beneath the robe,* he thought.

"I'll ask you again," he said, and his voice barked out far more harshly than he had intended. "What are you doing here? How did you get here . . . in this house? How did you find me?"

"You were easy to find. I simply asked where you had been transferred. One of your orderlies pointed out your quarters in this house. It wasn't locked, or guarded in any manner. I let myself in. You should be more careful. The city of Richmond is teeming with refugees, some of them desperate men. Some people are fleeing the city again, afraid of Grant, and stealing everything in sight on their way out. Amazing, isn't it? Our countrymen aren't all noble soldiers and physicians. Some are simply cowardly thieves."

"Mary, *why* are you here?"

She tossed the brandy down and set the glass back in a deliberate gesture, her eyes downcast. Then they met his again.

"You said that I owed you; I always pay my debts," she told him.

"What?"

"I'd heard that you were here. My father . . . I owe you for all that you did for my father. I—I always pay my debts. It's Christmas. It seemed like a good time."

"So . . . you're here to . . . pay a debt?"

"Yes," she said quickly, her eyes falling from his once again.

He couldn't help it. He reached out, caught her hand, and pulled her to him. She wasn't wearing a thing beneath the robe. He lowered his head, kissed her. Her lips trembled. God, they were sweet. His kiss deepened. Her lips parted. Her body, pressed to his, was warm and supple and perfect. He cupped her breast, marveling at the feel, shuddering as the sensation in his fingertips seemed to work into his groin.

He caught himself, pulled away from her. "Damn you, Mary!" he swore angrily. "You don't owe me! I was angry when I told you that; you owe me nothing at all for your father. What the bloody hell do you think of me, that I wouldn't help any man when he was dying?"

She stood just feet away from him, shaking, her eyes shimmering like sterling with a hint of tears.

"I do owe you for what you did for him."

He took the single step back to her, taking her into his arms, lifting her chin, meeting her eyes. Her lips trembled. He felt himself shaking. "Mary, Mary! You little fool. I will not make love to you because you feel that you owe me any debt! I was angry, jealous, hurt—an idiot."

She lowered her eyes, leaning her head against his chest.

"Would you . . . would you make love to me . . . if I told you that I simply wanted to be with you? That I've spent every day since you left trying to figure out how to come to you, how to tell you . . ." Her voice trailed away in a whisper. He wasn't even sure he had heard her correctly. His fingers shaking, his blood burning, he caught her chin, lifted her eyes to his once again.

"What?"

"I want to be with you. I need to be with you. I have nowhere else to go now."

"Mary, you shouldn't be here just because there is nowhere else—"

"It's not that, you fool man! I want to be with you. I admire you, I am intrigued . . . I am curious—for the love of God, I am willing! Don't tell me you can't use me—"

"Use you?" he interrupted, frowning.

But her thoughts were elsewhere. "Here, at the hospital. You know that I'm more than competent, that I can anticipate your needs."

"Can you anticipate them all?" he murmured softly.

"Brent, please. I know I've arrived quite strangely, out of the blue. But I had to come here, and I had hoped that at Christmas . . . well, you would feel at least something for me."

"Mary, it wouldn't be right. You are not that kind of woman."

"What kind? Sensual—seductive?"

"Oh, my God! Mary, trust me . . ." He paused, looking at her. Silver eyes glittering, hair streaming down her back, robe parting to provide just a peak at the roundness of her breast, the rouge of her nipple, the narrowness of her waist, curve of her hip . . . "Trust me, you do know how to seduce!"

"Brent . . . please . . ."

"Mary, please . . . what?"

"Hold me tonight. Let me be with you. Make . . ."

"Make love to you?"

"God, yes!"

"But Mary, come the morning . . ."

"Brent! I planned this for a very long time. Yet in my dreams, you made it much easier for me. Brent—I am all but throwing myself at you. You must not be so cruel as to refuse me!"

He was lost—or found. He was not sure which. "God forbid that I should be cruel," he said.

She smiled. He swept her up. Her arms curled around his neck.

"Merry Christmas," she said softly.

Merry Christmas indeed. It was cold outside, but it was as if he had died and gone to heaven.

Chapter 8

He had ruined all hope of sleep.

As Tia paced across the floor in her bedroom, she kept hearing his voice over and over again, mocking, taunting. *Godiva.* Had he been threatening her?

Yes, of course, he was threatening her. Sometime, tomorrow, he would tell her father the truth. Tell him who she was, what she was doing.

Her father would kill her.

Worse. He would be disappointed. *Shamed.*

She had to see Taylor. Talk to him.

What was she, mad? She couldn't just go tapping on his door; she might wake up her parents, or her brother, or Alaina, Reeves, Lilly, someone else in the house.

She opened her doors to the balcony. The night had grown cool, but not cold. She stepped out in her bare feet. She'd seen him just outside on the rear balcony, near his room. Without really planning out her intention, she suddenly sped around the balcony, came to the guest doors, and hesitated. No, don't think, you won't *act!* she warned herself. She opened the door, slipped inside.

It was dark, but a whisper of moonlight filtered in. She could just make out the bed, and she tiptoed over to it.

She saw his form, shoulders bronze, the muscles starkly defined against the white sheets. In the shadows, he seemed to be soundly sleeping. She hesitated, then sat at his side. "We need to talk. Please, listen—"

She nearly cried out as he turned, arms sweeping

around her, bearing her down into the bed. He whispered something. She couldn't make it out. A name?

She strained against his chest with her palms, her anxiety growing. "We need to talk, I need you to listen to me."

Beside her, one leg draped over her, his arm around her waist, she suddenly realized that he hadn't been sleeping at all. He had probably seen her from the moment she'd reached his doors to the balcony.

"Miss McKenzie! Just what game is it you're playing now?"

"Colonel Douglas—"

"Yes, it is. Surprised?"

"No, of course not, I—"

"What the hell are you doing? Wrong room, Godiva? Were you looking for your gallant Southern lover? He who would accept anything from you, anything at all?"

"You wretched eavesdropper! You are the rudest individual—"

"Rude? For repeating the truth? I could be far worse."

"We need to talk."

"We? You and me? Oh, so you came in the dead of night—dressed, I'll admit, but my Lord, Godiva, this is seductive material!—to talk. To me."

"I was not looking for Raymond!" she insisted.

"As you say. How charming. You were looking for me in this lovely sheer gown. Coming purposely into my room. I'm deeply flattered, and not a little stirred, I must say."

"Stop it! I'll call my father, my brother, the whole Confederate army!"

"Stop it? May I remind you, you came after me."

"I didn't come *after* you."

"And make up your mind—are we calling your father, or the Rebel army? My defense will be based entirely on the identity of whom we summon."

"Listen to me, I wasn't coming after you—"

"You're in my bed."

"Please—!"

"So you *were* looking for good old gray-clad Colonel Weir," he said. "Mistake, I might add."

"How dare you insult Colonel Weir! He's loyal and fighting for his state, and he is determined, and a gentleman still, and—"

"A good man. That I don't doubt."

"Then—"

"He is a fanatic. He has read too much Machiavelli. The end defends whatever means is required to reach it. He will destroy this state before he allows it to return to the Union."

"We haven't lost the war!"

"You will."

She stared up at him, the tawny eyes now on hers in the night, the very handsome, currently grave structure of his face. She felt almost compelled to reach out and trace the line of his cheekbone. Nor did it seem quite so terrible to lie there, being touched by him, and she suddenly thought of her brother's closed door and all of the things she had missed by committing herself to the war. She gritted her teeth, furious with herself, wondering what was wrong with her that she could lie there with an avowed enemy who seemed to take the most perverse pleasure in taunting her and want to touch him. The warmth that spread through her seemed like a taste of evil, and yet—heaven help her—she desired it.

"I didn't come to talk about the war."

"Now I'm really flattered. You've come to seduce me?"

"No!" she protested, then realized the volume of her voice and swore softly at him. His smile further infuriated her. "Damn you, stop it!"

"I haven't done a thing."

"Stop doing what you're not doing!"

He smiled again, shook his head, then sobered. "All right, Godiva, talk."

"You haven't given me away as yet," she breathed, looking into his eyes.

"I have great respect for your father, brother, and

mother," he told her. "It would not benefit them to know of your evil deeds."

"What I did was not evil. It was accidental. You must understand. You were there."

"I was there once," he said softly. "Godiva also led a company of men down a merry path when they had nearly taken Captain Dickinson and his troops. How many other times has she ridden since then?"

"That's the only time, I swear it. I didn't mean to—"

"You are quite frequently naked by sheer accident for a well-bred Southern girl, are you not?" he demanded.

"I wouldn't say 'by accident'; it was spur of the moment, sheer desperation—"

"I really should tell your father. Because you have to stop what you're doing."

"You can't tell him, please—"

He leaned closer to her. "You will get yourself killed. And when your body is found, they will know, and their grief will be compounded again and again. And I will be guilty of a terrible crime against them, because I knew."

"Please . . ."

"Tell me that you'll never do it again. No matter what the circumstances."

She caught her breath, staring up at him.

"It's the only way, Godiva."

"I won't do it again. I didn't mean to do it, as I said—"

"No matter what the circumstances."

She gritted her teeth very hard. "No matter what the circumstances."

"Then your secret is safe with me."

Barely daring to breathe, she looked into his tawny eyes, praying he was telling the truth. Then she realized again her circumstances. She lay flat on his bed, his leg cast over her, his hand upon her waist.

This time, *he* was naked.

And she realized it in such a manner that her eyes widened in panic and her flesh burned with a flow of blood. "Well, then, I—I—"

"Ah, you suddenly see the real danger in the enemy!"

he taunted, leaning close again. "Good. But you needn't try to run so suddenly in sheer panic, dear Miss McKenzie. What did you think, that I would suddenly lose control in your father's house, rape his daughter in his own home?"

"No, I—I—my God, it's just that—"

"Shush!" He suddenly brought a finger to his lips. She had heard nothing. Yet he quickly moved over her, leaving the bed, striding to the doors to the balcony. He held still there, and she bit her lip, trying not to watch his lithe, bronze form in the shadows. His broad shoulders and well-muscled arms seemed to ripple with each play of moonlight, and she couldn't help but notice the way his torso narrowed to a lean waist, that his buttocks were as tightly muscled as the rest of him, that his legs were long and powerfully built.

He moved like one who had grown up with danger— like her Uncle James and her cousins, who had known the suffering of the Seminoles. In silence, he watched at the latticed doors, and heard what she did not. He turned back into the room, finding his trousers and slipping into them.

"What are you doing?" she whispered.

"Be quiet, and stay there," he commanded.

A second later, he was out on the balcony. And a moment after that, she heard him cheerfully hailing someone who was also out on the balcony.

"Ah, Colonel Weir! Did you find you couldn't sleep as well?"

"Colonel Douglas," Weir returned. He sounded awkward.

"It's a beautiful night." Taylor said. "From here, this gracious house, with the sky so dark, the stars so bright, it is almost possible to forget the war."

"I never forget the war, sir."

"No, I imagine that you do not," Taylor agreed, and Tia could hear a note of irony in his voice.

What had Ray Weir been doing on the balcony. By her room?

"I think, sir, that what we accomplished here tonight

has been good work," Taylor continued. "There is so much bloodshed; when lives are spared, it is a decent thing at last."

"But freedom, sir, has always come at a cost! Sometimes, lives must be the price paid for a nation to survive."

"True enough. That lessens the value of no one life." Taylor said. "Well, sir, I didn't mean to interrupt you if you desired a private vigil in the night. But then . . . is that the door to your guest room? Were we given such close quarters? How interesting an arrangement by our gracious host."

"That . . . no, that is not my room. I am around there to the river side of the house. I—I merely decided to walk around the house, admire the architecture."

"Ah, I see. Oh, of course, I believe that is one of the family rooms. Ian's room—no, it is his sister's room, I think."

"Perhaps," Weir said stiffly.

"Good God, I didn't interrupt a secret tryst—" Taylor began with horror.

"No, indeed, sir, that you should suggest such a thing against the daughter of the house!" Ray said angrily.

"No offense intended, sir. It is simply that your admiration for her, and hers for you, is quite obvious."

"She is the most beautiful creature I have ever seen," Raymond said. "I have loved her forever."

"Curious that you never married. She was of age before the war, I believe?"

"I should have pursued my suit, sir. The lady longed for travel and adventure. I thought that she should see the world she craved to see, before becoming a proper wife. Yet, I always believed that she loved me."

"Well, the war will end," Taylor said.

"One day, indeed, I believe she will be mine."

"Good luck to you, sir."

"Yes, good night," Raymond told Taylor. "Were you returning to bed?"

"I thought that I'd enjoy the stars awhile longer.

Don't let me delay your stroll around the house any longer, sir."

"Yes, er, good night, then."

Tia waited, sitting up in Taylor's bed. A minute later, he reentered the room and came to the bedside. Now, somewhat decently clad in his trousers at least, he sat at the side of the bed. She noticed for the first time that he wore a gold chain around his neck with a medallion; it rested against the bronze of his chest.

She noticed, as well, that he wore a gold band around the ring finger of his left hand.

"I believe your lover was looking for you—heading for your room. I would not deprive you two of a romantic encounter, but I didn't think you'd want him discovering that you weren't in your room—indeed, that you were visiting me. You might want to slip back into your own room before someone else comes looking. There probably will be bloodshed here this evening, should someone find you here."

"No one would think that I had come for an illicit affair with a Yankee," she assured him.

He smiled. "Then just how would you explain your appearance?"

"You suggested that I come here, because . . . because I might know who Godiva is! Because I must warn her . . . that the Yanks may know who she is, that—"

She broke off. He was laughing softly. "And you think that your parents would believe that I enticed you into my bedroom *to talk about the welfare of a strange woman*?"

"Why not?"

"Oh, come, Tia, you're not a fool. You know that poor Colonel Weir lusts for you, in agony, so it seems. You teased an army with your perfection—and they followed you blindly. No, either your father or brother—or Weir—would want to kill me. There would be duels, and three people would die."

"And those people would be?"

"I would not be among them."

"My brother is one of the best swordsmen—"

"I am better."

"Your arrogance knows no bounds."

"Godiva, go back to your own bed, and leave me be."

"There would be no contest, sir!" she said, angrily rising. "I would simply tell my father that it was the truth, that you dislike me, have no desire for me—"

"Godiva, I never said that I had no desire for you!" His voice was deep, husky, and yet, for once, it seemed to hold no amusement. He stood before her, and though she was angry enough to strike him, she found herself not doing so, but standing very still as he reached out, his fingers touching her face. His head lowered to hers. She remembered the feel of his kiss. His lips were so close. They nearly touched hers. And still, she didn't move. His body was close as well. She could almost feel the hard-muscled structure of his torso against her breasts. "But," he murmured, "thank God, I would never be like that poor besotted Colonel Weir, never fool enough to love you, Godiva."

He was no longer touching her. Nowhere near so close. She felt a rush of cold air, as if wind swept in around her.

Fury filled her.

And she lashed out, her palm a blur, ready to hit him hard.

She never touched him. Her arm was captured, she was spun around, and she found herself enwrapped hard against him, her back to his chest, his arms around her tightly, fingers lacing just below her breasts. And his whispered warning touched her ear where he spoke softly against her. "You need to take care with that temper, Godiva. And with your welfare. Behave, I warn you. Keep your promise, keep yourself safe."

"What do you care?" she choked out furiously, her fingers working at his to earn her release.

"Your brother is my friend, your cousins are my kin, and your father is a truly great man."

"They are not your concern."

"Then perhaps I should simply tell them the truth."

"No!" she said, and went very still. "No."

"All right, then. I'll be careful not to mention you at all, should I be speaking with any of your kin. You take care not to talk about me as well."

"I wouldn't be talking about you."

"I could come up in conversation. And I wouldn't want you discussing various aspects of my person with which you shouldn't be familiar—after all, we have now both seen one another in the all-together."

He was taunting her now, he knew, and ready for the explosion of anger that ripped through her. Chuckling softly, he held her tightly until the fullness of her fury had abated. Then his amusement seemed to fade, and a somber quality fell over him. "Go to your own bed, Godiva. But heed my every warning, because I will tell the truth of the matter if I see no other way."

She stood some distance from him, still so livid she couldn't find the right words to say.

"I might be reprieved," she managed at last.

"I don't think so."

"It's a war, sir. You could be killed."

"And you could be killed, you little fool, and that's the point of this."

"Good night, Colonel. With luck, we'll never meet again."

She turned to flee with dignity.

He caught her arm. She wrenched at it. "Wait!" he grated. "Don't you want to see if the coast is clear?"

She bit her lower lip, drawing blood, lowering her head. He stepped past her.

A silent tread.

"Go," he said softly.

And she did.

Christmas Eve.
There was no reason why Sydney couldn't have gone home to Florida. Her husband lived in Washington, so it was where his wife should be, but since she hadn't seen her husband since their impromptu marriage in prison, she *should* have gone home. She didn't even live in his apartment. She still shared with Sissy and with

Marla, an Irish friend, widowed in the war, who had helped in her old spying days. Her borrowed space, her only privacy, here in Washington was a tiny ten-by-ten room in the apartment the three women shared near the White House.

Washington was cold. Wretched. Patches of ice, a vicious wind. Home meant the sun, and during those very few times when the temperature dipped into the thirties, there was still warmth from the sun. Home meant her mother, her father, her new baby sister. Perhaps Jerome would even be there; God knew, her oldest brother could move with unbelievable speed when he chose. And even if she hadn't made it home—Brent was less than a hundred miles south of here. She could have, perhaps, reached her sister-in-law in St. Augustine, or cut across the state and spent the holiday at Cimarron with her aunt and uncle.

She had to quit thinking that way. There were a dozen other things she might have been doing rather than what she was . . .

Risking her life again like an idiot!

Driving her wagon, Sissy at her side, she neared the Southern picket line.

"Ho, there!"

Today, the officer in charge appeared to be about twenty-five, lean, sad looking, and very cold. He wore a lieutenant's insignia. A worn scarf was wrapped around his neck. He shuffled back and forth on his feet, his rifle held easily in his hands. She drew in on the reins, ready for his questions. He smiled at her, bringing his hands to his face. Blowing on them. He wore gloves, but they were riddled with holes.

"Good evening, ma'am. May I have your papers? State your business."

She handed him her traveling papers. "I came south with letters from the fellows at Old Capitol, with proper permission from the Yankee authorities to do so. There, Colonel Meek, whose troops have headed on back toward Harper's Ferry, received the letters, and signed for my return to Washington."

The officer stared up at her. "Mrs. Sydney . . . *McKenzie* Halston?"

She nodded.

He smiled suddenly. "If you see your husband or your cousin Ian, tell them Rafe Johnston sends his best."

"You rode with my cousin Ian?"

"And your husband. With Magee. I heard your brother married Magee's daughter. Always thought it would be Ian."

"They're all doing very well," Sydney said. "I . . ." she began. But then she froze. The sound of a sneeze came from the back of the wagon.

Johnston stared at her. She stared back. She felt the blood drain from her face. Even as he looked at her, she saw the future flash before her eyes. He would arrest her. She was an avowed Southerner-heading north with runaway slaves. There could be a trial. There might not. They might hang her tonight, make an example out of her, prove that the South could not tolerate spies and traitors, even among their womenfolk.

She saw Johnston lower his eyes, and then he looked at her again. And he knew exactly what she was doing.

But he handed her back her papers. "Merry Christmas, Mrs. Halston. It's a good time to pray for peace."

She exhaled on a soft sob. "Merry Christmas, Lieutenant . . ." She lifted the reins. Her fingers were numb. She couldn't hold them. She inhaled again, remembered the embroidered bag she carried at her side—and the gift she had carried in case she had managed to see her brother.

Gloves. Good, calfskin gloves, both soft and resilient. "Lieutenant . . . these were for my brother Brent. I was never able to see him. Please . . ."

"No, ma'am, I can't take those." His eyes told her that they might be considered a bribe.

She shook her head. "Please, I wanted so badly to give them to someone to whom they might mean something. Please . . ."

He looked at the gloves in her hands, looked at her,

into her eyes. He took the gloves. "Thank you. Hurry on now."

She grasped the reins, cracked them, calling out to the mules. They rode on.

"God bless us!" Sissy breathed.

"We're still in Rebel territory. And we've the Yanks to get through. If we encounter a wretched son of a gun the way we did last time . . ."

"We won't," Sissy said with assurance.

Sissy was right. It was Christmas Eve. The Yankee pickets, like their Southern counterparts, were melancholy. They wanted the war to be over. They wanted to be home. All along the lines, they sang Christmas carols.

The officer who stopped her on the road barely looked at her papers.

No one sneezed.

They passed on through to the city, and arrived at last in a dark alley off South Capitol Street, near the African Methodist Episcopal ministry of Reverend Henry Turner. Washington might mean freedom for the slaves, but it did not assure them a good life, or even a decent meal. Reverend Turner had always been a passionate man about helping his fellows, so tonight, Sydney drove Sissy and the two men and three women they had met just below the lines to the alley where Turner would meet them, and find them a place to stay.

They blessed Sydney as they came from the wagon, one of the men carrying the beaten, pregnant young girl whose story had inspired Sydney to risk her own life again and come south for the contrabands.

One of the women came around the front of the wagon, looking at Sydney with her huge dark eyes. She grabbed Sydney's hand and tried to kiss it.

"Please!" Sydney whispered. "Go on now. Merry Christmas."

"God bless you, ma'am!" said one of the men, a huge black field hand.

"And you," she murmured. She was flushed; embarrassed. She shouldn't be doing this. But when the message had reached the house about the dying girl, she'd been busy feeling sorry for herself, and angry with herself for not leaving Washington.

"I'll go with them to the Reverend," Sissy told Sydney. "Are you going to be all right?"

"Yes, of course."

Sissy shook her head. "Marla isn't even at the apartment. She went off to spend Christmas with old Mrs. Lafferty and the orphans."

"I'll be fine. I'm very tired."

"I'll be back tomorrow morning sometime."

"We'll find a good Christmas dinner somewhere," Sydney agreed.

She left Sissy, and took the wagon back to the livery near the apartment. "It's late for you to be heading home alone, Mrs. Halston," the night man told her.

"I'll be fine."

It was past midnight, she realized, but not so strange, for in wartime, there always seemed to be someone out and about. She passed a group of officers sharing a flask over a street fire. They tipped their hats to her, watching her curiously. She nodded, and hurried into her apartment.

A fire burned in the cozy living room. There was a note left on the mantle from Marla:

> Syd,
> I'm off to play Santa the best I can to the little ones. Major Cantor brought a roast—it's on the dining room table—and a delicious claret. (I know it's delicious; I tried it.) Left you a steaming bath and my gift, lavender soap. It may not be steaming when you return. Left a kettle by the fire.
> Love to you, Marla.

Sydney smiled. She might be far from home, but at least she had a few friends. She shed her cloak and her boots in the living room. She walked into the darkened bedroom, where even there, a fire had been left burning. It was the only light in the room, illuminating the tub. She touched the water. Still warm. The kettle rested by the fire. Taking a thick pot holder, she poured the steaming water into the bath and began to shed her clothing. As she stepped from her skirt, her travel papers fell from the pocket. Weary and anxious for the warm water, she left them where they lay, and sank into the tub.

She closed her eyes and leaned back.

After a moment, she felt a very strange, uneasy sensation.

She opened her eyes.

She froze.

Jesse was there. Across the room, seated in the one armchair in the far dark corner. Stripped down himself to uniform trousers, boots, and white cotton shirt, eyes grave, handsome features somewhat leaner than they had been when last she'd seen him. He watched her in silence.

"Jesse . . ." she breathed, stunned.

He stood, walking toward the tub.

"Where have you been?"

"Been?" she echoed.

"It's after midnight. Where have you been?"

She thought desperately for an answer. Her mind was blank. She shrank into the water, hugging her knees to her chest, greatly unnerved. "I . . . I can't discuss the situation right now, Jesse. I wasn't expecting you."

"Obviously."

Her eyes narrowed. "I haven't heard from you in six months!" she snapped. "In fact, you told me to get an annulment."

"But you didn't. Where have you been?"

"Out!"

"Out where?"

"It's really none of your business, and you have your nerve, interrogating me here, now, in the bathtub. If you'll just get out of my room and let me finish and dress—"

"I married you, Sydney," he said softly, leaning down, bracing his hands on the side of the tub. "Then I did the very gentlemanly thing—and rode off to war. Tonight I'm back. Where have you been?"

She met his eyes, sharp, hazel, and unrelenting. Six
months. A long six months. He had changed. She lowered her head, remembering when he had been a Confederate prisoner and she had been his nurse. She
remembered the way he had looked at her then, the
charm in his voice, the sound of his laughter, the gentle-
ness of his touch, the way she had longed to see him
each day.

She looked up again. He wasn't the same man.

"I was out—with friends."

He turned away, picking up the papers that had fallen
from her skirt. He read through them. They fell from
his hands, drifting back to the floor. "Letters from dead
Rebs, eh, brought south?" he asked.

Then suddenly he turned. And his hands were on her
shoulders, and he was dragging her dripping and protesting from the tub. "My God, you promised, you
swore!" he raged at her. "You swore there would be no
more espionage, and I gave my word for you, that there
would be no actions against the Union in which you
were involved. My word! I gave *my* word for you!"

She had never, ever seen him like this. He was the
one always in control, a man who did the right thing,
thoughtful, considerate, courteous—if determined. When
he had prevented her from leaving the city with Jerome,
when he had arrested her—when he had married her—
he had been in control. Even after the wedding. *He had
walked away.* Not now.

She couldn't even respond. She stood before him with
soap and bath water sluicing from her form, and she
couldn't find the right words to defend herself. No! She
hadn't betrayed the Union, but she had ridden south . . .

His arm suddenly jerked back and she braced herself,
gritting her teeth, certain that he meant to hit her. Six
months, six months between them, and this was how
they met.

No blow landed upon her. But his hands were suddenly upon her again, and he was shaking her, and then
he thrust her from him, and in the small space of the
tiny bedroom, she fell back, tripping so that she fell into

the tub again. Water spewed up and around her. Her fingers closed around the soap.

She threw it. He saw the missile coming and ducked. Then he stared at her, and she knew she was in trouble.

He made a dive for her in the tub again. She struggled, trying to free her arms. She was dragged back out anyway and caught again before the fire, where she kicked and writhed to get free. "Let go of me, you oaf. You want an annulment, you'll have an annulment so fast your head will spin, Colonel Halston!" she swore. It did her no good.

"Liar! I trusted you!" he hissed. "Like a fool, I thought your word meant something." He didn't begin to release his hold, but used his weight to press her toward the foot of the bed. This time, she fell backward on the mattress. He followed her down.

"Get away from me, get out of *my* apartment. My word does mean something, you horrible *Unionist.*"

"Rebel spy."

"Yankee bastard."

"Indian!" he shouted at her.

"And God help me, but I'd love to scalp you!" she taunted him in return.

"Where have you been?" he repeated.

"None of your business. Leave me alone!"

"Not this time. You're going back to Old Capitol, my dear wife. This time, you will stay out of trouble."

She sucked in her breath. "Fine! Send me back. There will be an annulment."

"I will."

But he hadn't moved. He still lay atop her, his shirt as soaked as she was.

"Send me back!" she whispered. But she didn't mean it. God, she didn't mean it. She hated prison. And hated the fear that one of her brothers, her father, or her other kin would die to free her from such a place. And yet . . .

"Do it! Send me back!" she repeated.

"Not yet."

"Yes, now . . ." The feel of his body was a fire against her. She'd been so afraid so many times that he didn't

come because he was dead. He wasn't dead; he was alive
and well—he had just stayed away from her. "Do it!"
she cried, and she started slamming her hands against
him. "Do it, do it, do it . . ."

He caught her wrists, shook his head. "I came home
to spend Christmas Eve with my wife. It is a long, hard,
lonely war. I intend to spend it with her."

His mouth found hers. Seared into it. She tried to
close her lips, twist her head. Tears stung her eyes; her
lips parted in a sob, and suddenly she was kissing him
back. She'd fallen in love with him easily. Trying to hate
him had been hard. Fearing for him daily had been torture. Waiting, and waiting, and waiting . . .

And now this. His kiss, the touch of his hands. A
feeling of hunger, of rage, of fear. His wet clothing was
a tangle around him. She was chilled and hot at the same
time. Aware of where they were going, and thinking that
I should never have been miserable, praying that she
would love him . . .

Just his kiss, his touch. Heated, evocative. Awakening
a hunger that left her clinging to him, and still afraid of
the unknown. He was passionate, but impatient with his
anger. She tasted his lips; her fingers curled into his hair.
The kiss did things, and still . . .

She screamed and choked, and wanted to die. Her
nails dug into his shoulders. He went rigid, waited. His
eyes met hers. Hers closed. And he began to move
again, giving no quarter. She still thought that she would
dic. The pain remained . . . but something grew out of
it as well. She gritted her teeth, trying to push him away.
She burrowed against his shoulder, his chest, suddenly
wanting more, moving with him, wanting . . . wanting . . .

Sweet mercury filled her, as molten as a spill of steel,
sweeping away strength and anger and every other
thought except elation for the moments that lifted her
to ecstasy. She clung to the magic, and to his arms, and
then she was drifting down again, and she was cold and
sore and caught in the tangle of the sheets and his
clothing.

He lay beside her, no apology spoken. After a few

moments, he rose, shedding his disheveled clothing. She shivered, watching his body in the moonlight. He was perfect—except for the scars. The bronze of his shoulder was marred by the white line where he had been injured at Gettysburg. He'd probably receive another promotion because of that scar—bravery under fire on the battle-field. And of course, so many officers had died. It was a time when replacements might readily be given credit.

She looked lower, swallowing. There had been that time when they had both been intrigued, when they had flirted, when they had fallen in love. A time when they had been friends. Then there had been their marriage . . . and now, when nothing seemed right at all, there was this time of intimacy. God, how she had dreamed of being with him! Laughter, champagne perhaps, all the right tenderness, whispers in her ear. She hated him, hated him for con-demning her. An echo of pain seemed to linger within her, and still . . . she wanted him to lie down beside her.

He came back to the bed, wrenching the covers with her still upon them. "Get under the sheets and blanket," he said brusquely. "You're shaking."

Ah, what gentle, endearing words on this occasion!

"I'm not cold. I'm angry. I want you away."

"You're freezing. Do as I say—for once."

"Because this is Washington, and you think you have all the power?"

"Because it's logical."

She rolled away from him, trying to rise. She was drawn back; the covers brought over her. He lay down beside her. She stiffened. He didn't allow her to do so. He drew her against the warmth of his own body, held her there. She closed her eyes. There were so many things to say. She didn't say any of them.

Then she felt him.

His lips, a brand against her nape, her shoulder, her backbone. His hands, cupping her breasts, sliding down her ribs, her belly, to her groin. Fingers pressing, stroking . . .

This time, something suddenly caught within her. Wildfire. She turned to him, guided by instinct, touching, tasting, kissing, in a frenzy. Desire spit, rose, spiraled, teased, and taunted. His mouth was everywhere on her. Each touch elicited a burst of fire. She twisted, writhed, and trembled, and when he was within her again, she arched to his every thrust, feeling impassioned, fevered, hungry . . .

The world seemed to explode. The war was over; life had ended. Diamond glimmers of bursting light broke a black satin heaven, then there was nothing more. And it seemed to take forever and ever to drift down and realize that he was with her, shuddering as well in the aftermath of climax.

It was wonder, pure wonder. And she was in love again, ready to admit to him what had happened, how she had become involved, how it was actually the South, her own heritage, and everything she stood for that she had betrayed. She'd never do it again. If it hadn't been for the kindness and justice of Lieutenant Johnston, she might have been caught, but . . .

He stroked her hair. "There will be no question of an annulment now," he said.

"No," she whispered, turning into him, her face against his chest. He smelled delicious. Muscle rippled beneath her touch. His warmth was encompassing.

"My God, I shall be sorry to see you back in prison."

She stiffened. Drew away. "In prison?"

His eyes touched hers. Deep hazel, grave. "Did you think that I was so desperate for your love that I would be seduced and demented—and forget that you *lied*— *that you made a liar and a fool out of me*?"

She jerked away from him. He reached out, preventing her from fleeing when she would have left the bed.

"Get away from me! Get your hands off me! Call your guards and have me arrested tonight, though on what charges, I do not know! Call them now! Old Capitol seems a wonderful place to sleep, as long as you do not sleep there as well! You're right, I'll be among my own people, my own kind, sleeping with Rebels rather than *snakes*!"

"Get back in here."

"No!"

"Sydney—"

"You intend to arrest me again; do it."

"Not tonight."

"Why not tonight?"

"There's time."

"No, there's not! I could cause an entire uprising; force the South to win the war while you sleep!"

Aggravated, he caught her around the middle and pressed her back down. She couldn't believe the pain she was feeling.

"I hate you!"

"Sorry. It's a war."

"Yes, it is. So arrest me this minute—or let me go."

"No."

And he didn't let her go. He lay down beside her, keeping a firm hand upon her. She twisted, turning her back to him, but aware of his arm around her.

Christmas Eve . . .

A time of peace.

She had never felt more at war.

Chapter 9

~

Dawn.

The sun was rising; the sky was clear; the day was beautiful. And far in the south of the Florida peninsula, it was warm.

James McKenzie stood by the little inlet of salt water that created a lagoon on his property and looked out far past it—far to the sea beyond. He stood shirtless, his bronze chest muscled and honed, and barefoot, the warmth of the salt water running over his feet. He loved the water; he loved the sea and the warmth. His attire might not be exactly proper, but then, they were far to the south of real civilization, and he'd been called a savage often enough in his life. Down here, on his own property, his attire was his own concern. He gave it little thought as he continued to stare at the sea.

His son was out there. Somewhere. His oldest son, Jerome, trying to find new ways to slip the Union blockade and bring supplies to the state and the Confederacy. He had watched the water through the night and into the morning, hoping against hope that Jerome might make it home for the holiday.

There was no sign of a ship. He didn't despair. He had to believe in the ability of both his sons—and his daughters!—to survive the war. At the moment, however, he wasn't particularly worried about the girls. Jennifer, his child by Naomi, his first wife, was home with him. She and her son, Anthony—now a handsome, precocious young boy of six—had been with him since Jarrett had brought her home after her husband's death. Disguised as a man, she had begun some very dangerous spying activities, been caught and nearly hanged. His nephew, Ian, had managed to save her, and since then, she had tried to exist without thinking about the war—despite the fact that the state remained Rebel, and Union navy ships out of Union-held Key West far too often came near their shore.

Then there was his daughter Mary—born just last year and quite a surprise to both him and his wife, Teela. She had given him tremendous fear at the time of her birth, fear that she would die in childbirth, but she and the baby were well now, saucy, sweet, toddling around, allowing them to smile in the midst of their worry for their other children. James had lost a wife and child to fever during the Seminole War; he knew the anguish of it, and often prayed that, were he to be given one gift from God, it would be to *not* outlive any more of his children. Brent, he thought, might be safer than Jerome; Jerome was brash and reckless, and renowned for his daring escapades against the Yanks. Brent was a doctor, a surgeon, dedicated to life. James liked to believe that he would have the sense to take care for his own.

But then there was Sydney . . .

Reckless, passionate, as any warrior of old. She had been with Brent in Charleston when South Carolina had seceded. She had become a nurse in Richmond. She had gone to try to exchange a Yank for her brother when Jerome had been captured.

Then, recently, she had married the Yank.

A damned fine fellow, he had been assured.

But Sydney had been living in Washington ever since, and he longed to have her home. Staring out at the water, he wondered about heading north to suggest to her new husband that Sydney might fare better back in her own home while the war raged.

No one thought, of course, that he should do it. Teela told him he had too hot a temper, that he'd be demanding his daughter—something he didn't have a right to do, since Sydney had married the man by choice, had written about him before, and apparently loved him. But it was too long for a father to wait to see his child. Especially when it was Christmas.

"Father?"

He turned, surprised to be discovered there, by the lagoon pool, at this early hour. It was Jennifer. She was maturing now, in her mid-thirties, into a very serene and dignified woman, more beautiful, he thought, with each passing year. She had her mother's hazel eyes, a nobility to her native features, a gentle smile, and at least, an inner peace. She came to him, and he slipped an arm around her shoulders. "Father, he is smart enough not to come. He knows the navy men will be keeping a close eye out for him now! They know Jerome loves his family." She was silent for a minute. "I imagine Risa is by the sea today, as well. Looking out."

"Risa is in St. Augustine. Teela urged her to come to us, but she was afraid that she would hear he had come to the north of the state somewhere, and she wouldn't be able to reach him."

"He's not a fool. He is safe. And we just received that letter from Brent; he is well, but very busy—"

"You'd think they'd stop killing for Christmas, wouldn't you?" James said softly.

"We have a long letter from Sydney, as well, you know, brought by one of Captain Dickinson's men."

"I know."

"Father, I wish I could ease this all for you somehow."

He drew her closer, setting his cheek against her dark head. "You do. You and Anthony and Mary. Have I told you how much I love you lately, daughter? How very precious you are?"

"Father, I—"

Abruptly she stopped speaking. "Look, Father, look!"

He'd been staring out to sea, and so he hadn't seen the man lying half in the water and half out at the far side of the lagoon beneath a giant palm.

"My, God, it is a man!" Jennifer breathed. She pulled from James, and started running around the pool.

"No! Wait!" James called firmly. He didn't know if she would heed him or not, and so he started to run himself. He caught her arm, pulling her back. "Wait! If he's alive, he may be dangerous!"

He passed his daughter, aware she still followed behind him, but at least she was at his back. As he neared the body, he drew the knife he always kept in a sheath at his ankle before falling down to his knees in the wet sand by the body. He rolled the soldier over, thinking that the man must be dead.

Not dead . . . a pulse ticked at his throat. Weak, but there. He looked at the uniform. Union cavalry. More cavalry—damn the cavalry! He was a lean man, young, with sand-encrusted blond hair and burned skin.

"Father . . ."

"He's alive."

James studied the man's face. A smear of blood grazed his temple, coagulated now with a matting of hair and sand.

"We have to bring him in! Help him," Jennifer said.

"He's Union, Jennifer."

"So . . . so is Ian! And Taylor stayed with the Union as well. They are both men you care about, nearly as close as your own sons."

"Jennifer, your husband was killed by Union fire."

"And I was saved by my cousin Ian from a hangman's noose. Father, you can't mean to let him die because he is a Federalist! What if a Union woman were to find Brent or Jerome or Julian injured? Oh, my God, does that matter—"

He looked at his daughter carefully. "No, I just want to remind you of the past, of the years gone by. There was a time when you wanted even Ian dead!"

"Perhaps. But both you and Ian taught me to live past bitterness. You wouldn't just let a man die. I know you!"

James sighed. This was trouble, pure trouble. But Jennifer was right; he wouldn't let any man die.

Yet he'd cut the bastard's throat himself without blinking if he awoke to threaten his wife or children or six-year-old Anthony.

"Father . . ."

"I have him, Jennifer. Run back and tell Teela quickly

that I'm bringing . . ." He paused, smiling ruefully. "Tell her I'm bringing her a wounded Yank for Christmas. It's just what she's always wanted!"

Christmas morning. Tia could not help flirting atrociously with Weir, aware that her easy laughter was heard by her enemy, that he listened to her teasing comments, saw the way she laughed with Weir—sharing conversations about the past. She intended to dazzle Weir, but she didn't know why, because it felt dangerous and wrong. She caught her sister-in-law's warning eye, and knew that Alaina was perplexed and worried. Still, she couldn't help herself.

The morning was, however, truly enjoyable after breakfast ended. The children awoke but weren't in the least hungry, since they were anxious only to open their gifts. They tore into the bright packages containing games and toys, laughing and running around. Their eyes were bright; too young to know that a dark cloud remained over the state and a country divided.

Then gifts were distributed to the adults as well, those that the family naturally exchanged, and those which Tara saw to it were available for her guests.

For Raymond Weir, a large smoked ham.

For Taylor Douglas, a miniature tintype of a woman, formed into a delicate silver frame that would easily fit into a soldier's knapsack or pouch.

Tia had never seen it before. She didn't even know what it was at first, but it traveled around the room and everyone complimented the workmanship. Taylor Douglas gazed upon the gift, then looked at Tara. "It's a kindness beyond all I might have imagined, Mrs. McKenzie. With all the responsibilities you have here, that you thought to do this . . . that you were able to obtain this likeness . . . well, madam, I am deeply grateful."

Tara smiled happily. "You sent this to James's wife, my sister-in-law, Teela, soon after you were married. Teela and James lost their home to fire a while back. During the rebuilding, she sent us many things which had been saved, to keep for her. This picture was among them. When I heard you were coming here, I knew that Teela would be glad for you to have it again."

The framed miniature had reached Tia. She looked down. The woman in the tintype was delicately blond and very beautiful. Her smile was sweet and winning. Her eyes had a faintly teasing nature to them.

She was his wife.

Her fingers felt cold and awkward. What did it matter? She had prayed she'd never see him again. He'd done nothing but humiliate her.

And now this.

They had shared a strange intimacy, and he was a married man.

He was looking at her. She handed the miniature to him. "She is very beautiful."

He nodded, and turned away.

"Tia, will you help me with the eggnog, dear?"

"Yes, of course, Mother."

"We'll move on into the music room, gentlemen."

"And ladies, Papa, and ladies!" Ariana, sitting in her grandfather's lap, reminded him.

"Oh, yes. And ladies, of course." He smiled across the room at his daughter-in-law. "Ladies, do forgive me."

The others laughed. Despite the very presence of the war in their house in the form of the opposing colonels, the house seemed filled with Christmas spirit.

Only Tia seemed to have lost her sense of joy. "Are you all right?" her mother asked her as they joined Lilly in the kitchen, preparing a tray of eggnog—with and without whiskey—for their company.

"Yes, of course, Mother, I'm fine."

"Has the colonel been pressuring you?"

"What?" she asked guiltily. Could her mother have possibly realized that there was *something* between her and Taylor Douglas?"

"Ray Weir. I do feel a bit sorry for him. He looks at you constantly."

"Oh . . . well. He did mention marriage again."

"And?"

Tia shrugged. "I reminded him there was a war on."

Tara nodded. "Then take care with him, my dear. Don't tease him too mercilessly. He's becoming very much a military man."

"And what does that mean?"

"That he might want to take the law into his own hands at some point."

"But—"

"Never mind, Tia. I didn't mean that many military men aren't fine human beings—such as your brother, Ian. But power is strange. Men take hold of it some-times—and want more and more. You just don't always realize your own power."

"What is that power?"

"Youth and beauty," her mother said, smiling.

"Oh, Mother—"

"Come, dear, you're going to deny me, say that I think you're beautiful because you're my daughter, and that is all. You're simply very, very beautiful, and the rest of the world agrees. Most obviously, Colonel Weir thinks so."

"Colonel Weir . . . and who else?" Tia said, surprised by the words herself, and very surprised by their wistful quality. "Oh, Lord, how silly of me, how petty in the midst of all this—"

"Tia, I will not say more. I'll not have it all go to your head!" Tara gave her a tight hug. "Let's go do carols. This is a very precious occasion, with you, Ian, Alaina, and the babies, and I will not see the day slip by!"

Drinks were served. At her father's insistence, Tia joined her mother at the piano. They had often played together and even more often, sung together. Her moth-er's stage training coupled with a really beautiful so-prano voice had made her an excellent teacher, and Tia knew that many of the harmonies she did with her mother were exceptionally pretty. She was tense at first, uncomfortably aware of both Weir and Douglas, but after a while, Ariana, joining in, had her laughing, and they did fun songs with the children, then medieval car-ols. Realizing that at one point Taylor Douglas was watching her with an intrigued speculation, she found herself suddenly striking the keys in a rousing rendition of "Dixie." Her playing was perfect, her voice even more so, full of the emotion that could make a song great.

Yet when she had ended, the room was in utter silence. She met her father's eyes, and saw his anger and his disappointment that she had forgotten that their guests were there for *peaceful* negotiations, not to fight the war in their living room.

Then Raymond Weir began to clap.

Politely, Taylor Douglas joined in. Then the others as well. She felt the blood draining from her face, knowing that her father did not applaud. She quickly began to play "Silent Night." Ariana crawled up on her lap. She sang with the baby's pretty little voice joining her own, a few sibilant *s*'s making it all the more charming. Still, she wanted to sink into the woodwork.

She had ruined the spirit of the day.

Finishing the song, she kissed the baby on her forehead, set her alone on the piano stool, and turned to her father. "Excuse, me, Father . . ."

And she fled.

She couldn't crawl into the woodwork, but she could go riding. Fly through the cool winter's day on Blaze, and feel cleansed by the air.

"Tia!"

Her father hadn't called her, her mother had. She pretended not to hear.

She didn't dare take time to change. Exiting the house by the rear, she ran down the sloping lawn to the stables. Billy Cloud, one of her father's Seminole men, was whittling by the door. "What are you up to, Miss Tia?"

"Just a ride, Billy."

"Take care that you follow the property line, Miss Tia."

She hesitated. "Why, is something wrong?"

He shrugged and looked up at her with sage dark eyes. "War is wrong, Miss Tia. The Vichy house due east of here was burned down last week. No troops will admit to it, but they say that Mr. Vichy was selling his cattle to the wrong group of people. You take care where you're riding."

"I will, Billy, I promise."

She went in for Blaze, bridled her horse, but didn't bother with a saddle. She left the stable, waved to Billy, then raced for the forest trail.

Sydney awoke slowly. She opened her eyes, wondering why she felt so groggy, sore . . .

And suddenly cold. She shouldn't be cold. It was Christmas, and she should be home, where it was warm . . . home with her mother, father, family.

She hadn't been home in a very long time . . .

But home was different now.

She sat up quickly, remembering that Jesse had come, remembering the night. Remembering the way that he had held her, infuriated her, and held her again. She was tired because she had barely slept; each time she had drifted to sleep, she had awakened to sweet sensation, seduced awake, and in dreams. The words that had come between them had made them more certain enemies than ever, but she had loved him before . . .

And she loved him still, despite the damage to her pride, the bitterness he felt for her, certain she had betrayed him.

She looked swiftly around herself in the small bedroom, and then saw that he was there, standing in front of the mantle. He was dressed, in full uniform, hair clean and smoothed back. He held his hat in his hands as he stared at the flames, his expression grave. Though he didn't turn, he knew that she had awakened, and he spoke to her softly.

"Sydney, I'm sorry. By God, so sorry. But I see no help for it!" he said.

"Help for . . ."

He turned to her. Ever the officer, gallant and straight, thoughtful now in his words. She thought of the way he had touched her in the night, and more; she thought of the way he looked at her, at the gentle, teasing things he had said in the past.

"I swore for you," he told her. "When we were married, I swore that you would cease all spying activities. On my own honor, I swore for you."

She looked down, not knowing what to say, whether defending herself with the simple truth would suffice or not.

"Jesse, I've done nothing. I swear to you now, I'm innocent of any wrongdoing against the Union."

"I wish I dared believe you."

"How can you care for me, as you claim, and not believe me?" she cried out.

He smiled with a bittersweet curve to his lips. "I've seen your work firsthand, Sydney. I know that you are passionate about your cause."

"Jesse, I haven't seen you in six months. I left here once to see my brother Brent—"

"Who happens to serve just outside Richmond."

"I wasn't carrying any government or military secrets, Jesse. I just went to see my brother. He's been assigned back to military hospital duty after having been on a special project . . . dealing with disease."

"Yes, I know where Brent is working, Sydney. I make a point of keeping track of your family, the best I can. Luckily—and with ill luck for the many who are killed— the Army of the Potomac and the Army of Northern Virginia are constantly circling one another. Brent was sent to try to educate some of the illustrious Southern camp followers, and stem the rising tide of venereal disease. Now he's back trying to patch up the wounded, who flow in as constantly as we circle one another. That explains the past. What now?"

"I went to see him again."

"You were not gone long enough to have traveled to Richmond."

"How on earth can you know that?" she began with annoyance.

Again, he offered her a very wry smile. "Spies," he said softly. "Sydney, why were you gone when I arrived? Where had you been?"

"I . . ." she began, then hesitated. Did she have the

right to tell him? Would he accept what she and Sissy had done as being a good thing?

She lowered her head. "I'm not at liberty to tell you," she said.

"Sydney, for the love of God—"

"Yes, for the love of God." She looked up at him, suddenly damning him. "There is no such thing as trust between us, is there?"

"Sydney, how can there be?"

"Then if you'll excuse me, I'll dress—and you can arrest me."

"Sydney, don't be ridiculous. I'm not leaving this room."

"Then stay if you choose."

She threw off her covers and rose, ignoring him as he stood by the fire. She gathered fresh clothing from the small wardrobe in the corner of the room, turning her back on him to dress. She had barely stepped into pantalettes when she felt his hands on her shoulders, his whisper at her nape.

"Sydney—"

"Jesse, leave it be!"

He spun her around to meet him; stroked out a long, tangled lock of her hair, ran his knuckles down her cheek. She wanted to fall against him, lay her head upon his shoulder, feel his comfort—and his passion. She pulled away from him, her green eyes hard as jade.

"Leave me be, Jesse. Leave me be."

To her surprise, he did. Uttering a harsh oath, he turned away from her, heading for the door.

He paused there.

"House arrest, Sydney. I won't have you thrown back into Old Capitol."

"Indeed—even Yankees might ask about my current crimes!"

"If you won't tell me—"

"I can't!"

"Then you leave me no choice," he said.

The door opened, and he exited. The door slammed in his wake.

It was Christmas. He would come back, she thought. But he did not.

Following Tia, Taylor reached the stables to find a tall, muscular fellow standing at the stable doorway—swearing. If Taylor remembered correctly, it was Billy Cloud, Jarrett McKenzie's head groom, whose features more than hinted of his Indian blood. He saw Taylor, flushed, and excused himself. "Colonel! I beg your pardon, I was in thought regarding a problem."

"No explanations are necessary, sir, but what's the problem? Perhaps I can help."

"Her father's the only man who can ever help with that hellion!" Billy said, shaking his head with exasperation.

"Are we referring to Tia McKenzie?" Taylor asked, grinning slightly.

"We are." He peered at Taylor suddenly. "You're kin to James McKenzie. And to Osceola."

"Distantly, yes."

"We'd heard you were coming. I remember you from many years ago. It's good to see you again, sir—though in a strange uniform."

"Billy, the men who brutally pursued our people in this uniform have split, just as the nation has split. I thought about it long and hard before I chose the path I did."

"Did your dream visions lead you to your quest?"

Taylor smiled. It had been a long time since he'd been with the Seminole people. "Under the influence of the black drink—and stone-cold sober—I made my choice. You have stayed with Jarrett McKenzie."

"Oh, I think some of those swaggering braggarts in Confederate uniform are complete asses," Billy said, and grinning, he added, "I will get your horse. You're leaving?"

"I'm going after Miss Tia."

"Good, you will save me the trouble. Her father's men guard the circumference of the house, but outside the grounds here . . . I tell her not to ride into danger. She promises she will not and does so anyway. She doesn't think she lies because she refuses to see danger when it stops her from doing what she will."

Billy brought Friar from his stall and went for the saddle while Taylor bridled his horse. He thought that Billy's assessment of young Miss McKenzie was right on the money—she didn't think, and she didn't see danger. She did what seemed right for her at the moment. She didn't even see the danger she was causing in her father's own house. She had no idea how her every word and movement were affecting Raymond Weir.

"Thank you, Billy," he said, and grinned, stepping back.

Taylor followed the path Tia had taken. It was a clear shot to the woods, and once there, he could easily follow her trail. The area was exceptionally beautiful, the floor blanketed in pine needles, the trees forming canopies of green darkness overhead. He cantered through the trails at first, then slowed, certain she had stopped somewhere ahead. He dismounted, walking the distance, until he came to a copse around a beautiful, freshwater spring. She was seated upon a log, legs curled beneath her, staring at the water.

"Too cold to dive in?" he inquired.

Startled, she swung around, eyes widening, then filling with anger as she looked back to the water. "How did you find me? Billy told you where to go?"

He walked over to her log and stood by it, then hunkered down, folding his hands before him, staring at the crystal clarity of the water as well. He didn't gaze at her. He didn't need to. It seemed that she was a memory in his mind's eye. Her eyes were very dark, mahogany dark like her father's—a strange twist of inherited traits, since James's family, with their Seminole blood, all had light eyes, blue or green. Tia's very coloring was part of her beauty. The depth of her eyes seemed endless. The color seemed to match the sable luster of her hair. Her cheeks were fair. Pure ivory and cream. And her features were delicate and beautifully formed. Soft rose naturally blushed her cheeks, her lips were the deep red of wine,

generous, full, beautifully formed. He remembered too
clearly the taste of them.

"No one needed to tell me where to go," he said.
"You're easy to follow."

"Why did you follow me? I left the house to escape."

"To escape what?"

"Mainly you," she said, turning to stare at him.

"Or perhaps your father's disappointment?" he suggested. She turned away quickly, and he knew that he
was right. She had wanted to get to him—and so her
stirring rendition of "Dixie." She hadn't gotten beneath
his skin at all—he liked the song. But she had disturbed Jarrett.

"I'm not your concern. Why did you follow me? Why
couldn't you just leave me be?"

"Billy was about to come after you—he said he
warned you to stay closer to the grounds of the house."

She shook her head, staring at him. "You're in danger.
I'm not. I serve with the Rebel militia. No one is angry
at me."

"You don't need people to be personally angry at you
to attract violence, I'm afraid. But I told you before—
I'm angry with you."

"Well, are you a threat?"

"Oh, yes. I've certainly warned you of that, too."

"But you've given me your word that you will not
reveal my secret."

"As long as you keep *your* word."

"I said I would."

"But will you? You like to play with fire."

She sighed, then stared at him. "Why is it that a man
is brave and a woman foolish when they both want to
fight for something in which they believe?"

"I don't consider all women fools."

"Only me? How selective of you!" She shook her
head angrily, loosening the coil that had held the length
of her hair. It rumbled down her back. He rose, but she
saw him coming and jumped off her log, retreating from
him. She backed into a tree, and he reached around her,
capturing a long tendril of her hair. It curled around his

fingers like a silk sheath. "I should slice this off here and now, force you to keep your word."

"My father would kill you."

"For what—assault upon your hair?"

She tugged at the lock. "Let go."

"Maybe. After we have a conversation. Tell me, Miss McKenzie, who do you know better? Weir—or me?"

"What on earth are you talking about, Colonel?" she demanded impatiently. "We've known Colonel Weir forever; he is a friend of the family."

He leaned toward her, laying his free palm flat against the tree at her back. "No, Miss McKenzie, you misunderstand me. Who do you know better? Was there a serious relationship between you two?"

"It's none of your business, is it, sir?"

"Perhaps."

"How can it be?"

"Well, I feel that I've come to know you rather well. And having learned how well versed you are in the art of seduction through intimate experience, I feel obliged to ask. Does he know your lips the way that I do? Or the feel of your bare breast in his hands—"

She was quick. She very nearly caught his cheek with a serious slap—one which might have left it reddened for hours to come.

But, she realized, he had goaded her on purpose, he had expected the slap—and so he had caught her hand in the nick of time.

She lifted her chin, her eyes flashing. "You tell me, sir—how does the feel of my bare breast compare to that of your wife?"

She might as well have managed to strike him, the sudden pain that seared him was so very sharp.

Abby was dead. For what felt like many years now.

Yet her question seemed to rob him of breath, to tear at his heart, his soul.

She didn't realize that his wife was dead.

But he had no desire to inform her. He stared at her blankly, fighting the reminder of the pain and impotent rage that had filled him at her death. He had learned to live with it. He'd been with other women since her death. He didn't understand what affected him so, until he thought, *she's like Abby in this, too much like Abby.*

He hadn't seen it at first, because they were so different. Abby was pale in her beauty, golden, with eyes bluer than the morning sky. But she could be so stubborn as well. Set on her own course, refusing to see the danger . . .

He could still hear her, crying out that she could reach the injured men. He could hear himself shouting to her, "Abby, no!"

She had turned to smile, but had kept hurrying forward.

"I can reach them."

But he couldn't reach her.

"Abby, no!"

He had run after her. The day remained loud with the sound of fire. So loud that he didn't hear the individual shot. Her eyes were still on his.

Abby, Abby . . .

Huge, blue eyes, so very wide on his . . .

But she was falling, and when he caught her, confused, unable to believe what had happened, he lowered her to the ground. Pulled his hand away.

And it was red, so very red; God yes, a sea of blood seemed to drip from his hand, blood from the hole that had pierced through her back, and straight into her heart . . .

His fingers tightened. He didn't realize that he had unintentionally pulled Tia's hair until she cried out.

He eased his hold. Stared at her hard. Yes, in her way, she reminded him of Abby. And then again, she did not. She attracted and intrigued him. She didn't know the power of her own passion. She made him feel a hunger stronger than what he'd felt with even the delicate wife he had loved so much. She infuriated, compelled, repelled him. She was the daughter of a friend; not a woman to be any man's plaything, and yet, she didn't know what she did. Best get the hell away. He had no power over her, no power to stop the tempest that surged around her. He gave himself a mental shake. Let go. Stepped back.

"Everything about Abby brings perfection to mind, Miss McKenzie, her breasts included. Turn around. Get on your horse. Ride back to the property where those who love you can protect you."

"You can't tell me what to do. Go tend to your own perfect Abby!"

She spun around and walked away—just in time, perhaps. He was knotted with the anguish and fury she reawakened within him.

Let her go, let her walk away. You couldn't change fate for a woman who loved you, who listened to you. Here you are the enemy, loathed and despised . . .

He didn't make a move to stop her. Staring into the water, he swore that he would ride away, and leave her to her own destiny.

When he awoke on Christmas day, Brent thought that he would turn and find her gone, or discover that the night had been a dream. But it was not. She lay beside him, curled into the covers, appearing as innocent and untouched as she had come to him, and yet forever changed.

He slid carefully from the bed, washed and dressed. Without awakening her, he left the house and walked the distance to the hospital. His aides greeted him with coffee. His patients, even those dying, seemed to awaken with a certain cheer for Christmas. Nurses and orderlies gave him home-cooked treasures, often small but given with love. He attended to his men, and the time passed far more quickly than he had known.

At last, he could return to the house, and again, he feared that she would be gone.

But there were delicious aromas arising from his house. When he entered, he found her in the kitchen. She offered him a beautiful smile. "No turkeys, I'm afraid. Nor could I get my hands on a ham. We've a rather sickly chicken, but there are two of us, so I think he will do."

He followed her with his eyes, and then came to her, taking her into his arms when she turned toward the stove with knit wool potholders in her hands. "The chicken will be the best I have ever tasted, though I admit to my greatest hunger wandering in other directions."

She flushed, telling him, "It will burn . . ."

"Rescue the chicken."

She did. She had sweet potatoes, turnips, and canned tomatoes as well. Canned peaches rounded out their feast. Conversation was polite; she asked about his current patients, and he told her what he could. They didn't talk about the war, or the ravaged South, or the fact that they might well be losing, or that this time, Lee might fail and Grant might take Richmond.

When they were done eating, he helped her to pick up the dishes, but then, in the kitchen, he could wait no longer. He pulled her into his arms, kissed her. She fumbled with the buttons on his jacket. He nearly tied her into her apron for all time. And still, breathless, laughing, they shed their clothing on the way to the bedroom. They made love, and made love again, and sated for the time, Brent stoked the fire, and she had risen with him, so he wrapped her in the blanket and sat with her in the chair before the flames, watching them burn.

"Mary . . . why did you really come here?"

"I told you—because I wanted to be with you."

"But I thought you wanted to be alone."

"I needed to be alone for a while. Because of my father. But I also needed to be with you. Because I can't just be somewhere and pretend the war doesn't exist. And because I can't just be somewhere . . . and forget that you exist."

"You're sure?"

"Of course, I'm sure."

"You have to marry me," he said gravely.

She touched his face. "No, Brent. You don't have to marry me because I came here, because I wanted to be with you. I knew what I was doing. You don't owe me anything. I was afraid that raised as a gentleman, you would think you owed me for my innocence, but you will not marry me for that reason!"

He smiled. "What about the reason that I want to be with you?"

"Brent, there is a war, you were alone—"

"Alone all my life until I met you."

"That is so kind."

"It is also true. Marry me . . . because I love you," he said firmly.

"Oh, Brent . . ."

"Well?"

"Well . . ."

"Say it!"

She smiled. "Yes, I love you!"

"It wouldn't be at all proper for a respected surgeon to live in sin!" he told her.

"Not at all!"

"And I simply won't let you seduce me anymore if you don't intend to do the right thing!" he teased.

She stared at him, and started to laugh.

And she kissed him, and they made love again, and it was the best Christmas he might have ever imagined.

Chapter 10

Tia returned to the house, riding hard. When she saw Billy, she realized that she had really frightened him.

She dismounted from Blaze, and set her hand on Billy's upper arm. "I'm sorry. Honestly, Billy, I wouldn't want you upset."

He nodded. "Please, Miss Tia, become aware of what is going on around you."

"Billy, I've been gone from home most of the war."

"But the war changes every day."

"I'll be careful, Billy, I promise."

"Your father came here, looking for you."

"Thank you, Billy, I'll find him."

"I told him you were with Colonel Douglas."

Billy said the words as if her being with Taylor had made everything all right. She tried to swallow down her feeling of hostility. She couldn't. It galled her to remember the morning by the river, when she had set out to seduce him so that her green Rebel boys could take him down. She grew infuriated with herself when she thought of the things that had happened between them, the way that she had felt being with him, how quickly she had fallen to the force of his touch, how she had felt his kiss, his hands . . .

And he was married.

She forced a smile for Billy and hurried back toward the house, clenching and unclenching her fists. She reached the house, ran up the porch steps and into the front hallway.

Her father's office was to the right. She walked to it,

tapped on the door. There was no response. She opened the door and stepped in. Her father wasn't about.

With a sigh she went to the large plush leather chair his mother had ordered made for his last birthday. The leather was soft; the chair was deep and encompassing. She sat in it and leaned back, wondering why it should seem her soul was in such a tempest. She opened her eyes. A cut glass decanter of sherry sat on the occasional table across the room. She leapt up, and helped herself to a large glass of sherry.

Her father chose that minute to enter the room.

She was, as her mother had told her, her father's daughter. She knew that her dark eyes were his, that she had inherited his rich ebony hair. But he was very tall, and though gaining more silver in his hair with every year, the expanse of his shoulders remained broad while his torso was as lean and hard as ever. He had been a wonderful parent, stern, a teacher. But she had always felt that she could run to him, and he could solve all problems. In many ways, she had certainly been a spoiled and privileged child. But he had expected manners, intelligence, ethics, and compassion from his children. They had all been taught courtesy, to give way to the elderly and injured, no matter their color or ethnic derivation. His employees worked hard for him, and they were rewarded for their labors. He was, however, a typical father in many ways. His sons had certainly enjoyed a few days of carousing. His daughter he had always protected and pampered—and he expected her to behave with modesty, even if he had encouraged her education and even her free speech in almost every conversation.

He arched a very dark brow at her, eyeing the sherry she'd poured.

"A bit early for you, isn't it?" he said, moving on into the room, his hands folded at his back. He went to the window. His office looked down the river at the far slope of the land. His back remained to her.

"I'm sorry, Father!" she cried.

She wanted to go to him. His back seemed stern and aloof.

He turned around. She saw his eyes and knew that he loved her—but that he was baffled. She set the sherry glass down and ran to him, feeling his arms around her. He kissed the top of her head. "Whatever demon got into you today?" he asked her. He tilted her chin so that he could meet her eyes. "I was always grateful that Julian was a doctor, that he joined the militia as such. And though it tore at every paternal muscle in my body, I knew that you needed to go with him. But I have never lost sight of the fact that we were becoming a strong nation because we were so many states together, and though we went to war over states rights, the argument had always been over slavery—an institution that is obviously morally wrong, and should be legally wrong. And I can't believe that you don't agree with me."

"I do agree with you!" she said. "I just don't agree with . . ."

"With what?" he asked.

At the moment, she couldn't remember.

"Father, it's our state I support. My God! Dozens of men were against secession, but when their states seceded—"

"Yes, yes, I know, even the great Robert E. Lee was against secession!"

"Well, yes, I wasn't going to mention his name, but since you did . . ."

"Men from both sides are guests in this house," he told her. "We were to show no offense to either. Ian has managed to be very circumspect."

"Ian is treading on dangerous territory!"

"Not in my house," her father said firmly. "Then there is the matter of danger to you."

"I'm in no danger here."

"I've held on to this plantation, Tia, because I've held on with an iron fist. Everyone knows that my employees include Seminoles who are familiar with war—they fought the government long enough to become excellent soldiers. My men also include immigrants I supported from their first step on this soil, ex-gunfighters, Highlanders, fighting Irish, and more. But my scope extends only so far. The war has grown bitter. Bad things happen, Tia. Rapes, burnings, murders. Bodies are never found; criminals don't find justice, but blame the war for every deprivation. God knows, a disgruntled commander could come after this house one day—he would simply need a small army to take it. But outside the boundaries of the house . . . Tia, you *are* in danger."

"Father—you know that I intend to return to Julian's field hospital."

"Yes, with Julian or his very loyal men accompanying you at all times."

She didn't protest that statement. Let her father think that she was always under heavy guard.

"I won't ride into the woods again," she promised.

"Go and get your sherry," her father told her. "I'll take a brandy, I think."

"Yes, sir."

She walked to the table to pour him a drink.

"Taylor came after you?" her father asked.

"Yes," she said, turning back to Jarrett as she poured the liquor.

"You apologized to him, I hope."

"Apologized?" She almost spilled the brandy.

"You baited him with that song, Tia."

"Oh . . . I, yes, of course, I apologized."

She suddenly felt as if they were not alone. She turned to the doorway. Ian and Taylor were just entering the office. Had they heard her words? She damned herself for flushing so easily. She tried not to betray her feelings.

"Ian . . . Colonel Douglas. May I pour you a drink?"

"What are you having, Father?" Ian asked, doffing his plumed hat on his father's desk and taking a seat in the leather chair. "This is a magnificently comfortable piece of furniture!" he applauded.

"Yes, it is," Jarrett agreed. "I'm having brandy. Your sister has acquired a taste for sherry."

"We seldom drink in the surgery, and nothing so refined as this," she told her father.

"I'll have a brandy with you, Father."

"Taylor, what can my daughter get for you?" Jarrett asked.

"I'll join you gentlemen for a brandy, sir. Then I'll be on my way," Taylor said.

Tia poured the brandies, keeping her eyes downcast as she delivered the drinks to her father, brother, and Taylor. Her fingers brushed his as he took the glass. Even that brief contact seemed to cause a rush of blood to her veins. She wanted to throw something at him— or quite simply, tie him up and beat him to a pulp.

"Which way are you going, Taylor? How are you headed out?"

He was silent for a minute, taking the wingback chair opposite Jarrett, too near the occasional table where Tia stood again.

Then she realized that he was looking at her. "I'd rather not say, sir."

"My daughter is not a combatant, Taylor," Jarrett said.

Taylor's eyes were riveted on her father's. "No, sir. But she is friends with many."

"Well, there's an exit line if I've ever heard one!" Tia said with false cheer. "You Yankees just discuss away. I'll remove myself."

"Tia . . ." Jarrett said, frowning.

"It's quite all right, Father!" She returned to him, kissed his cheek, and fled, closing the office door behind her.

She wondered where her mother, sister-in-law, and the children had gotten to. The house itself seemed quiet. Pushing away from the office door, she exited the house by the river side again, thinking they might have gone out on the lawn. She didn't see the children.

She walked down to the docks. Rutger, in charge of the docks and much more in her father's life, waved a hand to her from the bow of one of her father's ships. She waved in turn, and then watched as the men worked along the dock, loading the ship with beef, the Florida beef they raised, that fed so much of the Confederacy.

She sat on the dock, watching for a while. It seemed that life went on here as it always had. Men worked the fields. Horses ran free in the paddocks. Crops grew. It was a good life, a sweet life, and it might have been the same as ever except that she could see armed men at the storehouse windows.

And her father, brother, and Taylor Douglas were discussing Yankee plans in her father's den. Or were they still? She had left sometime ago. Christmas day was fading to dusk.

She rose suddenly, thinking that her mother or Alaina might be around the side of the property. As she walked across the expanse of the lawn, she suddenly found herself drawn to the fence that enclosed the family cemetery. She reached the gate. Strange, it was open. She slipped into the little private plot and thought that, in the dying light, the graves were somehow beautiful.

Before the war, her mother had come here once a week to decorate the graves with flowers. She came more often now, telling Tia that she was grateful every day that none of their family had died in the war, and that the graves were now growing old.

Her father's first wife lay within the cemetery, a grave that was very carefully tended by Tara, who always had a special sympathy for her predecessor. Lisa Marie McKenzie's gravestone was a beautiful sculpture, centermost in the graveyard. There were a number of Seminole graves in the little cemetery as well—most of them relatives of her Uncle James.

Like Taylor Douglas.

She cursed silently to herself. Even coming here, she was reminded of the wretched man.

"Tia."

She turned quickly.

Raymond Weir had followed her. "Raymond," she said.

"I'm glad to find you alone," he told her.

He looked very handsome, in his full dress gray and butternut uniform, his plumed hat in place over his long golden curls.

"Why? What is it, Raymond?"

"I believe they're discussing plans in your father's study."

Her heart skipped a beat. "Raymond, surely not. You are a guest here just the same as Taylor Douglas. If you were to go to the study—"

"No, Tia," he said. Then he looked at her and asked, "I was wondering if you had been in the study."

She inhaled sharply. "I was, and I left. You know, I am passionate myself in the Southern Cause, and I am willing to do a great deal for it, but surely, Ray, you're not suggesting that I spy on my father in his own house?"

"Tia, not only that. I am suggesting that you do something about your father while there is still time."

"Time?"

Raymond shook his head impatiently. "Tia, your father has always been a maverick. When the whites fought desperately to survive during the Seminole Wars, he stayed neutral to foster his half-brother's cause—the Seminole cause."

"Take care where you tread, Ray!" she warned softly. "I love my uncle, and my father prevented untold bloodshed during the Seminole Wars. And, I might add, my uncle's sons have served the Confederacy with sacrifice and honor."

"And I admire your cousins, as you know," he said. "But men such as your father have fostered a line of half-breeds like Douglas—a man who would better himself by joining with the enemy. God knows, most of the Indians have the sense to realize that it was men in Union uniforms who massacred them."

"And those who changed uniforms with secession? Are they different men in different uniforms?" she heard herself asking.

"They have the sense to fight for their state, for a new way of life."

If the South won the war, she didn't think that most white politicians would worry more about the Indians who had helped them.

"Douglas may be half-Seminole or half-savage, Ray, but I believe he went to West Point, and was with the military before the outbreak of war," she said evenly.

"The point is, Tia, that he knows the state. He was bred to the land. He is a dangerous man as an enemy. He knows the swamps, the hammocks, the pine country, the red hill region . . . If you were to know what was happening . . . if we were able to stop Douglas now . . . well, it might be a very good thing."

"I don't think that now would be a good time to attempt to stop Douglas!"

Tia jumped back, dismayed to see that Taylor Douglas was in the cemetery, leaning against a tall oak in the far corner. He must have been there for some time.

He must have heard every word spoken.

Just what had she said? She'd definitely suggested that he was half-savage.

He pushed away from the tree, coming forward.

Ray drew his cavalry sword, ready to face Taylor.

"Put your weapon away, sir," Taylor said contemptuously.

"We'll fight—"

"No, Ray!" she cried. "Please, Ray, no, not here."

She started to run toward him. She was stunned when Taylor caught hold her arm before she could reach Ray.

"No, Tia!" he snapped angrily. "This is not your fight."

"It's my father's house!"

"Draw your weapon, man!" Ray demanded.

"No please!" Tia said. Taylor had a hand on her arm. She placed a hand on his, pleadingly. His eyes, glittering gold, touched hers.

"Coward!" Ray accused.

"This is my father's house!" Tia repeated. "Taylor—"

"Be that as it may, you'll not stand between us!" Taylor said. His grip upon her was fierce.

"Let her go!" Ray bellowed. "You let her go. Others in this house may be traitors, but she is not, sir, and you will cease to be so familiar with this *Southern* lady."

"This lady you so cherish—you would suggest she engage in spying?" Taylor demanded.

"Taylor, let go—" she began.

"I will run you through, Douglas!" Ray insisted.

"Yes, well, I will keep you from running her through in your stupid, irresponsible passion!" Taylor returned, but as yet, he held Tia. He had not drawn a weapon.

She dreaded him doing so. The tension in the air was palpable. Ray was determined that blood would be shed there.

In the graveyard.

She was very afraid that if they fought, he would be the one to die!

"Both of you, please . . ." Tia tried. But she didn't need to go further.

Her father had seen them all. He was coming across the lawn to the cemetery. Ian was behind him.

"My God, stop! What is going on here?" Jarrett demanded, swinging the white picket gate open again with such a fury that it nearly snapped on its hinges.

For a moment, no one answered. The squeaking of the gate as it banged shut again was all they heard.

"I repeat, what is going on?" he demanded. "Colonel, why is your sword bared on my property?"

"Because there is war," he said, staring at Taylor Douglas. He looked at Jarrett. "There is a war, sir, and this property is in the state of Florida, and we are at war with the Union! Colonel Douglas should not have been hiding in the cemetery, intent upon spying on your daughter and me—"

"I came to visit a great-great-uncle," Taylor interrupted dryly. "Tia happened upon the cemetery after me, sir—you made the assumption that she was alone."

"You did not make your presence known, Colonel!" Weir snapped. He spun on Jarrett. "This man is a threat to your daughter, sir! See how he holds her? You must order him from your property!"

Jarrett looked at Taylor, a brow arched. Taylor lifted his hands, releasing Tia.

"Colonel Weir!" Jarrett said impatiently, turning from

Taylor to Ray. "I agreed to use my home for your negotiations. I was assured you would both be proper gentlemen—"

Ray was incensed. He interrupted, barking out a command like a drill sergeant. "Order him from your
home!"

"I will not!" Jarrett snapped back indignantly.

"Because you are a Yankee, sir!"

"Take care, Raymond!" Ian said, speaking for the first
time. He had meant to defer to their father here, Tia
knew.

"As your son is a Yankee."

"Colonel Weir, Taylor Douglas is a guest, as you are
yourself."

"You refuse to take appropriate measures here?"
Weir demanded.

Tia had seldom seen her father so angry. "I repeat,
you are a guest in my house, as is Colonel Douglas, and
I made a promise to your government, Raymond, that I
would host these negotiations and keep the peace. If you
wish to do battle, I implore you, return to your
battlefield."

"Sir, there is something you continually forget—this
is a Southern state. A Confederate state. You are against
all that your own land stands for, you—"

"There is no one more dedicated to this state than I
am, Colonel Weir. I built what I have out of dreams. I
know this land as you never will. I know the people, who
grow weary of the conflict, who desire again to build in
our paradise, rather than destroy. Don't tell me about
my state, sir; I know it as well as any man."

"Then surely you realize you could find yourself under
fire—"

"Sir!" Jarrett countered. "Look around you. Look
carefully, and well. Down to the river, at points by the
pines. My home is defended."

Weir knew the truth of that statement. He sheathed
his sword slowly, then stood stiffly, staring long and hard
at Jarrett. "Sir, you will deeply regret this day. I will
take my leave, and you will have no further threat of

trouble here from me this Christmas. Colonel Taylor! I pray for the honor of killing you in battle. Look for me. I always ride at the front of my troops!" He started to walk away, then turned back. Sweeping his hat from his head, he bowed to Tia.

Then he continued on toward the stables.

"I, too, shall take my leave, Jarrett," Taylor said, causing them all to cease watching the departing Weir and turn to face him.

"There is no need," Jarrett protested.

"Oh, but there is, sir!" Taylor told him. "I'd not have it said that I lingered when you argued with a Southern colonel, and that you fraternized with the enemy."

"It is still Christmas day," Jarrett said. "Raymond will say what he will, and there is no way to silence him. But there is no need for you to leave."

"Thank you. However, it is time I moved on."

"Then we'll not hold you," Jarrett said.

Tall, dark, an imposing figure in his navy frockcoat, Taylor Douglas also departed the cemetery, leaving Tia alone with her father and brother.

Her brother, she knew, was puzzled.

Her father was staring at her.

"And what, daughter, caused this near disaster?"

She opened her mouth to explain. Did she tell him that Ray Weir had been suggesting that she spy? Or that she had been surprised by the presence of Taylor Douglas in the cemetery? Did she try to tell him what had happened?

She shook her head, suddenly angry. "Men!" she exclaimed. "Men! They are always harping on women, Father. We're to be careful, we're to be ladies, we're to guard life! Well, men are all fools. They swagger with their swords. They fight like little toddlers in the dirt. Don't look at me so, Father. I did not cause this, I swear it!"

He walked over to her. She bit into her lip, forcing herself to meet his angry dark eyes. "You'll stay out of this war!" he told her harshly. He swung around then, heading back to the house with long strides.

She looked at her brother. "Ian, honestly—"

"You heard him!" her brother interrupted sternly. Blue eyes seemed to bite into her as if she were a child.

"Ian! I didn't do this! Father has a right to his beliefs, and Raymond has been a complete fool, but the state is Confederate! Weir and Douglas have been like a pair of pit bulls since they met. They are, I repeat, like little boys, far too ready to go to war!"

"Raymond is living with some ridiculous ideal of what the South should be," Ian told her, "but Taylor Douglas has seen enough death to last a lifetime. You are baiting a weary man."

He, too, turned and started for the house.

She ran after him. "Ian, wait."

He swung around on her. "Tia! Life is no longer a barbecue or a ball. Don't you understand that?"

"Of course I understand that! How can you say that to me, Ian? You know that I've been with Julian throughout all of this. I've seen the fevers, the saber wounds, the shrapnel, the stumps, the shattered limbs . . . and I've seen my share of death, too!"

He touched her cheek, shaking his head, and she knew that although he understood that she had been as involved as anyone else, he was, after all, the far superior older brother—and a male of the species.

"Then be careful what men you tease, little sister. I would die in your defense, but I would hope not to do so because you played some childish game."

"Ian, I . . . I'm not playing any *games*. I'm grown up, Ian."

"That's what's so scary."

He kissed her forehead, and started for the house again.

She watched him go. Then, feeling a sudden chill settle over her, she left the graveyard, closing the gate behind her. She strode to the house, torn and in a tempest, sincerely hoping that both their Northern and Southern guests were gone.

The breezeway was empty. She went to her father's

study. Alaina was there. Sean was on her lap as she read a book.

"Our guests are gone?" Alaina queried.

"I hope so. I hope that Ray goes and sits in a swamp and that Colonel Douglas—that Colonel Douglas returns to his wife and finds out that she's turned into a real shrew who thinks he's a savage. When he walks into their house in the middle of the night and surprises her, I hope she scalps him for safety's sake alone!"

She felt Alaina staring at her, and she looked at her sister-in-law, puzzled.

"Tia, Abby Douglas is dead."

"What?"

"Taylor's wife is dead. She was shot down by accident at the beginning of the war."

Tia gasped. A strange knot was forming in her stomach.

"Shot?"

Alaina nodded. "It was a terrible situation. Apparently, people in Washington thought that the first major battle was going to be pure entertainment, quickly fought and quickly won. Dozens of politicians and civilians dressed up and came out—and of course, it turned into a deadly conflict, and the Rebels thrashed the Yanks. Abby hadn't thought it would be a picnic, but she came in a carriage with some other cavalry wives. Taylor didn't know she was coming out. When she found Taylor's position and saw all the injured men in the woods . . . she tried to help. She was shot by stray fire. She died in his arms."

"I'm . . . so sorry."

She was more than sorry. She felt ill. Her words to Taylor had been taunting and brutal under the circumstances.

She stared at Alaina, then hurried from her father's study. Racing up the stairs, she found her mother just coming down the landing. "Have you seen Colonel Douglas?" she inquired.

"I believe he's gone to the stables. Tia, what's—"

She tore down the stairs and ran hard across the lawn

again. She slowed as she neared the stables. *Her father might be there, saying goodbye to an invited guest . . .*

Hearing her father's voice from within, she skirted the stables—she didn't want to see Taylor Douglas there. She turned and ran down the slope of the lawn toward the forest, certain he intended to take that trail across the state, where he could surely meet up with many a Yankee unit.

She stood by an old oak and waited in the growing darkness of twilight. A few moments later, she saw Taylor ride out from the stables.

As she had suspected, he came her way. His horse cantered at a brisk pace across the lawn, slowed as it neared the trees.

She stepped from her place by the tree.

"Colonel Douglas!"

He reined in, seeing her. He frowned at the sight of her. "You're at just about the limits of the property, Tia."

"I know; I'm going back."

"Good. Because I did warn you, I will not just give you away if you risk your games anymore. I'll see to it that your father is aware of your actions, and that the authorities—"

"You don't need to threaten me again! I didn't come here to argue. I just—"

She broke off.

"Yes?"

He inched Friar closer to her. Despite his Union frockcoat and plumed cavalry hat, he suddenly seemed . . .

Threatening. The strength of his Seminole blood seemed evident in his features, in the way he watched her. He could move too quickly. Too quietly. Like a savage. Or *half*-savage, as she had called him. And as he had certainly heard. She could see only the stark planes of his face, the dark length of his hair, and the powerful breadth of his shoulders.

She was afraid, she realized. And yet, she was not

afraid of any violence. Force, perhaps, yes, the force of his touch . . .

"I'm sorry."

He inclined his head, his chin tilting, a dark brow lifting, his curious eyes glittering in the half-light. "You're sorry? About . . . ah, calling me savage. A slur on your own relations?" he queried dryly. "I'd no intention of mentioning the matter to our mutual relations, who might have taken offense."

"No! I'm not sorry about calling you savage, and it has nothing to do with my relations! You can be savage and very rude and—"

"Then?" he queried softly.

"I'm really sorry, terribly, terribly sorry about your wife. I didn't know. I thought that, well I thought that . . ."

"Yes, I know what you thought."

"You let me think that . . ."

"Yes, I suppose I did." He was silent for a moment, studying her. "And, I'm sorry for what I let you think. Tell me, then, is it less horrible to be seduced by a widowed enemy than a married one?"

"Oh, what arrogance. I was never seduced by you!"

"Hm," he murmured. "You would have been."

"I beg your pardon!" she said regally, bringing another wry smile to his lips.

"You do know me better than you know Weir, Tia. And you may not believe this, but you want to know me better than you know him."

"You are sadly, sadly arrogant, sir! As are most of your kind!"

"My kind being savage Indians—or Yankees?"

"Unionists! Enemies of a people who seek only their freedom!"

He shook his head. "You don't really believe that."

"I do!"

"Tia, I don't believe that I'm the enemy you want me to be. In fact, I think that I could have had you in the woods. Before you even knew my name."

"Never!" she cried indignantly. "What a wretched, conceited—indecent!—thing to say. Never—"

"What a violent protest!" he interrupted, laughing.

"Look," Tia snapped, trying quite hard to control her temper—and the strange tremors that were suddenly rippling through her limbs. "I came here to say I was sorry, truly sorry about anything rude or cruel I said about your wife—she was very, very beautiful, and apparently kind and compassionate as well." She hesitated. "You must have loved her very much."

"I did," he said simply. His laughter had faded.

The breeze rustled around them. She didn't know what to say then.

She felt him looking down at her, silent for a while. Then, he dismounted, and she backed away—sorry she had come.

But she couldn't back away fast enough. He touched her cheek, lifting her chin, studying her in the red-gold darkness of the dying day. She held very still, oddly paralyzed by this touch.

She couldn't pull away. She felt the gold fire of his eyes. Looking for something within her own.

Finding it, perhaps.

"Thank you," he said after a moment. She felt the bark of the tree at her back. And the heat and form of his powerful stance before her. She didn't think that she had ever been so aware of another human being. His fingertips ran over her cheek. "Take care of yourself, Tia," he said softly.

Then he was gone.

He leapt up on Friar and looked down at her again. "Remember, if I catch you in the woods again, Godiva, you will truly regret the day. I promise you. You will pay for it dearly."

He nudged Friar, and in seconds, he had disappeared into the twilight.

Chapter 11

Julian arrived at Cimarron toward the end of January, with his wife and newborn son—a very *McKenzie*-looking little fellow with bright blue eyes and a head full of thick dark hair. Rhiannon and the baby, Conar, would spend at least the next several months there, out of the range of danger and fire.

The prisoner exchange took place the day Julian arrived, with different officers, North and South, in charge. Tia was glad that it occurred—the men were a sad-looking group, both Yanks and Rebs. Several were wire thin, suffering from dysentery, and probably too weak to have survived a number of the prison camps. She knew that Andersonville, where most of the Union soldiers would have been taken, had a reputation for being a death camp. Watching the official exchange take place, she slipped an arm through her father's, very proud of him. He played a much bigger role in the war than she had ever realized.

Ian had departed soon after Christmas. Alaina and the children had remained at the house as well for the time being. Tia was glad that her sister-in-laws and nephews and niece were at the house; she knew that made it easier for her parents when the day came for her to ride away with Julian.

Though it was always painful to part from the rest of her family, Tia was glad that Julian needed her. She knew, however, that the battle they were heading for this time would be different from the skirmishes and fights they had faced before—this was a direct assault with the intent to split the state.

It was especially difficult to leave her parents, just as

it had been difficult for her to say goodbye to Ian. She was always afraid that she would be seeing him for the last time. She was glad that he sailed away—she didn't want to think of him fighting in Florida. Too many people grew bitter about the war. It seemed especially dangerous to be a military man many considered to be a traitor.

She hoped that Ian had been ordered to the North. Very far away.

She felt an uneasy certainty, though, that Taylor Douglas was heavily involved in the assault. He had been ordered back to Florida when the Yankee powers had determined that the state must be given far more aggressive attention. As a cavalry officer, he had asked *not* to fight in his native state, and it seemed that his superiors had heeded his request for years yet ignored it now. Ian had often been sent home because of his knowledge of the terrain; she was sure they expected the same expertise from Taylor Douglas. He could move quickly about the state; he probably knew every small Indian trail and cracker pass in the entire peninsula. He could ride circles around troops unsure of the often marshy and swampy landscape, assess the number of the enemy, and give information on positions and strengths as few other men would be able to do.

The closer she and Julian drew to the gathering of troops, the more she began to realize that a good-sized battle would indeed be staged. General Joe Finegan was in charge of the Confederate forces. When the Federal forces arrived in the state, he had only about twelve hundred fighting men, scattered throughout East Florida. He quickly sent out a call for reinforcements, however, and men began moving north from middle Florida and Georgia. Since the battle was taking place near the Georgia border, many of the troops were Georgian. By February thirteenth Finegan had selected a position near Olustee Station, a place that offered the best nature protection in a land that was flat and riddled with pine forests.

On the fifteenth, Julian and Tia had reached the chosen position, and began setting up their field hospital.

By the day of the battle, the Yankees had already done serious damage. They had taken Baldwin, where the railroad met from Fernandina to Cedar Keys, and from Jacksonville to Tallahassee. They had also seized Confederate supplies valued around half a million dollars.

But the Rebel troops had dug in, ready to fight. Their defensive works formed a line from Ocean Pond on the left to a small pond just south of the railroad station.

February twentieth dawned as a beautiful day. Clear, crisp, slightly cool, with rays of sunlight streaming through the pines. The troops raised a cloud of dust, and they became motes in the sunlit air. The battle commenced with the Union sending out a skirmishing party.

General Finegan had ordered forth his own men, convinced that the Union general, Truman Seymour, would be too careful to attack so well defended a Confederate position. As it happened, they came to meet one another on a fairly even playing field. The Federal forces had one cavalry and three infantry brigades, and sixteen big guns. The Confederate had one cavalry and two infantry brigades, and three batteries. The Federals numbered about five thousand five hundred; the Rebs about five thousand two hundred.

Right before twelve, the first cavalry skirmishers met.

After twelve, General Finegan made his decision to send his men out to meet the Yanks on the open field, determining that they couldn't be coaxed to his line.

Soon after, the surgeons were busy.

At her brother's side, Tia quickly felt as if she had been bathed in blood. Word coming in with the orderlies kept them informed about the battle.

The Rebel line had been formed with cavalry on each flank, infantry in the center. Information quickly came that General Seymour had wanted to put his artillery in the center of his line, with infantry on each side.

The deployment of his troops was proving to be his downfall.

A soldier, his left leg riddled with shrapnel, came into the surgery with a smile upon his face despite his pain. "Oh, ma'am, you should see it out there!" he told Tia.

"I'm seeing enough in here, I'm afraid," she told him, busily cutting his trouser leg so that they could see the damage to the limb. A cannon exploded in the pines, far too near. She braced herself, but didn't duck.

"No, ma'am, it's just that . . . well, you know, we're fighting for a victory here! Why, those Yanks are so confused . . . they're hitting their own troops with their fire."

"We're winning the battle?" Tia asked. She flushed, dismayed to realize that she found the thought of a Confederate victory here surprising.

The soldier nodded. "The Georgians and us, ma'am. There's so much bad and sad news coming from Virginia and Tennessee way . . . we're running out of goods and men. But here we are, winning. They aren't going to take our capital ma'am. They will not take Tallahassee!"

"I hope not, soldier!" His pant's leg split, she could see the shrapnel in the leg. One piece was very large, lodged, she feared, against an artery. "This man next!" she called to an orderly, wiping her hands on her apron. She looked beneath the canvas tenting, where Julian was conducting surgery.

They were just removing a young man from the operating table. Her brother was known for his ability to save limbs.

This time, he had not been able to do so. Nor had he been able to many times throughout the day. Sometimes, the screams of those coming under the knife had been deafening. There were several doctors here today. They all worked without pause. There were more women working as well. Officers' wives, some of the privates' wives. There was one woman who Tia had been certain was among the camp followers, but she moved with precision and no thought of hesitation in helping the wounded. Tia had met her eyes once. "I'm good at what I'm doing. I belong here," she had told Tia somewhat defiantly.

"You're very good, and apparently you do belong here," Tia replied.

The woman smiled. She might not have intended to do so, but she had made a friend.

The look on her brother's face was hardened, sad, and grim. He watched his last patient leave the table. With the bottom half of his left leg missing, the young man was singing as the orderlies carried him from the tent to the mule-drawn ambulance conveyance which would bring him south to Confederate-held land and better facilities.

"We've enough morphine?" Tia asked her brother. He had spent part of the last year with the Army of Northern Virginia, and he had grown accustomed to the horrible pace of a real battlefield surgery. She realized she was just beginning to see what he had lived through for months. He had tried once to describe the battle at Gettysburg to her, but words had failed him.

"God knows," he said, waiting for his next patient. There were other surgeons at work. While the soldier with the shrapnel in his leg was set down for the scalpel, another doctor called for help quickly. Tia raced to his side. A lieutenant with a scruffy beard that gave away his youth was spurting blood from a severed artery. She caught the vessel at the doctor's command, using all her strength to exert the needed pressure while the doctor fixed a forceps at the proper point.

"Tia, here."

She hurried back to Julian. Again, her small fingers were needed. "I'm trying to save his limb. I may not be able to. Catch the blood vessel. Hold tight, and be prepared to hold for at least a half a minute." Her brother's eyes touched hers, making sure she understood. She nodded. Once again, she deftly reached through a sudden rain of blood to capture the necessary vessel. The blood was slippery; she nearly lost her hold.

This man was singing as well.

Singing "Dixie."

She didn't know why the sound of the song made her stomach plummet.

"Ease off now . . ." Julian said. "You've got it, fine. Can you stitch up the opening here, Tia?"

"Yes, I've got it."

Their next patient was engulfed in mud; a cannon ball had exploded directly in front of him. Tia busily began cutting off clothes while orderlies soaked cotton cloths in cold water and soothing plant extracts—he was badly burned as well. It was hard to tell what was dirt and what was charred flesh. She talked while she worked on him, cutting cloth while Julian supervised the two orderlies who delivered morphine through a small canvas bag set over the man's mouth and nose. "It's all right, soldier, take it easy, take it easy!" He twitched in his pain, then slowly went still. "Hold on, young man, please hold on . . ." she whispered.

"Miss Tia!"

She looked closer through the dirt.

It was Gilly.

"Gilly, good God . . ."

"I'm dying, Miss Tia."

"No, you're not. I won't allow you to die, do you understand?"

He closed his eyes, tried to smile. "My foot . . ."

She winced, looking at his foot. It had been halfway blown off. She had seen a lot that day, but she nearly vomited at the sight of the bloody stump.

"Julian will take your foot. You'll walk with a crutch. You'll live, do you hear me?"

He stopped twitching. For a moment she froze, biting her lower lip. Had he died?

More cannon fire exploded. She winced. Liam, one of her brother's men, an amazingly capable amputee, came to her side, setting a hand on her shoulder. "He's alive; he's just passed out."

"His foot—"

"Your brother is ready for him."

More cutting. Julian hated being a butcher.

The day was no longer beautiful. It was filled with a miasma of flying dirt, black powder, the screams of dying horses.

The screams of dying men.

A rider came to the hospital, crying out with a bone-chilling Rebel yell.

"We're taking the day, gentlemen! Confederate artillery has riddled the center of the Yankee line! The Rebs are on the move, pushing back the Yanks."

Julian's eyes met his sister's above Gilly's body. She didn't know if either of them felt the general jubilation that quickly spread throughout the surgery. If they were winning, why were they patching up man after man? Losing so many . . .

Finishing with Gilly, Julian told Tia that he thought the boy would make it. "You know as well as I do, though, that it's infection that kills the boys more often than the wounds."

"But you lose fewer men to infection than other surgeons."

"Usually," he told her ruefully. "I always use a clean sponge on each wound. Today . . . we're running out."

That was not all they were running out of. Toward the late afternoon, a man brought in with a broken arm told him that they'd run out of ammunition. His arm had been broken by the strike of a Yankee bayonet—he and the enemy had tried to beat one another to death. The arrival of a friend who had crushed the Yank's skull had saved his own life.

She listened, feeling very sick.

Orderlies were drawn from the hospital to help as officers, and anyone available rode back and forth at utmost speed with supplies from a railcar held far to the rear of the line. Cartridges were carried back in hats, pockets, haversacks, and even the skirts of some of the other women assisting.

New ammunition, and the last of the Southern troops held back at the line, arrived at the front nearly simultaneously.

There was a mighty advance against the Federal line.

Soon after, with night almost upon them, Federal wounded began to be brought in. The Yanks had been forced to leave them behind during their retreat.

"We won! We won!"

Across the field, the shout went up. Among the standing, there was a feeling of victory so great that it seemed like a cry upon the very wind. "We won, Florida won, the Yanks will not be taking Tallahassee, they'll not be taking our state!"

Bugles could be heard.

Shots that signaled victory.

"The battle has been won," Julian said quietly. "Our night has just begun."

The battle could definitely be called a victory, but the fight wasn't over. The Rebs were pressing the Union forces back, back. God knew how far they would follow; what territory they would gain.

The night was horrible. With the fighting over; it was time to search the battlefield. While Julian remained in the surgery, Tia rode out with his orderlies, trying to find the living among the dead.

"Miss Tia?"

Liam, who had learned to ride with his one leg, was with her, ready to summon orderlies with stretchers and litters when they found men who could be saved.

A remnant of the sun remained, as red as the blood that covered the ground.

They dismounted and studied the uniforms on the corpses.

"Mostly Yanks here," Liam said.

"Yes." She turned to him. "I'm so afraid, Liam. Of who I will find."

"Your brother Ian isn't here," he said gently. "He was ordered to Virginia after Christmas."

"You're sure? How do you know?"

"We brought in a cavalryman Julian knew. He told us."

Tia suddenly saw a cavalry officer, lying facedown. He wore a navy frockcoat, and his hair was dark as pitch, straight, long . . .

"Oh, God!" She fell to her knees at his side.

"Tia, I told you, Ian isn't here."

Yes, but Taylor Douglas is! she screamed inwardly.

She touched the man, carefully drawing him back toward her. He moaned. He lived. He had a bullet through his shoulder.

He wasn't Taylor.

"We've got one to bring back!" she called to Liam. He nodded, and whistled for the men with the litters and stretchers. Tia moved on.

And on.

During the night, she still thought that she heard the sounds of moans and cries from the battlefield.

She thought that she would hear them forever, for the rest of her life.

During the next six days, the Confederate forces pushed the Union soldiers back to within twelve miles of Jacksonville. The battle had been a disaster for the Union.

Yet the Confederate victory at Olustee Station did little to lighten the mood of the South.

Supplies grew ever scarcer during the spring of 1864. Throughout the South, battles were being waged, and mostly lost. The Union grip was tightening; the Northern generals were considering new ways to tame their Southern counterparts. A "scorched earth" policy became popular—where Yankee armies went, nothing was left for the surviving civilians.

In the weeks that followed the battle of Olustee, Tia could afford little concern for the rest of the Confederacy. Julian was left with the seriously injured to be tended.

During the first few days after the battle, they moved their surgery to an old house at Lake City. Local matrons came to read to the soldiers, to bring whatever food treats they could improvise, and to write letters.

A week after the battle, she and Julian were invited to dinner at the home of General Victor Roper, a septuagenarian who had served during the Mexican War, and a passionate secessionist. A number of officers still in the vicinity had been invited, militia and regular army. The local men brought their wives and daughters. To fill in for those men from other Southern regions, a number of young ladies from the nearby towns were present as well.

It was the closest thing to an old-time Southern party that Tia had attended since the war began. She had been too tired at first to want to come, but Julian had convinced her.

Raymond Weir was there.

At first, she avoided him, but she was glad—after all she had seen on the battlefield—that he was alive. He and his militia troops had been involved at Olustee. His troops had been too far south to be called in for the battle, but he was there because he had ridden quickly northward in anticipation of trouble to follow.

He was persistent, following her until she would listen to him. He apologized for the trouble at Christmas, telling her he was sorry to have ruined her Christmas.

She accepted the apology on the surface.

He did not say that he was sorry for threatening her father, or challenging Taylor Douglas. But to her, he was so earnest and sincere that she couldn't help but forgive him, he seemed so desperate that she understand.

There were musicians from the 2nd Corps of Engineers. Tia danced with her brother, with enlisted men and officers—and with Ray. She was touched again by his affection for her, but equally determined that this was not the right time for her own involvement. To her annoyance, she continued to wonder about Taylor Douglas, and pray that his had not been among the bodies at Olustee that she had not seen.

"Marry me, Tia," Raymond Weir said, looking at her gravely as they danced.

"Raymond, do you think that my father would let me marry you right now?" she asked innocently.

"You're over twenty-one, Tia. You don't share your father's beliefs."

"I share his love," she said softly.

"If he understood what I felt for you, he might readily agree."

"I can't marry until the war is over," she said. "I have to work."

They came to a halt by a table laden with a punch bowl. He poured them both a glass, and looked at her gravely.

"You shouldn't be involved in such work, Tia. It isn't fitting for a proper young woman."

Their hostess, Amelia Roper, a resplendent woman with a huge bosom and assumed dignity to match, stood by the table chatting with a young soldier—until she heard the comment. She tapped her glasses on Tia's arm and joined in, uninvited. "The colonel is quite right, my dear. The work you do is better managed by the order-lies—and by the injured. In Washington, they use the convalescing men to work in the hospitals. The amputees make useful nurses."

"There are never enough nurses. Especially here in Florida," Tia said. "You know that our men are constantly drawn from the state to serve elsewhere. Even Julian, who has dedicated himself to his fellow Floridians, was ordered north last year. I believe I can be helpful."

"What are our men fighting for if not our Southern honor—and that of our Southern womanhood, Tia McKenzie?" Amelia demanded indignantly.

"They are fighting—for us all," Tia said, surprised by the attack on her effort. "And if they fight, then I feel that I must help as I may."

"If you were to marry me, Tia," Ray said, "I would see to it that you were removed from the ugliness and indecency you endure for this passion to work with the wounded."

"Ray, I have said many times: it's work I feel I must do. My father, mother, and brothers know what I do, and they are not appalled. They are proud of my commitment to life."

"Even your father and your oldest brother, dear?" Mrs. Roper said tartly. "I imagine they might be happier were you to cease work, and allow for more Confederate dead!"

"No one wants men to die, Mrs. Roper."

"No? Well, it's quite bad enough in the state as it is. Your father and brother aren't the only traitors among us."

"Quite a number of people in the state were against secession, Mrs. Roper," Tia reminded her.

"Oh, I know! And some of our brightest military stars failed to see the error of their ways!" She shook her head, glancing at Raymond, and speaking bitterly. "My husband—a brilliant leader when he was on the field!— has studied the battle at Olustee carefully. Do you know who was one of the first cavalry officers on the field for the Yankees? *Taylor Douglas!* My God, but I remember when that man was a guest in my house. They say he moves like the devil, faster than the wind. He is a traitor to us now—a thorn in our side when he should have been a hero for the state."

Tia didn't want to appear overly interested in Taylor, but she felt as if she were dying within herself, and needed what information she could garner.

"I met Colonel Douglas just before Christmas, Mrs. Roper. He is actually kin to my uncle, my father's brother. I hadn't heard that he was at Olustee."

"Dead center of the battle, dear, leading troops out to the very first of the skirmishing and beyond. It's a wonder he wasn't killed."

Thank God.

She almost said the words aloud, but realized that Ray Weir was watching her closely.

"He led troops out—and wasn't injured?"

"Not by our men—or his own!" Mrs. Roper said with a sniff, then smiled. "Though I have heard the Yankees killed nearly as many of their own as they did Rebs! Young lady, don't you go getting it into your head to tend to Yankee men! You will assuredly die with no proper husband!" With another sniff, she shook her head. "This war! It is amazing. The things going on . . . have you heard of the new heroine being hailed by the soldiers? A woman dashing through the woods, leading the Yanks astray. In the buff, completely in the buff.

The little slut! Godiva! They call her—Lady Godiva. Now, there's a girl who will have no husband! There is war, and there is total indecency!"

"Isn't the greatest indecency of war seeing a young human body totally broken and bloodied and maimed? Isn't the greatest horror the destruction of human lives, of dreams, families . . . isn't death the indecent tragedy of it all?" Tia queried, amazed at the tumult suddenly inside her.

"A lack of honor is the greatest indecency! Honor is everything! What is life without honor, without society, without rules of what is proper and what is not? What do men fight for, if not their quality of life—and the honor and chastity and virtue of their womankind?" Amelia Roper demanded, and she waved her reading glasses in the air. "You remember that, young lady!"

"Perhaps we can have honor—and compassion!" Tia said.

Mrs. Roper let out another of her sniffs and turned her back on them.

Ray shrugged to Tia. "Many, many people don't approve of your activities."

For a moment, she froze. *To which activities was he referring? Did he know about Godiva?*

No, Godiva was a story to them here, nothing more. She let go of the breath she had scarcely realized she had held, and answered.

"I thank God, then, that it is only the approval of my own family that matters to me, for as I have said, they are proud of my work with my brother."

"Ah, Tia!" Ray took her hands. "I know that you care for me . . . I feel it when we touch, I see it in your eyes. I wish I could make you see that wrong is just that—wrong. Your work is wrong, and Mrs. Roper is quite accurate in her assessment—many men would refuse to marry you, considering what you have seen and done entirely indecent. And you must realize . . ." His voice tightened suddenly. "You must realize that your father is wrong. Very wrong."

She drew her hands from his. He spoke to her so

earnestly. Her feelings for him were very confused. They had been different before the war. She had liked him . . . she had been tempted. He had liked horses, riding, agriculture, good brandy, and even books. Something had changed with the war; she did care for him, but with a strange reserve. It was still hard to hurt him.

It was made a bit easier, however, by some of the things that he said to her. She was defensive against any criticism of her father.

"If you find my father a fool and me indecent, it's amazing that you would marry me."

"Ah!" he said softly. "But I love you. All men might not. And," he admitted grudgingly, "I know that there are other women working with the wounded. Few of them, though, hold your place in society."

"My father is a man who taught me to respect other men and women for what they do, and how they behave—not how much money or property they possess. Perhaps that's because he was raised by a Seminole woman, my half-breed uncle's mother," she said, the words far too pleasant to convey the reproach and anger she was feeling.

"Your uncle managed to overcome his birth—"

"My uncle is proud of his birth."

"Tia! The Seminole Wars are over, and I don't care to fight them again with you here and now; there are other matters at hand—"

"Just think! Marry me, and you'll be cousin-in-law to *redmen* yourself!"

"Tia, I will tolerate many things for you."

"Tolerate," she mused.

"I believe you have feelings for me as well. There is no need for you to die an old maid. Perhaps what you do is not quite decent, but at least you are not a whore such as that woman the men are all cheering as such a great Rebel—that—that Godiva creature Mrs. Roper was talking about. She has been everywhere, so it is said, leading dozens and dozens of Yankees to their doom."

A gross exaggeration! Tia thought.

She longed to slap Ray—then her anger faded. *The*

*things he said were things that he had been taught! And
there was nowhere in him where he might open his heart
and mind to new thoughts, or to understanding . . .*

"If I do not marry, I will not consider my life a dismal
waste. And I would be loathe to marry a man who did
not love me under any circumstances. I appreciate your
kindness, that you would love me enough to marry me
despite my tarnished character. But you have your beliefs, Ray. I have mine—"

"Do they really matter between a man and a woman?
Think about it! Marry me."

"I must refuse you. The war does matter. You can see
that, surely."

"Perhaps. Yet still, I must ask each time I see you!
And if ever you need me, want me . . . you only need
to come to me."

"Thank you. But . . . you must excuse me—I see my
brother waving to me."

She fled from him, hurrying to Julian—who had not
been summoning her. "What's wrong?" he asked.

"I have been hearing about my indecency."

Julian grinned. "The old biddies! What you do is good
work, Tia. You save lives. Don't let anyone ever tell
you differently."

"Thank you, Julian."

"My pleasure. Are you tiring of life here in this bed
of good and decent society?"

"Tonight, yes."

"Good. I'm ready to start back for our old grounds
outside of St. Augustine. I want to take some of the
wounded to convalesce in better circumstances. There
are too many wounded here, and not too many admira-
ble men and women to look after them."

"I'm definitely ready!"

God, yes, she was ready.

Chapter 12

She could see the child, a small child, with a quick, mischievous grin, charming, delightful. A handsome little fellow, dark-haired, with a will of his own, and a way of behaving badly in so sweet a manner that he managed to get away with quite a lot. He was playing, as children were wont to do.

The dream was murky, as if there were a fog in the bedroom where the child played. There was an open doorway, leading out to the balcony. There were other children, but she couldn't really see them . . . there was the fog, of course, but more. The little boy was the focus of the dream, and so she could see him clearly. He had a dimple . . .

There was a balcony. He crawled upon the railing . . .

"No! No!"

She tossed in her sleep, trying to tell him, trying to stop him. "No, don't do it, oh, God, please, no, no . . ."

And then he was falling, falling, falling . . .

"Rhiannon! Rhiannon! Wake up!" She felt gentle hands on her shoulders, and looked into the concerned, beautiful blue eyes of her mother-in-law.

She jerked up, petrified, terrified. Where was she?

Julian's house, safe in the haven of Cimarron, though Julian was far away. Despatches had already crossed the state; she knew that her husband was safe, that Tia was safe. In his personal letter to her, Julian had sounded very weary, not certain if he cared whether the South won the war anymore. The flow of injured at Olustee Station had seemed endless, almost as bad as when he had been serving with the Army of Northern Virginia, and by sheer numbers of combatants, the battles had been horror-filled from the start. But it was over, Julian was well, her sister-in-law was fine as well, and she was here, recovering as she must, away from Julian, because of their infant son, a Christmas present unlike any she might have imagined. A gift of life in the midst of so much death!

"Conar!" Rhiannon shrieked, leaping from her husband's bed. Heedless of her concerned mother-in-law, she flew to the wicker bassinet where the baby slept. Too panicked to leave him at peace, she swept him into her arms. So brusquely awakened, he started to cry.

"Rhiannon, you're shaking. Let me take him from you," Tara McKenzie said softly.

Rhiannon looked from the baby in her arms to Tara, then handed the baby over and buried her face in her hands.

"It was a dream . . ."

"About the baby?"

"Yes . . ." she said, then hesitated. She sat on the bed, and Tara sat beside her, soothing the baby and still managing to show her concern for Rhiannon.

Rhiannon let out a long breath of relief. "No, not my baby!" she whispered. And yet the pain remained in her heart.

The boy was someone's baby. Someone's beloved baby.

"No, an older baby. A toddler. Not Alaina's Sean! It didn't happen here . . . it was at a different house. A large, beautiful house, on a busy street. People are always coming and going. There's an entry to the house with that wallpaper that is made to look like marble. There's a child's room with a little rocking horse—like the one in the nursery here that was Tia's. There are dolls . . . toys . . ."

"But it definitely isn't this house," Tara said softly.

"No. I'm certain."

"It can't be where Alaina has been living in St. Augustine. She and Risa have just a small place together, without so many rooms, and there is certainly no grand stairway!"

Tara McKenzie had tended many a small child with her own three, nephews and nieces, and grandchildren. Conar's little eyes were already closed again. Rhiannon was tempted to take him, crush him to her, even let him cry again, she was just so grateful to see that her own child lived. Had her dream been of Conar at some later date? No, she would know, surely . . .

"It is someone else's child. If I could only warn her . . ."

"Rhiannon, perhaps the time will come when you can do so," Tara said. She had never doubted her new daughter-in-law's ability to see strange things through dreams. Julian had told her that Rhiannon's predictions had saved many men from sure disaster. Even generals had paid heed to her warnings.

But Tara's heart bled for her daughter-in-law at times.

There was a child, in danger. And she wanted so desperately to help . . .

Tara set the baby back in his bassinet. She took her daughter-in-law in her arms, and rocked with her, smoothing back her long dark hair. "Rhiannon, you mustn't be so upset. It's a blessing to be able to help anyone the way that you have. We'll all be very careful not to let any toddlers we know play unsupervised on a balcony. We will make a difference."

"A difference . . . my God, one day, it's the children who will have to make a difference. The children who will have to lead us from the devastation of this war we have cast upon them!"

"Yes, they will have to make a difference." She drew away and smiled. "In a way, I envy them. They will have to fight and struggle—and forge a new world."

"It will be miserable for years."

"Growth and learning are often difficult. But they are the only ways to forge a new world! Shall I get you a drink, warm some milk, perhaps."

"No, no, thank you, I'm sorry I disturbed you. I know that I'll be able to sleep now."

Tara kissed her on the forehead, and left her.

Rhiannon didn't sleep, but lay awake. In a few minutes she rose, and very gently took her precious child from his bassinet. She didn't wake him, but laid him beside her, and she watched him throughout the night.

Tia and Julian moved southward the day after Mrs. Roper's party. Julian warned her the journey would be long and slow.

It was indeed very tedious; a few of the men were in poor shape. Still, it felt good to be away from the constant reminders of the battle—a field that smelled more and more of decay. Towns where so many men were without limbs. They traveled with the medical supplies they needed, and the days were cool and pleasant, the nights chilly but not too cold.

Toward the end of March, Julian was summoned late at night by a rider sent by General Finegan. One of his most important aides had been wounded by a sharpshooter. "The bullet is lodged in his shoulder," the messenger explained to Julian. "There is no man but you to perform so delicate a surgery."

"I would very much so like to help any man," Julian told him. "Especially an officer the general values. But I have only one whole man among this sorry group!"

Tia, who was at her brother's side, cleared her throat.

"Tia, I don't like leaving you—"

"Sir, will you have some coffee?" Tia asked, addressing their visitor.

"Ma'am, with pleasure."

His name was Arnold Bixby, and he was a Georgian. He sipped his whiskey-laced coffee with real pleasure as Tia tried to sound casual and convince Julian that she would be all right at the same time. Julian hadn't quite seemed to have grasped the concept that he wasn't being *asked* to accompany Bixby, he was being ordered to do so.

"Julian, I can manage very well."

"Tia, I don't like leaving you."

"Julian, we had to split up once before in like circumstances, and I was just fine." It was a lie, but he had never learned that she had met up with any difficulty before reaching Dixie and his men before Christmas.

"We've just won a major battle! The territory is safe. Liam is with me."

"Liam has lost a leg."

"Liam remains as fierce as a bulldog," she insisted.

"If you can reach this point by the river here," Bixby said, drawing a map on the dirt floor of the the tent, "you'll tie up with Dr. Lee Granger. He's keeping camp there with more survivors from Olustee. In fact, we can ride there on our way north and let him know that your injured will be joining his."

Julian kept staring at his sister. "I don't like leaving you."

"Julian, I don't *like* being left. There's little choice, however, and I can manage. I wouldn't perform surgery without you, but I think that I can manage to keep bandages clean and a party on the road. I've done it before," she reminded him.

"Bixby, I don't like this. If anything happens to my sister . . ."

"Julian, I'll be fine," Tia insisted. "If we should happen upon the enemy, it might well be men I know. Many of the officers in this war went to school with Ian or are friends with Father. Julian, no matter what, I would be in no danger."

And she would be fine. She would take no chances. They had sorely beaten their enemy. The Yanks were like dogs with their tails between their legs now—running away from, not after, the Rebels.

"I'll pack your things," she told her brother.

The next morning was beautiful. Tia awoke feeling confident, washed at the stream, drank the coffee Gilly had made, and saw to it that her wounded men at least sipped some of Liam's hardtack stew before she arranged for them to start out.

Gilly and a man who was fighting an infection were placed in the back of the wagon. The mules were docile, and a fellow who had lost his lower leg could manage them easily enough. Tia, Liam, Hank Jones, and Larry Hacker, who had lost his lower arm, would ride.

The day started off very well. They moved very slowly, careful not to jostle Gilly any more than absolutely necessary. By noon, she was proud of the distance they had covered. They could reach Dr. Granger's camp by tomorrow morning if they kept up their pace.

Soon after she congratulated herself on her success, the wagon hit a pothole. The wheel broke; the wagon lumbered, and Gilly screamed.

Frightened, Tia looked at Liam, then hurried to the back of the wagon. Gilly's foot—or rather his ankle— had flown up and crashed down on the planks. It was bleeding profusely.

"Help me get a tourniquet together!" she called to Liam.

Accustomed to working with Julian as well, Liam quickly found her a stick. She ripped up her skirt, and together they wound the tourniquet around the injury. The bleeding stopped. She had Gilly taken down by the water and cleaned the wound. The stump had been cauterized, but the accident had left a tear in it. Gilly fought the pain bravely, but Tia could see the tears in his eyes. "We have whiskey—let's share it." She took a drink first herself; Gilly came next. Liam arched a brow at her then took a long swallow. Returning to the wagon, Tia got out her needle and the surgical thread she was lucky to still have. Sometimes, she sewed wounds with horse hair.

Gilly got enough whiskey in him to pass out, right by the water. Liam set up a camp for the others with Hank Jones. When the camp was done, Liam came back to her. "I'll stay here by the water for a while with him," she said softly. The poor fellow remained passed out. She smiled at Liam. "I think I'm wearing half his blood. I may try to wash out some of this."

"You want me to keep guard, Miss Tia?"

She smiled. "If you will."

Liam watched her for a long moment. "You're a fine leader, Miss Tia."

"No, I'm not, but thank you."

He left her. Gingerly she approached the cold water. She could smell the blood that covered her. She stripped her blouse over her head, shivering. She wore a corset today, but it didn't give her any warmth. Still . . . she slipped out of her skirt. She had to wash her clothing. Liam could bring her the extra set of clothing she carried in her bag. She could leave these to dry on the rocks. She had to bathe. The smell of the blood that covered her made her feel sick to her stomach. She felt as she had the night at Olustee, as if she'd never get the blood out. No matter how cool the night had become, she had stripped down completely and scrubbed until the scent of blood was gone.

She washed her face, then sat back, thinking she could hear something.

She did, and she froze. Looking through the trees, she saw glimpses of blue uniforms. *Yankees.*

She was low against the riverbank. Gilly slept upon it. It was possible that the Yanks on the other side of the trees might pass by without ever noticing them.

But they were close. So close.

"Captain, can we stop here; get some water?" one asked.

"All right, but we can't take long. They say there are Rebs here; we just have to find them."

"What then, Captain? Can we kill them, make it a massacre like Olustee?"

"We're not murdering men, Private Long."

"What if they're half-dead already?" the one named Long asked. "I heard it was nothing but Confederate wounded moving through here."

"Any wounded Rebs we take as prisoners," the captain said sternly.

Tia heard him moving away. Then she heard Long chuckling to a fellow soldier. "Wounded, yeah. So we can't mow them down the way they murdered us. Hell, yes, wounded. Well, they can just happen to die on their way."

There was a slight rustling behind her. She turned

quickly to see Liam coming. She brought her finger quickly to her lips.

Liam didn't see the soldiers, but sensed the danger. She indicated that he should drag Gilly back. He hunkered down by her, catching Gilly's shoulders and frowning.

"Where's Blaze?" she asked him in a hushed whisper.

"Just yonder—"

"Take Gilly. Break camp, and ride through the night. Get to Granger's camp as quickly as you can."

"And what are you going to do?" Liam demanded.

"Lead them astray with Blaze."

Liam shook his head. "No. No. Absolutely no. Your brother—"

"My brother will never know."

"Miss Tia, I'll lead them astray—"

"No!" she said quickly. These particular Yanks were out for blood. "We can't spare you—I can't help Hank lift Gilly and the others; I have to be the one to create a diversion. Besides, I can just be a good local *Unionist* out for a ride. No harm will come to me. All I have to do is mention Ian's name, and I'm perfectly safe with the Yanks."

"No—"

"Liam! You have to listen to me. That is the truth. You all are in danger from the Yankees; I am not. I'll be just fine. If there's a Federal camp near here, I may just sashay in for dinner!"

She spoke lightly, and with assurance. But he frowned, looking at her. "Where's your clothes, Tia McKenzie?"

"On the rock there. Go now, please, please! Get Gilly out of here. Get to Lee Granger's camp, and don't worry about me. I'll deal with any situation as it arises."

Gilly shifted suddenly, moaning.

"Get him out of here, quickly! They'll hear him."

Liam gave her a stern look. She frowned fiercely back. But when Gilly made a deep, moaning sound again, Liam came to life, hobbling on his one leg, but very strong despite that fact. He had barely moved Gilly before Tia saw one of the Yanks come through the trees, heading for the water.

He didn't see her at first. He dipped his head into the cool stream, then made a cup of his hands and drank deeply. She stayed perfectly still, barely daring to breathe.

He drank, and drank. He splashed his face.

Finally, he looked up.

He wasn't old himself, though not as young as most of the Rebs she helped patch up these days. He had a round face, thick beard, and ruby red mouth. He was round himself, as well.

She hadn't seen a heavy soldier in a very long time!

He stared at her; she stared at him.

He opened his mouth as if he would cry out. No sound came at first. She rose slowly. She was in her pantalettes and corset. The latter boasted the tiny pink rose centers of her breasts.

"Ah . . . hello," said the soldier.

"Hello," she returned.

He kept staring at her. She let the seconds go by, hoping she was giving Liam enough time to get moving.

"Ca-Ca-Captain!" he cried at last.

She waited. Waited, counting the seconds. She wanted the captain to see her.

In a minute, the captain appeared. He was more the soldier she expected. Tall, slim, his lean face hardened and saddened by the years of war gone by. She had a feeling he had been in it from the beginning.

He looked across the water at her.

"Are you looking for the enemy?" she called.

"Who do you call the enemy, er-ma'am?" he called back.

"I'll show you!"

She scampered up the embankment, through the trees. She looked to the place where they had been forced to stop.

No sign of the troops.

She whistled; Blaze came trotting to her. The mare wasn't saddled. Tia took a running leap and careened on top of the horse. She headed back through the trees, not wanting to lose the Yankees.

She could hear them, splashing through the trees, shouting. There were at least a half-dozen of them, or maybe more, since she could hear many different voices calling out.

"Where'd she go?"

"Who is she?"

"What's she up to?"

"Where can she lead us?"

"She's naked—"

"Half-naked—"

"Tons of hair—"

"Godiva!"

"My God, yes! Godiva—who has led hundreds of men to their doom."

"That's her, yes!"

Her, yes? Hundreds of men to their doom? Dear Lord, how on earth could truth become so horribly exaggerated?

It didn't matter how she had become such a villain. Her estimate was right—there were six or seven men after her. Seated on Blaze, she tried to count their exact number.

She didn't want to play the wretchedly "dooming" Godiva, adding more fuel to the fire of rumor, but she had to.

She rode hard down to the embankment again.

"This way, fellows!"

She turned Blaze, and started racing first downstream. The Yankees needed to retrieve their mounts. She slowed her gait, making sure they were behind her.

She left the river embankment, heading for the road. She heard them following. She turned, making sure they could see her.

A branch slapped her in the face. Hard. She decided to give more attention to the direction in which she was going.

Ten minutes, twenty. She kept ahead of them by at least fifty lengths, trying to think of a place where she might lose them. Finally, she thought of the pine hammock to the north. The area was riddled with streams and small lakes and ponds. She could plunge into the hammock, follow around the pond, through the pine trails there, cross the stream and the pines on the other side, then head straight out to the copse.

She could hear Blaze breathing as they raced. How long had she run her horse? The Yankees would have to slow when she did, she assured herself.

She reached the hammock, then veered into it. She heard the shouts far behind her when they first followed. They had even lost one another.

She smiled, circling around the pond, at last slowing her gait.

Dismounting from Blaze, she quickly led the horse through the thicket of underbrush, heading again toward the trail of pines along the stream's edge.

She could still hear the Yanks behind her. They remained mounted, without the least idea of where she had gone. They wandered in circles. They couldn't run through this terrain; they didn't seem to realize that neither could she. But she knew where she was going. Once she cleared the pines and passed through the stream, she'd be free. She'd have reached the copse, and so many ways to go it would take a bloodhound to track her. One of the trails led southward. Along that trail there were a multitude of abandoned Indian cabins where she could hide—and perhaps find clothing.

She moved quickly, running through the shallow water, swimming across where it deepened at the river, finding the slender flow of the brook again beyond the main body of the small river. She slipped into the pines, still leading Blaze, but running herself as she realized she neared the copse where she could mount up and ride again.

Yet at the fringe of the trees, she came to a dead stop, startled and dismayed.

There was a camp in front of her.

A Yankee camp.

Tents were pitched; fires burned. It was an organized

camp, with pickets down the length of the pines. A large tent far to her left appeared to be a hospital. Wounded men sat about before it. Elsewhere, soldiers cleaned their weapons, cooked over the fires, smoked pipes and eased back against the trunks of trees. A few had books. Some wrote.

Pickets walked the outer circumference of the camp as well, watching the east and west trails, assuring the men who rested that no large body of men could come crashing through the pines to destroy them.

It was an excellent position; easily defended, well placed for water, food, the best of the sunlight.

She hadn't imagined that the Yanks would know it; it was not an area that had been well mapped in the past.

Ah, but the Yanks were learning the state. And there were, of course, more and more Unionists in the state daily. Those who tired of the war. Those who had voted against secession. Those who might have organized the territory this side of the state into East Florida—with a Unionist government to run it.

She heard the men behind her.

She cursed the camp.

It would be her death! she thought.

The soldiers behind her remained lost in the maze of trees, rivers, and ponds.

But they wouldn't stay lost for long.

Dozens of Yanks lay before her.

She hugged a pine, trying not to panic. She searched the camp, shivering. It was growing dark. A large tent, probably an officer's quarters, held a prime position right by a little inlet of water pulsing from the stream. The pines encroached upon the very back of it. The positioning of the tent allowed for privacy within, and escape to the brook—should a man desire his own counsel under the stars.

As she stared at the tent, her heart quickened. A man exited from the canvas flap—tall, dark, imposing. She saw nothing but his back. He wore no jacket, just a bleached muslin shirt and Union-issue cavalry trousers. He had to be an officer; she was certain by the assurance with which he moved. Command was visible in his carriage, in his manner.

He paused by a young, sandy-haired, freckle-faced soldier at a cooking fire some distance from the tent. She didn't hear what he said; he spoke with a deep, low voice and his back remained to her. She did hear the sandyhaired soldier's reply since he was looking in her direction and his voice seemed to carry straight to her.

"Yessir, I understand. You're meeting with Colonel Bryer, and will be with him for some time. If the scouting party returns, I'll tell Captain Ayers that you're with Colonel Bryer, and he may find you there, or wait to speak with you here later, but you wish to see him tonight."

The officer moved on. Tia looked down the length of the pines. She could hear the soldiers coming closer. She ran along the pines, leading Blaze.

Behind the officer's tent, she gave Blaze a firm pat on the rump. "Go on now!"

The horse trotted off as bidden. Tia watched her horse, fingers clenched into her palms. Blaze wouldn't go too far—she hoped. Tia didn't want her horse to give away her position. She hoped, as well, that Blaze would stay deep within the pines, and avoid the copse that was so heavily laden with men and tents.

She didn't want her well-loved mare stolen by the enemy.

"Go on, girl, go on!" she whispered.

Tia watched her go, glad that Blaze soon discovered a nice thicket of grass concealed by the pines.

Sure that the mare had moved on far enough, she plunged quickly through the trees, and then, just as quickly, she drew back, hesitating.

Carefully she viewed the area. She could make it into the tent without being seen, she was certain. She could bide her time, perhaps find more clothing, then slip back through the pines after the soldiers had given up searching for her.

Yes, she could. Easily, if all went well.

But what if the officer who lived within the tent came back before she dared slip back into the pines?

He wouldn't! He had just informed his sergeant that he would be gone for several hours.

She sped the short distance to the tent, fell to her knees on the soft grass, and crawled beneath the canvas wall of the tent.

Within the enclosure she rose, shivering. The night was growing very cool. She was soaking wet. Her hair lay like a cold, damp cloak around her shoulders, trickling little droplets of ice down her spine. Her fear didn't help. Her teeth were chattering. She needed a blanket. Searching for one, she surveyed the strange refuge she had so desperately chosen.

The tent was large, a welcoming place. There was even a throw rug over the earthen floor. A large camp bed lay beside a camp desk. A map of the area was stretched out across the desk. An officer's frockcoat was draped over the folding chair in front of the desk. There was a standing shaving mirror, a chest that housed eating utensils, and a small table that was piled high with books. She found herself looking at the titles. There were military manuals and medical periodicals. Books on engineering and books by Audubon. They were well-read books, and she was tempted to go and look through them. Her father's library at Cimarron was extensive, and he had encouraged his children to read. Her mother loved books; she had told them often enough that books were like luxurious voyages—they could take you wherever you wanted to go from the comfort and warmth of an armchair. Books were teachers as well, opening up the world to those who cared to learn. They were friends with whom to curl up on a rainy day, company when you were lonely, cheer when you were feeling the weight of the world.

She almost walked over to pick up a book. She stopped herself firmly.

She wasn't here to read! she warned herself. She had come to hide—and find clothing. She could not wear a book!

And so, she kept looking around the tent. Another traveling chest was at the side of the first. There was a clean white cotton shirt folded atop it.

Everything in the tent was neat, and yet, the space seemed to have the indelible imprint of a personality upon it. She was intrigued by who might be staying here. The tall, dark-haired officer she had seen leaving. A Yankee, the enemy. Yet the term "enemy" was best when it was a faceless term. Her brother was the "enemy," and yet a cherished face within her life. More than ever, she despised the war.

The second chest, she told herself firmly, probably held clothing. She could use the shirt folded atop it to begin with. There must be trousers within. Too big, certainly, but she could find something with which to tie them on. She hurried to the chest, still shivering. She opened it. Trousers. Nice, warm, navy wool trousers. She lifted them out, then laid them back on the trunk and looked nervously to the flap opening of the tent. She hurried to it, carefully moved the canvas aside, and peeked out. The soldier at the fire seemed to be keeping guard. The other men were busy about the camp. No one knew she was there.

She dropped the canvas, and returned to the trunk where the dry shirt and trousers lay. Seriously cold now, and nervous that she might be interrupted, she quickly stripped off her corset and pantalettes. Her fingers were numb and she could barely untie the strings of her corset and pantalettes. At first, she freed herself from the sodden remnants of her clothing and bent over and reached for the shirt.

As she did so, she froze, a feeling of fear sweeping over her. She was somehow aware that someone had come. No sound, but the air . . . yes . . . she felt a whisper of air from the flap of the tent. Someone had come in with an uncanny silence. Without the sound of a single footfall.

Someone had come, yes. And her back was to him.

She heard the click of a gun as the trigger was set.

"Who are you, and what are you doing?"

The voice was deep, commanding an immediate reply.

She spun around, looked up. She saw the man holding the Colt six-shooter and gasped, horrified.

She was staring at Taylor Douglas. Tall, dark, imposing—as she had noted before. Features betraying no emotion, no surprise, hard-set.

And angry. Merciless.

Yes, he was the officer she had seen leaving the tent. *She should have known, she should have seen, she should have thrown herself in the river before coming here!*

But of course. Taylor was the Yankee officer who knew about this copse, who knew the area, the defensive possibilities of such a position.

And yes . . . the books . . . the sense of clarity here, and of character as well.

Oh, yes, it was his tent.

And he had returned.

Chapter 13

~

Instinct.

Foolish perhaps, illogical, but there. Within her soul. She turned to run.

She didn't get anywhere. His arms were around her waist; he was lifting her from the ground, throwing her down.

The camp bed was hard. It knocked the breath from her as she landed on top of it. She instantly, *instinctively,* attempted to rise again. But he was there beside her, a booted foot on the edge of the bed as he leaned over her.

"Godiva!" he declared.

She gnawed her lower lip, staring at him.

"Well, well. So we meet again."

She couldn't speak. She just stared up into his hazel eyes. She crossed her arms over her breasts, feeling tremors snake along her spine and cause her to begin to shiver anew.

"Cat got your tongue? I never imagined you being silent. But speak up. To what do I owe the pleasure?" he mocked.

She gritted her teeth, swallowed hard, blinked—and then faced him with her own features hard set. "It was a nice night for a ride," she said smoothly.

"Ah, now, that's a poor lie, Godiva, for you. No imagination to it whatsoever."

"This is a social call?" she suggested blithely.

She was amazed that he smiled, yet the amusement didn't reach his eyes. "I warned you, remember, about riding out naked—"

"I didn't come naked!" she said, pointing to her clothes.

He didn't follow the direction of her finger. He arched a dark brow. "Ah, so you came with clothing. You stripped to wait for me? How decadent—and charming, of course."

"Oh, you should truly rot in hell, Taylor Douglas. You're supposed to be having dinner with Colonel Bryer!" she informed him. "You're supposed to be gone for hours."

"Yes, well, forgive my bad manners. I came for some despatches. How rude of me to unexpectedly return while you were stripping—and stealing my clothing, so it appears."

"Borrowing," she murmured.

"You were going to return them?"

"Of course I—" she began, but she broke off, hearing footsteps approach the tent. She paled. If someone entered the tent . . .

"Get under the covers," he told her.

"What?"

"The covers!"

She jumped up, shivering. He pulled up the sheet and blanket, and she crawled beneath them. He tossed both back on her—covering even her head.

"Sir!" a soldier called.

She heard Taylor lift the canvas flap.

"Colonel Bryer was called to the infirmary tent. Colonel McKenzie is on his way here now. He'll take the despatches and join you for dinner in your quarters."

"Thank you, Sergeant Henson."

She heard the footsteps retreating. She didn't move the blanket or sheet that covered her face. A second later, they were ripped away.

"You'll suffocate, you little fool," he told her.

She didn't even look at him. A tempest seared through her heart. Ian. She would be grateful to see her brother. She had learned that she must always be grateful to see him alive.

But . . .

"Ian!" she whispered miserably. "My brother is here—now?"

"Your brother arrived yesterday. Thank God. I'll turn you right over to him. I imagine facing Ian will be worse for you than the prospect of incarceration at unknown Yankee hands. Perhaps he can trim your feathers."

"No, please, Taylor, you can't!"

She didn't look at him. She was dazed. She stared at the canvas roof of the tent. Death, she thought, had to be so much easier than this.

He sat on the edge of the camp bed, caught her chin with his thumb and forefinger, and forced her to look at him. His features were hard and set, eyes damning. "I warned you. You broke your word."

She shook her head, twisting from his touch. "I did not! I swear to you, I never intended to do so. I was covered in blood; I was bathing. I heard the Yanks—"

"You heard men from this camp. You didn't need to lead them on any wild chase. They were looking for injured men."

"If they found Rebel injured, they were going to kill them."

He let out an impatient sound. "Captain Ayers is a good officer and an ethical man. He wouldn't murder injured men, not even enemy soldiers—"

"Maybe Ayers wouldn't—but the men with him would!" she insisted.

"I don't remember allowing you any extenuating circumstances when I asked for your word. You swore you wouldn't do it. You broke your word; you decided to play Godiva."

She shook her head. "I didn't. I had just taken off my shirt and skirt to soak the blood from them. You really can't imagine what it's like, all that blood."

"I believe I could," he murmured darkly.

"The scent of it was . . . never mind. And it all happened so quickly. We were by the river, fixing Gilly's bandages—"

"Gilly?" he said, and she was startled to realize he remembered the young soldier he had met.

"He was horribly burned, and lost a foot at Olustee. Your troops happened upon the exact spot at an importune time."

"And you were convinced they were going to *murder* your injured?"

His disbelief was evident in his tone, in the sharp narrowing of his eyes.

"I'm telling you the truth!"

"With no faith that the men would have a leader who would prevent such butchery?"

"How dare you disbelieve me! You! My mother told me that Federal soldiers—the same army as yours—butchered Seminole women and children during the Seminole Wars. What makes you think that certain men wouldn't consider Rebs as much vermin as they considered the Indians?"

Her angry appeal just seemed to irritate him.

"The same men who were in that army are many of the same men who are in the Confederacy now, and you know it damned well. There were no conditions, Tia. My men just happened upon you. Well, your brother just happens to be here. By God, I warned you that I'd turn you over to him!"

"It was all an accident," she insisted, trying to pull the covers to her breast and rise, and gain some distance from him.

He set his hands on her bare shoulders, pushing her back down, leaning closer. "I take back any insult to your ability to weave a story. You are the most imaginative actress I have met in quite some time, Tia."

"Taylor!" came a call from just outside the tent.

Tia went completely rigid. *Ian!*

Then she felt hysterical laughter rising in her throat. Ian was right outside—no, Ian was coming through the flap. Maybe Taylor would get a chance to tell Ian what had happened. Maybe Ian would kill Taylor.

Maybe Taylor would kill Ian.

"Taylor, I sent word that Bryer was called back to a wounded man—"

Ian was in the tent.

She was in the bed. Naked. Taylor was leaning over her.

"Tia?"

Her brother's shock was evident in his voice: the depth of his indignation and absolute fury became evident in his eyes. He looked from her to Taylor. "Douglas, by God, I don't know what's going on here, but I will know and—"

Ian's hand was on his sword hilt.

"Ian!" Tia cried. Taylor stood, facing down Ian. He had instinctively set his own hand on his sword hilt.

Tia grabbed the covers to her chest and leaped from the bed. She didn't know what she was doing, but she rushed to Taylor's side, putting an arm around him, preventing him from drawing his sword.

"Ian, thank God! At Olustee, with all the Union dead and wounded, we were so afraid! I'm so glad to see you. I was told you were out of the state, sent back to Virginia. We were so relieved to hear that . . . there were just so many dead. So many, many men dead." She was babbling, not getting anywhere. She lowered her voice, filling it with feigned emotion. "In fact . . . I had to see Taylor. I was told that he had been part of the battle, and so . . . well, I had to find him. To make sure that he was all right."

Ian's jaw was locked in a way she knew too well. "You had to see Taylor?" he queried, his teeth on edge.

"Of course . . ." Tia said, letting her voice trail off suggestively. "Oh, Ian, of course, I thought you'd realized that we'd met before."

"Tia, when we were last home, I warned you that you couldn't play games! By God, you are my sister and I will defend you at any cost, but—"

"Ian, I swear, I didn't cause the trouble at Christmas. But neither is there trouble here. Oh, God, I have to make you understand. I did know Taylor before Christmas. You see . . . we had become—well, more than acquaintances."

Her brother's scowl at last showed a hint of confusion. "Taylor, what is she talking about?"

"Your sister—"

"He was scouting to the south," Tia interrupted quickly. "We ran into one another. I couldn't say anything at the house during Christmas time. It's all been so very hard for me. You must understand—after all, Alaina was passionately involved with the South when *you* first met. I was angry, confused. I'd come to know Taylor, and . . ." Again, she didn't exactly lie; she just let her voice trail off. "We were so involved, but he was the enemy. Is the enemy. But . . . Ian . . ."

It wasn't enough. Her brother was still as rigid as a steel pike. He was still going to kill her. Or try to kill Taylor. There would be an awful, explosive fight any second. Taylor wouldn't just let Ian kill him because she had decided to take refuge in his tent. She had to say something else, do something . . .

"Ian, we're married," she lied swiftly.

"What?" he said incredulously. "I don't believe you! If so, Tia, someone should take a switch to you, after the way you played with Weir at the house during Christmas. Taylor, good God, explain this!"

Tia held her breath. She stared at Taylor. He stared at her.

Time seemed to go by. An eternity.

Taylor didn't deny her.

Nor was he going to help her. "I'm sure she'll explain," he drawled softly. "Tia is just so—enthusiastic. I'm dying to hear her description of what has occurred myself."

"Tia?" Ian questioned. "Start talking. I really don't understand. Father was upset with your lack of manners to a guest. You were rude and hateful at the house—"

"Oh, Ian! That's what I'm trying to explain. This is so hard for me! I couldn't admit what I was feeling at first. I mean, he is in a Union uniform. Like you. Only you're my brother, and we've managed, except for the awful fear when there's a battle. I didn't want to come here!" It was the first truthful thing she had said. "Though, now, of course, that I see you . . ."

He was waiting. Demanding more of an explanation.

"Ian, I never wanted to care about another enemy! It's bad enough to have my brother . . . fighting against his state. But you've got to understand. There were so many dead, Ian! Yes, I was wretched. And I was afraid. Afraid, terribly afraid, when I'd heard that Taylor was leading cavalry at Olustee. I knew that I couldn't wait, I had to come to him. I had to see him . . . it didn't matter anymore that we were still at war."

Was there even a prayer that he'd believe her?

Taylor slipped behind her, pulling her close to his chest, his arms holding the blanket against her nakedness. "Imagine. Can you believe such a story?" he asked huskily.

She thought it a miracle that Ian didn't hear the sarcasm. But apparently, he didn't.

Because he knew Taylor; trusted him.

He just stared at her, his deep blue eyes troubled, brow knit in a frown.

"Taylor . . . you and my little sister!" Ian said, looking from her to Taylor at last. "Who would have imagined . . ."

"Certainly not me," Taylor added smoothly.

"Oh, right, who would have imagined!" Tia breathed. It was a miracle.

"My God, Taylor! You and my little sister!" Any minute he was going to step forward, pump Taylor's hand, kiss her cheek. But his hand still hovered at his sword hilt.

Ian's hand fell from his sword hilt. He came forward, grinning now from ear to ear.

He shook Taylor's hand. Kissed her cheek. "This calls for a celebration. I've nothing good enough for this occasion, but I did bring a red wine—do our parents know?" he demanded.

"Uh—no. This just happened after Olustee!" she said very softly.

Her brother's palm touched her cheek with real affection. "They'll be glad, Tia, trust me, they'll be glad, I think. Glad of your choice. I think Father was afraid that you were becoming too involved with Ray Weir, and that would have been disaster. Taylor, welcome to the family. Well, you are family to part of the family, but I'm damned happy to have you as a brother-in-law. Good lord, though, I've come at a bad time—"

"No, no! There's no bad time to see you, Ian!" Tia cried out.

"I didn't even imagine that I'd be able to see you at all this trip, Tia. I thought you'd be in the woods with Julian and the wounded."

"No. Here I am," she said lamely.

"Here you are, a married woman, little sister!" he exclaimed. "My congratulations! To you both. I'll go for the wine, and make other arrangements for my sleeping quarters this evening. Tia, get dressed. We will drink a red wine toast. It should be champagne. If only I'd known . . ."

Ian turned and slipped beneath the tent flap, leaving them alone. Tia was suddenly shaking so hard she thought she was going to fall—except that Taylor was holding her with an iron grip. He turned her in his arms. Stared down into her eyes. "Now that was clever. Really clever."

"What should I have told him?" she whispered desperately. The blanket didn't seem like enough of a barrier between them.

"How about the truth?" he queried hotly.

She closed her eyes, opened them, met his gaze again, seeking understanding. "I—I couldn't."

"So you came up with one really damning lie!"

"I'll think of a way out of it."

"Oh, no. I've had it with your fabrications."

He pushed her back against the rear of the tent and walked to the flap, lifting it and exiting. She heard him calling to his sergeant, speaking softly, then, as he reentered the tent, he gave a few last instructions. "Sergeant Henson, tell Father Raphael he must come immediately. And bring Private Allen as well; we'll need another witness. It must all be done very quickly."

"Yes, sir!" Henson called from beyond.

Clutching the covers to her breast like a lifeline, Tia stared at him. "Father . . . Raphael?"

His eyes seemed like knives, cutting into her with irritation and fury. "We're getting married."

"Oh, no, we can't possibly. I can't marry you."

"Oh? You're the one who created this disaster."

"Marriage would be a worse disaster—"

"Well, guess what, my sweet? Your brother is coming back to celebrate. He expects you to be staying with *your husband* through the night. Did you want to become my mistress and continue to pretend to be married?"

"No, of course not—"

"Ian is staying at this camp. You will not be leaving this tent tonight."

"But marriage is a bit drastic—"

"So is death—even in warfare."

"There has to be a way—"

"There is a way, and damn you, I'm offering it to you. This was your lie, not mine. I assure you, I haven't the least desire in the world to marry you."

She couldn't help but take offense. She lifted her chin. "Then why do it?"

He shrugged. She still felt the razor's slash of his eyes. "I have no desire to marry again ever. So . . . since you have begun this charade, we'll carry it through. I don't really give a damn what commitment I make on paper."

She didn't know why she felt so hurt. The situation was a catastrophe she had created herself. She started shaking again, standing at the rear of the tent. Her eyes stung with tears. The truth. She could tell Ian the truth rather than do this. This was serious, awful, forever. If she told Ian the truth about what she had been doing . . . that she was the woman gaining fame as "Godiva," and given credit for far more excursions than she had ever taken . . .

She couldn't do it. She was desperate to find a way out. He seemed to have it for her. Calculated perfectly. But it couldn't work.

"But . . . what about the rest of your camp? They'll

know . . . that I wasn't here before. You're in a scouting and foraging situation—what will your superiors say to the sudden arrival of a Rebel bride?"

"There are no superiors here. Colonel Bryer has equal rank, but I'm the command officer, in full charge of the camp. Colonel Bryer has a daughter here, and there are two young women of excellent reputation working with him in the hospital tent as well, not to mention the laundresses, who also perform other duties for the men. Those with money and inclination. I'm sure you know what I mean. Henson will never breathe a word of when this wedding took place, neither will Father Raphael."

"But . . ."

Outside the tent, a throat was cleared, and there was a call from Henson. "Colonel! I'm out here with Father Raphael."

Taylor threw her the white shirt. "Put it on."

She did so, shaking, managing badly, feeling his hard gaze on her all the while. The shirt was a dress on her. She didn't need trousers.

"This is it. The moment of truth," he said.

"Can it . . ."

"Save you?" he inquired sharply. "Yes."

"I didn't mean that. I mean, can it work, can it be believed . . ."

He was silent for a minute. "Oh, yes. It can work, and be believed. And it will be legal," he added softly, as if in afterthought. "Time, however, is of the essence."

"Call them in," she said.

He stepped beneath the flap of the tent. For a wild moment, she was tempted to crawl beneath the canvas and disappear. But her hands were frozen; she was frozen . . .

He entered again through the flap. Alone. He stared at her. She felt the rage of anger behind the sharp gold glitter of his eyes. "We're just waiting for Private Allen. A few seconds' reprieve! Time to reflect! And I'm really doing you one hell of a service, Miss McKenzie."

Her teeth were chattering. "You don't have to—"

"Yes, you see, that's the point—I do. Yet bear in mind

that you trapped me into this. And I haven't forgotten that you broke your promise. Marry me, and I swear, I'll halfway kill you if you break it again."

She felt flushed. "You don't understand. I didn't mean to—"

"No excuses, or conditions. Marry me, and it isn't a game."

"I don't understand—"

"You're lying; you do."

She shook her head with sudden anger and passion. "I came up with the lie, yes, but you came up with this solution. We don't have to do this."

"We do, unless you want your brother's blood on your hands."

"Ian is damned fine swordsman—"

"You can try to tell him the truth. He still found his sister naked in my tent. His sense of honor and duty will call for him to demand satisfaction from me. He may be a damned fine swordsman, but so am I. You take your chances. It's a pity that any man should die for your recklessness, but there it is."

She felt the gold sting of his eyes a moment longer. Then he turned and moved quickly. He stepped out of the tent and returned with Henson, another soldier, and a man in a white collar. If they were in any way surprised or nonplussed about the strange situation, they gave no sign. "Father Raphael, Tia McKenzie, Ian's sister. Tia, Father Raphael. And these gentlemen are Sergeant Henson and Private Allen. They're two of my best men, discreet in every matter."

"Ma'am!" Henson said, offering her an awkward smile. "We're glad to have you. Mighty glad the Colonel's to have a wife again."

"Thank you, Henson," Taylor said, his voice grating.

Private Allen was a very lean fellow who looked as if he had been called out of an accounting office to serve in the war. He didn't speak, but he smiled at her.

"Father Raphael?" Taylor said.

Father Raphael was a white-haired Frenchman. "You both enter this willingly?"

"Yes, Father," Taylor said.

She would burn in hell, Tia thought. "Yes, Father," she echoed.

"Father, if you please, we need to do this quickly," Taylor reminded him.

The priest cleared his throat. He began to speak. Taylor came to stand beside Tia.

A white cotton man's shirt. This was to be her wedding gown! She was marrying the enemy in the enemy's own shirt . . .

There was no elegant ring for her finger; just Taylor's West Point class ring, made to fit her with a piece of string.

The words were all said; she signed the papers the priest carried. He made a hasty exit along with the officers who had stood as witnesses to the event.

When they were gone, she still stood barefoot, shivering, looking down at the ground. "My God, I could die . . ." she breathed. "Just die!"

He didn't intend to let her be at all. He jerked her chin up angrily, staring at her. "Lord no, my love, you're not going to die. You're not going to be allowed to die. There's plenty of torture in store for you before I would begin to let you escape into death! Ian is coming back. You have to play the loving, dutiful wife. You didn't just happen to bring clothing, did you?"

"I told you—"

"Oddly enough, he'll now be expecting you to be dressed. That he interrupted a passionate encounter with us as having been recently married is something he'll accept—he sees his own wife infrequently enough. But now, with you knowing that he is returning, he'll rather naturally be expecting to find you respectably clothed," he told her, then shook his head. "I'll go see if I can find a fairly slim camp follower."

"A camp follower!" she said with dismay.

"Yes, a good, loyal camp follower! One who probably wouldn't dream of doing anything so wanton and dangerous as running around the woods naked."

"You bastard!" she whispered.

"How do I explain to your brother that you haven't any clothing?" he demanded. He didn't expect her to answer. He started from the tent, then ducked back under the flap, tense as wire, voice a whip crack, eyes lethal fire. "Don't leave. Do you understand me? You'll wish you'd thrown yourself on your father's mercy a hundred times over if you take a single step from here and I catch you."

Again, he expected no reply. After he'd left, she sank down on the bed, staring at her ring finger. This couldn't be. She had married hastily in a small canvas tent, wearing only a man's white shirt.

Taylor was back almost immediately with clean clothing.

Chaste clothing. A pale-blue skirt with a blue smocked blouse to match. And a pair of shoes, thank God. He handed her the garments. "You'll have to wear them as is. Godiva's fashion accessories remain quite soaked," he said, indicating her corset and pantalettes, still lying in front of his trunk.

She ignored the comment, rising to dress. Her hands continued to shake; he continued to stare at her. If only he'd leave her alone! But he wasn't going anywhere. His arms were locked over his chest. She didn't attempt to tell him that he was making her so nervous she could barely function; she turned away from him, slipped from the white shirt, and into the new garments. She was struggling with the back hooks when he at last came around to help her. He was fixing the last of the tiny hooks when she heard her brother hailing them again.

"Taylor, Tia!"

"Come on in, Ian," Taylor invited.

Ian carried the wine—and long-stemmed glasses. "They belong to Colonel Bryer," he informed them, setting everything down on the camp desk, then working with a knife to open the bottle. "He is well packed for a surgeon in the field, but a good man, I hear."

"So it appears," Taylor said. He accepted wine from Ian.

"Colonel Bryer had no idea that your wife was here,

or even that you had married my sister," Ian informed
Taylor.

"I hadn't told anyone she was here. Well, Sergeant
Henson knows, of course, and Father Raphael. He married us. Truthfully, I don't want the matter known. It
could cause your father further difficulty with the Confederacy if it's known that his daughter has married the
enemy," Taylor to him.

"Perhaps that's true. Well, Tia," Ian said to his sister,
providing her with a wineglass. "It might have been far
more proper had you asked Father's blessing, or taken
the time for an announcement—"

"Oh!" she exclaimed. "You're going to tell me about
being proper! If I recall, Ian, you made an appearance
at a party with a bride, none of us knowing a thing about
it, and rumor circulating that you' had seduced your new
wife in a spring on our property!"

"Sons are allowed more liberty than daughters, Tia,"
Ian countered. "But I suppose you do have your point,
and I'm delighted for the both of you. Very delighted. I
could begin to imagine what situation I might have come
upon! To your health! To your long lives, to happiness!"

"Our thanks!" Taylor lifted his glass, took a swallow
of the wine. Tia did the same.

"Sirs!" Henson called from just outside the tent. "I've
arranged for dinner to be served."

"Please, bring it in," Taylor told him.

Flushed, Sergeant Henson brought in an amazing display of field culinary achievement. He'd managed a
snowy tablecloth, China plates, silver flatware. The camp
desk became a table complete with a softly glowing
candle.

Taylor seated Tia with a mocking, "My love!" whispered at her nape. She sat down to an amazingly complete and intimate meal.

Union foragers had apparently happened upon Florida
cattle Tia thought, but she was resigned rather than bitter. They had done an excellent job with it—the cuisine
was the finest she had ever tasted in the field. The food
consisted of steaks, potatoes, okra, and wild winter ber-

ries. Tia thought that she wouldn't be able to eat, but she was famished. And thirsty. Her wine went down quickly. Too quickly. Despite it, conversation was an effort. She had to explain to Ian that Julian had been called to serve one of General Finegan's men, and that no, he wasn't aware that she had left his Rebel troops to find Taylor.

"Tia, that was foolish! You don't know who you might have encountered along the way."

"I came straight to Taylor. Straight to him!" she protested, amazed at how easy it was to smile, then frightened because the smile threatened to turn to laughter, and if she began to laugh, she would cry and she wouldn't be able to stop.

Taylor was staring at her. He looked at Ian. "Oh, yes. She came straight to me."

By the end of the meal, she was giddy and exhausted, worn out with her own efforts at pretense and charade. Her brother had asked about Julian's infant son, and she had happily described him as the spitting image of his own child, Sean. "A little McKenzie pea in a pod," Tia said. "Beautiful blue eyes, thick dark hair—a totally cherubic little face."

"And he and Rhiannon are well?"

"Very well. She was, however, unhappy about staying at Cimarron when Julian left." She shivered suddenly. Many people called her sister-in-law a white witch. She had what they labeled "sight"—sometimes, an ability to see the future. She had seemed to know that Julian would be safe when he had ridden with his sister to join the regulation army for the battle at Olustee.

What a pity she hadn't warned Tia about the dangers of tending to the wounded when Yanks were in the territory! "Though I think she knew," Tia added softly, "that the Rebel forces would turn back the Yankee invasion."

They were both staring at her. She hadn't realized the passion with which she had spoken. She had forgotten that she was in a Union encampment.

"There can be but one finish to the war, I'm certain,"

Ian murmured. "There are things which have now taken place of which you might not be aware."

"What has happened? Our own forces just took the battle here!"

"Surely you've heard that things do not go so well elsewhere."

"Ian, why are you back here so quickly? You were ordered north after Christmas."

"Tia . . ."

He stared at his sister. Tia realized that Taylor was watching him, and she wondered what Taylor knew of the war that she did not. Obviously, Ian wasn't going to share his orders with her, even if she was his sister—and now the wife of a Unionist.

Ian leaned toward her. "Tia, England has officially refused to recognize the government of the Confederacy. No more ships will be outfitted there. The rest of the European powers have refused to recognize her as well—other than the Roman Pontiff. Don't you see—it's over, except for the additional deaths that will follow, on both sides."

"They'll shoot any man—as a deserter?"

"No government has ever had such a harsh law, Tia, and God knows if they can implement it or not. Communications are destroyed in many areas."

She thought he must have seen some deep unhappiness in her eyes then because he suddenly rose. "I pray it ends soon," Ian said briefly, and walking around the table, he pulled her up to her feet, offering her a warm, brotherly hug at last and speaking to her with deep affection, "Enough sorrow for tonight! I wish you every happiness. I'm pleased to see you wed to so fine a man, though you disagree with his beliefs and loyalties. The rest of us have managed under the duress of supporting opposing sides; I imagine you two will do as well. I'll leave you alone now, for I'm very aware of how precious time can be in the midst of war."

"No, no, Ian! You don't need to leave!" Tia said in a panic. She suddenly realized that she was choking on unshed tears. She loved her brother so very much. And with him there, that night, she suddenly thought of the import of his words. She could remember, before the war began, when her brother had scandalously arrived at a party for their father with a new bride himself. And then the violence had broken out, and Alaina had been such a Rebel, and she had believed that her husband would resign from the Union army . . .

But he had not.

"Stay, Ian," she said softly.

He smiled, lifting her chin. "I'll be here in the morning, Tia, though I cannot stay long. We'll be together again."

She desperately wanted to cling to him, and beg him not to leave her.

She couldn't do so.

"I'll walk you out, Ian," Taylor said. He smiled at Tia—like an angry alligator might grin at a crane.

"Good! There are matters we need to discuss."

She couldn't let him go so quickly. She threw herself into her brother's arms, holding him very tightly.

He kissed her cheek, unwound her arms from around his neck. "Good night, little sister!" he said.

He left the tent with Taylor. She paced. She gazed longingly at the canvas at the rear of the tent. The pines were just beyond. Hammocks, rivers, streams—trails that led south and west, back to Cimarron.

"Mrs. Douglas!"

Sergeant Henson was just outside. Calling. Calling her, she realized.

"Yes?"

"I'll just clean out the tent, ma'am," he said, entering. "The dinner things."

"Oh, yes . . . thank you," she said.

He smiled at her and went about his business, quickly and efficiently. "I'm sorry to be a bother," she heard herself telling him.

"No bother, ma'am. Sometimes, other officers have their wives along. Some of the men from St. Augustine are able to have their ladies . . . Colonel Bryer is a New Yorker, but his wife is with him frequently. She defies all Rebel fire! Confidentially, they call her an old battle-ax, but she's a great lady to have in a fray!"

"Well, good for her!" Tia applauded.

He grinned, and slipped out of the tent. Tia turned longingly to stare at the back canvas again. She was startled as she heard another voice in the night. "Colonel! Colonel Douglas!"

A second later, a man was slipping through the tent. It was another man she had seen earlier; the tall, sad-looking captain from the river.

He started, staring at her. "Excuse me, please, I'm so sorry, I didn't know that the colonel had company. I was ordered to report to him this evening."

"He's with Colonel McKenzie," she advised. She bit her lip, wanting to blurt out the fact that his men were monsters.

Yet, he was staring at her equally strangely.

At that moment, Taylor returned to the tent. "Captain Ayers!"

"Yessir," the captain said, saluting. "I have a report for you, sir." He was trying not to stare at Tia.

"Captain Ayers, my wife. Tia, dear, Captain Kenneth Ayers."

"How do you do?" Tia murmured.

"I do apologize for staring. It's just that I'm sure we've met."

"Never, sir," she said, afraid she would choke over the denial.

"I didn't know that your wife was in camp, Colonel Douglas."

"She's just been able to join me," Taylor said smoothly.

"Well, I've come to report—"

"We'll discuss the day's business outside, shall we?" Taylor ordered.

"Certainly, sir."

"Excuse us—my love?" Taylor said, staring at her again.

He and Ayers departed. She paced again, sat on the

bed. She stared at the rear of the tent, then jumped up with horror.

Blaze!

Was she still wandering within the pines? She had to find her horse. She would never let some wretched Yankee killer seize her horse!

She stood, then paused. She'd be right back. She had to come back; surely Taylor would realize that. After all, her brother was in the camp. But she had to find her horse.

She ducked low, plucked at the canvas, and exited the tent by the rear. The moon was half-full, the stars were out, and she had some vision. She slipped quickly into the pines and walked among them. "Blaze! Blaze!" she called. She whistled, dismayed when her horse didn't come. She began running along another path, glad Taylor had provided her with her soft leather slippers along with the clothing.

She came to a halt on the trail, listening. She thought she heard a movement among the trees, and she turned hopefully.

No, Blaze hadn't appeared.

Taylor had.

Arms crossed over his chest, his stance rigid, he watched her with his eyes like the rays of the sun, piercing and hot.

"I told you not to run."

"What? Don't be absurd! I was only—"

She broke off. He was coming toward her. "No! God spare me another of your stories! You have a tale for every occasion; you lie with the same ease with which you breathe."

"I wasn't about to lie to you!" she protested angrily.

"Good," he said. He was almost upon her. Heat seemed to bounce from him like the sun from the earth on a sweltering summer day. She could almost see it on the air. She unwittingly backed away from him. He caught hold of her arm, jerking her to him. "My God, but you have your nerve! You twist me into your wretched games, and then think to escape!"

"No, I didn't—" she tried to protest, struggling against his hold.

"No game, Tia. You forced me to marry you—"

"Forced! Did I hold a gun to your head?"

"No," he drawled sarcastically. "Your brother was about to draw a sword."

"Oh, but you would have killed him with your amazing prowess."

"To my great sorrow, yes, it might have happened."

"Or you might have lain dead."

"Either way, Godiva, you are not worth the bloodshed!"

The words hurt as much as his hold upon her. "You don't understand—" she began.

"No, you don't understand," he assured her. "But you're going to."

It was as if something within him had snapped. He ducked against her midriff even as she struggled, throwing her over his shoulder. A raw sense of panic seized her as she realized the full implications of what she had done. Her chin slammed against his back. She bit her tongue as it did so. Tears stung her eyes. How could things come out so badly when her efforts had all really been so noble?

"Let me down, Taylor, please, now!"

She might as well have not bothered to speak at all.

"Please! I'll cry out, I'll let out a Rebel yell unlike any you have ever heard before. I'll create such a fuss! My brother—"

"Your brother would not interfere between a husband and a wife, Tia. You changed the battlefield today, Godiva. Now I am responsible for you."

Again, he walked with such a fervor that her face slammed against his back. Her nose was crushed. Tears again formed in her eyes. She was unaware when they left the pines. He slipped beneath the back canvas of his tent swiftly and smoothly, as if she were not a burden at all.

He set her down upon the camp bed none too gently, exhaling as he did so with a grunt. She scrambled to a sitting position. They stared at one another. The look in his eyes as they met hers was not at all reassuring. Gold, sharp, incensed, his eyes seemed to cut into her with the sharpness of a bayonet. The veins at his throat and temple pulsed with the depths of his anger. He stood before her, hands on his hips. She could hear his teeth grinding with his efforts to remain still, see the lock of tension that held his body dead stiff from head to toe.

She braced herself for whatever he was about to say—or do. She prepared to fight—a war of words she must win quickly. She was good with words—even he said so. But she couldn't come up with the right ones—despite her innocence at the moment.

She didn't need to speak. He did so.

"All right, Godiva. Here we are."

"Here we are," she repeated. "Look, I tried to tell you—"

"I don't want you telling me anything anymore. Every word out of your lips tends to be sheer fabrication."

"I want my horse—"

"So you said. Well, she is safe, and will be taking you nowhere tonight."

"I didn't mean to run from you—"

"Good. Because you have not managed to do so."

"So . . ." she murmured carefully, very aware that he still stood less than a foot from her, his temper dangerously explosive.

"So. Well. Get on with it," he said curtly.

Not what she had expected. He suddenly seemed cold and distant, and calculating. Brief in the extreme.

"Get on with what?" she whispered warily.

"My love!" The term was spoken in a voice that was deep, husky, masculine—and so mocking! "You are always so eager to shed your clothing. And I admit," he said wryly, "to have chastised you in the past for your tendency to lose them, but . . . here and now would be the proper time. You *married* me today, Godiva. So here and now, you have your chance. My love, my dearest wife—your constant penchant for carelessly casting your clothing aside is what has brought us here to this—this all-decisive moment in life. So . . . Tia, get on with it. Now."

Chapter 14

Just what the hell am I doing? Taylor wondered. By God, since he'd come back tonight and found her in his tent, he hadn't really known a thing he was doing—until he'd done it.

Actually, his own emotional state didn't matter, he told himself, except that he was angry. He really wanted her to suffer—something like the pain of the damned, which he felt he was enduring now, though he wasn't at all sure why.

"Need help?" he queried, his tone polite. *Talk,* he told himself, *talk. It will keep you from thinking.*

"I'm more than willing to assist you, my love, though one would think you'd have removal of your garments down pat by now, since you so frequently shed them," he told her, and he heard the sarcasm in his voice, knew what he was doing to her, and yet, he couldn't stop himself.

She had brought them to this.

He saw the change in her as her temper flared. Burned.

She jumped up, careful that she did so across the camp bed from him, staring at him, hands on her hips, seething. "Say what you will. It's cruel and untrue—"

"Untrue!"

"Yes, untrue. Everything is greatly exaggerated. What you've heard is all lies."

"Tia, I found you tonight," he reminded her. He lifted his hand in a pretense of realization. "We should have consummated the marriage first—done the legal deed later. What a fool I was!"

She shook her head passionately. "I told you what happened tonight. And every word was the truth. You have men who mean to murder injured Rebels if they come upon them. If you weren't such a self-righteous fool, you might at least take the time to wonder if such monsters do exist beneath your nose!"

"I still found you here—"

"Excuse me, sir, but if they had murdered injured Rebels in cold blood and I watched, do you think they would have left me alive?"

"Tia, it is farfetched, and you have lied a dozen times before—"

"It's—"

"Just as you lied to Ian tonight. Well, it was a lie neither of us could live with. A lie which has now become the truth. That being the case, I do intend to reap the benefits."

She didn't intend to respond to that.

She started walking around the camp bed and he realized that she was leaving again—this time, via the tent flap. He caught her arm, swinging her back around to face him. She stiffened, teeth gritting so that they crunched, trying to free herself from him. Flashing dark eyes met his.

"Where do you think you're going now?" he demanded, as angry as she.

"To Ian! I'll tell him we've had a lover's quarrel."

"The hell you will!" he retorted.

He could feel the defiance in every inch of her body, but he had no intention of letting her go. He drew her tightly against himself, one arm pinning her against his length, the other catching her chin.

She meant to protest—wildly. But he didn't allow her to. His mouth crushed down upon hers and he gave her no mercy. She tasted blood where their lips met. His fingers tangled into her hair, holding her, and his tongue pressed past her lips, deep into the crevices of her mouth. He felt her breasts against his chest with her every breath, felt the heat within, the pulsing of her heart, the shivering that had seized her. And he allowed no quarter, could give no quarter, for it was suddenly a battle he meant to win. She tasted sweetly of the evening's wine, of warmth, of slow-building fire, and it seemed, in a matter of seconds, that her lips were molding to his, that they had parted of their accord, that he no longer battled the wall of her teeth for the depths of his kiss.

She was no longer straining against him. Her hands lay upon his chest, but not with struggle or resistance, and when he lifted his mouth from hers at last, her eyes were closed, dark lashes sweeping her cheeks.

"Tia."

She didn't open her eyes. She had decided to play the martyr, he realized, and he couldn't help smiling, because he could see the erratic pulse point beating a mile a minute at her throat. "I have married you, Taylor, and therefore will pay my debts."

His smile deepened. "That you will, Mrs. Douglas!"

He lifted her, swinging her into his arms. With a little gasp, she clasped him around the neck, afraid she would fall. He took the few steps that led to the camp bed and lay down with her, not about to give her another chance to rise. She let out an indignant and garbled protest when he rolled her over to find the buttons at the back of her blouse. "Want to destroy the garment?" he demanded. "I don't know just how many outfits I'll be able to find out here in the midst of nearly nowhere in the middle of the war!" he warned her.

She went still for a moment; he undid the last of the buttons. He could still taste her lips, feel her . . .

He eased the blouse from her. Still at her back, he slipped his arms around her, his hands cupping her breasts. His palms slid over the hard peaks of her nipples, and he feathered the aureoles with the tip of his fingers, stroked them softly, cradled the fullness of her breasts. He pressed his lips to her throat, to the pulse there, and felt the thundering fever of his own arousal begin to pound within him. He stroked the length of her spine slowly with his tongue, and found the buttons to her skirt, opened them, rose enough to drag the garment away. He sat up, drawing his shirt over his head, and cradling her into his arms once again, turning her, so that the stream of her black hair fell away and her breasts teased the flesh of his chest. Her eyes were closed again. He allowed her that, kissing her eyelids, finding her mouth again. Her lips gave way easily to his; he felt her hand upon his shoulder, upon his cheek, touching him, and this time, he felt that her lips melded naturally to his, that she sought as much as she gave, quested, searched.

The length of her shaped itself naturally against him. Their flesh melted together in a sweet inferno. He slid down her body, bathing the tips of her breasts with his tongue, taking the nipples into his mouth, teasing, stroking, sucking, drawing from her lips an exhaled gasp. Her fingers dug into his shoulder. He continued to move against her, nuzzling the satin of her belly, drawing lower, feeling the shaking in the length of her, finding the center of her sex, touching it with his tongue, breathing in the musky scent of sex, tasting the woman, rising to an anguish of desire. His sex throbbed against his trousers. He jerked them open to free himself, shimmying from the length of them, kicking them to the floor. She barely moved, barely breathed, then he touched her, and touched her again, and suddenly she was shaking, and writhing against his wet caress, and murmuring, protesting . . . arching against him. He rose, and hovered over her.

Her eyes were closed.

No mercy . . . and yet, he would allow her that.

He sank slowly into her, and began shaking with the depths of desire she had awakened within him. She went rigid; her nails scraped his chest and she gasped, twisting her head. He saw that she bit into her lower lip to keep from crying out, and for a moment he was shamed, remembering. She had dared the world, risked life and limb—she knew so much about men and war, and yet she was so innocent. He closed his own eyes, feeling the force of his desire trembling like a drumbeat through him. He fought for control, moved slowly, slowly, sheathed in warmth and fever, wanting her . . . every muscle in his body tortured and rigid. Slowly, slowly, deeper, withdrawing, deeper . . .

Her fingers tightened upon him. Breath escaped her lips. His rhythm increased, and the fierce anguish in his limbs burned with a greater fever as he sank again, and again, and felt the subtle change in the woman beneath him, the hunger awakened in her, the way she began to move, arching to his stroke, accepting, taking . . .

Wanting.

He cradled her hand against him, and the fever that swept him seemed to take them like the power of the wind. Guns might have thundered, swords might have clashed, the world and war might have exploded around him, and he would have given them not a care. Compulsion ruled him, the searing need, the desperate desire to reach the pinnacle. He had seen her, yes, he had known her, tasted her kiss, tasted her flesh. He hadn't imagined that she could drive him so far, reach so deeply into him, bring him to a fulfillment of something more than he had expected or known. Sleek, damp, twisting, moving . . . she suddenly strained against him, and he shuddered into her, and into her, and into her again, flooding her with his seed, with the force of his climax. He fell to her side, pulling her into his arms again, and lay there panting, wondering what she had done to him, what spell she had cast upon him, why there was something so unique about her that . . .

That he could forget.

Not just feel hunger, want sex. But forget . . .

The sound of gunfire. The war all around him. Abby . . . running.

Abby . . .

The blood on his hands.

He lay in silence. So did she. Soft tangled webs of ebony hair lay upon his chest. The top of her head was beneath him. He couldn't see her face. Although he'd been almost violently certain he hadn't wanted a wife, he couldn't regret the events of the night. He had wanted Tia McKenzie. She wasn't a lonely widow, divorcee, or prostitute. She was Jarrett McKenzie's daughter,

Ian's sister. There was only one way to have such a woman. Marry her.

She was also Godiva, he reminded himself, and he suddenly felt a greater anger at that fact. She still didn't realize what she had risked, even after tonight.

"Do you think you're going to survive marriage?" he queried.

"Don't!" she whispered.

"Don't what?"

"Don't—talk. Don't, I beg you, add insult to injury!"

Insult to injury? She had taken a heady slug at his masculine dignity and pride, and he wasn't going to ignore it. He turned to her, finding her face hidden in a web of her hair. He delved through it, smoothing it to the side, capturing her hands when she tried to twist away. Being Tia, she put up a fight. He straddled her, leaning low, pinning her wrists down, meeting her eyes. "You were injured?" he demanded.

"This was your idea!" she accused him.

"Marriage was your idea."

"But this—"

"This goes with marriage!"

He saw that her thick dark lashes were spiked with unshed tears. Compassion and anger stirred within him simultaneously. "You were wishing for a gallant Southern gentleman, I take it?"

"You were thinking of your wife!" she accused him in a pained whisper.

Something seemed to thud against the wall of his chest.

"You are my wife now," he told her quietly.

"I have married the enemy."

"So have many women. You will survive it."

"Will I? Will we survive the war?" she asked, and her voice sounded desperate, pained, frightened. He suddenly knew her vulnerability, and the courage it had taken to do the things she'd done. And prickly little enemy that she was, he wanted to protect her.

Enemy . . . wife. *His* wife.

"Yes! We will survive! I will see to it!" he promised

her. Her eyes were beautiful. Shimmering mahogany. And for once, she looked up at him as if she trusted him. He leaned down to kiss her again, and her lips were salty with the taste of tears. But she made no protest to his kiss; indeed, she kissed him in return with a sweet, hungry yearning. Kissed him, and kissed him . . .

It was he who raised his lips. "Insult to injury?" he queried huskily.

"Must you always talk?"

He smiled. "Certain talk has its place . . ." he murmured. "Such as . . . madam, I love the way you move. I love the way you look, the scent of you, and though other wives might be cold and dutiful, making love swathed in voluminous nightgowns, I would not dream of enduring such a situation, since you are quite stunningly beautiful, and you seduce by your very existence."

Her ebony dark eyes were upon him, still glittering with a certain moisture, but his words brought a rueful smile to her lips.

"I don't *dislike* you, Taylor."

"With endearments like that, it is amazing that I can control my ardor at all!"

Her smile deepened. "Taylor?"

"Yes?"

Her cheeks were flushed. She wet her lips. "You . . . are . . . it's not so awful to be with you. You're right . . . you've somewhat seduced me before. I don't think that I could have been with anyone else . . . as I am with you."

"Thank God!" he said.

She was dreaming again. She saw the big white house with the grand entry. Then the toddler, the boy, the beautiful child, was on the balcony . . .

Falling, falling, falling . . .

She awoke screaming. Once again, her mother-in-law was there, waking her, holding her, arms around her, assurances coming softly from her lips. "It's all right, it's a dream, and we'll take care, we know it's a warning. We'll warn everyone we know with a little boy, Rhiannon. It will be all right, really."

Her mother-in-law wasn't the only one with her. Alaina was there as well, holding little Conar, who screamed in resentment at being awakened again.

"I'm so sorry!" Rhiannon said, "I keep waking you . . . causing so much trouble."

"Waking isn't trouble, Rhiannon," her mother-in-law assured her.

"I just wish that we could help you somehow. Tell us about it," Alaina said. "Perhaps if you talk it out, detail by detail . . ."

And so, Rhiannon talked. Detail by detail. She described all that she had seen in her dream, all that recurred, all that was new.

And when she had finished. Alaina was as pale as the sheets. Her eyes were immense, their deep blue in stark contrast to the ashen shade of her cheeks.

"Alaina, what is it?" her mother-in-law asked with alarm.

"I know the house!" Alaina said. "I know the house she is describing."

When Tia awoke, she was alone, and she lay pensive on the cot for a long time.

The events of the evening seemed overwhelming and unbelievable to her at first. But with the increasing daylight, they became very real.

She didn't dislike Taylor. She was often furious with him, very often wished she could just slap him once really good and force him to listen to her point of view. But he had always intrigued her. And it was true that she had been strangely drawn to him from the beginning, true that she had been fascinated by him, that she had wanted to touch the bronze texture of his flesh. True, she had never imagined that anyone could awaken in her the sensations she had learned in her first night at his side. True, she was even anxious to see him again, feel his gold eyes upon her again, and feel again that sense that she was his, somehow protected, even cherished . . .

Even if he hadn't wanted another wife.

Remembering where she was, she rose quickly then, anxious to wash and dress. A bucket of fresh water and a towel had been left by the camp desk; she assumed they were for her. She also found Taylor's brush in the first compartment of his trunk, and she struggled to brush the mass of tangles out of her hair and wind it into the semblance of a neat chignon.

After making herself presentable, she stepped outside the tent. Sergeant Henson sat on a makeshift chair constructed out of a fallen log, and he whittled a little wooden figure as he tended a fire with a coffeepot. He looked up as she exited the tent, greeting her cheerfully.

"Good morning, Mrs. Douglas." He knew a great deal about her, she mused. What had he thought of her last night, having suddenly arrived in Taylor's tent—and becoming a wife in a large white uniform shirt?

Whatever he thought, he could not have been more cheerful or polite.

"Good morning."

"There's a meeting this morning, occurring in the doctor's tent since your husband wanted to let you sleep."

Because Taylor wanted to let her sleep? She doubted it. *Because no one wanted her around while they discussed Yankee strategy!*

"Thank you, Sergeant."

"Coffee?"

"I would love some."

He poured her a cup, and she sipped it. It was the best coffee she had tasted in a very long time. "Sergeant, is my brother involved in the meeting, too?"

"Why, of course. Your brother arrived with despatches and information, Mrs. Douglas."

"I see." Information they would assuredly not share with her.

Of course, they were both the enemy—her brother, her *husband*. It didn't seem real.

She looked across the camp of army-issue tents, hitching lines for the healthy horses still held by the Union, fires, and men. From a large, extended bleached canvas tent, she suddenly saw a woman hurrying across the grounds. She was young, thin, attractive, and seemed to be coming straight toward them.

"Sergeant," she said softly. "Who is that?"

"Cecilia Bryer, the doc's daughter. A fine young lady, at his side throughout this fight!"

"Mrs. Douglas!" the young woman called, hailing her.

Cecilia Bryer was about Tia's own age, slim, pretty with soft red hair and green eyes. She had a quick smile for Henson, but she looked tired, worn, old for her age, as did most people who involved themselves too deeply in the realities of war.

"Miss Bryer, how do you do," Tia said carefully.

"Well enough, for myself." In a no-nonsense manner, the woman offered Tia her hand. "We heard about your arrival, of course. News travels swiftly in a small camp such as this."

"I arrived unexpectedly."

"Through great difficulty, I understand. Your husband explained the going was quite rough, that you traveled hard to reach him. Those are my clothes you're wearing. I understand that your things were terribly muddied and damp."

"Yes—something like that," Tia said. "And I'm so sorry, I didn't know I had your belongings. Thank you, I apologize . . ."

"There's no need. I'm glad to have the luxury of several changes of clothing. I believe we are far better supplied than our Rebel counterparts."

"We make do," Tia said quietly.

Cecilia arched a delicate, flyaway brow, as if surprised that a woman in a Union camp who was married to a Union colonel would still align herself with the South.

"Well, my father is glad to help any man."

"So is my brother," Tia said quickly. The girl frowned, thinking she was speaking about Ian. "My brother Julian, a Confederate surgeon."

"Oh, yes, we've all heard about Julian—he was spirited into St. Augustine once to help General Magee!"

"Yes."

"Well." The girl smiled suddenly. "Whatever your affiliation, Mrs. Douglas, I'm glad that you seem to have a generosity of the soul. There is a young man in our infirmary who is dying—and he is an old friend of yours."

"Who is it?"

"Canby Jacobs. He said his parents have a little cattle ranch a few miles west of your family home near Tampa."

"Canby, yes. I went to school with his sister, years ago."

"Come with me, if you'll see him."

"Of course I'll see him."

"He said that you may not. That you might consider him a traitor, and not want to have anything to do with him."

"I will see him gladly."

"Good. Follow me."

Tia followed Cecilia Bryer through a number of single soldier's tents. She saw in the distance that some of the men were going through drills. A few were at leisure about the camp, tending to their laundry, writing at makeshift desks, reading. One lone soldier played a sad lament upon a harmonica, but stopped as they passed him by. "Mornin', Miss Cecilia," he said, nodding to them both.

"Good morning, Private Benson," Cecilia said. Tia noted that he had no left foot.

They continued on to the large hospital tent. There were at least forty, maybe fifty beds in it. Flies buzzed; men groaned. Orderlies and nurses, male and female, moved about, changing bandages, talking to the soldiers, bringing water and what aid they could.

It was not as bad as the battlefield had been. They were not lying strewn about in pools of blood with slashed, missing, and mangled limbs.

But the soldier on the bed to which Cecilia led Tia was in very bad shape. A large, fresh bandage, already beginning to show the color of blood, covered half his torso. The left side of his face was covered with a bandage as well. She wouldn't have recognized him as Canby Jacobs if Cecilia hadn't told her his name.

"His lung is mostly shot away," Cecilia whispered to Tia. "There's nothing more we can do but keep the wound moist and clean. Take care if you change the bandage again."

Staring at Canby, Tia nodded. She walked over to the bed. His one good eye was closed. His hand was upon his chest. She clasped it in both her own. His eyes opened. Deep and blue. The visible half of his lip curled into a smile. "Miss Tia, can it be!"

"Canby! Yes, it's me. It's good to see you."

"Good to see me, but I don't look so good, eh?"

"You'll get better."

"No, I'm dying," he said flatly. "It's all right. I made my choice. I knew what I was fighting for, and what I'm dying for, and I believe that I was right, and that God will be glad to greet me. I'm awful glad, though, that you agreed to see me. Thought you might not. My folks split up over this, you know. My mother is in Savannah now. Pa died with the Massachusetts Fourth Artillery last spring."

"Canby, I'm so sorry. I'll write to your mother."

"You needn't write to her, Tia. She said that her son was dead the day I signed up with the Union."

"She can't have meant it. No mother—"

"Not all folks were like yours, Miss Tia!" he said, then smiled again. "I always had such a crush on you. Even now, I can see you when your father had his fine parties at Cimarron! Why, you danced and you teased—and you were nice to every fellow there, including ugly poor boys like me!"

"Canby, you were neither ugly nor poor!"

"So you married Colonel Douglas—now that's mighty fine. He's a good fellow, Miss Tia. You'll see that more when the war is over. Reckon, though, I shouldn't be so surprised that you did come to see me. Your father is one mighty fine man, one I sure do admire. He loves both his sons, no matter what path they chose. Guess he taught you the same."

"I do love both my brothers."

"And Colonel Douglas."

"And my friends, Canby, no matter what side they chose!" she told him. She didn't want him to see the way she was noting how quickly his bandage was filling with blood. "Canby, I need to change this bandage for you."

"No, just leave it be."

But she called to an orderly for a fresh bandage. The limping fellow who glanced her way knew what Canby needed.

As he came over with fresh linen for the wound, Canby said, "Tia, I do need you to write for me—to my wife. I found a right pretty little thing while I was in training camp first of the war, up in D.C. Her name is Darla. Darla Jacobs. And we got us a fine little boy, a real beauty. Can you tell her that I died thinking of her, loving her, and not to grieve too hard or too long, but raise our boy to be a happy child and a good man. Will you tell her . . . tell her that I died with faith and courage."

"Of course, Canby."

The orderly had arrived with fresh linen. Tia carefully started to remove the old bandage. Her heart seemed to stop in her throat. Half his chest had been blown away; the lung was raw and exposed.

She quickly applied the new, dry bandage.

"Sing to me, Tia. 'Amazing Grace.' I remember when you and your ma used to do that at the piano at Cimarron. Your pa would gaze on you both so proud, and you were just like a pair of nightingales, or Rose Red and Rose White, your ma so blond and you so dark! It was so beautiful, I thought the angels could hear!"

"I'll sing, Canby. You save your breath."

"Miss Tia, there ain't nothing to save it for! I got the one lung left, so might as well speak while I can. Father Raphael is on his way over. Most companies have Episcopal ministers, but here we got lots and lots of Irish fellows. So we've got ourselves a Catholic priest!"

"I'm sure he'll be here soon."

"Sing for me. I think the angels will listen to you, Miss Tia, more than a priest."

She smiled, squeezed his hand, and began to sing, very softly. But as she drew in breath for the second verse, another soldier called out, "Louder, please, miss, for all of us!"

And so she did. And when she had finished the last verse and looked down, Canby was already dead. He had died with a slight curve to his lips, as if he had, indeed, seen the angels coming.

She had seen so many men die. They died the same in Union blue as they did Confederate butternut and gray.

She lowered her head, tears sliding down her cheeks as she held his lifeless hand.

In Dr. Bryer's private quarters, Ian had spread a number of maps over the camp desk, describing the main situation of the war as he had seen it in the last meeting he had attended in D.C. "As far as the situation here, little has changed. I have often given my opinion—that nothing less than a major thrust against the peninsula will work. The people here are tenacious, and those who would declare for the Union are often too afraid of repercussions if they state themselves Federals. To win a major battle, you would need a major army. The blockades, however, are tightening. Colonel Bryer, you're to have a few more weeks in the field, then I'm afraid that our captured wounded and missing must be abandoned. You're to return to St. Augustine, the men will be given light duty there, and then returned to heavier duty with the Army of the Potomac."

"These men have been through a lot," Colonel Bryer said. "It was an even battle, and a bloody one, and these men were wounded by swords, cannon fire, bullets, and bayonets, as in any other battle."

"And so the time spent in St. Augustine will be considered a vacation by many of the soldiers," Ian said.

"I fear the war will go on here as it has—with neither side gaining much in victory, but losing many in death,"

Taylor said. He looked at Ian. "I assume you have new orders for me as well?"

Ian nodded, handing him a leather-bound, waterproofed case. Reading the paper within, Taylor looked up at Ian. "This will be like looking for a needle in a haystack!" he said.

"I know. I admit—I'm glad they gave you the duty, and not me."

"And why do you think they have done so?"

Ian stared at him for a minute. "Because you're Indian," he said flatly. "They will always believe that because of your blood, you know the swamp a little better, you are a little craftier—more able to manage such a duty."

"What is the duty?" Bryer asked curiously. "If I am allowed to know. I have served some time now with Colonel Douglas. I have served with no better man."

Taylor glanced at Bryer, somewhat surprised by the crusty old soldier's dedication to him. "Thank you, sir," he said. "But I'm afraid that the mission is to be confidential. I'll be leaving you in a few days' time."

"Colonel Douglas," he began, "I know my rank and I know my work, but I am a medical man, and not prepared to lead this camp as you have done."

"I had thought I was to be leaving this morning," Ian said, "but a messenger arrived from St. Augustine this morning, asking us to delay bringing in so many units of cavalry along with your sorely wounded men. I will be staying here for a time before taking the companies to St. Augustine. Then I, too, will rejoin the Army of the Potomac, just a little later than I had expected." Ian turned back to the maps again. "On the ninth of March, Lincoln put Ulysses Grant in overall command of the armies. These are the goals: Meade remains head of the army under Grant and is to attack Lee's army, as we have attempted throughout the war. General Butler is to take his forces up the south bank of the James River from Fortress Monroe, Siger is to sweep through the Shenandoah Valley, Sherman is to attack Atlanta and Banks is to ride on and assault Mobile."

"And it will end the war?" Ayers asked.

Taylor let out a grunt. "If it all succeeds."

"Grant doesn't care how many men he kills," Bryer added.

"Ah, but we complained that too many of our generals were overly cautious! Meade should have chased Lee after Gettysburg. This fratricide might have ended by now," Taylor said.

"But do you think we can win soon?" Bryer asked.

Taylor stared over at Ian, then shrugged and pointed to the map. "Renowned Confederate General P. T. Beauregard is in here somewhere—and he'll do his damned best to detour anyone from Richmond. Jubal Early could catch up with the men in the Shenandoah—"

He broke off suddenly, listening. Someone was singing. A plaintive ballad, in a high, clear voice, both sweet and powerful.

"My sister," Ian murmured.

"I know," Taylor said, rising. He slid his despatch into the inner pocket of his frockcoat and started out of Bryer's living quarters. The small tent was not far from the larger one where the colonel and his nurses tended to the wounded they had managed to gather. Since the day was warm, the canvas walls had been rolled up so that the breeze could cool the injured men.

Tia was seated on a camp chair in the middle of the tent. Someone had supplied her with a guitar; she strummed the chords lightly as she sang her song—one popular with both Northern and Southern soldiers, promoting neither side, but ruing the cruelty of death.

She had a rapt audience.

The soldiers with camp cots lay upon them; amputees with bandaged stumps sat on the ground or leaned against trees just outside the enclosure. Nurses and orderlies had halted in their tasks. And even Cecilia had stopped her busy fretting around "her boys" to enjoy the fact that, for once, they seemed to have forgotten their pain.

When Tia finished her song, they applauded.

"Play 'Dixie'!" someone called to her.

Her eyes shot up with surprise as she looked for the speaker.

"Ma'am, it's me, over here. My name's Corporal Hutchins. I was born right smack on the Suwannee River, though I went to school up in New York. I'm still a Southerner—I just don't cotton to the idea of breaking up the Union. So play 'Dixie' for me, if you will. The boys won't mind."

"You could play any danged thing you want, Mrs. Douglas, and we won't mind a bit!" another man called.

And so she sang "Dixie." Then someone asked her that since she was in a Union camp and they had all enjoyed "Dixie," would she mind terribly doing "The Star-Spangled Banner," and she hesitated, but then she sang the song. And when she was done, she handed the guitar back to one of the men and thanked them.

"Don't you worry none about Canby Jacobs, Mrs. Douglas!" the man who had asked for "Dixie" called out to her. "We fellows will put in money from our pay, get him properly embalmed so that he can be returned to that young wife of his!"

"Maybe he wanted to be buried on Florida soil," she said softly.

"He loved Florida, but he loved his wife more."

"Then that will be very kind, sir, if you can see that his body is returned to his wife. Properly put back together."

She started walking through the tent. Taylor was still some distance from her, and he was sure she hadn't seen him yet.

Captain Ayers, leader of the company he had sent out scouting yesterday, suddenly stepped in front of her.

"Mrs. Douglas, hello, how do you do. Excuse me for waylaying you . . . but I could swear that we've met before."

Taylor saw her hesitate; saw her pallor. *Yes, of course, Ayers had seen her yesterday. As Godiva. Leading him from the Rebs—back to their own camp.*

"My brother is with the camp here, sir. Colonel Ian

McKenzie. Perhaps I bear quite a resemblance to him. He and my other brother, Julian, are so much alike they could be mistaken for one another; even the cousins in my family bear a close resemblance to each other."

Ayers was smiling. "Ma'am, you don't look like any man I've ever met; that is certain."

"Perhaps you've been to my father's home, Cimarron."

"No, ma'am, it's not that . . ."

It had gone too far. Taylor strode through the tent of injured, reaching Tia's side. He set an arm around her shoulders. "Ayers!"

"Sir!" Ayers saluted. He was a fine young cavalry captain, steady, brave, and dependable. "Forgive me. I have this uncanny feeling that I have met your wife before."

"Well, Captain Ayers, I agree that she resembles no man—but if you know her brothers and family as I do, it's true, there are features they share, such as the shape of their eyes, the structure of their faces. I am kin to Colonel McKenzie's cousin myself, and I can tell you, that even the Seminole McKenzies bear a striking resemblance to one another."

"Perhaps that is it. Forgive me," Ayers said again. "It's been a pleasure. It is my understanding that you served with Rebel forces in your brother's field hospital. It was kind of you to bring your talents here today."

"I pity all men maimed by this war, sir," Tia said. With his arm around her, Taylor could feel that she was shaking.

"Amen!" Ayers said.

"Captain, we've yet to fully discuss certain events. Tia, my love, if you'll forgive me, I have business with Captain Ayers. I'll not be long."

"Taylor, you must do your duty!" she said, turning to him. Her dark eyes on his were grateful. Her hand, laid against his chest, felt oddly right.

He stared down at her. Had they reached some strange sort of truce? Brought on by the absurdity of a lie turned real?

He caught her hand, smiled, brushed a kiss on her fingertips.

There was a general call of appreciation from the men—hoots and whistles.

"Aye, there, Colonel, you've found yourself a really wild Rebel to win!"

"That I have!" he agreed.

But smiling still, he stepped around her. And his heart seemed to squeeze. Had he won her? No, he had not really begun to do so.

His future with her, like the war, remained to be seen.

Chapter 15

With an oath of impatience, Rhiannon ripped up the fifth letter she had tried to write, gnawed at her lip, and started again.

Dear Mrs. Davis,

My name is Rhiannon McKenzie and I am the wife of Colonel Julian McKenzie, surgeon, Florida militia. I believe that the name McKenzie is familiar to you; my brother-in-law, Ian, was well known to President Davis before the division of the states. Ian was a West Point graduate and serving in the army when President Davis was Secretary of War. Jerome McKenzie, a cousin-in-law, is with the Confederate navy and captains one of the most successful blockade runners of the war. Though I admit to grave antisecession sentiment myself, I have worked with my husband in the field saving the lives of Confederate men. I have seen the tragedies of this war, North and South, and have come to put a great value on all life, yet most of all, on the lives of our children. Madam, I have often heard of the love you bear your own. I am sometimes haunted by dreams and visions, and I fear an accident could befall one of your children. Please, I beg you, heed this warning, and do not think me insane from the depravities of war. I see a child falling from a balcony. I have found that though sometimes my dreams are cruel pictures that I can do nothing to stop, sometimes they are but warnings, and so I beg of you, take care with your children on the balcony of your beautiful house. With all prayers and best wishes for you and yours, I can

*only hope to understand the full burden of all that you
carry with the war.*
        Sincerely, Rhiannon McKenzie

She looked pensively at what she had written this
time. The first lady of the Confederacy might very well
think that she was totally insane, and throw the note
away.

It might never reach her.

She still had to try. The dream was far too haunting
to ignore.

Rhiannon laid her head on the table. No, she could
not prevent all the awful deaths of the war! And still,
knowing that a child could needlessly die . . .

Her own sentiments remained staunchly antisecession-
ist—and antislavery. She was comfortable in her father-
in-law's house.

Alaina, though married to a Union officer, remained
a Rebel at heart.

Could either of them make a trip to Richmond?

How could she, with an infant? How could she risk
her own child? And if Julian knew what she was even
thinking . . .

He would say that he would get the letter through.
And surely, he would. But would it be enough?

Alaina could not go. She had her own two small chil-
dren, and since Christmas . . . well, it seemed likely that
Alaina was going to have a third babe. If Alaina could
get to St. Augustine where her new cousin-in-law, Risa
McKenzie stayed, waiting for some word from
Jerome . . .

There was also Sydney, an ardent Rebel—but married
now and in Washington, D.C.

That left . . .

Tia. She was out there somewhere near St. Augustine.
Assisting Julian in her place. If she could just reach her
sister-in-law . . .

Yes. Tia was perfect. The Southern sister of a Southern surgeon who had tirelessly pledged himself to the
lives of so many. Captured for his Cause, in the South,

fighting for life once again. Tia, the daughter of Jarrett McKenzie, respected and consulted by leaders from both sides.

Who could not be faulted for going to Richmond.

She rose suddenly, quickly. She would give her letter to Jarrett, and ask him for an escort across the state. To join Julian. She had lingered behind her husband long enough. The baby was strong, big, healthy—and she had never felt better. She was longing to see her husband; her in-laws would understand.

Yet as she swung around, she saw that Alaina was standing in the doorway.

"Rhiannon, what are you up to?"

"I'm going to find Julian."

Alaina stared at her for a minute.

"I'm going with you. You're not really looking for Julian, are you?"

"Of course I am. I love my husband."

"I didn't say you didn't," Alaina told her stubbornly. "I'm still going with you!"

But she paled suddenly, her palm going to her stomach. "Excuse me!" she said, and turned to flee to her private quarters.

Rhiannon got her traveling bag from the wardrobe and started to pack.

Alaina appeared back in her doorway. "A Christmas present from *your* husband, I think," Rhiannon said, flashing Alaina a smile.

"I was never so sick before."

"You never had twins before."

"Twins!" Alaina grabbed the door frame.

Rhiannon had to laugh. "I'm sorry; I was teasing. I don't know. But you can't come with me—and I have to go."

"You're not going to try to get to Richmond, are you?"

"No, I'm just going to find someone who can. Without causing trouble, of course."

"Of course," Alaina agreed. "I'll help you pack."

*   *   *

Tia was exhausted. She had meant to leave the oppression of the hospital tent, feeling as if she had done her duty. She had held Canby's hand as he died; she had sung more songs when the other injured men had asked her to continue for them.

And in the midst of it all . . .

Captain Ayers had recognized her. Thank God, he didn't know why he had recognized her. Taylor had come to her defense. Perhaps he'd had to do so. He had his sense of honor. He had married her. She had cast him into the situation, and he had seemed very bitter, but then . . .

When Taylor had left with Ayers, Cecilia came to her side. "We can use more help, if you're willing."

And so Tia had turned back to assist the wounded. Most were very brave, grateful for the water she brought them, the quinine with which she dosed them, the bandages and poultices she carefully applied. It was at the end of a very long day when Cecilia slipped an arm through hers and led her from the hospital tent.

"We'll walk down to the stream. It's cool and beautiful there. This is a wonderful place, I think! With pines and ponds and a river and little brooks everywhere! I understand why people come here. I had never thought in a hundred years I would want to come to such a new and *uncivilized* place at this, yet I love it!"

"Where are you from?"

"Massachusetts. And it's very, very cold there!"

The soldiers smiled or nodded as the two women walked through the camp. Tia was so accustomed to running that she had to remind herself that no one was after her.

The pines were shadowed as the sun fell. Cecilia knew exactly where she was heading; along a well-trampled trail that must have been used often by the people in the camp. It led to one of the ponds in the pine forest, fresh spring water that was cool and delightfully fresh. She doused her face with it, drank deeply, and sat back on the embankment, feeling the cool spring air wash over her.

"It's wonderful to have you here," Cecilia said, leaning back beside her. "You're so very good."

"I admit to thinking that you are quite incredibly competent, organized, and efficient yourself!" Tia said.

"I am," Cecilia said, laughing.

"You're also well supplied with bandages, quinine, poultices, morphine, laudanum . . ."

"Yes, we're lucky in that."

"Lucky in many way," she said. "Like my own father, yours is willing to risk himself to help others."

"Oh, my father is wonderful. I remember, at the beginning of the war, when I wanted to help him—as I always had before!—I was given such a miserable time by some of the good society matrons. Nursing was not ladylike, so they said. I shouldn't see the soldiers, touch the soldiers—"

"Really?" Tia asked, startled to realize that someone who seemed as serene, feminine, and dignified as Cecilia Ayers could have possibly faced the same censure she had known. "I thought women were persecuted only in the South."

"No, I think we have all been vilified for wanting to be sensible and help. Even though I am a doctor's daughter, I have had my share of criticism. Oh, it was inevitable that women would be needed to help, and when Dorothea Dix was appointed superintendent of women nurses, *some* women were even welcome." She smiled, her dimples showing. "But not me! She said that I was too young and too pretty to work in a hospital in Washington, and she wouldn't have me. Her nurses had to be thirty and plain—no young ladies with romantic notions were going to work with her! So I turned to Father, and although he really hadn't wanted me on the field at that time, he said that no one could tell him who could or could not help him there, so I have been on the field with him ever since. I *hope* that by now I am good."

"I keep hoping that I'm good, too," Tia said. "When I started with my brother, our skirmishes were small, and we could deal with our injured. Then we had offshore battles, and bombardments, and bigger skirmishes.

I'll never forget the first time we had a large number of injured. Julian told me to wash a soldier's face. The poor fellow was even worse than my friend Canby today—a ball had torn away part of his nose and both eyes. I thought I'd be sick. I somehow managed to clean his face, but then I needed air. Julian had had to amputate a number of limbs, and I tripped over them trying to leave the tent. I fell right into the pile of arms and legs. But I knew then that if I gave way, I'd probably panic and run and never come back. So I stood up, decided I didn't need the air as much as the injured needed me— and I went back. There is still so much that is so painful, so melancholy, and yet now, when I see men shattered by their injuries, there is not much that I flinch from anymore. So many 'niceties' seem nothing more than silly to me."

Cecilia nodded in understanding. "You can't let petty things concern you—I learned that long ago. To be honest, in a way, I did not blame Dragon Six—that is what many of her nurses call her! Some women cannot take the horrors they see. And some do think that they will find romance—not wounds that exude pus and blood and stumps on which one must change bandages without causing arteries to bleed! Some young ladies thought they would find officers to marry—not enlisted men with wives and children poor and dying and needing real help!"

"On both sides, it's the same," Tia murmured.

Cecilia smiled. "Well, I have been in the war all these years, and I am truly afraid that I may end up an old maid! So I have decided what I will do when the war is over."

"What is that?"

"I'm going to medical school. I'm going to be a doctor myself. Father says it's a fine idea. There's a woman named Elizabeth Blackwell who is the first of our sex, they say, to have earned a medical degree, and she was one of the very first to realize that we would need medical supplies and all manner of things for our troops—

including things as simple as socks! There are other women doctors now, not many, but I intend to be one."

"You should do it. If you have the desire, yes, you should!" Tia applauded.

Cecilia stood. "Thank you for your encouragement. But now I must get back to my father. Don't get up— you look relaxed there at last by the water. Thank you also for what you have done for our men, be they your enemies."

Tia smiled at her. "Thank *you*—for trusting me."

"I think you are a friend, a dear friend," Cecilia told her, and turning, she walked away, back through the pines.

Tia sat awhile longer, staring at the cool water, feeling the soft breeze that wafted through the pines. She closed her eyes, realizing how tired she was.

Then her eyes flew open. She had to go back now. She had become so involved with the men, she had forgotten that Ian would be leaving.

She leapt to her feet, spun around—and froze. Taylor was there, had been there, she realized. Leaning against a pine, watching her.

"I wasn't trying to escape anything," she murmured defensively.

"I wasn't accusing you of trying to escape any*thing*. If you were trying to escape, I assume it would be an any*one*. Me."

"But I wasn't—"

"I didn't say you were."

He continued to watch her, still leaning casually against the pine.

"I am really well aware that, as you said, you have done me a tremendous service."

"Nothing so deep and grave that I cannot endure," he said lightly. "I apologize if I caused you a tremendous amount of guilt."

"Well . . . I . . . you made it quite plain how you feel about marriage."

She backed away awkwardly as he left the pine and came toward her.

"Actually," he said, a slight smile on his features, "you have somewhat managed to change my mind."

"I'm glad it's not the torment you expected."

"And what is it to you?" he inquired. He'd reached her. She couldn't go anywhere else or she'd be backing into the water.

She hesitated, meeting his eyes. "Not torment."

"That's right. You don't dislike me."

"And I honestly wasn't running."

"I'm glad. I grow wearing of dragging you about."

Her eyes fell. "I need to see my brother. If he's still here, if I haven't missed him. I can't believe I became so involved I forgot that I might not have much time with him before—"

"He isn't leaving anytime soon."

"No?" she inquired, uneasy. He gazed at her in a strange way, not angry, not mocking.

She was surprised when he looked away for a moment, then his eyes were back on hers. "No, he will be with the camp several days here, I believe, then he'll be going in to St. Augustine."

"Oh!" she said, pleased. If she was going to live with the enemy, at least her brother would be among their number.

"Yes," he said, and his voice had a husky and slightly harsh quality to it. "Yes, you'll be with your brother. For a while, at least. So there is no need to hurry to him now."

She felt the breeze again, touching her cheeks. They felt very warm. This was so strange. The night before had been a tempest of emotions, tangled lies, a swiftness of events. But now, seconds stretched out as he stared at her. Dusk turned darker. Though the sky still remained somewhat blue, the moon began to appear as a half-crown about the treetops.

"You managed quite well today."

"Did you think I would falter?"

"You didn't turn away from your enemy."

"We treated Union injured at Olustee Station."

"Of course . . . as we treated Rebs."

She lowered her head. "An old friend of mine was here."

"An old Yankee friend?"

She nodded. "He died."

"You comforted him?"

She nodded. "His . . . lung was blown away. And half his face." She was feeling very uncertain, afraid she was going to cry.

"He talked about my father . . . Cimarron. Times that are now long gone by . . ."

She suddenly covered her face with her hands. And she was glad to feel him pull her into his arms as tears began sliding down her cheeks.

"It's all right, Tia."

"It wasn't all right. He had a wife and a child to live for, and he was so terribly hurt—you could see what remained of his lung. It was amazing he lived so long."

"Sh . . ." he said softly, easing back down to the pine embankment with her. He held her against him, rocking slowly. "Tia, you have done this so long! It's the bitter truth of the war—men die, and they do not do so prettily."

"But his wife, his poor young wife—"

"There are thousands of poor young wives out there. Thousands of young widows who may live another fifty years or so, and who will live those years full of bitterness and regret."

"Widows and . . ." She broke off suddenly, remembering the picture her mother had given him at Christmas. The picture of Abby.

"Oh!" she murmured suddenly. "I'm so sorry, really, I forgot . . ."

Instantly, she felt him stiffen. His arms did not seem to hold her so closely. *He hadn't wanted to marry. She wasn't his real wife; his real wife lay dead. She was the Rebel liar who had cast a shadow upon his honor, and forced his hand.*

"It's all right," he said.

"How can it be?" she whispered, lifting her damp

cheeks to seek out his eyes. "I heard that she was shot, that she died in your arms—"

"It's all right," he said again. "If you don't mind, it's a painful memory, one I don't care to relive."

"But—"

He suddenly set her from him, rising. "I believe that Ian is in his tent. One has been set up for him not far from mine. He is probably anxious to see you as well."

She was embarrassed to realize that she had been dismissed. Cleanly, clearly dismissed.

"Oh, course," she murmured coolly. "Thank you. I'll find my brother."

He didn't say anything. She rose, but he didn't even seem to notice. He was watching the water.

She walked back through the pines.

The camp was busy with dinner preparations. Sergeant Henson waved at her. She waved back, then seeing the large, newly erected tent near Taylor's, she walked toward it with a purpose. "Ian?" she called.

"Tia!" he replied from within, then appeared at the flap. "Come in!"

She did so. His home away from home already bore marks of Ian. A locket with Alaina's likeness and a tendril of hair, a common piece of jewelry, especially for a soldier, lay on his camp desk. Letters lay strewn next to it, along with the manual he was reading, a text on gunshot wounds. His frockcoat hung on his folding chair, and his shaving paraphernalia had been set up at a standing mirror.

"Sit!"

He indicated the foot of the cot. She sat there, and he took the folding chair himself.

"I was so afraid I'd missed you," Tia told him. "The day was strange, passing by so quickly. I'm glad you're still here."

"I never would have left without saying goodbye," he assured her. "And making certain that you were happy, well cared for. And that you understand what you've done."

"What I've done?" she echoed.

Ian was quiet for moment, then he rose and went to the camp desk and fingered the locket carrying the likeness of his wife. "Tia, you've married a very well known Union cavalry officer, renowned for his abilities to find anyone, anywhere, anytime. And for his ability to shoot the wings off a fly at a hundred feet."

"Well," she breathed. "Thank God I did not marry an inept cavalry officer!"

Her brother turned toward her, apparently seeing the attempted humor in her words. "You have gone from working in a Rebel camp—to working in a Yankee camp."

She lifted a hand in a weak gesture. "The men bleed the same."

"And do you treat them the same?"

"Of course! Why would I be any different from Julian or Brent? I worked well today with your Yankees, Ian. Very well. You may ask Miss Bryer—or the men, for that matter."

He came to the bed, sitting down beside her, searching out her eyes and staring at her very sternly. "Tia, I'm sorry, I can't help but find this very suspicious."

Her throat tightened. "Why?"

"You didn't come here to get into Taylor's papers, did you?"

"No!" she denied heatedly, jumping to her feet.

"You're certain?"

"Ian," she said, frowning at him, "it never occurred to me that Taylor would carry papers that meant anything to me. I was tending to wounded Rebel soldiers throughout the war—*not* attending high-level strategy meetings!"

"The point I'm making is this: You have changed your life. Your own side will mistrust you for the Yank you have married; the Yanks will mistrust you for what you have been in the past."

"I've no interest in the opinions of others."

"You should. Opinions make people dangerous."

"I did not marry Taylor to pry into Yankee secrets,"

she said, agitated. "Oh, Ian, I don't want to argue with you."

"I don't want to argue either, Tia. I just want you to understand that there is no turning back."

"I don't want to run anywhere. I served well here today. I didn't even rifle through the pockets of the dead or dying!" she said bitterly. "Though some of *your* men are butchers who would kill helpless Rebels."

"What?"

She paused, horrified at what she had said. How could she explain to Ian that she had heard the men in the woods and that was why she had wound up running here to Taylor?

"Nothing."

"What did you say, Tia? That wasn't nothing!"

"All right. I think that some of your men would just as soon kill an injured Reb as touch him!" she said.

"And why do you think that?"

"I-I heard them talking today." She wished fervently that she wasn't going to have to fall into another length of lies.

Last time she had lied to him, her world had made a total inversion.

"Whom did you hear talking?"

"Just—just a group of the men. By the hospital tent."

"If you see these men again," he said sharply, "show me who they are, and we'll find out the truth of the matter."

"You'll find out the truth? How can you? You're leaving."

"No, the despatches gave different orders."

"But . . . I'm not sure that Taylor will believe this either, and—"

"I will take care of it."

She frowned. "But if Taylor is in full command—"

"Taylor will be—" Ian broke off. "He didn't tell you?"

"No—he didn't tell me! Tell me what?"

"He's been ordered out on special assignment. I'll take his place until these troops return to St. Augustine."

"He's been ordered—out?"

"I'm very sorry. I wish they had given me the assignment. As it is . . . well, you'll have to stay in St. Augustine. Risa is there. She'll be glad to have you with her."

She was surprised at the way her stomach wretched. *He was leaving; Taylor was leaving.*

And he hadn't even thought to tell her.

She shook her head, feeling her fingers clench into fists at her side. "I'll go back to Julian then. It's insane for me to live among the enemy if Taylor isn't with me. I'll—"

She was interrupted by the sound of a deep voice at the entrance to the tent. "You'll go to St. Augustine, as Ian said!"

She leapt up, startled to see that Taylor had come quietly into the tent. And had issued his command.

"I'm sorry, Taylor," Ian said. "I didn't realize you hadn't told her, that she didn't know."

"It doesn't matter. She knows now," Taylor said. "What does matter, Tia, is that you will not return to *your old ways!*"

"*I* will not return to my old ways!" Tia repeated angrily. And suddenly it all irritated her, not just the war, but the world itself seemed unfair. "And Alaina must watch her step as well, and Cecilia shouldn't work in a hospital becase she isn't homely enough! This is all so absurd and bizarre! Oh, the hell with you both!" With angry force, she slipped beneath the tent flap, exiting in a sudden passion.

"She's really upset," she heard her brother say. "I understand, of course. She didn't realize that you were leaving. I honestly thought you'd had time to tell her."

"It's all right," Taylor replied. "Let her go. There is no way out of it."

Let her go! he'd said.

So she went.

With long, angry strides, she walked away from her brother's quarters. She headed straight back for the pines, glad of the welcoming darkness that was beginning to fall around her. She stood before the cool pond beneath the pines.

My horse! she thought. *Where is my horse? If only I had her—*

She nearly screamed with surprise when a hand landed on her shoulder. Instinctively, she jerked free, backing away in a circle.

Taylor. Damn him. Damn him for his ability to move like a panther in the pines. Too quick, too swift, too silent. Too . . .

She hadn't thought that he would come.

"What the hell are you doing?"

"I am walking through the pines. What does it look like I'm doing?"

"Trying to find a way out of the pines," he said flatly.

"Oh, really? Who will chase me once you're gone? What difference does it really make? You said—*let her go*. I heard you."

He folded his arms over his chest. "So just where was it you thought you were going?"

She crossed her arms over her chest and stared back at him. "Just where was it that you meant I should go?"

"Back to our tent."

"*Our* tent? How generous you've suddenly become. Our tent. A Yankee tent. Thank you—I don't want part ownership in a Union tent."

"Tia, I don't have much time. I'm not going to spend it arguing with you."

"Good. Save yourself any aggravation. Don't spend the time with me at all."

"Tia, walk back, or I'll take you myself."

She stood tall and stiffly, staring at him. And then she was absolutely amazed at her own language when she told him what he should do with himself, and she didn't even understand herself, didn't know why she felt so angry and so much like crying, all at the same time.

"All right. That's it. I've had it."

"You've had it?" she repeated. "*I've* had it!"

"Run, then. Go on, run."

"What the hell is this game you're playing now? Quit

that, or I swear I shall slug you right back, and I have
a very good right hook, I grew up with two brothers. I
didn't come here to run, you fool. I never intended to
run—"

"Oh, yes, you did. You very much so wanted to run.
So go on. Do it. Go. Let me give you a little help . . ."

He shoved her shoulder. Outraged and feeling a
strange trickle of real fear down her spine, she backed
away slowly.

"Do it!"

His fingers were knotted into fists, and she was suddenly certain he intended her real violence.

She turned and ran. She was right on the edge of the
pond and she stepped into the shallows. The water flew
at the impetus of her flight, it turned to a shower, and
she felt it as it catapulted up around her and fell back
in huge splatters.

Stupid! she charged herself. He had goaded her into
this. She was encumbered by her skirts, growing heavier
in the water.

But she couldn't stop now. He was behind her.

Oh, this was insane. Madness.

And yet she ran. She was swift and fleet, and she knew
it, but she had chosen the wrong path, and she was
quickly bogged down.

She heard him behind her and sped forward then suddenly spun back on him. He was there, just feet away,
but he stopped as well, calculating the distance—planning his pounce.

She wondered if she could outswim him.

Not with a heavy, soaking skirt . . .

But she was wearing her pantalettes.

She slipped out of her shoes then reached behind her,
keeping her eyes on him. She found the buttons on the
skirt—and shed it. His brow shot up with amazement.

"Ah, my love. When in danger—strip?"

"When cornered, use whatever means are available to
elude the *enemy*!"

The skirt gone, she plunged into the water.

And she was very, very good. She'd spent a lifetime

in the water, in the rivers, in the bay, in fresh springs, in salt water.

But so had he.

The far side of the pond stretched before her. She realized, far too late, that he probably let her reach the shoreline first.

When she rose, she saw that he had stripped off his frockcoat, shirt, and boots, and was coming behind her. He didn't even seem hurried. Bronzed shoulders were knotted and tight fingers remained clenched into fists at his side. He didn't run; he walked with steady purpose and menace.

She swore and turned to run again. Then she felt him. A touch of energy and heat in the air at her back, a sound like the wind . . .

And he caught her by the flying length of her hair . . .

Chapter 16

S he cried out. He released the tangle of her hair caught in her hands, but his iron grip wound around her upper arm.

He swung her around and she briefly felt the barely suppressed force of his anger. She cried out again to no avail; they crashed down into the shallows together. The pond erupted. The water cascaded around them. He lay atop her, half in the water, half out, and she shivered. She was soaked, and suddenly cold, as she hadn't been before, as she hadn't been when moving.

He's gone mad, she thought, *totally insane,* and she might die right there and then at his mercy. He seemed a misplaced Othello, his length atop her in the ever-darkening chill of the night. The sun hovered barely upon the horizon; the moon was rising. The glitter of his eyes seemed terrifying in the lengthening shadows.

She closed her eyes, gritting her teeth, rigid, yet shaking, waiting. His voice was as tense as the whipcord length of his sinewed body, deep, harsh.

"You can never run so far or so fast that I will not find you," he warned her. "You should know that now. Wherever you go, I will know. Wherever you might be, I will come for you. You have cast us upon this trail; this is your lie come true. So this is your game, but now, there are new rules in the game, and you'll abide by the rules, my love. Do you understand?"

"Whose rules?"

"My rules!"

"And therein lies all my argument!"

"You must understand—"

"I understand that you will not be here, that you are going on a quest for the enemy—your enemy, not mine—and I am suddenly expected to live among the enemy—my enemy, not yours! The Rebel camp is very close. I can find it. I am almost as good as my brothers in the woods."

"You'll go to St. Augustine!"

She shook her head, feeling tears form in her eyes. "Why can't you understand?" she asked him.

"Why can't *you* understand? You brought this about, but I have married you, Tia."

"A paper commitment which means nothing to you!" she reminded him.

Something passed within his eyes; she didn't know what. "My wife doesn't spy on Union soldiers, strip naked, and lead them astray."

"But it's all right for you to trap or kill Rebel soldiers. To spy on them, scout them out—"

"I'm not off to murder any soldiers!" he interrupted harshly.

"Oh? Are you planning on taking your wife with you?" she inquired.

Again, a shadow over the angry gold of his eyes. And his face was suddenly nearer hers; his thumbs moved over her cheeks. "My love, I dare not!"

"Then understand that I must return to Julian—"

"No."

"I'm not asking your permission! I'm telling you what I must do."

"There are some cells available at Fort Marion," he told her.

"What?"

"The castillo. That beautiful old Spanish fort in St. Augustine, now housing Union men! There are cells in it, I'm sure you know. James McKenzie was imprisoned there once with other savages—or *half*-savages."

He took her face between his hands. And he lowered his head even closer to hers. She felt the water wash up on the shore around her, shivered, and was then warmed. His lips came down upon hers, passionate and hard. Her face lay imprisoned within the walls of her hands. His very passion forced her lips to give way to his; the hot sweetness of his assault seemed to permeate swiftly within her. The depth of his tongue seemed to reach to unexplored places, newly discovered. The deep searing stroke of his kiss elicited fire; she had wanted to touch him—now she yearned, itched, ached to feel more.

Pinned to the embankment, she felt a rush of cold, a rush of hot. The pond against the lightning texture of his body, the air against the inferno of his kiss. She briefly recalled that the blouse she wore was borrowed; then it didn't matter because he was so determined to free her from it, and quickly. The thought touched her mind as well that this did not seem real, possible, to want someone so much, to feel such raging hunger, when she had so recently learned what such a hunger could be like to be appeased. She murmured just one protest. A sound in her throat against the force of his kiss. But he didn't seem to hear. His mouth remained upon hers, lifted, returned, touched, drank, penetrated . . . all while his fingers found buttons, ties, and ribbons. She shivered in the air, against the water, writhed when his fingers covered her breasts, when his mouth opened wetly over her nipple, that dampness so hot, so wickedly hot, where the other had been so cold . . .

His hand slid between her legs, pressing them apart. She felt his fingers there, probing. Felt a burst of sweetness erupt, a fire between her legs. Still he kissed her lips, then her breasts. His thumb moved deeply within her. She writhed, arched, longed to escape, longed for more. Even where the air touched her now, the sensation seemed erotic. He stroked mercilessly within her. Touched, stroked, excited. She had longed so for his touch. Her hands moved wildly over his shoulders. Down along his spine.

He shifted, tore at his trousers. Pressed her deeper and deeper into the embankment, then he was within her, hot, slick, vital, moving like a thunder in the earth, drawing her into the fever of his tempest. They seemed to burn at a million degrees, move more swiftly than the winds of a storm, fly higher than the sky. It was a fever seized and ignited, then burned with an energy of passion born of fury. She lost all thought of past and future, even of the present, for the damp ground did not matter, the pond did not matter, nor the onslaught of night, the concept of intrusion. She simply wanted him, wanted to feel every sensation of him within her, every pulse, every thrust, and each escalating her higher, steering her toward the ecstasy that, once tasted, became ever sweeter. Elusive, so barely known, yet awakened with the scent of his flesh, the feel of his kiss, a brush of her fingertips against the sleek bronze texture of his skin. And culminated with this so very intimate feel of him inside her, the length of him flush against her, lips, hands, sex . . .

She felt the jack-knifing of his body as he climaxed. The warmth filled her, permeating her, erotic and sweet, creating the same sweet lightning within her. Bursting sweet, erasing the world, the war, the embankment, the night . . .

So wonderful, so good. Almost a taste of death, and surely, almost a glimpse of heaven. With her eyes closed, she could see the velvet of the night, the bursting of the stars. There was a plain upon which she drifted, and she stayed there . . . stayed, not wanting to come down. And yet, at first, when she did, she did not mind so much, for she still felt him with her, in her, reposed, not yet withdrawing. She loved the feel of his body still pressed to hers, the intimacy of his arms around her, the scent of him, the way his arms remained around her . . .

Then she felt the water. Cold now. Each little lap of it against her seemed to chill her more. A night wind was coming indeed; the breeze picked up with every passing second. He seemed not to notice the cold until she began to shiver. He withdrew at last, rising, while she drew into herself. He adjusted his trousers and collected the damp clothing he had strewn about, then he came to her, reaching down a hand to her. She didn't accept it at first, but she took her wet pantalettes from him. Shivering violently now, she stepped into them, then he helped her into the corset, his fingers working the ties where hers most certainly could not, and then buttons of her blouse as she donned that wet piece of attire as well. Yet, when she was dressed in her sodden clothing, she found out that she could soon get wetter.

"It's shortest and safest to return the way we came."

"Safest?"

"There may be pickets around the opposite shore, but your skirt and my frockcoat are there. We need to swim back."

She nodded, starting out. She was still shivering. She felt him at her side and she knew that she would never escape him on land—or water.

He didn't know that she really had no desire to escape him, but it was best that he not learn such details.

She reached the shore from where she had begun her reckless plunge, yet as she hovered in the water, too cold now to exit, she wondered if he had not purposely baited her. Perhaps neither of them had known it; they had achieved the outcome they'd desired.

"You're not going to get any warmer remaining in the water," he told her, taking her hand, helping her to her feet. She stumbled, having to cling to him as she rose.

He had her skirt. It was thoroughly soaked, yet she put it back on—the easiest way to return to camp. Which was what she wanted to do quickly now. She was numb with cold, her borrowed clothing as drenched and heavy as the midnight mass of hair spilling down the length of her back.

His frockcoat was dry; he slipped it over her shoulders, then collected her shoes and his boots and shirt. With an arm around her, he started leading her through the trees.

"There is a faster way," she told him.

"Oh?"

"The way I came yesterday."

"Lead on."

"You know where it is—you followed me last night."

"Um, I had forgotten." He turned, leading her along the twisting, slender trail through the pines that was scarcely a trail at all. They emerged from the trees at the rear of his tent, hurried across the few feet from the edge of the pines to the tent, and crawled beneath the canvas. A kerosene lamp had been set on his desk and lit, filling the tent with a shadowy yellow light.

He dropped their footwear and his shirt by the trunk, then turned to her.

She was still shaking. He took his frockcoat from her shoulders and ordered, "Get out of those things now."

She felt too cold to move. She wanted to protest, just for the sake of argument. She didn't. She just stood there, and he returned to her, spinning her around to work at the tiny wet buttons and ties. When her clothing fell to her feet, he cast a blanket around her, collected the wet things, and started out of the tent.

"Taylor!" she murmured, pulling the blanket tightly around her.

"What?"

"What—what will you say?"

"That your clothing is wet."

Her cheeks burned. "But—"

"No one will ask questions," he said, then left the tent.

She hugged the blanket tighter, sitting on the cot, trying to get warm. He returned within minutes, bringing with him a small soldier's-issue pot filled with something that smelled delicious and steamed invitingly. "Henson's famous chicken soup," he said, offering her the pot.

She accepted it, glad of the warmth that thawed her fingers first, then filled her inside as she swallowed down some of the contents. It was freshly made.

"Henson's been stealing Southern chickens again, so it seems!" he said with mock concern.

She ignored the bait of his comment and asked, "What about you?"

"I ate earlier with the men."

She didn't argue. She was starving, and Henson's stew—be it made with stolen chickens or not—was delicious.

He watched her for a moment, then turned away, left

the tent, and returned with two cups of coffee. She had finished the soup; he took the pot from her, exchanged it for the coffee.

She drank the coffee as well. She almost felt warm.

He took the cup from her, but she stood, holding the blanket around her, moving away from the bed. She heard him peel away his damp trousers, then lift the glass and blow out the lamp.

She kept her distance from him, standing in the darkness.

She heard him crawl into the camp bed, and then a moment later, sigh.

"Come to bed, Tia."

"When are you leaving?"

"Soon."

"I'm not tired."

"Then come for the warmth."

"I'm no longer cold."

"Get in here then, to be eased."

"I'm not in any pain."

"You will be—damn it! I don't have much time; I refuse to spend it alone. Come to bed."

She walked slowly toward the camp bed. With his hawklike vision, he saw clearly while she was blinded by the darkness. He was up when she came, drawing her down beside him, keeping the blanket around her, drawing her close to warm her. She felt his hands, his touch, the length of him, something wonderful about being with him. She wanted to sleep beside him, awake beside him.

But he did not intend to be there long.

Yet she was surprised to hear him whisper, "Tia, do you think I *want* to go?"

She turned against him, burrowing her face against his chest, breathing in the memory of him. His hand smoothed her hair; she inched closer. And then, in a few minutes, she heard his breath quicken, and she knew that she had been seducing him, her knuckles running against his chest, then the hardness of his belly, grazing her sex . . . just barely, again and again. A hint, a tease . . .

Soon, she was in his arms again, and he made love very slowly then, so, so slowly, and she didn't even know just how thoroughly she had been seduced in return until she found him kissing her suddenly to silence the cry that was escaping her . . .

Then the reality of night was with her again. The night, the darkness, the camp beyond the intimacy of the Yankee tent. And again he repeated to her, "There is nothing I want less than to go."

"Then don't go."

"I must."

"You are *ordered*."

"Because I believe in what I'm doing."

"And so do I," she whispered passionately. "So do I!"

Then she wished that she had not said the words, for she realized that though he didn't answer her, and though he held her, he lay there awake. Thinking that she did believe in what she was doing. And that made her dangerous.

"Taylor, if I swear to you—"

"You've lied too many times!"

"But—"

"You'll go to St. Augustine. And you'll be there when I come for you."

"Good morning."

One very strange fact of marriage seemed to be that she awoke far more tired than she had been when she went to bed. Yet, this morning, the voice that greeted Tia was a startling one. She had barely opened her eyes, but at the sound of these words, they flew open. Gathering her covers around her, she twisted, and to her amazement she saw Risa, her cousin Jerome's wife, seated comfortably in Taylor's camp chair before his folding desk. She looked wonderful—fresh, beautiful, relaxed, out of place and time in the camp, elegant and composed. Her auburn hair was neatly bound at her nape; her eyes, green as the pine forests, were bright and amused. Risa was the daughter of Union General Magee; once, before the war, she had very nearly married Ian. The war made for strange bedfellows, most certainly, because Ian had married Alaina, an absolute paragon of the virtues of the old South, and Risa, who was very nearly a walking, breathing image of the "Battle Hymn of the Republic," had married Jerome—a blockade runner still doing just that, running circles around the Union navy.

"Risa!"

"Tia McKenzie—excuse me, Douglas. My, my, what will this war come to next!" Risa teased.

Tia longed to hop up and hug her cousin-in-law; but in her state of undress, she did not. Risa looked at the book she had been reading. "I admit, I should have been reading *Shoals and Sandbars off the Florida Coast*! she told Tia. "But your husband does have some wonderful literature here, beautifully bound Shakespeare, Bacon, Defoe . . . I wonder if he ever has the time to read for pleasure, though I've heard that many of the men most responsible for the war do find that reading is what allows them to keep their sanity."

"Risa, I'm so pleased to see you . . . but what . . ." Tia began, and then her voice trailed away. She drew the covers to her chest and sat up. "I was about to ask you what you're doing here, but I think I know. Either my brother or my husband sent for you—to keep me under control."

Risa smiled. "Something like that. An escort party arrived for me yesterday. I felt a wee bit guilty myself, leaving a new doctor in St. Augustine with many wounded coming in. But there are a number of male military nurses there to help him at the moment, what with the situation at Olustee Station being recent and so many men from the army still in the state . . ." She broke off, shrugging. "Were you in some kind of trouble?"

"Who sent for you, Taylor or Ian?" Tia asked, rather than reply to the question.

Risa hesitated, but then apparently decided to tell her the truth. "Taylor sent for me. Ian knew about it, but I don't think he was overly concerned. He still sees you as his little sister, and despite your wrong-headed opinions, he assumes you will listen to him. He can't begin to imagine that you would disobey him or your new husband if what they asked was surely for your own safety."

Tia looked away for a moment. "Then, I'm sorry to say it, but my brother is a fool, and he should have learned better dealing with his own wife!"

"But his wife didn't love him at first, did she?" Risa reminded her. "While now . . . they share everything. And he assumes, of course, that you love him."

"I love both my brothers, and they know it. I've been with Julian through the majority of the war and Ian has known it."

"But that was before you married a Federal officer, wasn't it? And then again, Ian has no idea what else you may be doing."

Tia stared at Risa again. "Are you implying—"

Risa leaned toward her. "Yes. I'll tell you exactly what I'm implying. There's a rumor out about a new Southern spy, the likes of whom rival Belle Boyd and Rose Greenhow."

"Oh, that's preposterous."

"If you know nothing about it, how can you deny the rumors so quickly?"

"What did Taylor tell you?"

"Taylor told me nothing. I simply know the war rather well—and I know you."

"I never spied on anyone," Tia said angrily.

"Rumor does have a tendency to become exaggerated," Risa agreed. "You don't have to answer me, but I'll tell you exactly why I'm here. I think that you are this 'Godiva' they talk about—I admit, I've never met anyone else with the hair to create such a disguise, and I'm amazed more people haven't figured it out."

"Now that's ridiculous! Many, many women have very long hair."

"Very long, sleek, raven-black hair, and the form and figure of a Circe! And it has to be someone very, very familiar with the area. Then, I've actually had Godiva described to me. You see, I've met a few of the men led astray by Godiva.''

"Risa, I never—''

She broke off, alarmed by the sudden sound of gunfire and a barrage of shouts. Her eyes met Risa's. Risa, she saw, was as startled as she by the commotion.

"My God, what—''

Tia leapt up in alarm, dragging the covers with her like a cloak. Both Taylor and her brother were out there. She had to find out what had happened.

"Tia, wait—you don't go running out when you hear gunfire!'' Risa, always the general's daughter, called. But Tia was already heading out, her heart in her throat. Men were running everywhere. Risa caught hold of her.

"You can't run out like this! At least get dressed.''

Torn, Tia wasted several precious seconds thinking that someone may lie dying while she was taking the time for concessions to society. She was totally encompassed in the covers.

"This might not even involve Taylor or Ian!'' Risa insisted.

"But it does. I know it. Help me! I haven't anything—''

"Tia, but you do. I brought you all kinds of clothing.''

"Then give me something quickly, please!'' Tia said.

"All right. I'll help.''

Tia stepped back into the tent. Risa was as good as her word, ready with a cotton print day dress to slip right over Tia's shoulders as she let the covers fall.

Tia muttered a quick "Thank you,'' eschewed the concept of looking for shoes, and went tearing outside. By then she could see that the men were gathering around a large circle by the hospital tent. She wedged her way into the circle, felt hands upon her shoulders, and knew that Risa was there. She became aware that there was a pileup of men in the center of the circle. All around the circumference, the men were cheering—and throwing out suggestions.

"What's going on?''

"Fight—big fight!'' one of the soldiers said cheerfully,

then he looked at her. "Oh! Mrs. Douglas, it's . . .
um . . ."

Taylor.

Taylor was in the midst of it all. As she watched, she
saw that there were actually three other men in the circle, and that the three of them were coming at him. One
of the men she recognized. Private Long. The soldier
who had talked about killing Rebel injured.

Taylor was in his navy trousers and cavalry boots; his
jacket and shirt—and weapons—were gone.

"There are three of them against him!" she said indignantly. "There were shots . . . and now this! What's
going on?"

The soldier looked at her again uncomfortably.

"There was an incident . . . with some Rebs," he said
uncomfortably.

"Get him, Colonel, get him!" someone cried, and the
soldier turned from her again. "That's it, Colonel, damn,
sir, but that's a good right hook."

Tia saw her brother then, on the opposite side of the
circle. She tried to break through the men.

"Ma'am, you mustn't interfere now," one soldier said
politely, stopping her.

She tried to break in elsewhere. A graying sergeant
stopped her. "Why, Mrs. Douglas, we couldn't let no
harm come to you, ma'am!"

"Tia, calm down, wait!" Risa called to her.

"They'll kill him! And Ian is just standing there!" Tia
said indignantly, escaping Risa's touch upon her arm.

Wrenching furiously from the next man who tried to
stop her, she made it around the circle to where Ian
stood. At that point, one of the men lay on the ground.
Two of them were making a calculated and coordinated
running leap for her husband.

"Ian! What's happening? Stop this! My God—"

She tried to rush past her brother, but there was no
way to do so. He grabbed her back, not in the least
afraid of using force with her, as any other man might
have been.

"Stop, Tia. Stop here, let it go."

"Let it go! He'll be pummeled—"

"He chose this."

"He chose this! But he'll be killed!"

"Tia, have faith. He knows his business."

Shouts were going out, calls, cheers, jeers.

"Ian . . ."

The men were down in the dirt on Taylor. She struggled with Ian, staring helplessly as fists and earth flew. Then, she was startled when the two soldiers on Taylor went flying. They literally seemed to soar, up and away from him, and into the dirt.

Then Taylor was standing.

Hands on his hips, he looked at the downed men. His torso was muddied; there was a long scrape down his chest. His cheeks bore evidence of the brawl as well. But the three men who had attacked him lay in the dirt without moving. For a moment, Tia thought they were dead. Astounded and confused, she listened to the roar of the men, congratulating their colonel. She could still feel Ian's hands on her shoulders.

She twisted in her brother's hold, anxious to see his face. "What happened?"

"What you wanted, I think."

"What are you talking about?"

Ian's cobalt eyes fell on hers. "They came across some Rebs, wounded at Olustee or during the skirmishing as we were chased back toward the coast."

"And?" she breathed.

"One of them has nearly died."

"Oh?" Her heart seemed to be in her throat. "You said I should be glad for this. Is the Rebel someone we know?"

"Not an old family friend, but if he is an acquaintance of yours, I don't know." He sighed, shaking his head. "We've been on an opposite side for years now. I don't know who you know, Tia," he reminded her.

"But—there was a fight in a Yankee camp over a Rebel prisoner dying?" She couldn't help sounding skeptical. There had to be enough concern here over their own dying men.

Ian's eyes fell sharply upon her again. "His condition has become much worse since he arrived."

"How?"

"A bandage was ripped from him. His sutures gave; the artery was exposed. He nearly bled to death."

"A bandage was ripped from him . . ."

"Tia, you said you heard men talking about killing wounded Rebels. Taylor listened to you, more than you realized. He asked some questions among the men, found out who it might have been. The Rebs had just been found and brought in. He kept an eye on the suspects and caught them in the act of trying to kill the fellow. He took them by surprise—and they shot at him. He was furious; he dragged them out here . . . and a crowd gathered."

"They tried to shoot him! He should have shot back—"

"They claim they thought they were being attacked."

"They tried to murder a man!" she whispered. "They shot at him—"

"If he'd shot back, he wouldn't have missed. And he might have faced a court-martial."

"*They* shot at *him.*"

"But they claimed to think themselves under attack by Rebels coming for their wounded. And after the fiasco at Olustee . . . Taylor might have faced an inquiry at the very least. This way, the men will be sent to St. Augustine. And they'll stand trial."

She turned back to look for Taylor. He was gone. And the men who had grouped around him were also gone. The soldiers he had fought and beaten were being dragged away by other men.

"Where is he?" Tia asked anxiously.

"By the water, I would think," Ian said. "He'll want to bathe. It looked like he was wearing half the mud in Florida."

"Ian—"

His hands fell from her shoulders. "I think it will be all right if you go to him now."

Freed from her brother's hold, she ran across the camp,

through the men and to the pines. There was a picket on duty near their tent, but he smiled and waved her on. She ran quickly through the trees, bursting out on the copse before the pond where they had been the night before. As Ian had suggested, he was there, his back to her as he sat on a log. He used a yellow regulation-issue cavalry scarf to squeeze water over his shoulder.

She stood dead still for a moment, wondering if he would want her there. But without turning, he knew that she had come, and he talked to her.

"My love, please don't just stand there and gape. Come over here and be helpful."

She walked around to him, inhaling sharply as she saw the depth of the jagged wound across his chest. She'd spent so much of the war treating injuries; it was instinct and habit to fall down on her knees before him where he sat on the log, take the cloth from him, soak it, and dab carefully at the wound. "Ian told me something of what happened, but I still don't understand . . ."

He caught her hand, and still holding it, he placed his fingers under her chin, causing her face to rise, her eyes to meet his.

"You were right. There were a few men determined that the only good Reb is a dead Reb. Last night, a foraging party came across a small band of wounded Confederates, and brought them back. This morning, I thought I should look in on them—I didn't want to believe that there were such men under my command, but I can tell you, it has been a bitter war. I knew the most fanatic of the men serving beneath Captain Ayers, so I knew who to watch for." He lifted his hands. "To kill a man so vulnerable would have been cold-blooded murder. They panicked and tried to shoot me."

"You would have been within your right to shoot back."

"Thank you, no. The temptation was great, but I have no desire to defend myself on any trumped-up murder charge. I think I broke a few bones, made my point. And the men will be out of here, and under arrest."

"But this slash on your chest! This is fairly serious! It should be stitched."

"Ah, I see! And I think I've gotten your gentle touch at last, when all you want to do is stick a needle into me!"

"Taylor, I'm serious."

"So am I," he murmured wryly, but he was smiling.

"I do excellent stitches. And if you're afraid of me, your camp is well enough supplied with morphine!"

He stroked her cheek. "No morphine, not for such a trivial wound, and certainly not now. I want to be in full control of all my senses for the time I have remaining, thank you."

She flushed slightly, her eyes downcast, but persisted. "Taylor, the wound really does need to be stitched. If you don't trust me—"

"But I do trust you," he said, and her heart seemed to warm. Then he added, "In this, I trust you."

Her eyes flew to his again. "Yes, well, I know how you feel otherwise. Risa is here—to keep an eye on me, of course."

"I was under the impression that Risa was a friend, as well as Jerome's wife."

"Yes—the wife of a really wicked Rebel blockade runner."

"That wicked blockade runner is my relative as well, Godiva."

"Don't call me that!" she whispered, dabbing carefully at the wound again. "Take an injury like this too lightly, Colonel Douglas, and you'll find yourself falling prey to a fever. Even with this, gangrene could set in."

"It will be all right." He caught her hand again. "Get what you need from Dr. Bryer. Meet me back in our tent. I just want to wash the rest of this mud off. Go."

She rose, hurrying to do as he had said; the wound needed stitching. As she moved back into the camp, she was surprised when she was suddenly stopped by Captain Ayers. "Mrs. Douglas! I just wanted you to know . . . well, I'm sorry. Most soldiers would never attempt to kill an injured enemy; they know that they, too, could fall into the hands of those they fight. You must believe me. I didn't know I had men capable of such heinous actions. Don't despise all Northerners for the cruelty of a few men who have fought in one battle too many."

"I do not, sir," she said quickly, uneasy with the way Ayers watched her. She couldn't help wondering if he wouldn't one day figure out that she had been the woman he had surprised by the stream that day.

"Excuse me, please, I must see to my husband . . ." she murmured.

When she had obtained what she needed from the hospital tent, she hurried back to their own. Taylor had returned. His trousers and his hair were damp; he had washed away the dirt and blood and mud of the fight. The wound at his chest, cleaned much more briskly by his hand than hers, was bleeding afresh.

He sat at the camp desk, a bottle of whiskey in his hands. He took a long swig from it as he beckoned her to him. "Ready?"

She nodded, bringing sutures and a needle to the desk. He looked at her gravely, then offered her the whiskey bottle.

"*You're* supposed to drink for the pain, not me," she told him. "You want small, neat stitches, right?"

He smiled. "I was handing you the whiskey to pour on the wound," he told her, and poured the whiskey over his chest himself. He winced with the pain, gritting his teeth. She rescued the bottle from his fingers, knelt down beside him, and began to sew. She did so as quickly and efficiently as she could, and when she had finished, tying a careful knot, she met his eyes again. Watching her, he took another long swig from the bottle.

"You did that very well."

"Did it hurt?"

"Did you want it to?"

"I asked you first. Did it hurt?"

"Not too badly. Disappointed?"

"Not really—except that maybe some real pain might have made you more careful in the future!"

He stroked her cheek. "I was careful. I knew what I was doing. And I thought that you would have been pleased that this matter was settled."

Her eyes fell. "I *am* pleased. I was saddened to learn that a vulnerable man was made worse. I am grateful to you."

"Don't be grateful to me for this, Tia. I didn't do it for you—I did it because it was the right thing to do."

She drew away from him, rising. He caught her by the tangle of her hair, not hurting her but pulling her back. She wound up on her knees before him again, and he caught her chin, meeting her eyes.

"I didn't do it for you—but I'm not unhappy if what I've done has pleased you."

"Why did you need to let them attack you?"

"Because I was angry. And I wanted to hurt them for what they had done. But I can shoot the wings off a fly, and God knows, in this war, there are those who might have been against me if it came to a matter of military law. Frankly, I wanted very much to bash in the one fellow's face—and I did so." He hesitated a long moment, his eyes on hers, his fingers moving gently through her hair at her temple. "Tia, it was Gilly."

"What?" She felt the blood drain from her face. Her men, the men she had wanted so badly to protect, had been taken anyway.

"Your friend, one of the young fellows with you when we met."

She started to rise. "I have to go to him! I have to see what I can do."

His pressed her back down, shaking his head. "Colonel Bryer is a really good man, one of the best surgeons I've ever had the pleasure to work with. He is also compassionate. He has done his best. Cecilia is there with him now. Risa is helping out with all the injured. You are surely wanted, and may see him in time. But you're not needed in the hospital tent now."

"But—"

"I need you here."

She nodded, trembling slightly. Her hands rested on

his thighs; she felt very close to him, as if they were
almost carrying on a real conversation between man
and wife.

"Taylor—"

"He was one of the men you were trying to protect
when you played your Godiva act and came here, isn't
he?"

"Taylor, I didn't play any act on purpose."

"So you came here, and now you are married and
trapped in a lie, and it was all to no avail. Your injured
have been taken by the Yanks."

"You know the truth now of what I heard the soldiers
say! I had no choice, Taylor."

"That's debatable. You heard the men. If you had
brought what they said to Captain Ayers—"

"How could I know that Ayers was any better?"

"But look what your recklessness—or courage—had
brought you to."

His eyes were so intently upon her; the almost tender
massage of his fingers had not ceased. She lowered her
head, then raised her chin. "Well, there were a number
of people worried that a woman as decadent as a *nurse*
would never find a husband."

"But you've married a half-savage."

"I know," she replied gravely.

He leaned forward, his knuckles grazing her cheeks.
"I know your innocence, and your recklessness, I know
that you are rash and determined. I know that you are
loyal and headstrong, and that though your heart and
passion are often in the right place, you are more likely
than Robert E. Lee to take chances! Whatever any old
biddies might have had to say, you could have acquired
dozens of husbands, before, during, or after this war.
But you have done the deed!"

"Yes—a commitment on paper," she reminded him.

"A commitment you will live with!" His thumb pad-
ded over her cheek as he continued to stare at her. "I
have to leave soon," he said.

"I know. In a few days' time—"

"Today."

She was startled by his words, and startled by the pain that seemed to strike deep inside her. "But you're injured—"

"A scratch."

"I warned you—"

"I know how to keep a wound clean. I will not die of gangrene."

She stared down again. "How long will you be gone?"

"A matter of weeks. I don't know what will come when I return; Olustee Station was a total debacle for us—they may give up on penetrating into Florida again, and sit tight with what the Yankees hold along the coast. I may be ordered back to action in Virginia. But I'll return to St. Augustine from the south, and I want you to be there."

She closed her eyes. It almost sounded as if he were *asking*.

"I'll be there," she said softly. She looked at him, shaking her head. "I was with Julian for years without incident," she told him. "I did nothing but help with injured men. I was never in danger." Her head lowered again with the last. "I don't think you understand. We can be so very *desperate* for help. I did nothing wrong."

"No, there was nothing wrong in what you did. But it isn't a matter of right and wrong. To the Confederates, Godiva is a serious heroine. The problem is that what you were doing was dangerous. Very dangerous. Look at me," he commanded.

She did so.

"Swear that you'll not ride out as Godiva again, and I'll believe you."

"I swear!" she said very softly.

"Come into my arms," he said.

"Taylor! You were wounded and bleeding—"

"And I will lie alone with only memory and desire— a far greater injury—in the days and nights to come. I haven't much time left at all. I want it to be with you."

"But Taylor . . ."

"Yes?" His hazel eyes looked gravely at her.

"It's day."

"Tia, trust me. We will not be disturbed."

She stretched higher upon her knees, and wrapped her arms around him. She lay her cheek against his chest where he was not injured. She eased her fingertips down the muscles of his arms. "I'd not hurt you . . ." she said hesitantly.

"My love, you will not hurt me," he assured her.

He rose with her, cradling her into his arms.

And in minutes, she didn't care that it was day.

That the sun rose, that the wind blew, that the war and the world went on. Time was precious, and she didn't know what she thought, or even exactly what she felt.

She only knew that she wanted to be with him.

Chapter 17

With Taylor gone, Tia thought she'd be very unhappy.

She had no idea of how she could miss a man, none at all, until she lay awake at night, thinking about him, wanting him. He had touched something within her from the first time they'd met. She should have wanted to escape this place, their marriage, all that had happened since her desperate run to this camp.

But she didn't want to escape. She wanted Taylor to return.

Nor could she despise the Yankees here.

Ian was in charge of the camp, and Risa was with her, and Colonel Bryer and Cecilia were wonderful people. Captain Ayers continued to study her upon occasion, but he remained baffled as to why she might be familiar to him. It was beyond the range of his imagination that Colonel Douglas would have married so notorious a Rebel as Godiva.

There was plenty to keep her busy in the hospital tent. Every morning when she awoke, she was glad to be able to assist the injured men. She was especially happy to be with Gilly.

Each day, he grew a little stronger. He seemed to have complete faith that he would eventually get better, because she was with him.

By the third day after he was nearly killed, Gilly was conscious again, his fever was down, and he seemed on the road to recovery.

She sat with him, carefully tending the rebandaged stump of his lower calf.

He watched her, shaking his head.

He had been startled to see her, but then she whispered what had happened to him. He smiled when she said that she was married to Taylor Douglas. Gilly knew perfectly well who he was, and he didn't seem surprised by the marriage part of it all.

"So you married Colonel Douglas!" he whispered to her one day, eyes bright as he shared the secret. "Did you have to?" he whispered.

"Gilly!"

"No, no, I didn't mean, did you *have* to in that manner. I mean, were you in trouble as Godiva?"

"I married him because I chose to," she said, and it might have avoided the truth, but it wasn't a lie.

"He's a darned good fellow. For a Yank."

"A Floridian. A traitor, some might say."

"Like your brother," Gilly reminded her shrewdly.

"Like my brother," she admitted. "But—"

"There's a strong man who can go against the tide of a raging sea to follow the convictions of his own heart and soul. Far harder to see, and understand, the losses, and be willing to fight the battle despite all that. Taylor Douglas, like your brother, may be the enemy, but he's proven himself one good friend to me. And he's been a good and honest man by you as well, Miss Tia McKenzie. Douglas," he added, then smiled. "And he knows about the Confederate secret weapon, eh?" Gilly seemed amused by it all.

"Secret weapon?"

"You."

"I never intended to be a secret weapon," Tia told him in return. "It just happened that way."

"But quite a legend. It will live on and on—with a happy ending, because you'll never be caught and killed now!"

The last gave her a shiver. "Gilly, it's all good, because you're here, and I'm with you, and you're going to get better."

"And be half a man," he said sadly.

"Never half a man, Gilly. A man is on the inside, not the out."

He squeezed her hand. "You tell that to the girls who'll refuse to marry me for being half a man, Miss Tia."

"Gilly, one day, the right girl will know you as I do, and she'll love you, and you'll never be half a man to her. I can promise you that."

"And how can you promise that?"

She decided a little blunt and rough-edged love would be in order then. "Gilly, half of the men won't even be half a man—they'll be dead and buried and six feet under or rotting in a forgotten and abandoned cornfield somewhere. You're going to live. And a woman who wants a man is going to love you one day, and that's that. And you can still have children—that part of you looks to be in fine working order! You're very young, and you're going to live a full and productive life."

"But what do I do?" he asked her.

"Can you write?"

"Of course!"

"Don't go getting huffy there, young man! I know plenty a planter who can barely sign his name and think that the words 'Francis Bacon' refer to a man's favorite pig! But if you can write, you can help me with letters to the families of the men we've lost—North and South. You can be honest about their bravery in battle; you can help their families through their grief, and make them proud."

"I like to write," he admitted.

"Good. You probably have saved the fellow's life," Colonel Bryer told her later that day. "Half the struggle for any soldier is the desire to live. He was convinced that he would die here—murdered probably, and I can't say that I blame him. But with you here . . . well, he believes in me as well."

The men responsible for the attack on Gilly were gone, and the others were really decent enough fellows. When she wasn't with Gilly, Tia helped Cecilia with other men. She wrote to Canby Jacob's wife, as she had

promised the first day, and told the young woman how
her husband had died a hero to his country, with forti-
tude, dignity, a deep belief in God, and a tremendous
amount of love for her and their child. She hesitated,
then wrote as well that her husband's last words instructed her not to mourn too long, but to live a good,
long, and happy life for his sake, and to raise their child
to be a compassionate man without thoughts of revenge,
but with a desire to structure and repair the country.

She found a certain peace in writing letters, and a
certain horror in time with nothing to do. During the
day, she worked hard with the men. At night, when most
bandages had been changed, meals served, supplies in-
ventoried and doled out, she wrote more letters. For the
soldiers who lived. She helped them describe the camp,
the state, the battle, the situation. She found out that
she could aid them in writing vivid descriptions, letters
that were personal and informative, without being morbid. Gily followed her lead. In time, in the hospital tent,
he became known more for his help than for being a
Rebel. And she knew, in this very strange little outpost,
that many of the soldiers had come to realize the fratricide of what they were doing. In writing home, they
were forced to see all that they shared—love for family,
fear of what would come if they were not there to provide when the war ended, fear of the future, regret for
the past.

Risa had moved into the tent with her. Her cousin-
in-law's company was good; they talked often and long
at night.

No one wanted the war over more than Risa. She
worried constantly about her father, a Union general,
and even more constantly about her husband, a Rebel
blockade runner. And now, she missed her baby, Jamie,
on top of all else. He had been left behind in St. Augustine with Chantelle, nanny, maid, and housekeeper,
when Risa had ridden into the interior.

"You had to leave the baby to come baby-sit me!"
Tia said one night after they had both crawled into bed
exhausted at the end of a long day. The black of night,

beyond the tent, was broken by a full moon, and they lay in shadow and pale, ivory light. Taylor had been gone about a week.

"That's horrible. Taylor had no right—"

"He knew what he was doing," Risa told her firmly. "The baby is fine, and he needs this time to be without me, to learn to share . . . because we're going to have another."

"Oh, Risa, that's . . . so wonderful!" Tia said, but she knew that there was a catch in her throat. Naturally, men and women wanted children. North and South, men wanted sons to carry on their names, while mothers often longed for daughters to love, to dress up, teach, and raise to be beautiful young ladies, their very best friends in the years ahead. But in Tia's experience, childbirth was also dangerous, complications far too often resulted in the death of the mother. She knew of many women who arranged for their babes to be cared for by others long before their babies were born.

"Everything is going to be fine," Risa said, as if reading her mind.

"Of course."

"Rhiannon told me so."

"I wish she'd told me a few things!" Tia muttered.

"She doesn't have a crystal ball; she can't plan what she sees and what she knows," Risa reminded Tia. "Just sometimes . . ."

"Is it a boy or a girl?" Tia teased.

"Another boy."

"Oh, well, we have baby Mary and my little niece to dress up."

"Well, my dear cousin-in-law, there is nothing wrong with boys!" Risa told her.

Tia laughed. "I wasn't suggesting there was—men, yes, little boys, no." Although, she thought, watching those who had fought sometimes, she realized there was often a thin line between the two. "I was merely thinking about keeping the sexes somewhat even here."

"Then you'll have to have a girl."

Tia was startled by the sudden, uneasy pitching of her

stomach. "I—I wasn't planning on children, not in this war."

"I can't say that I actually *planned* my own," Risa said.

"Yes, come to think of it, when did you manage to . . ."

Risa laughed, rolling on her camp bed to look at Tia. "I knew not to leave St. Augustine at Christmas! Jerome came down the St. Johns, slipping past all the Yankee gunboats . . . he left far too quickly, but we did have Christmas!" she said, and her voice, filled with amusement at first, faded to a husky pain.

"I'm glad you had Christmas," Tia said.

"And I hope you get your girl."

"I have barely married."

"Tia! You are no naive little hothouse flower! You don't need to be married at all to have a child; indeed, you need no more than one night. Or morning—or afternoon."

Tia rolled to her side, away from Risa. She loved children. But not in this war.

"Good night," she whispered.

"Sleep well."

She didn't sleep at all.

The next morning, it was determined that the camp had fulfilled its usefulness; all the soldiers who could be found had been found, and it was time to break down and move into the city of St. Augustine.

By horseback, even alone, the trip south would have taken Taylor nearly eight days, and that would have been hard riding, moving Friar along at fifty miles a day.

However, Taylor was able to find passage on a small, three-gunned ship heading from St. Augustine south to Key West. They were able to take him as far south as an abandoned dock fifty miles north of the Miami River. The trouble with taking too many chances close to the coast was that the sandbars shifted frequently, and it was dangerous territory for a gunboat to run aground, even if the Union blockade was strong and the Federal navy was far more in charge of the seas than the struggling Rebels liked to admit. There was dockage to be had south; in fact, even as far south as Taylor eventually intended to go, but Union navy ships didn't seek safe harbor near James McKenzie's property. Not that James McKenzie had proclaimed himself a sworn enemy; his sympathies were well known and his ties to the Seminole society were also well known—the Union was fighting hard there for little enough gain without adding an Indian conflict into the mixture. But no matter what the possible dockage, the coast offered dangers because of the shifting sandbars and shallows that had to be navigated. It was because of a shipwreck that Taylor was going there now, and he didn't want his mission to become the cause of a greater loss. Besides, there were places just to the north where he needed to go. Population in the south of the peninsula was sparse; white population in the south was even sparser. Taking the time to garner a little information might prove to be well worth the effort.

On their first evening out, he was standing on deck before the helm when he noticed the quickly dimmed lights of a ship that lay southeastwardly of their position. Before the lights had gone out, though, he'd a moment to study the ship.

"Colonel!"

He was startled by the whispered call of the helmsman. "Aye?" he replied as softly.

"Did you see her?"

"The ship that lies ahead?"

"Aye, sir, I thought I might be seeing things."

Taylor was quiet for a moment. "I think we need to steer clear of her!" he said.

A third man, young Captain Henley, who was in charge of the small gunner, joined them on deck then. "Colonel, sir! You may have the rank on me as far as the army goes sir, but this is my ship and we are at sea. Sir, I offer no insult, but I suggest that you're advising we avoid her because the ship is a notorious blockade

runner belonging to your own kin, Captain Jerome Mc-
Kenzie, of the *Lady Varina*."

Taylor replied to the captain, leaning against the teak
of the helm. "Indeed, Captain, I think the ship ahead is
the *Lady Varina*."

"Then, sir, I'm afraid whether she carries your kin or
not, we should attack her."

"Really? I had not suggested we avoid her because
she is captained by my kin."

"Oh?"

"She outguns us by at least three cannons, sir."

Captain Henley flushed. "Perhaps she is wounded already, drawing into shore. Perhaps—"

"Perhaps she has seen us, and thought what a magnificent prize we might make!" Taylor suggested.

Henley's color deepened. "Helmsman, hard to port,
avoid her if we can."

He called orders to his first mate, who called the men
aboard and ordered them quickly to their stations.

A cannon shot was fired from the darkened Rebel
vessel. The shot fell just short of their ship.

"See? We have outrun her!" the captain declared.

"I don't think so. I believe it was a warning," Taylor
said quietly. "If Jerome had meant to hit us, he'd have
fired more than one gun."

Apparently, Captain Henson saw the wisdom in his
words. "Keep her hard to port!" he ordered, and the
command was shouted down the ranks.

They passed by the phantom Rebel ship with no further fire.

The following night, at dusk, Taylor and Friar disem-
barked at an abandoned dock Taylor knew very well.

He was the one who had ordered the dock abandoned,
long ago.

His father had built the dock and that had been even
longer ago.

They had dredged out the inlet to give the bay there
the depth to accommodate a small gunboat. The land on
the coast was his, and since it was mainly undeveloped
and bordered what most white men considered to be a

mosquito-riddled swamp, he doubted if the state government had made any efforts to confiscate the property. Besides, deeper inland, the terrain was considered dangerous. It was alive with cougars, 'gators, snakes—and Indians.

Despite the growing darkness, there was still enough of a moon in the sky for him to move through the beach and shrub, into thick foliage, and deep, lush pine trails. He rode for an hour, soon becoming aware of the sounds in the forest.

There were eyes in the night.

He was being watched, and he knew it.

He called out loudly in the night, a greeting in the Muskogee language. He drew in on Friar. A moment later, a young man appeared. Tall, muscled, with long black hair and strong, dark features. He wore European-style breeches, a patterned cotton shirt, and a handsome headdress of shell and silver. He grinned, his teeth wide and white in the moonlight. He replied in perfect English.

"What is a White Wolf doing so far to the south, especially when he wears the blue of the slaughters?"

"Charlie Otter, wolves come home," he said, dismounting from Friar. He clasped his clansman's arm in a fierce grip. "We always come home," he repeated.

"Then welcome, cousin," Charlie said, and turning, he let out a birdcall. Three children, two young braves and a little girl, came running out of the bushes. "This can't be the baby?" he asked. "She was just a little pea in the pod when I left!"

"This is the baby. She has grown. Time goes slowly in war, doesn't it?" Charlie asked. "Sometimes," he said, "I think it is all we know . . . except that in this war, the whites kill one another, and do nothing but try to persuade us that we should join them and kill again as well."

"So you've joined neither side?"

"I don't choose to kill white men by sides," Charlie said softly. His eyes were hard, and he grinned again. "No, I do not like killing. But as the war goes on . . .

the refuse of the white armies runs here, and when the deserters come after my wife, our women, cattle, food, children . . . yes, then I make war again on the whites. They don't fight with armies against us now, so when I kill a man and he falls, he is buried in the swamp, and the tale of his evil is buried with him as well. A kindness for a white widow, don't you think?"

"If a man has deserted his army and run to the swamps to steal from the Seminole and rape and murder his wife or children, then yes, you, like any man, have a right to defend yourself."

Charlie grinned. "Come to my chickee, quarter-cousin-wolf. Friends remain forever."

Charlie's wife, Lilly, was a shy, gentle girl. She prepared food for Charlie and Taylor and some of the other men of the small village. She served it, but then moved away to the women's chickee, as was the custom. Sitting on the platform that rose about three feet from the ground, Taylor ate deer and a porridge made from the koonti root, and with the men, he shared the black drink, a strong brew, known to give men visions. He was careful to appear to swallow much more than he actually did. He spoke with the men, honestly, telling them what was going on in the white men's world, how the war went on, how many of their number fought for the Confederates—because of the uniform.

The men around him were grave, listening, judging, nodding.

Then Charlie spoke.

"You didn't come here to teach us about the war, Taylor Douglas. You wear your blue uniform but come to us as White Wolf, our cousin. You don't ask our aid to fight white men in the state. So why are you here?"

"I'm looking for a man, a soldier. One who wears this uniform as well. He was on a ship that went down in a storm. The ship was wounded by an enemy gunner, then she was caught by the wind and waves, and wrecked. Some men survived and were picked up by another ship. Some men were drowned, and their bodies were found floating. But one man was carrying papers important to

our government, and he carried information in his head
that mustn't fall into Rebel hands. I need to find him,
or find out if he drowned and if the papers went to the
bottom of the sea. Have you heard of such a man, living
here somewhere? The swamp is vast, but still, word travels here. News about a white man from the sea would
not be common."

He knew, before they answered him, that they knew
of the man. His heart quickened; he hadn't begun to
pray that he might find the man he was seeking.

"Charlie?" he said.

"White men are not so unusual as you think. More
come all the time. Even with the war. They run into
the swamps, as we ran into the swamps, to avoid their
governments," Charlie told him. "The man you are looking for could easily be dead."

"Is he dead?"

Emathla spoke quietly. "There is a white man, nearly
dead from the sea."

"Where?"

Charlie smiled. "You have come to us . . . when the
man you seek is south."

"South where? Will I be able to find him?"

"Such a man is with your grandmother's nephew,
James McKenzie. A white man, nearly dead from the
sea . . . yes, indeed, there is such a man. Go south to
your family there, and you will find what you are looking for."

Taylor frowned. "Is he dying? Is James caring for
him?" He felt a strange chill. James was a Rebel, and
though he would never murder the survivor of a shipwreck for being a Yankee, would he care for an enemy
in his own home?

"Go see James McKenzie, and you will understand,"
Charlie told him. "Will you stay here with us tonight,
and ride south tomorrow?"

"I accept your gracious invitation.

"You never need an invitation. You are among your
mother's people."

He inclined his head in acknowledgment of Charlie's

words, making no further protest. He was glad to see that his mother's small band was doing well; they had cattle and pigs, and were growing pumpkins and other fruits and vegetables. There were a number of strong, sturdy chickees built in a circle within the copse, space for the band to grow. They had already fought their wars and had come to this place, and though they seemed interested in his news about the war, they were not affected by the war itself.

The night was balmy. Taylor stripped down to his breeches to sleep, and felt the air wrap pleasantly around him. The mosquitoes weren't bad this season, the breeze was light, and the moon continued to give the sky a golden glow. He had a chickee to himself, and in the night, it was like being alone in the world.

From across the copse, he heard soft shuffling and whispers. Charlie and his wife making love. The stars and the air were good. Being alone was not. He felt the air cool as his body burned. Life certainly took strange twists and turns. Godiva had been enticing; she had intrigued him, and he had wanted her. But the reality of Tia McKenzie as his wife was far more than he'd ever imagined—in his most erotic dreams.

Eyes so dark, face so pale, the cascade of her hair a cloak of silk, encompassing them both, feather soft in his hands. She haunted him in the night; thoughts of her flesh, her lips, the way she moved, the way she looked at him, eyes shimmering ebony, like the deepest pond in a tempest of shadow and light, a tempest that spoke eloquently of the strange bond that had formed between them, of the desire that had burned with incredible brilliance, seizing them like the wind, taking them both unawares . . .

He groaned softly and sat up. Not enough of the black drink. He watched the stars.

Wanting her.

Chapter 18

Long before he reached James McKenzie's home, Taylor knew again that he was being watched.

A breakwater and lagoon shielded the property from the sea; at a distance, the house and grounds could not be seen. On land, the house was surrounded by thick pine forests, and the trails through the forests were known only by those who were familiar with the area.

The place had burned to the ground a year or so earlier, but it had been rebuilt and stood again as a spectacular enhancement to the natural beauty of the landscape. Built of wood, limestone, and coral rock, the house itself was back from the beach, designed to best embrace the north-south breezes, and painted a soft blue-green that blended with the colors of sea and sky. There were long sweeps of tended lawn right around the house, but then the grass grew sparse and sand began to intermingle with shrubs. Sea grapes shaded the lawn; pines and coconut palms dotted the ocean side of the house. In gardens that fringed around the house, Teela McKenzie grew medicinal herbs and beautiful flowering plants. Far from the back of the house, Taylor knew, the lagoon swept around to an entirely private pool, secluded by underbrush and trees, a paradise within an Eden. Before the war, white friends and neighbors had visited by boat while James McKenzie's native kin and friends had ridden the narrow Indian trails, many of them very old, down to the wild area off the bay. Taylor had journeyed to the property both ways. The McKenzies were as he was himself, both Indian and white, and sometimes, feeling like an outcast from both societies.

As a child, he had felt a strong affection for James, Teela, and their children—there were not many men who straddled the fences of such diverse cultures. Yet now . . .

He knew that many men would fiercely fight for James McKenzie, defend this place as they would defend him, if they felt that he were threatened. Taylor might well have been afraid here, but he was not. Whatever James's belief about the war, he would never allow his own kin to be gunned down on his doorstep.

Even as that thought crossed Taylor's mind, he was startled by a sudden sound that whistled through the air. He turned in time to prepare himself for the attack of the warrior who flew at him with a wild impetus of strength from the branch of a sea grape.

Taylor let the force take them both from Friar and down hard upon the ground. He knew how to twist to take the weight from another person in such a fall—and he knew how to twist to give his opponent the disadvantage as well. He did so, straddling the man, pinning the arm that wielded a long-bladed knife. His attacker was a full-blooded Seminole, a wiry, well-muscled fellow with his flesh bear greased and slippery as all hell. He wore nothing but a breech clout, attire often worn by a people who had learned that clothing fragments could cause infection and bring mortality from wounds that might not have been fatal.

The brave was young and strong, and angry. Taylor slammed his arm hard against the ground, aware that he had to force the weapon from his opponent before it became wedged in his own throat. The fellow grunted; Taylor forced the tactic again. The knife slipped, hitting the ground. Taylor reached for it, hurling it far away from them both into a bed of nearby crotons. The brave slammed a fist against Taylor's chin, a stunning blow. Taylor worked his jaw, hoping he didn't have a broken bone. He could have pulled a Colt, sent a bullet straight into the warrior's heart. In fact, such an action might have become necessary to save his own life because the brave beneath him was wild, twisting, trying to strike again. Taylor got in his own blow, however—a good one. Stunned, the brave lay still.

"Dammit, don't come after me again, you fool," Taylor warned him, standing up. "I'm not here to hurt anyone!"

"So why are you here?"

The question, in English, seemed to come from thin air. Taylor turned. A tall, thin Seminole with a remarkably strong and arresting profile stood before him. Taylor recognized the man, known as Billy Bones. In fact, he was a relative, the son of a cousin of his grandmother.

"Billy. It's Taylor."

"So I see," Billy told him gravely.

Billy was carrying a rifle. It wasn't directed at Taylor, but held loosely in his hand. If he chose to fire, however, it would all happen with the speed of lightning.

"I need to see James. I've come alone, not to do harm."

"This is a Southern state. You're wearing a Union uniform. Why have you come here in that uniform?"

"Because I'm not a spy, Billy. I've come as what I am, and I wouldn't pretend to be anything but what I am."

"What you are is not a friend."

"Billy, we are kin, no matter what clothing I wear. If I discard the uniform, I still believe in the cause I'm fighting for."

Billy watched him gravely. "You are sure you are alone?"

"When I had no father, James McKenzie was that to me and more. I would not come to his house except alone."

Billy Bones nodded after a while. Billy spoke in Muskogee, telling the boy to get up. The warrior who had attacked Taylor got to his feet, watching him carefully.

Billy raised a hand, indicating that Taylor should join him.

Taylor did so. Friar obediently followed along behind them. They followed the trail around to the rear of the house, where the porch let out by the lagoon. To the northeastern side of the house were the docks, and Taylor was sure that there were always more men on guard at that point. He was sure, as well, that Jerome often brought his blockade runner, the *Lady Varina,* into these docks.

James McKenzie stood on his rear porch, arms folded over his chest. Like Billy, he had been aware of his coming company.

"Taylor," he acknowledged gravely. Then he said, "Looks like you're acquiring a bruise on that jaw."

Taylor grinned. "But you should see the other guy."

James smiled, eyes downcast for a minute. "If you'd hurt that other guy, you would have been in some severe trouble."

"Did you think I would?"

"No," James said after a moment. "But I had to be sure. So—what are you doing here?"

"I'm looking for a man. A Union soldier. He was on a ship that went down, but he had despatches from Key West that carried a fair amount of information about naval movements."

"And what do you want with such a man?"

"Well, I want the despatches, of course."

"And the man?"

"And the man."

"Does the Union government suspect him of treason, of having changed sides to give the information to the Confederate government?"

Taylor hesitated only a moment. "Probably."

"And if I knew this man, why would I allow you to take him to be hanged?"

"A man who too easily changes sides may also too easily be a traitor to both."

Behind James, a door suddenly opened. A tall, slender young man with gaunt cheeks shuffled out on crutches. He was wearing a bleached white muslin shirt and dark cotton trousers. His one foot was bandaged; his other foot was bare.

James turned, saying firmly, "Michael, I told you to stay inside."

"Yes, sir, you did. But I won't bring the war to your doorstep. Colonel Douglas, I'm Lieutenant Michael Long. I'm the man you're looking for. The despatches remain in my coat pocket. They have not been touched. If I'm to face a court-martial, I will do so."

"No!"

Behind Lieutenant Michael Long, the door burst open again. Jennifer McKenzie, beautiful straight black hair flying behind her like a sea of ravens, came flying out of the house, slipping an arm around Long, and staring at Taylor with defiant, troubled eyes. "No, he came here half-dead! He can still barely walk. He nearly died of a fever!"

"Jennifer—" James began firmly.

"Jennifer," Long repeated.

The door opened again. Teela hurried out, coming to stand beside James and stare at Taylor. "Taylor, welcome. I think. Oh, dear, this is quite awkward, isn't it?"

From inside, he could hear a wailing. Mary, a little over a year old, the youngest of the offspring of James and Teela McKenzie, didn't like being separated from her mother.

Surveying the group before him, Taylor felt a sense of defeat. This was not what he had expected.

"Perhaps we could go in and talk," he suggested quietly. He smiled at Teela. "I never got to see the baby."

"Oh, she's beautiful!" Teela said. "James . . ."

"Yes, of course," James said after a moment. "Yes, we should go in and talk."

With that, Teela smiled, walked down the porch steps, and greeted Taylor with a hug and a kiss on the cheek. She smelled sweetly of jasmine, as she always had.

"Are you coming in, Billy?" she asked.

"I think I'll see to my nephew," Billy said. He looked at Taylor, nodded, and passed him by. It was the best he could expect. He was the enemy.

But it hurt. Teela slipped her arm through his. They walked to the porch together. He met James McKenzie's eyes, a startling blue against the bronze of his features.

James hesitated, then reached out and embraced him. Taylor closed his eyes.

God, how he was coming to hate the war.

James released him, and they entered the house. Teela went to retrieve her crying baby from the mixed-blood servant who held her. "Taylor, Mary. Mary, meet your distant cousin Taylor."

He was startled when the little girl stopped crying, reached out to him, then wound up in his arms, placed there by Teela. "Hello, Mary!" he said uncertainly. "You are very beautiful, very definitely a little McKenzie!" The baby was all McKenzie, with huge, blue green eyes and ink-dark hair.

"Let me get drinks," Teela said, turning to start down a hallway.

"Mama!" Mary cried, her little arms now reaching out for her mother.

"We're following her!" Taylor said, hurrying after Teela. He liked children, though he wasn't accustomed to them quite this young. Still, she smelled so sweet, like soap and talc. Her eyes were wide and trusting. Holding her, he remembered that once he'd wanted children, then Abby had died and he'd forgotten everything except the business at hand—the war. But now . . .

Now, he had a wife. A McKenzie wife, closer to this child than he was himself . . .

He could hear Lieutenant Michael Long limping after him, James and Jennifer in his wake. A few minutes later, he was seated in James's study, nicely redone after the fire. Mary had been rescued by Jennifer, who was watching Long with tears continually forming in her eyes. Seated in a leather chair with a large whiskey, Long explained the shipwreck, how he'd been unconscious for weeks and still woke up in the night with chills and fever. "The despatches are safe, Colonel Douglas. Completely safe. I'd not have betrayed my country, but . . . but . . ." he looked at Taylor. "I've prayed that the Union government would think me dead."

"They had to find the despatches," Taylor said. "You must have known that."

"Perhaps. Perhaps I just prayed they wouldn't find me." He glanced at Jennifer, then stared at Taylor again. "I don't wish to be a deserter. But neither do I wish to make war against the South anymore. Nor do I think, in all truth, that I may be able. I still can't walk. My ankle was broken and not set quickly enough."

"Taylor, please . . . isn't there something you can do?" Jennifer pleaded.

"You can see that he really can't go back to war," Teela whispered.

What he could see was that Jennifer had fallen in love. And that Michael Long seemed to be a very decent man. Tired of the war—and not about to fight the people who had saved his life. *He would let me shoot him before taking him from here,* Taylor thought—except that he wouldn't do that now because the man who had rescued him was kin. He wouldn't cause bloodshed among the family.

James seemed to understand Taylor's situation all too well, and maybe he was damning himself for not remembering that though Taylor was kin, he remained the enemy as well. "Do you think that Taylor can go back to the Union military authorities—and lie?" he asked harshly.

Long lowered his head. "There will be no bloodshed here. I will go back."

Jennifer started to weep.

Taylor rose, walking over to her. He hunkered down before her. "I can't lie, but . . . I can take the despatches to the fort at Key West. And see what I can do."

She looked up at him tearfully. "You won't take Michael?"

"No."

"Oh, Lord, Taylor, you'll be taking a risk."

"Well, I might be taking a risk if I tried to seize him as well, right?"

"How's that?"

"Your father could have me shot down."

"My father wouldn't do that."

"And neither, Jennifer, would I hurt a good man who

is wounded already. Or a cousin who has already felt the tragedy of this war too closely."

"Taylor . . ." She set her arms around him, hugging him. "Taylor, I'm so sorry for doubting you . . . I'd forgotten about Abby in my own pain. The war has cost us Lawrence and Abby and left you a widower."

He drew away from her gently, rising. "Well, I'll leave tomorrow and see what can be done. And I guess I should tell you . . . I'm not a widower anymore."

"You've remarried! How wonderful," Teela said. "Who, Taylor? Ah, a Yankee girl, I imagine, someone from the North! Will you stay there after the war, Taylor, do you think? Will there ever be an 'after' with this wretched war?"

"Teela, my love, you've asked him a half-dozen questions. Let him answer one," James advised.

"You know my wife. You know her well. She's your niece. I married Tia McKenzie."

Jennifer's gasp seemed loud enough to be heard at sea.

"Tia—married you?" she inquired incredulously.

He looked at her, arching a brow. "Yes," he said flatly.

"Oh, Taylor, I did not mean that."

"She means that you're a Yankee," James said.

"Um, well, no one is perfect."

"And *you* married *her?*" Jennifer said.

"She married me, I married her. We are married."

"I think I shall have another drink," Teela said.

"I didn't know that you knew one another," Jennifer said. "Well, of course, you and Ian have been friends—you'd been out here with all the boys since you all were young, but I don't remember Tia being around."

"We met recently."

"At Cimarron?"

"And before," he acknowledged.

"Well, perhaps we all should quit staring at Taylor," Teela said. "You'll be hungry. I'll see about dinner. Michael, dear, you really should be back in bed. Jennifer, give me Mary and help Michael along. James . . . Taylor . . . I'll call you as soon as dinner is ready."

Michael Long came up to Taylor. "Thank you," he said gravely.

"I haven't done anything yet. I make no guarantees."

"Thank you for the effort you have promised."

He nodded. Jennifer and Michael left. He was alone with James. He felt James's brooding, dark blue eyes studying him. "You know, Taylor, I feel, at times, that I helped raise you in a way."

"Yes, sir. I feel that myself at times. It was why I dared come here alone."

"I know you very well. Other than the fact that you've chosen the wrong side in this wretched fight, I'm proud of the man you've become."

"Thank you, sir."

"So what is going on? Why did you marry my hellion of a niece?"

"I . . . well, . . . sir, one need only look at her," he said, taken completely by surprise by the question.

"Hm." James studied him still. "What kind of trouble did she get herself into?"

"I—none. Unless you consider me trouble."

"I'm sure my niece does." James stood, walked over to the whiskey decanter, and poured himself another drink. "Tell me. I've heard rumors about a Rebel spy working the state. I would have feared that Jennifer was trying to take on the war herself again, except that she has been with me—and with this wounded soldier, Michael Long. And I would have feared for Sydney, except that she remains in Washington, married to an unknown Yank, but safe, at the very least. So when I heard the rumor and the description, I began to fear for my brother's daughter—it is a ridiculously dangerous game this young woman plays. Does this marriage have something to do with the capture of a spy? If Godiva happens upon the Yanks . . ."

"Sir—"

"Don't lie or hedge, Taylor. I expect more from you, I'm afraid."

"Sir, it isn't my place—"

"You married her. It is certainly your place."

"I am the Yank she happened upon."

James nodded after a moment. "Keep her safe, whatever it takes," he said. "My brother would, I think, lose his mind if anything happened to her. A man loves his boys, but his daughters are his treasures. God knows, it is terrifying enough to wake up knowing your sons may face a barrage of bullets that day. God help you, North or South, keep her safe."

"Sir, I intend to do my best." He hesitated a moment. "And for Jennifer as well. I'll take the despatches to Key West tomorrow."

James lifted his glass to Taylor. "To your success, Colonel Douglas. In all things."

"Aye, sir."

With all of the injured men, the trip to St. Augustine seemed very long, though they had not been more than thirty miles from the city. It took more than two days to travel the rough roads with their crude ambulances and the amputees who needed care that their stumps were not injured all anew by too much jolting. The men were excited, though, to be coming into the city. Tia found that she was pleased herself.

From the time Tia was a little girl, she had loved St. Augustine. When friends from more northern climes had teased her about Florida being new and raw and savage, she could remind them politely that St. Augustine was the oldest continually habited European settlement in the New World.

A Union flag waved above the city now, and it had done so since 1862. Union soldiers marched in the fields, and took their leisure by the water. Some Rebels had remained, determined to hang on to their property. Others had fled, giving everything up for their great Southern Cause. Since the Yankee invasion, Tia had been in and out of the city a few times to see Alaina, Risa, and the children. When they arrived this time, Risa went home immediately to see her son, little Jamie, but Tia stayed with Cecilia Ayers and the doctor. She didn't visit anyone at first, since she was so busy helping to settle the injured soldiers into their new hospital facilities, scattered throughout the city. When at last that night Tia rode with her brother to the place where her family kept apartments, she was as stunned as he was to find Alaina, who was supposedly back at Cimarron, standing by the house, waiting. Ian let out a surprised cry, leapt down from his horse, and went running to his wife.

Tia dismounted from Blaze, collected the reins for both horses, and followed more slowly. Alaina was in her husband's arms. Tia was so close that she had no choice but to hear their intimate whispers. Her brother spoke first, thrilled to see his wife, but chastising her as well.

"My love, my love, I thought you weren't well, that you were staying at Cimarron, not traveling," Ian protested while holding her.

"I knew you were going to be here. I couldn't stay away. God knows when you will leave the state again, when I'll no longer have such a chance," Alaina replied.

"But you shouldn't have come alone."

"I didn't! Rhiannon is with me. And your father arranged for an escort, of course. I had to come, Ian. I didn't intend to leave when I thought you were out of the state, but when you wrote from the camp saying you'd be here . . ."

"I wouldn't have told you if I thought you'd risk yourself and the children."

"But I'm here. Fine. And well. And the children will get to see you again. So soon after Christmas; they'll even remember you!"

Their voices were so filled with emotion. They were beautiful and romantic there—her very tall, dark brother, so handsome in his uniform, and his petite blond wife, framed there with him in the moonlight. It was a picture of the war: a greeting now, but soon it would be a goodbye as well. Tia felt as if she intruded, and she wished she could slip away.

"Tia!" Her sister-in-law noticed her, raced for her,

hugged her. "It's good to see you again! I'm glad you're with Ian; everyone worries about you so much."

"I'm fine, Alaina," she said quickly, not wanting another barrage of questions regarding her appearance at the Yankee camp and her marriage to Taylor. "The children—"

"Are sleeping, Risa's Jamie as well. And little Conar. Rhiannon is here with me. We came eastward together. She's anxious to see you, of course. Oh, and wait until you meet Chantelle. She is wonderful, the apartments are always neat and clean, and she's a marvel with the children. She came in with the new doctor. His name is Jon Beauvais. I think you'll like him very much. Anyway, Risa's door is there, mine is there, the doctor is across . . . and there, that door is yours, Tia. But, of course, Risa has tea on and is waiting for us all."

Tia smiled suddenly. "Alaina, neither you nor my brother want to have tea at the moment." She kissed her sister-in-law on the cheek. "Go with your husband. We'll be fine."

"Oh, no, but you've just arrived."

"Alaina, my brother is a much nicer human being after he's been with you. Go away; we'll manage! Risa, Rhiannon, and I will do very well on our own, thank you!"

Alaina grinned, raced back to Ian, and caught his hand.

"But the horses—" Ian began.

"I can see the stables—and the stable boy!" Tia called. Her brother stared at her, waved back. He slipped an arm around his wife and disappeared through one of the doors of the big old house that had been turned into apartments.

Tia walked the horses to the stable. She'd been here before, and she knew the layout of the street, the surgery, the hospital. She was far more familiar with it all than perhaps Ian realized—it was much easier for a young woman to cross enemy lines than it was for a man.

A young black stable boy took the horses from Tia. As she thanked him, Risa's door opened and her cousin-in-law came out. "Tia, come in now, come on in. You must be so tired." Risa's arm came around her shoulder and she led Tia into the small parlor area of her apartment. As they entered, she saw that Rhiannon was standing in front of the fireplace, her head lowered. But she heard the two of them enter and she turned, walking quickly across the room to greet Tia with a warm hug. "It's so very good to see you again this soon," she said.

Despite her sister-in-law's affectionate greeting, Tia felt uneasy. Rhiannon appeared tired, and Tia didn't think that it was due to the baby keeping her awake.

"What's wrong?" she asked quickly.

Rhiannon shook her head.

"Oh, my God, you didn't hear anything bad? Julian is all right—"

"Julian is fine," Rhiannon said. "I saw him briefly before coming here. I plan on joining him again shortly. He's working alone now."

"Oh, I know! I'm so sorry—"

"I planned on joining him anyway," Rhiannon reminded her, smiling.

"The tea is hot and we've biscuits and soup," Risa said. "Perhaps we should sit down now and eat. And by the way, Tia, your *husband* is just fine as well."

Startled, Tia stared at Risa. Her red-headed nononsense cousin-in-law was staring at her as well.

"Oh? And how do you know? Where is he?"

"I don't know where he is now."

"But he was . . ."

"To the south of us."

"And how do you know?"

"I received a letter from my mother-in-law."

"Aunt Teela? Taylor is with Aunt Teela?"

Risa sighed. "James McKenzie's aunt was Taylor's grandmother, you know."

"Or so I've learned!" Tia murmured.

"It's not so strange that he should have gone there."

"Except that Uncle James hates even the sight of a Union uniform."

"Did he ever hate Ian? No. Does he hate your father? No. Does—"

"None of that counts. Taylor was ordered there. Taylor is after something there."

"You'll have to let them all work that out themselves, won't you?" Risa said softly.

"But—"

"He's alive and well, we know that much," Risa reminded her dryly. "If they'd decided to hang him or shoot him instead of inviting him to dinner, I'm sure she would have mentioned it in the letter."

Tia cast her a frown. "This is hardly a joking matter."

"No, it's a war, isn't it? But my in-laws haven't disowned me for being General Magee's daughter, nor did they blame me when radical Union soldiers decided to burn their house to the ground. To fear that they would do some harm to Taylor does them an injustice."

"But what is Taylor doing there?"

"Negotiating, at the moment."

"Negotiating what?"

"They didn't say. But he will be in the south of the state for some time yet."

"Perhaps time enough for you to visit Brent," Rhiannon said.

Tia stared at her sister-in-law, thinking that the whole world was going insane. Risa and Rhiannon both had their reasons for being Unionists. But why Rhiannon should suggest that she travel through the war-torn South to visit Brent seemed ludicrous.

"Visit—Brent. My cousin Brent," she repeated. "You—Miss 'Battle Hymn of the Republic' herself, are suggesting that I go to Brent. The Confederate surgeon."

"I'm suggesting you visit your cousin who is a doctor—not that you carry military information to Longstreet or Lee!" Rhiannon said indignantly.

"Rhiannon! I'm not so sure that this idea of yours is possible at all. Tia can't go just anywhere anymore," Risa said. "She is married to Taylor."

"I know that—you told me that she married him," Rhiannon said with an exasperated sigh. "I'm not suggesting she do anything at all wrong, dangerous—or even pertaining to the war!" Rhiannon said.

"It does pertain to the war—" Risa argued.

"No, it pertains to a child!"

Tia threw up her hands. "What are you two talking about? I'm going to need whiskey instead of tea if someone doesn't start making some kind of sense soon."

"I had a dream," Rhiannon said.

"Oh, God, no! What about—my cousin Brent?" Tia asked, horrified. "Is he in danger? Can't we write to him? No, we'll have to send him a telegraph."

"It's not Brent," Rhiannon said.

"She keeps dreaming about a little boy in a big white house—falling from a balcony."

"A little boy we know?" Tia asked.

"Alaina says she knows the house I described. And Risa agrees. It is the White House of the Confederacy. And the child belongs to President Davis."

"Oh, but . . . are you sure?" Tia asked.

Rhiannon shook her head, distressed. She walked about the small room. "No, of course I'm not sure, I'm not sure at all. I've already written a letter . . . your father has assured me that he has given it to an officer who will get it through to Varina Davis. But what will she think when she gets a letter from a woman she doesn't even know? She may never read it. If she does, she'll think I'm mad, and ignore it. Then . . ."

"What?" Tia asked.

"It's the strangest set of dreams I've ever had. Once, I thought I'd go mad with the dreams, that they would simply torture me with visions I could not prevent. Then your brother showed me that sometimes I could avert tragedy with my sight. Sometimes . . . but this dream came several times. Then, the last time, while I struggled to wake up, I saw a man's face, such a sad face . . . and it was as if he was speaking directly to me . . ."

"And?" Tia persisted. "Please, Rhiannon!"

She shrugged. "He said that some things were fate, maybe not meant to be prevented."

"Rhiannon, who was the man?"

"I think it was the child's father. President Davis, perhaps."

"So you think you're dreaming about the death of a child—that can't be averted?"

"I don't know! But a child died, and I can't bear the thought!" Rhiannon cried.

"So many people die," Risa said softly. "That's part of life, Rhiannon. Death is a part of life."

"But too many are dying now. Saving what we can seems to be the only way to get through this war. I feel that I still must do what I can!" Rhiannon said.

Tia stared at her. "Someone should go to Varina Davis."

"You know her," Risa said. "President Davis was Secretary of War before this madness started. Your father and brothers were friends with him; you visited their home before the war."

"Yes, I visited them with my family before the war. But you've visited them at the White House of the Confederacy, where they're living now. You were there with Jerome at the beginning of the war. You're the wife of a great Southern hero—"

"And the daughter of a Union general. And . . . and I'm not sure I could make the trip right now," Risa said apologetically.

Tia felt a chill snake along her spine. No, she couldn't ask Risa to go. Not if she was expecting another child. And Rhiannon's little Conar was barely a few months old. "Alaina . . ." she murmured softly.

"Alaina is sick," Rhiannon said.

"Sick?"

Rhiannon shrugged. "Alaina is expecting another child as well."

"Another babe? Are we McKenzies trying to repopulate the South all on our own?" she murmured bitterly.

"Tia!" Risa said.

"Oh, I'm sorry. I'm delighted for you all. I just . . ."

"Are you afraid that Taylor will be angry?" Rhiannon asked.

"She should be," Risa said, staring at her sternly.

Tia suddenly felt defensive—and like a child who had been ordered to behave. "No, of course not. I mean, he is off to war, with no explanations for me, there is no reason I shouldn't travel to see Brent . . . but . . ."

"Ian will probably not let her go," Rhiannon said with a shrug.

"Ian will most probably not be here long," Risa said. "They are pulling officers and all the able-bodied men they can back out of Florida, preparing for a new offensive. General Grant has said that war must be hell, and that he intends to make it so."

"As if we were not in hell already," Tia murmured.

"Ian will be preoccupied. With Alaina. If we have to slip you out before he leaves, we can surely do so."

"Well, tonight," Rhiannon said, appearing very nervous and upset, "you should get some sleep. You can decide in the morning. That will be time enough."

Time enough . . .

As it happened, Tia didn't need the morning to come in order to make up her mind. She had barely crawled into bed when there was a pounding at her door. There had been a buggy accident that night. A man's leg had been crushed, his son had an injured arm, and his seven-year-old daughter had been seriously hurt.

The doctor, Jon Beauvais, was a skilled young surgeon. Tia worked with him throughout the night. The man's leg had to be amputated. The little boy's arm was broken, but they set it, and the doctor believed he would be all right. The fight to save the little girl lasted until morning. Tia tried to soothe her. She was very brave.

"Does it hurt badly?" Tia asked her. "The doctor will make it better. The medicine helps, doesn't it?"

The little girl offered her a tremulous smile. "Doesn't hurt too bad! It's all right, I know. If I die, the angels will come for me. They came for my brother, Daniel. He died at Gettysburg, and so he is in heaven, and if I die, he won't be so alone."

"You're not going to die. You're going to live. Listen, hear that? Your mommy is out there, and she's crying. You have to live so that she won't cry."

But no matter how hard the doctor worked with her, and despite the healing touch of Rhiannon's hands, the little girl died. Tia was at her side when, just before dawn, she struggled to draw in one last breath. She was a beautiful child with strawberry ringlets and cherry-red lips. In death, she seemed to sleep. Tia drew her into her arms and cried, unable to believe that the little girl was gone. She still held her tightly, crying, when the doctor came and said the mother needed to be with her child. Tia sat numbly in the doctor's surgery, listening as a photographer was called. It was common practice, she knew, for photographers to take pictures of dead children so that their parents could remember them. The mother sobbed, holding her baby for the photographer. The child did, indeed, look at peace, as if asleep, and yet it all seemed so horrible to Tia that she could scarcely bear it.

Both of her sisters-in-law went back to cradle their own babies. Risa as well went to her Jamie.

Tia sat outside the surgery, feeling ill. She could still hear the mother's sobs. They would haunt her all her life.

When dawn broke, she told Rhiannon she was ready to go to Richmond.

As it happened, things worked out very well. Ian's traveling papers had awaited his return to St. Augustine.

He'd be leaving by a Yankee ship in the harbor.

Tia would be leaving soon after, slipping out of the city and down river to board a blockade runner.

Taylor arrived late, having not received the documents he needed until late that morning. Then, though the weather was excellent and he had moved along at a fair clip, it was still nearly two hundred miles southwest from James McKenzie's home to the Union naval base at Key West. With the captain of the small vessel eternally nervous that he would meet a heavily gunned blockade runner along the sandbars and shoals that haunted the coastline around the islands, it seemed slow going.

Taylor came into the lagoon by dinghy, and though it

was late, again he was being watched. He rowed in alone, planning on rowing back out to meet the ship that night.

As he stepped from the dinghy onto the wet sand of the beach, he almost expected another ambush, but this time, as he dragged the dinghy high up on the sand, it was Jennifer who came running out to throw her arms around him. "Taylor! Taylor, what happened? Please tell me, quickly! Will it be okay, did they believe you, did—"

"Jennifer, Jennifer, whoa!" James McKenzie was right behind his daughter, slipping an arm around her, ready to draw her from Taylor before she could drag them both down into the sand.

Teela was there as well. "Let him get out of the water and into the house!" she chastised. "The night is cool; let's get inside."

But Taylor could see Jennifer's tortured eyes, and he felt a strange pain in his throat, in his gut. She loved the Yankee she had fished from the sea. He had never expected to see it; her first husband had been killed at Manassas. And she had mourned deeply, and recklessly. But seeing her eyes, hearing her voice, the passion, the care, the concern . . .

"Jennifer, they accepted the despatches, and my statement that he was far too ill to be moved."

"Oh, Taylor!" Escaping her father's hold, she threw her arms around him again. She kissed his cheek, hugged him. "Oh, Taylor!"

"Jen, Jen!" James warned quietly. "He'll eventually have to go back—"

"No, sir," Taylor interrupted quietly. "That's part of what has taken me so long. I have an honorable discharge with me. I took the liberty of suggesting that he'd never be much use to the Yankee Cause again. Of course, I swore in turn that he'd never take arms against the Union, as well."

"Oh, my God, I have to tell Michael!" Jennifer kissed his cheek again. "Taylor! Thank you so very, very much!"

She sped off.

Teela and James remained, staring at Taylor. He could hear the lash of the waves against the shore. The moon was dimming, but it still cast a gentle glow down upon them. Palms rustled gently in the breeze, a whisper against the night sky.

"For my daughter's sake, I thank you sincerely," James told him.

Taylor grinned. "Well, I admit, I'd thought about reporting him dead. I had that suggestion made to me a few times, and it did sound like a good idea. But one day, the war will end. And I don't want any of us to be haunted by this in later years. I was afraid . . . it was a gamble, and Jen might have wound up hating me, but the gamble has paid off."

"Come, let's go on into the house," Teela said, stepping forward and taking his arm. "It's a cool night. You need some hot food, and a good night's rest—"

"Teela, I would deeply appreciate sharing a meal with you and James. Afterward, however, I must return to the ship. I am going to be ordered back to Virginia, and I want what time I may have in St. Augustine with Tia."

Teela seemed to pale suddenly. "Um . . . well, let's have something to eat first, shall we?"

She turned and headed quickly for the house. Taylor looked at James, frowning.

"What's going on?"

"We received another letter from Risa. Tia has headed toward Virginia herself, to spend time with Brent at the hospital outside Richmond."

"She . . . what?"

"Perhaps she thought you'd be gone much longer. There was a ship on the river—"

"A Rebel ship?" Taylor asked tightly.

"Yes," James admitted. "Not Jerome's," he added quickly. "Under the circumstances, he might have refused her passage. I don't really know much; all I have is the information in my daughter-in-law's letter."

Taylor felt as if a band were tightening around his insides. Fear and fury combined to make him feel sick.

Damn her. He'd trusted her.

He pulled the papers he carried—correspondence and Michael Long's honorable discharge—from the inner pocket of his frockcoat and handed them to James.

"Sir, I beg your forgiveness, but I must forgo dinner."

"What is your intent?"

"I'm going after my wife."

"She will be in Rebel territory."

"I am accustomed to seizing her from Rebel territory."

"Take care, Taylor. Take the gravest care."

"Aye, sir, that I will."

He pushed the dinghy from the shore, hopped into the small boat, and picked up the oar, rowing with a vengeance.

What in God's name was she doing? What reckless game did she play? Was she torturing different troops now, leading them into an ambush? No matter how good she was, no matter how swift, how careful, how cunning, she would eventually be caught.

He felt a tightness clamp around his throat. He couldn't lose her . . .

He paused in his furious rowing, staring into the dark velvet of the night, listening to the water lap against the small boat. His heart slammed bitterly against his chest.

Prison. A Yankee prison camp. It seemed the only answer.

Chapter 19

Going north was precarious, at best. War was to be hell, the Yanks had determined, and they were practicing a scorched earth policy throughout the South. Train tracks had been destroyed, and travel by rail was very uncertain. The Yanks had constantly been bombarding the forts protecting Charleston, making travel by ship equally dangerous.

But throughout the journey, Tia cared little. She couldn't shake the vision of the beautiful little girl who had died. She couldn't forget the way that the photographer had posed the dead child to take her picture. Memories. Memories that would haunt her a lifetime, she thought.

She'd had little to do with her own travel arrangements, leaving all the details to Risa and Alaina, who argued over her route and just how and when she should travel. In a way, however, there was little choice—she would have to travel by the whim of the war, with little help otherwise. Her sisters-in-law and Risa were rather like a threesome of maternal hens, leaving St. Augustine with her and braving whatever dangers might face them to accompany her south down the river to the blockade runner. They made certain the captain was a respectable man, and obtained his assurances that he would see to Tia's welfare above all else.

The captain, a man named Larson, was a kindly, gnarled little fellow, a man dedicated to the south. Tia took her meals in his cabin, where he talked fondly about his two little girls, the wife he had lost in childbirth, and how he despised the men who claimed to be

Rebels but ran the blockade purely for the profit they could make. They were bleeding the South worse than the Yankees.

Charleston had been under heavy fire. He would best be able to deliver her to Wilmington. He didn't consider the seas a safe way for a woman to travel—not that there was a safe or sure way to travel through the South anymore.

As it happened, she was able to disembark in North Carolina just off of the Virginia border. Captain Larson received word from his contact at the port that Brent had arranged for an escort to bring her to the hospital where he was working, on the outskirts of Richmond. She was disheartened to meet the two men who would take her to her cousin; they were so thin, their uniforms so very threadbare. They had both been wounded, and weren't ready yet to return to the front line, yet were able to take on the duty of protecting one woman along a path that might be peopled by cowardly deserters or a stray Yankee. Both men were polite, courteous to a fault, and determined that she should have decent accommodations each night. Her first evening she spent at a small, still-functioning plantation that had thus far avoided Yankee depredations. Her hostess was the wife of a lieutenant who had known Ian before the war. The woman thought that Tia must now hate her brother.

She was careful not to mention that she had married a Yankee as well. Her blindly loyal hostess might have thrown her right out. Thankfully, the woman seemed to think that her cousin Jerome was single-handedly keeping the South in the war.

The next morning, they started riding early again. They avoided riders when they heard them coming; Sergeant Brewster, the older of her escort, told her that they never really knew just where they might run into a party of scouting Yanks. In the towns, however, they dared the main roads. They were able to buy meals, and there were places where it even seemed that there was not a war on. Everyone, however, seemed to be wearing a mask. They would win the war, yes, of course, the

South could still win the war, and though Europe had refused to recognize the government thus far, well, they would simply be proven wrong. The South could never lose. The spirit of the people still remained too strong. They were still thrashing the Union army at most engagements.

Whether that was true or not, Tia didn't know. The gaunt, weary soldiers helping her across the countryside didn't seem convinced that they were doing so well. Costs for food had soared—what little could be bought.

The second night she slept in a hotel thirty miles south of the city. She awoke the next morning to a fierce pounding on her door. She bolted out of bed in her nightgown, still exhausted from her long ride, startled by the pounding and blinded by the long tangle of her hair.

"Yes?"

"It's me, Tia, Brent."

"Brent!"

She didn't care the least about decorum but opened the door, delighted to see her cousin. She threw her arms around him, hugged him fiercely, then drew away from him. Brent looked good. He was all McKenzie, tall and dark, Seminole in his features but with a touch of his mother in the shade of his eyes and the hint of red in his hair. He was lean, as seemed to be the tendency with men in the South, but there was something about him that made up for his thinness and the slightly frayed quality of his uniform. He seemed alive with hope, as few people did these days, she thought.

"Tia . . . my God, it's been so long since I've seen you! You are still as beautiful as ever, little cousin, though I hear that the beaus of the South will be forever wailing. You have gone off and married a Yank—my own relation—so I am told."

Tia stepped back, still holding his hands, studying Brent. "Taylor, yes, of course. I keep forgetting that he is your relative as well."

"How is Taylor?"

"Very well, the last time I saw him," she murmured,

trying to keep all sound of bitterness from her tone. "I have heard that he went to see your father."

"You sound indignant!"

She shook her head. "Well, he was off on orders, and naturally, he shares nothing regarding his orders with me."

Brent shrugged. "It's a war, Tia. You're not on his side."

"Neither is your father."

Brent smiled. "Well, Risa's letter, informing me that you were coming, arrived just a few days ago, along with a long, long missive from my mother. It seems there was a Yank sailor tossed up on their shore after a storm. He carried confidential despatches. Taylor was sent to find him, and bring him back."

"Did he do so?"

"No. You see, my older sister had decided she wanted to keep the fellow, and so Taylor went off to return the despatches—and report the soldier unfit for duty so that he could get an honorable discharge."

"How wonderful," she murmured.

"So it seems. Jen has now married the young man."

"Jen remarried—a *Yankee?*"

"Ah, well, he's not a military man at all anymore, so I understand."

She lowered her head, amazed at the information about her cousin Jennifer. No one had been more passionately hateful regarding anyone involved with the Federal government. Jen had been ready to lay down her own life rather than give up the fight. And now . . . she had married for a second time. "Everyone is getting married, so it seems. I didn't know about Jen."

"I believe the wedding just took place." He cleared his throat. "Well, I guess I should tell you now—I have just married as well."

"What? Oh, my lord, Brent! We didn't know, we had no idea."

"Well, you didn't ask me about marrying Taylor. You didn't ask your own father, so I hear, young lady!"

"The war changes the way we do things," she murmured. "But tell me! What is her name, where did you meet?"

"Mary. You'll meet her later. I met her at the special hospital where I was last working."

"Brent! I know where you were last working! Did you marry a . . . a . . ."

He laughed, tapping her chin. "Prostitute—is that the word you're looking for? No, I didn't marry a prostitute. But I wouldn't have cared in the least what she did in her past. She's the most wonderful woman in the world. Her father was my patient. He passed away, I'm afraid, but thanks to him, we're together, and it's horribly ironic—I still spend my days patching men together, but I've never been happier in my life."

"Oh, Brent, I'm so glad!" she said.

"Well, you must know what it's like."

Know what it was like . . . to be loved, as Brent loved his Mary? No, she could not begin to imagine being so cherished.

She kept smiling.

"Marriage is . . . different."

He laughed. "It must be—with Taylor. Especially . . ."

"Yes?"

"Well, with you being so opposed on your views of the war. Frankly, I can't see how it ever came about, but then . . ." He shrugged, grinning at her. "Well, actually, I'm just very lucky that I do have Mary, I suppose. Still, you and Taylor! You are the very soul of independence and Taylor . . . well, Abby was the sweetest little thing in the world, living by his very word."

"You knew Abby?"

"Of course. Taylor is what . . . my second or third cousin or second cousin once removed, or something of the like. His family lived further north, but he came south often enough." He grinned at her. "You've got to remember, you're from the all 'white' branch of the McKenzie family—I'm from the branch with the red blood. Taylor has a similar background. Such a history in the world we live in can create a unique relationship."

"So Abby was—sweet?" she couldn't help but asking.

Her curiosity was morbid, she told herself. Abby was dead, gone. Yet Abby remained a ghost in her life. The perfect wife, while she . . . well, she was a decadent, infamous Rebel spy.

"Charming. But very strong when she chose to be. I can't imagine what he felt, watching her die . . . oh, sorry, Tia. Well, of course. That is the past. He's married to you now. And here you are deep, deep in Rebel territory. Does he know?"

She lifted her hands. "I—don't know. You know more than I do. I came here because of Rhiannon. I felt I had no choice."

"Yes, of course. I understand. Well, surely Taylor will understand as well. Pity he isn't on our side. He would have been quite an asset. I've never met a man with sharper vision, clearer hearing. When we were kids, he could put us all to shame in the Everglades. He could hear the flutter of a butterfly's wings, I think. See in pitch darkness. He's the perfect scout—the Pinkerton Agency wanted him to work with them, but he stayed with the cavalry despite his engineering skills."

"Engineering?"

Brent looked surprised. "Engineering. He studied at Oxford for a while, before entering West Point. He's a regular genius with bridges, roads, pontoons . . . his first love is actually architecture. He used to talk about the building that time would bring to Florida. You didn't know?"

"I . . . well, no." She hesitated. She didn't know much about the man she had married. "We haven't had much time together."

"Well, I must admit, I haven't seen him much myself lately, but then, I've barely seen my own folks since the war began. My mother, bless her, must spend hours writing letters—and then hoping they can reach us. Anyway, the letter I received from Risa said that Rhiannon had written to Varina Davis, but that she felt someone should see her in person as well."

"Do you know about the dream?"

"Something about a balcony, and a child. But I

haven't been able to see either the President or Varina in the last few days. He has been insanely busy, suffering from insomnia—and from crushing blows. You've heard that the Europeans have refused to recognize our government?"

"Yes."

"He is losing too many men—and too many generals. But I've sent in a request to see Varina. When we arrive, we'll see her. Set Rhiannon's mind at rest."

"She was so distraught. The dream keeps recurring. In it, there is always a little boy, falling from a balcony. She doesn't know whether she's dreaming about any of the Davis children, but she's so upset. She's described what she has seen, and both Risa and Alaina are convinced that the house she's seeing is the White House of the Confederacy."

"Well, cousin, get dressed. We'll go right away. I'll meet you downstairs. The executive mansion isn't quite as open as it was at the beginning of the war, but we'll go straight there and surely, since I sent my note, we'll get an audience with Varina quickly enough. Maybe Rhiannon's letter has already reached her."

"Thanks, Brent."

"I'll be downstairs."

She watched him go, closed the door, and dressed quickly. When she hurried downstairs, he was waiting for her. He had hired a carriage, and as they jolted along the streets on the outskirts, Tia was amazed at the changes that had taken place since the war had begun. All over, there were defense works set up. "In case Grant gets in close," Brent told her.

"How close has he come?" she asked.

"Close," he replied. He met her eyes, then squeezed her fingers. "But Lee meets him every time."

She nodded, and looked outside the carriage again. There were people everywhere. More and more, the closer they got to the heart of the city. Wounded men in worn uniforms were in abundance.

So many men without arms . . . without legs . . . limping on crutches. The expressions on their faces were so lost.

"The city has changed, I guess," Brent said. "Strange, I don't see it as you do, since I have watched as it has happened."

"Why is that building burned to rubble?"

"Ah, that was a munitions factory—burned by our own men when it seemed the Yanks might be getting in. People have fled the city, returned, fled the city, returned. It's the capital of a nation at war. This is the price that is paid."

In time, they came to the huge white house that was serving as the executive mansion for the confederacy. The street was lined with carriages there. Civilians and military men hurried about with grave faces. Fashionably dressed women—appearing just a little frayed about the edges—moved about on their business, most still accompanied by slaves and servants. There seemed to be a constant flow of soldiers on horseback.

"Here! We'll alight here!" Brent called to their driver.

He helped Tia from the carriage and they walked from the street to the elegant house. Tia was amazed to see how neglected and overgrown the grounds were.

"Once . . ." Brent said, pausing on the walk.

"Once what?"

"The house was beautiful, freshly painted, the grounds were beautifully cared for . . . Mrs. Davis's coach was usually ready to take her about the city . . . she had such fine horses. She sold them long ago now. She hasn't been about much lately. It's said that Davis considers himself surrounded by foes. Most people believe that spies have penetrated even the White House. Davis has been ill, sleeping badly. He forgets to eat. I was at a meeting with him not long ago. It was a dinner, but he barely touched his food. He has Varina quite concerned as of late."

"He must carry a great weight on his shoulders."

"He does, indeed. You should hear the furor over Fort Pillow—though I must say, whatever happened was terrible."

"What are you talking about?"

"Well—perhaps some of the fury from the Yanks has to do with our accusations against them. General Dahlgren was to attack Richmond—he didn't make it to the city. He had thought himself something of the conqueror, drinking blackberry wine at the home of our own Secretary of War, Mr. Seddon—with Mrs. Seddon. He was led astray by a guide—hanged the guide—but reached Richmond too late to tie up with Kilpatrick, who had already retreated. To make a long story short, he was killed. He had an artificial leg, acquired at Gettysburg, which was stolen—along with papers claiming that his intent was to fire Richmond and kill the Confederate cabinet. Lee sent photographic plates of the papers to General Meade, still directing the Army of the Potomac under Grant, protesting vigorously. The Yanks were up in arms over us, declaring the entire battle a massacre. Then, just a few weeks later, Bedford Forest's famed Reb Cavalry storms Fort Pillow—five hundred some odd soldiers are holding the place with more than a third of them being black troops. About two hundred and thirty are killed, another hundred are wounded, and two hundred something are captured. That is, I must say, an absurdly high ratio of killed to captured. So the Yanks are stating that we're all a lot of murderers, that it was a massacre—which it might have been, since over two hundred of the troops were black soldiers, and many men in the South are bitter and afraid of the blacks fighting against them—it might well have been a massacre. At any rate, all this goes on day in and day out, and there's no good news, so Davis is suffering the torment of the damned."

They had reached the house. Tia looked at her cousin, reflecting on the actions he had just told her about. It was no wonder there was so much hatred in the war. Both sides could be horribly ugly. She wondered if the bitterness would ever be lived down.

Not in my lifetime! she thought.

And suddenly, she just wanted to run away. From it all. She had dreamed of visiting the pyramids in Egypt, seeing London, Madrid, Rome. What a pity she hadn't gone! Before she had seen the dead, dying, and maimed soldiers, before she had come to all but bathe in blood. Before she had seen so many people die, the children as well.

"Here we are. Perhaps my message has been received."

They entered the foyer, and Brent gave his name to a servant, saying that they were friends and that he had written ahead to tell Mrs. Davis they were coming. They needed to see her as soon as possible, on a matter of urgency.

They were asked to wait.

Seconds passed, then minutes. The morning waned. Tia knew that Brent was anxious. He had left his patients to the care of others.

They stood outside, waiting. Brent talked more about Richmond, about the war, telling her that he had seen Sydney shortly before Christmas. Tia was glad to hear it, musing on the fact that Sydney remained in Washington.

"Well, she has married a Yank, you know."

"Of course, but . . ."

"No one made her return. She wanted to be in Washington, just in case he made it home for Christmas. There was some fighting then, of course, but the weather was wretched, halting the armies when God and mercy could not. She hoped that, due to the fact that the armies were most frequently up to their necks in snow, he might be spared—especially considering the fact that he had been injured at Gettysburg."

"I knew that he'd been wounded. Julian told me," Tia said.

"Yes, of course, Julian was there to perform the surgery." He tapped his hat against his leg, growing impatient. "I am a colonel," he told her ruefully. "But apparently, there are generals ahead of me."

"Brent, go back to the hospital," Tia suggested. "You don't need to wait for me."

"I had thought we might be more impressive together. Especially as kin to my brother. Jerome is quite the celebrated hero, you know."

"Of course. But you have patients who may be dying."

"There are many other doctors on duty."

"None so good as you."

He grinned. "That's true, of course, but they will manage without me for an afternoon."

She smiled, glad that he was with her.

Yet even as he spoke, they started to hear shouts coming from inside the house. Then, pandemonium. People were running everywhere; cries could be heard. Brent stared at Tia, then tried to regain entrance. They were stopped by a heavyset man.

"No one will enter now!"

"What has happened, man? I'm a doctor!" Brent declared indignantly.

The man shook his head. "It's too late now. There's been an accident. Young Joseph Emory has fallen."

Brent stared at Tia. She felt as if a river of ice suddenly filled her veins rather than blood.

"Excuse me, I will see the child!" Brent snapped forcefully, and pushed his way past the man. Tia followed.

But the boy and his family were on the ground level. There was too much confusion in the house for anyone to stop them as they saw the scene from above, then rushed back out of the entry and around to the ground level in the rear of the residence. As they came around the house, the sounds of sobbing seemed to be everywhere. Servants and children flocked about. They could hear the comments of the crowd that had formed.

"The President has been working so hard . . ."

"Mrs. Davis brought him lunch every day."

"She had just left the children, just left them to bring him his lunch."

"The boy fell."

"He was his father's favorite, so they say."

"He died right in his father's arms."

"Drew his last breath . . ."

"The poor babe!"

And there, beneath the deadly veranda, was Jefferson Davis, president of the Confederacy, down on his knees.

The grown man with worn, harried features held the lifeless body of his child in his arms. Silent sobs wracked his body. His wife was at his side, tears streaking down her face. She cried horribly. Tia bit down on her lower lip, noting that the first lady of the South was noticeably pregnant.

And in such a condition, she must endure this agony . . .

Soldiers stood by awkwardly.

"Sir . . ." A messenger had come with a despatch, Tia saw.

"Not mine, oh Lord, but thine!" Davis cried out. "Not mine, oh Lord, but thine! Not mine, oh Lord, but thine!"

Varina, tall, regal—and broken—stumbled to her feet. She said nothing, but looked at the soldier. The man turned away, his head lowered. The hardest heart would have felt a split. The beautiful child, five-year-old Joe, lay in his father's arms. No human enemy could have done the damage to him that God had wrought that day.

Whatever urgent business challenged the Confederacy would have to wait. Varina went back down to her knees by her husband and her dead son.

Brent gripped Tia's arm. She couldn't move. She could only stare at the little boy, so beautiful, so sweet in death. *How could they bear it? There was so much that was so very awful, she had seen young men cut down in their prime, and yet, this loss of a child seemed so unjust, so cruel, that she wondered if there could be a God at all. If there was, He must have been laughing at all of them, perhaps punishing them for the death they practiced so cruelly upon one another . . .*

Brent pulled Tia back, away from the growing crowd of servants and soldiers, onlookers and friends.

"Brent, is there nothing—" she whispered in anguish.

"He's dead, Tia," Brent said softly. "There is nothing I can do for a dead child."

There was nothing he could do for the child, but he and Tia stayed for a while, waiting in the parlor with Mary Chestnut, Varina's very dear friend, and others close to the Davises. Many people had come to help, yet few knew what to say or do—there was so little to say or do when a child was lost. As more and more messengers came and went, sent on to the president's military advisor, Brent and Tia found themselves waiting in Varina's little office on the ground floor. He was startled to see a pile of unopened mail lying on the footstool by her sewing basket. The top letter had a return address upon it: *Rhiannon McKenzie, Cimarron, Tampa Bay, Florida.*

His heart seemed to catch in his throat. Her letter had made it, just as they had made it. Too late. Perhaps destiny remained in God's hands, and He allowed his people only to think that they could change it.

Tia seemed drained, unaware of anything. Her beautiful fair skin was almost snow-white against the ebony of her hair and eyes, she was so pale. She hadn't seen the letter. When she turned away at last in response to something Mrs. Chestnut said, Brent unobtrusively picked up the letter and slid it into his jacket pocket.

It could do nothing now but cause the family further pain.

Taylor arrived in Washington aboard the ten-gunned steamer *Majesty,* a ship he'd boarded in St. Augustine. Coming ashore, he heard a newsboy hawking out the information that God had smitten the President of the Confederacy—little Joseph Emory Davis was dead.

Disembarking and leading Friar from his confinement in the ship, Taylor bought a newspaper, anxiously looking for word of Brent or Tia in the story. There was none. The anger which had begun a slow burn inside him when he'd heard of Tia's journey had cooled once he'd returned to the base at St. Augustine—and he'd spent an evening with the McKenzies, especially Rhiannon, who had seemed more distraught than ever.

Yet, he still felt a churning turmoil within. A feeling of *helplessness.* Yes, he damned well meant to get down to Rebel territory and find her. But what then? What power did he have over her while the war raged? He wanted her safe.

Out of the range of fire.

She was in Richmond—and he wanted her back. That simple. He damned well meant to find a way to do it.

Reading the dire news regarding Davis, he discovered that the reporter was not nearly so judgmental as the newsboy hawking the papers. There was sorrow in the article for the loss of a child. The writer didn't believe that Davis had lost his child because he had sinned before God—President and Mrs. Lincoln had lost a child during the war as well. The President's beloved little Tad had died of sickness rather than a fall, but the pain endured by the parents had been the same.

Having reached Washington, Taylor reported to Magee's offices, only to discover that the general was in the field. His presence in Washington, however, had immediately been reported to higher places. He was summoned from Magee's base headquarters straight to the White House, where he found that Lincoln himself had decided to see him.

Though it must have been difficult enough just to keep up with the movements of his generals, Lincoln was aware that Colonel Taylor Douglas had been sent back to duty in Florida. Though other losses were far greater, he knew about Olustee, and he knew, as well, about Naval Lieutenant Long who had been lost with important despatches regarding navy movements. Taylor was able to report that his business in the south of the Florida peninsula with Long had been successfully concluded. "The despatches are returned, and he has been discharged, sir. He is in no state of health to continue pursuing this war."

"We have lost him to the other side?"

Taylor shook his head. "We have lost him to the concept of war; he is weary and broken."

"We are all weary and broken."

Indeed, the President had aged greatly since the war had begun. The battles showed on his face, as if the loss of life lay in his heart at all times.

"No, sir, you do not break," Taylor countered, and grinning ruefully, he meant his every word. "I am surprised that you can be so aware of such small events within the magnitude of this war."

Lincoln shrugged, lifting his large, long-fingered hands. "Little things win a war, in the end. The Europeans helped us more than a dozen victorious battles when they refused to recognize the government of the Confederacy. As to Olustee . . . well, I had hoped for Florida to return to the fold."

"I am afraid she will not be so easy, sir."

"But so many of her citizens are Unionists."

"That is true, but my state is divided. And our best military minds have decided that the vast effort needed to win the state is not worth it—not when they have decided that Richmond must be taken and the deep South slashed in half."

"I'm afraid that our greatest military minds are fighting for our enemy!" Lincoln murmured.

"Are you referring to General Lee, sir?"

"And others. But I think I have a man who will fight now."

"General Grant?"

"You know him?"

"No, sir. He was fighting in the western theater; I was in the eastern campaigns until I was ordered to assess strengths when we undertook the Florida campaign."

"You'll know him soon enough. However, if we had Lee . . . I understand he was your good friend."

"A friend to many of us, sir. He was my teacher at West Point. A fine instructor, and a better man."

"It's been said he could be heard pacing a mile away the night I offered to make him head of the Union armies. He had such a beautiful, gracious home—now we bury our dead in his lawn. It is a bitter, bitter war, sparing no one. Old Jeff Davis apparently paced away the night his boy died. God knows, I can sympathize with the poor man, and he is, indeed, in my prayers. It's far too easy to love our enemies and feel their pain—but much harder to know they must be beaten. I'm sorry to see the destruction and death we reap, but God help us, if we can just end it . . . then we will reach out the hand of friendship, we will take our brothers back into our fold, and we will weep for our dead and our lost together."

"I pray it will be so, sir."

"Many men will feel the need for revenge when this is ended. Tell me, Colonel Douglas, will it be so for you? The war has made many widows—you are one of the few men standing to have lost a wife in this sad conflict."

"I did bear a grudge, sir. A bitter grudge indeed."

"Time has healed the wound?"

"Most wounds scar, sir. But like you, I am eager for the conflict to end." He was quiet for a moment. "I have remarried. A woman with Southern sympathies. You know her brother, Colonel Ian McKenzie."

"Indeed, so I had heard. You have married young Miss Tia McKenzie, the belle of your home state, daughter of Cimarron, renowned for its gracious hospitality, far and near. As your new wife is reputed to be a rare beauty, wild-spirited and entirely charming, I am happy for you, Colonel. It is rare to find moments of peace in this war."

"Very rare," Taylor said wryly. Moments of *peace*? "You are remarkable, sir. You not only know your officers, but are able to keep up on their marital affairs!"

"A house such as Cimarron is known far and wide. As are Jarrett McKenzie's services—not in the name of North or South, but in the name of humanity."

"The family is divided in loyalties, you know. Passionately divided."

Lincoln smiled. "You know, most of my wife's family fought for the South. So many are now dead! She has been accused of Southern sympathies herself. Poor Mary—her brother was killed, but because I am who I am, she didn't mourn him. Rather, she announced publicly that he should not have fought against our Union. When this all ends, the wounds will be terrible. And as you say, even with time, there will be terrible scars. Make peace with your Southern wife, Colonel Douglas. God knows, you have fought the war with faith and vigor, and are deserving of peace." He turned from Taylor, writing on his desk. "There will be fierce action soon, Colonel Douglas, and your expertise will be needed. Tomorrow you must head out and find General Grant himself to give assistance in the coming conflict, but this order which I am now writing will give you three weeks' leave. The order is undated, sir, and you may take the time when you feel that duty will allow it and circumstance demands it. There will be another attempt to sway Florida—she is a giant breadbasket, and though it saddens me, there seems no recourse other than to starve the South. God go with you, sir. I promise, once you find General Grant, you will no longer deal with the frustration of running from the Rebs!"

Taylor accepted the orders the President handed him, the one directing him to General Grant, and the other allowing him a leave of absence. "Thank you, sir. I've no desire, however, to leave a war half-fought."

"You won't leave the war, Colonel. But God alone knows when a man may need time."

Taylor nodded. Watching Lincoln, he wondered if he didn't have some of the precognition that plagued Julian's wife, Rhiannon. It was said that the President had dreamed himself in a coffin; good friends said that he saw his own death. He wondered uneasily if the man weren't foretelling an occasion—tragic? deadly? dangerous?—when Taylor would need time away.

"Thank you, sir."

"You've a night of leisure in the city, Colonel. Go home, rest, enjoy your time."

"Yes, sir," he said, but he didn't intend to head home at all.

When he had left his audience with the President, Taylor headed straight to a tavern often habited by cavalrymen. He would not go to his own Washington town home—he had avoided it since the beginning of the war. Abby's clothes still filled the closet; he'd never had the time nor the inclination to move them. Her touch was everywhere. She had even begun to knit clothing for the baby she was going to have, and they'd had a mahogany cradle carved.

In the tavern, he found a number of injured friends, politicians, men assigned to the forts that circled Washington, and men who had just received a change of command. In March, Grant had been in the city, conferring with Lincoln. Two known assaults would be occurring with the fine weather—the continual, Grant-determined pursuit of Lee and Richmond, and a slash across the deep South, hopefully breaking the backbone of the region. Louisiana had been drawn back to the fold; a new pro-Union government had been formed. South Carolina needed to be beaten to her knees—there lived the heart of the insurrection, and there it should be smashed and damned.

Taylor was in the middle of his second whiskey when a soldier at his side cleared his throat loudly. "Colonel Douglas, sir!"

He turned, not recognizing the man at first. He was old, with gray whiskers and a round face. He wore a sergeant's uniform.

"Sergeant," he said, acknowledging the man.

The old fellow grinned. "It's been a while, sir. I was cavalry back then, a private, with you at Manassas, back at the start of the war. Got a bullet in my leg, never could ride decent after."

"Ah . . . yes. I remember. Granger. Your name is Granger."

"Yes, sir, it is. Sergeant Hal Granger."

"Well, it's good to see you, Sergeant. Glad to see you alive." He swallowed the rest of his whiskey.

"Thank you, sir. And you as well. I don't mean to bother you none, Colonel. Looks as if you and that whiskey bottle are keeping company enough. But I'm assigned down to Old Capitol now, and I heard tell you were kin to folks named McKenzie."

Taken by surprise, Taylor frowned. "That I am, Sergeant. Is there some news about one of the McKenzies?"

"Nothing ill, sir, nothing bad happening at all, I'm glad to say. I've met a number of folks by that name now. Why, the Rebel sea captain was my guest awhile, but he's been back, a devil on the water, for some time, so I hear. Had the Doc McKenzie—Dr. Julian McKenzie—and Miss Sydney McKenzie."

"Sydney was in yes, I'd heard, but . . . Sydney married Jesse Halston."

"Right. But Colonel Halston, he's been at war for some long time now. And Miss Sydney, well . . ."

Taylor's jaw tightened; his features locked into a frown. "What about Miss Sydney?" he asked.

"Ah, well, sir! Nothing's amiss . . . but she doesn't seem to get out much, sir, that's all. Thought she'd be mighty uplifted by a visit from you, if you're able, before riding out."

Taylor nodded. "Where is she?"

Granger gave him the address. Taylor paid his bill, thanked Granger, and left the tavern, suddenly feeling sober and anxious.

Twenty minutes of riding brought him to the street where Sydney had taken her apartment. He frowned, seeing a uniformed soldier seated on her porch. His hat was pulled low and he was leaning back comfortably in his chair. Sleeping, Taylor thought.

Dismounting from Friar, he tossed his horse's reins over the hitch and approached the soldier.

The man didn't move. Taylor kicked the chair.

The fellow came to life. "Hey, what the—"

Straightening, pulling his hat back, he started to bellow—but then noticed Taylor's uniform and rank. "Colonel, sir—" he began, leaping to his feet, saluting.

"What the hell is going on here, Private?"

"I just dozed off, sir. It's traces of the fever. I had the malaria. That's why I'm on this duty, sir."

"What duty is that?"

The private reddened. "Well, the lady who lives here is a known Rebel spy."

"Who says so?"

"Her, uh, her husband, sir."

"Oh?"

The soldier grimaced uncomfortably. "She's been caught in the act, sir."

"Ah. Well, you can doze right back off again, soldier. I'll be watching her tonight."

"Oh, no, colonel, sir. I mean, I can't—I mean—just who are you, sir?"

Taylor folded his arms over his chest. "The lady's cousin, soldier."

"Oh, jeez—you must be Douglas, sir! I should have known, sir!" Suddenly, he was saluting all over again. "We've heard about you, sir. Every soldier has heard about you. Of course, I should have seen it right away. You're also an In—"

"Indian," Taylor finished for him, but he felt no rancor. The young soldier seemed to be a decent enough fellow. "My cousins are Rebels, but I was under the impression that Colonel Halston had vouched for his wife, and that she had been set free."

"Well, yes, sir, but she kept slipping back down to Richmond, sir."

"Doing what?"

"Well, no one rightly knew, sir. That was the problem."

"She's in there now, I take it?"

"Yes, sir."

"At ease then, soldier. I'll be with her now."

Taylor stepped past him, entering the house, closing the door behind him. It was a small but cozy place. It smelled like fresh-baked bread; a fire burned in the hearth. "Sydney?" he called.

There was no answer. He walked to the bedroom door, looked in. The bedroom was darkened. He could see a form beneath the covers.

"Sydney?" he whispered.

He walked over to the bed. Pulled back the covers. The shape of a body had been formed with pillows. No human being slept therein.

Mary was charming. Pleasant, thoughtful, and lovely with her warm, serious, silver eyes and long dark hair. Tia tried, really tried, to greet her with enthusiasm, to appreciate the woman who had made Brent so happy. When they were introduced, Tia hugged Mary and welcomed her to the family. Brent poured Tia a sherry, and she drank it, then started to cry.

She couldn't eat that evening. Brent told her that little Joseph Emory's death was terrible and painful but she couldn't make herself sick over what had happened. She didn't know how to explain to him about the little girl who had died in Jacksonville, how it was all too unfair to be endured. He was helpless, telling her that if she didn't calm down, he'd be wasting good opiates on her to *make* her calm down. Mary understood her better. She and Tia sat together for a very long time, and they cried together, but in the end, Brent did slip laudanum into Tia's drink, and she fell into an exhausted sleep.

In the middle of the night, she awoke. She sat up, staring at the fire, unable to sleep anymore. Unable to cry.

Brent really didn't understand.

She had failed Rhiannon. Rhiannon had known what was going to happen. Tia hadn't managed to move fast enough, and so another child had died.

Brent found her there, hugged her, tried talking to her. "Tia! This isn't like you. Where is your courage, where is your fire?"

"Gone," Tia told him. "Dead—like the children. Like the young men we kill on a daily basis."

"Tia, you're really going to make yourself sick. You're married now; you could be expecting your own child—"

"No!" she told him, swinging on him violently. "No! I will not have children, I will not let this happen, I will not have any more death!"

"Tia, you can't say that. You don't know that you won't have children. You can't will yourself not to have children—"

"I will *not* have them. I don't care what I have to do or not do, but I will never, ever have children!" she swore.

"I'm not sure that will be agreeable to your husband, Tia. Abby was expecting a child when she was killed. Taylor wanted children."

"Then Taylor will have to find a new wife!" she snapped. "Unless . . . unless . . . he gets himself killed!"

Suddenly, it seemed that flood gates were opened and she started to cry again, and cry, and Brent decided not to argue with her anymore. He fixed her a sherry with more laudanum, and he held her until she fell asleep again.

This time, he had assured himself, she would sleep through the next day.

Taylor sat in the rocking chair before the fire in his cousin's room, rocking, watching the blaze. He waited an hour, then grew worried.

Instinct warned him she wasn't returning anytime soon. The smell of the fresh-baked bread was a front. Just like the pillows tucked into the bed.

Maybe she had meant to make it home. Maybe she was in trouble.

He walked to her bedroom window and studied the sill, then opened the window and looked to the ground below. This was obviously the way she had left. A man didn't need to be any kind of a scout to read so clear a sign.

He left by the front door, saying nothing to the soldier on duty. Mounting Friar, Taylor rode around Sydney's street, picked up the trail, and followed it to a livery, where a man on duty remembered Sydney well. She was a beautiful woman who often rented conveyances from him. She had a brother she visited behind the lines, sick relatives just south of Alexandria.

"She's a sweet one, she is, and a beauty, and hey . . ." He paused, studying Taylor in the lamplight. "Colonel, you her brother?" Taylor was certain the man would think that anyone with Indian blood looked like anyone else with Indian blood, but the livery keeper really seemed to admire Sydney, and wanted to help.

"Cousin. And I'm afraid for her. Running into danger behind the lines."

"Well, I found something in a carriage when she returned it one night. Keep forgetting to give it to her. Perhaps it will help you."

The fellow limped into his office. He saw Taylor watching him as he limped back out. "Bullet in the ankle at Antietam," he explained. "Took me out of the army right fast; they thought I'd lose the foot. Here, it's what I found. Don't know why I kept it. It's just an old wrapping—for material, maybe, or a piece of clothing. But there's an address on it. See there? Bailiwick Farm, Virginia. Do you know the place?"

Taylor did. Northeast of Fredericksburg, in continually disputed terrain. He thanked the fellow, and quickly took his leave.

From the livery, he rode out of the city.

He was well aware of the mounting tensions. Washington itself was surrounded by forts. The father he traveled outward, through Alexandria, Union territory by sheer proximity, the more he heard about the way the armies were forming. They would meet soon.

Heading south, he was challenged several times by the Union pickets. He readily stopped at the lines, handing over his papers.

By dawn, he was far past the lines and into Virginia, into no-man's-land. Troops from both the North and the South vied for every advantage here. He avoided the main roads, taking side trails through the foliage. At one point, he barely avoided a small troop of Southern cavalry—scouts and skirmishers, he thought, watching the men from the cover of a huge oak. He could hear only bits and pieces of their conversation, but enough to know that the whole body of Lee's army was not far away.

By noon, he had reached the farm. Time had taught him caution; he watched the house from the untended apple orchard to its northwest side before deciding how to approach it.

The place had never been ostentatious; the house itself had two stories with trellises but no balconies. Spring flowers tried to climb along the trellises, but they were withered and dying. The paddock fences were broken in places; paint peeled there as it did from the house. The place looked neglected and sad.

A few skinny chickens roamed the dirt in front of the front porch area. One bony mule hung its head sadly in the paddock to the left of the house.

There was a large barn to the right. Its double doors were closed.

Taylor placed his hand on Friar's nose. "Stay here, boy. But come for me right away if I whistle, will you?"

He moved quickly from the orchard to the rear of the barn. Flat against the rear wall, he searched the wooden structure until he found an area of rotted planking. Slamming it with a fist, he winced as the beam itself gave with a creak. He pushed through, rolling into a stall filled with stale, damp straw. He immediately came to his feet, surveying the area.

The stables were empty—except for the wagon in the center of the work area. He walked to it; the horses hitched to the wagon were solid workhorses, in far better shape than the mule in the paddock. He moved to the double doors at the front of the structure. They weren't latched; he could push them open and see toward the house. He watched. And waited.

He didn't now how long he'd stood there, but then he saw a slim black girl come out of the house and start toward the stables. Frowning, he turned around and saw the ladder to the loft. He skimmed up it quickly, and went flat against the rotting hay.

A moment later, an older black man came from the house, then two youngsters, and finally a big, well-muscled black man in his prime. A field hand, Taylor reasoned.

As the older man entered the barn, Taylor saw clearly through the doors. A young, strikingly pretty black woman was racing after him—followed by Sydney. What in God's name was she up to?

Even as Sydney ran, he heard the sound of hoofbeats.

"A Rebel patrol!" the black woman cried.

"Get in, I'll fend them off!"

The black woman entered the barn and hovered at

the entrance, hidden against the doors. Even from his perch in the loft, Taylor could see the pulse beating at her throat.

The hoofbeats came to a halt. "Hello!" Sydney greeted them cheerfully. "Gentlemen, tell me, are the Yankees at bay?"

Barely able to see out the slit in the door, Taylor tried to count their number. "Is there about to be a battle near here? Dear Lord, gentlemen, I haven't much, but we've sweet fresh water—"

"Ma'am, there's word you're harboring an ex-slave known as Sissy McKendrick, and that you are committing treason by giving her aid."

"Sir! How dare you accuse me—"

"Check the barn—and if you find that black demon with any other darkees, hang 'em on the spot. I don't care if Jeff Davis thinks they ought to be returned to their masters—I think they're dangerous!"

"Wait!" Sydney protested. "You can't just kill people."

"Maybe I won't quite hang a white woman, miss. Definitely not right away. Maybe I'll just give you a chance to convince me and the boys that you shouldn't hang. Though they say you're a traitor—a Southern woman taken to thievery and spying for Abe Lincoln!"

"No honest soldier under Master Robert E. Lee would ever talk to a woman that way."

"Maybe I just don't care what Bobby Lee would say, ma'am. Bobby Lee isn't here right now, is he?"

The doors burst open. Taylor was able to get a full count of the men. Seven of them, including the leader, who remained mounted, staring down at Sydney. His six men entered the barn. The blacks had tried to hide in the musty hay once they'd known the soldiers were coming in, but one of the soldiers picked up a pitchfork and started to aim at a too-large pile of straw. Sissy cried out, and the man stopped, turned, and grabbed her. "I think we got the one we're after—damned pretty piece of black baggage, sir!"

"Hang her—hang her now, and fast, and get the rest

of them out here. Let 'em know that they'll die for this,
and others won't be quite so willing to run!"

"No!" Sydney cried. "Stop it, stop it now, I'll report
you—"

"You won't be reporting anything, miss. You're the
worst traitor here. When I finish with you, sweet little
belle, there won't be a pretty thing about you, and you
surely won't have lips and teeth to do much talking."

He dismounted, grabbing Sydney before she could
turn to flee. She fought him, catching him in the eye.
The blacks in the barn were beginning to scream. One
of the soldiers drew his gun. Taylor had wanted a clearer
shot, but he didn't dare wait.

He drew his Colts, aimed first for the man getting
ready to shoot, and caught him straight through the
heart.

Then taking a split second longer to make sure he
didn't hit Sydney, he caught her attacker dead center in
the forehead. Screams rose all around him as the slaves
in the barn feared for their lives. The five remaining
soldiers pulled their guns; five more shots from the Colts
brought the Rebels down, all dying while still trying to
find the position of the enemy.

Sydney saw him. She hadn't moved; the man who had
assaulted her lay dead at her feet. She stared at him.
"Taylor?" she whispered incredulously.

He came down the ladder quickly. Sissy stood by the
doors again, staring at him as well. "Get your people
into the wagon fast," Taylor ordered, "and get them the
hell out of here as quickly as you can. Stick to the small
trails—most regular troops are going to be too concerned with the major battle coming up to mind much
about a wagon going by."

"Yes, sir," Sissy replied. "Come on now, people, you
heard the man. Get in the wagon, under the straw in
back, fast!"

Her elocution was perfect, her voice soft and melodic.
She gazed at him with steady brown eyes, and he realized that she had never been really afraid. If they had
chosen to hang her, she would have been willing to die.

Sydney, a little wobbly, walked into the barn. "Taylor, I . . ." She stopped, staring at the dead men around her.

"Sydney," he said flatly. He came to her, stopping two feet in front of her, suddenly sickened by what the war was doing to all of them. "For the love of God, Sydney, what he hell are you doing? Sweet Jesus, you could have died here!"

"Oh God, Taylor, they're all—dead."

Sydney looked at him, stricken. But Sissy came to life with a vengeance. "Sydney , they were going to kill us, every last one of us!"

"But they were . . . Rebels. I never really meant to betray my people."

"Sydney! They weren't your people. They were the scum of the earth!"

Sydney stared at Taylor again. He thought she was going to crack.

"You killed them all," she said.

"I hate killing people, Sydney. I just didn't see a choice."

"No . . . no . . . it was all my fault!" she cried, and she suddenly threw herself at him, and she was shaking very hard. "Taylor, if you hadn't come . . . oh my God, they were going to hang us! Without a judge, without anything legal, without—"

"They were scum. White trash!" Sissy said. She was staring at Taylor. "Thank you, sir. I don't know you, but I am mighty beholden. It's a miracle that you're here."

"Not a miracle. I went to Sydney's house. I thought . . ." He shrugged. "I thought she was running intelligence behind the lines."

Sissy was very still, her chin high for a long moment. "Not intelligence. People, Colonel. Black people. Yes! She's slipped behind Rebel lines. And she's slipped back through Yankee lines. Saving lives, Colonel, saving lives, saving people!"

Taylor drew away from Sydney, slowly arching a brow. Her face flooded with color. She lifted her hands. "Jesse would still want to throttle me!" she said hoarsely. "And if Jerome knew . . . or Brent, or my father . . . Julian. Tia . . ." Her voice trailed.

"You've been working the underground railroad," he said incredulously.

"No!" Sydney said. "Not really. I didn't mean—"

"Yes!" the beautiful black woman declared defiantly. "She has been incredible."

"By accident!" Sydney said. He shook his head. Accident? He'd heard those words before. What happened that people were drawn into this conflict?

He smiled slowly, gravely. "Sydney McKenzie! I will be damned."

"Taylor, you understand then? You won't tell—"

"Sydney, you turned into a *Yankee?*"

"No! I'm a Rebel in all things . . . but this!" she whispered. "Taylor, you must keep my secret, you must—"

She broke off because he was shaking his head. "Sydney, I can't keep your secret. Jesse thinks you're spying for the Confederacy, so what you are doing has to be better. But he'd be angry because what you're doing is really dangerous. You've been branded a traitor. Go home, and stay under house arrest."

"Taylor, you can't mean to tell Jesse—"

"Sydney, I'm afraid that I do."

He leaned forward, giving her a kiss on her cheek. "I think he'll be very proud of you, too. After he throttles you, that is. But no more outings, Sydney. A good soldier knows when to lay down his arms."

Sydney lowered her head. "I know."

"We've got to get moving. I can follow you for about ten miles—that should bring us to a Union outpost, at the least."

Sissy was staring at him, smiling. "You one mighty fine man—for a white boy, that is. Are you married, Colonel?"

"No, he isn't," Sydney said.

"Yes, I'm afraid I am married," he told Sissy, grinning in return. He looked at Sydney to explain. "I've remarried."

"You have? When? Who? I'm so happy for you, Taylor. I know how deeply you were hurt when Abby died. When did this happen, where—"

"Tia."

"Tia!"

"Yes. Tia."

"Tia *McKenzie?*" she asked incredulously.

"The same. But now, if you'll excuse me, you have people beneath straw in that wagon, and God knows if these fellows had any friends following behind them. Sissy, it's been a pleasure meeting you. You are one of the most courageous—and beautiful—women of my acquaintance. Sydney, again, I'm very proud of you, but I've just left your father, and he would want to flay me alive if I didn't make you swear you'd never take such a chance again. Ever."

"I do swear, but—"

"Then let's get going."

"Let's get going, just like that!" Sydney protested, her emerald eyes as wide as saucers. "Taylor, wait, you can't really have married Tia—"

"I did, but we've no time to talk. Sydney, for the love of God, get in the wagon!"

She stared at him, threw her arms around him, and hugged him fiercely. "Thank you, Taylor, thank you so much for being here to save my life! I do swear that I'll guard it now myself!"

He didn't have to tell her again. She slipped from his embrace and into the wagon. Taylor dragged the dead man who lay outside the barn into the center of it, slapped the Rebel horses on their rumps, and whistled for Friar.

He followed the contraband wagon to the first Union picket he could find.

Then he turned back for the battle lines himself.

Tia lay in what felt like a strange state of twilight. She wasn't sleeping, but she wasn't awake. She didn't want to wake up. Waking meant the most awful sensation of loss. Just now, she was numb, and she liked the feeling.

Suddenly, she was being jarred out of sleep.

"Wake up, Tia!"

Brent was shaking her hard. Almost brutally.

"Stop it, Brent!" she protested angrily. "I want to stay here in bed. I want more laudanum."

"Not on your life. I've given you too much already. You've grieved for the dead; it's time to care about the living again. Get out of bed and get dressed. Fast."

"No."

But her cousin wrenched her covers away, caught her arm, and dragged her to her feet. "Tia, there's a major battle going on. Injured men all over. I'm being sent out to a field hospital. You're coming with me."

"No . . . no. You've got Mary. Nurses, orderlies—"

"Mary is coming. And you're coming with me, too. You're experienced. You've worked with Julian. You know me, and you'll be good with me."

"No, Brent, I don't care anymore. I'm sick of injured soldiers and chopped-up men."

"Oh! You're suddenly sick of them? Well, believe me, Tia, they're sick of being chopped up!"

"I don't care." She closed her eyes.

She was startled when her cousin suddenly seized hold of her, shaking her. "Damn you, Tia, now! I need your help—they need help. They're suffering. Not crying over what they can't change!"

"Brent!" She pulled free from him, taking a deep breath, meeting his eyes. What was the matter with her? "Brent, I'm sorry . . . I'll get dressed. Quickly," she told him.

"Good! I really need you, Tia."

Within a few minutes, she was ready.

With Brent and Mary, she rode down the street to the hospital, where dozens of wagons were being prepared with canvas tents and medical supplies. Men were shouting orders, horses were neighing, bugles were blowing, drums were pounding.

"The engagement has begun!"

"The bloody Yanks are everywhere."

"They say there will be thousands fallen."

"The Yanks don't give a bloody damn how many they kill, not even of their own!"

"Lee will beat them back. He always does."

"They're fighting right near Chancellorsville again."

More troops were amassing—cavalry, infantry. The street was filled with those leaving, and with those looking on.

And those afraid that Grant would ride into Richmond.

Soon their wagons were ready, and they were riding. Out to the Wilderness, an area of no-man's-land near Fredericksburg where the forest and foliage were nearly as thick as the earth.

And none of them knew just what kind of an inferno was about to be set loose.

Chapter 20

Almost a year earlier, the same ground had been traveled by both armies—to fight the battle of Chancellorsville. Both Union and Confederate troops had died in the forests of the Wilderness.

Riding hard along the trails as they sought the best ground to establish their field hospital, Brent, Tia, and their party passed by sad and ghostly remembrances of the deadly battles gone past: bones, bleached white by the sun, stripped of all flesh by prowling creatures, lay in piles far too numerous all about the roads and among the trees and foliage. Tia tried to tell herself that they were the bones of horses, but a human skull kicked forward by her horse's hoof dispelled whatever illusions she might have cherished.

They found a copse far back in Rebel lines. Brent began to shout orders, and men were quickly setting up the tents, folding tables, chairs, stretchers, and instruments. Before they were set up and prepared, the injured began to come in, some screaming in pain, some silent, some awake, some unconscious. There were five surgeons beneath Brent, ten nurses including Tia and Mary, and six husky orderlies.

Within an hour, the tables were stained with blood.

Tia forgot the strange apathy that had seized her, yet it seemed that she remained numb. She was glad, for she worked with an insane speed, fearful only that her haste would cause her to drop and lose the instruments the doctors called for. She was reminded of the battle at Olustee Station, and yet, within a few hours, she felt that Olustee had barely prepared her for this.

The day seemed endless. Tia felt as if she wore a second skin of blood. *Stay numb,* she urged herself. *Yes, numb. Just keep moving, and moving.*

That night, there was no end. Darkness had brought an end to the fighting, but not to the arrival of the injured. Yanks came into the surgery along with the Rebels.

She kept hearing where the different armies, divisions, and brigades were deployed. Information that meant little. The armies had met and clashed in the Wilderness, and it was highly unlikely that any of the commanders really knew where to find their own men.

Tia slept on a saddlebag by the field hospital, but only for a few hours. In the tangle of growth, injured men were lost and forgotten, found when another group of men stumbled upon the same scene of battle.

Dawn came without much light. The woods and copses were so filled with powder from the cannons and guns that it was hard to discern day from night.

She thought that it was midmorning. Mary had left with a wagon of wounded, desperate to obtain more supplies from a railway deposit that had been expected during the night.

Tia worked across from Brent, clamping an artery as he removed a minie ball.

He looked at her over the man's body, shook his head. "We've lost this one."

She lowered her eyes. There was no time for sorrow. The orderlies were already coming to take the man away and bring another in.

Flies buzzed all around them.

In a corner of the tent, a pile of limbs rose very high. The stench of the blood was almost overwhelming.

"Kneecap is shattered; the leg has to go," Brent said.

There was a sudden, whizzing sound that made even Brent flinch. "Who the bloody hell is shooting off artillery into woods like that?" Brent swore.

Soon they began to hear the sounds of screaming.

Then, the smoke began. Worse than the powder, it began to fill the air.

One of the wounded men brought in was shouting wildly. "God, God, God, someone has to stop it, stop it! They're burning alive out there, oh my God, burning alive, burning to death, sweet Jesus, sweet Jesus . . ."

An orderly rushed over to Brent. "Colonel McKenzie! Colonel McKenzie, it's true! The Wilderness is burning. Men are . . . are burning to death. Caught in the trees. The fire is coming this way. We've got to move the hospital. Quickly!"

Taylor left the women at the first Yankee picket post, then turned and rode back for the main army lines. He rode into hell already taking shape.

Owing to the troop movements in place, Taylor rode around half of both armies before finding Grant's headquarters.

He wasn't assigned to ride with the cavalry, or to lead troops, though he discovered that both Jesse Halston and Ian were out there somewhere, both in the midst of the fighting. His orders from the unassuming Grant sent him circling around the rest of the action, trying to discern the positions and number of the enemy. By reaching the general alone, at his headquarters near the woods, he had garnered a lot of the information about the Rebel units that the command had needed.

General Grant, chomping on a cigar, told him quietly that he was weary of the Confederate numbers being exaggerated—something which had happened frequently from the days when McClellan had been leading the Yankee troops on down. Union officers had been far too cautious. And far too often, even after taking a victory, Union officers ordered a retreat.

"We're not going to retreat, Colonel. We're going to fight."

By nightfall after the first day, Taylor had managed to circle a number of the Rebel divisions, discern the leadership, then meet back with Grant and his officers to point out their current situation and how they had come to it. After leaving the general, Taylor found out where some of the captured Rebels were being kept. A number of the men had been taken that morning, and he hoped that someone might have news about Brent McKenzie.

The Rebs were on a small hill, watched over by a number of Union infantrymen. Captured, they were at their leisure, many of them eating Yankee provisions, and most of them looking as if they needed many more decent meals. Their uniforms were more than frayed, and most of them were hardly regulation anymore. Many wore pants taken from dead Yankee soldiers, and ill-fitting boots taken from the feet of the fallen as well. Some were nearly barefoot. Yet when he first arrived among them, they remained defiant, no one answering when he first asked about the surgeon, Colonel Brent McKenzie.

"Why are you askin', Colonel?" an infantry captain asked him.

He turned to the man. Tall, lean, and grave, he watched Taylor with careful eyes.

"Because he's kin," Taylor said. "And I believe that my wife is traveling with him."

The captain was quiet for a minute, then told him. "McKenzie was working at the hospital just outside Richmond; he had been called out to work in a field hospital right after our first skirmishers ran into one another. Last I heard, he was doing just fine, setting up his surgery down the Plank Road." The captain kept studying him. "You're married to Tia?" he inquired.

Taylor had heard that note of skepticism so often. "Yes, captain, I am married to Tia McKenzie. The war does make for strange bedfellows. You know my wife?"

The captain nodded. "There was no finer place to be asked than Cimarron, sir. I hailed from South Georgia, and attended many a ball and barbecue at Cimarron. No one would ever forget the daughter of the house, sir. She possessed such beauty and grace in those days . . . and yet I had heard that she quickly turned to compassion once the war began, discarding fashion and finery for blood and death. My congratulations, sir."

"Thank you, Captain. You are certain she is with her cousin now?"

"No, I'm not certain. I did not see her myself, but I heard from mutual friends that she was with Brent, and I cannot imagine they would be wrong."

He thanked the captain again, then asked him if there was anything he could do for him. The captain hesitated, then pointed to a man seated by a tree. "Private Simms received a wound some time ago that continues to plague him. I know that we will probably be sent to different prison camps in the North . . . is there any way you can see to it that he goes to Old Capitol? I have heard it is the best, since it is beneath the nose of many Southern sympathizers, and that Old Abe is actually a man of compassion himself."

"I will see to it," Taylor told him. "You have my word. And for yourself—"

The captain offered him a hand. "For myself, I am in good health. I am nothing more than weary. I will survive the war and return home, and until then, I will go to bed nightly praying for it all to end."

"Amen to that!" Taylor told him and, soon after, left the man for what sleep he might acquire during the night.

Tomorrow . . .

Tomorrow would bring more savage fighting. And he would follow orders, and do his duty to his country.

And yet . . .

God help him, he would also try to find his wife.

Musket flashes ignited dry timber. Pine and scrub oak immediately caught fire. The woods were blazing.

Pandemonium broke out in the hospital at first. Tia, trying to calm a soldier with a shattered leg, heard her cousin's voice rise above the shouts in a deep tone of command. Order began to return; those who could walk were up. Ambulances were loaded; soldiers threw wet towels over the heads of the panicking horses. The conveyances began to leave. There were still soldiers to be moved when the trees surrounding the hospital began to smoke, smolder, and catch. Tia was busy tying a temporary bandage when Brent came behind her, picked her up by the waist, and set her on one of the wagons next to a soldier with an arm wound.

"Get going."

"Not until you leave."

"Stay on that wagon!"

"Brent—"

"I'm right behind you. I'll make it out much easier without worrying about you. For the love of God! Corporal O'Malley!" he said, addressing the man at her side. "Keep her there beside you! Get her out of these woods!"

"Yessir!" the slender, graying O'Malley said.

"Brent—"

Brent stepped back, shouting to the driver. The reins snapped, and the wagon started off along the trail.

"Brent . . ." Tia said, ready to hop off the rear of the wagon and race back for her cousin, no matter what his command. But she couldn't do so. The soldier at her side had her in a firm grip with his one good arm. "Miss Tia, I've been told to get you out of these woods. That was an order, ma'am."

The wagon moved down the road. Tia stared back toward the place where their field hospital had been. Her cousin was back there. Brent wouldn't leave until every last man had been moved from the path of the fire.

She heard the snaps and crackling sounds of the blaze as more and more of the brush and trees caught fire. The air began to fill more and more with the blinding smoke.

And even as they moved along the trail, above the din of the creaking wagons and the gunfire that remained, they could hear the screams of the dying.

Men caught in the field of trees. Hurt, fallen, not dead . . . seeing the flames.

"Oh, God!" Tia cried, covering her ears with her hands. But she couldn't block out the sounds, and she was suddenly certain that a cry she was hearing was coming from just ahead.

Taking Corporal O'Malley by surprise, she leapt down

from the wagon. "Wait! Give me just a few seconds!" she shouted to the driver.

"Miss Tia!" O'Malley shouted from behind her.

"A few seconds!"

She ran along the trail, desperately seeking the source of the cries she'd heard. Were the cries real? Or were they just more of the awful sounds of the forest, the rat-tat-tat of guns, the thuds, and bumps and crackling of burning, falling trees?

"Help, Jesus, oh sweet Jesus, oh God, if I only had a bullet . . ."

The words were real. She burst through the shrub on the side of the road. "Where are you?"

"Here, here . . . help! Oh, Mother of God, help me! Sweet Jesus, pray for us poor sinners now . . . oh, God, oh, God, and at the hour of our death . . . Amen . . ."

"Where are you! Talk to me, help me find you!" Tia shouted.

"Here, here, are you real, please, for the love of God, my leg . . . can't move it, caught, the branch is burning. The heat, here, here, please, please . . ."

She burst through the trees into a little copse. She saw that already the tinder-dry fallen leaves on the ground were beginning to catch in clumps. Then, across the copse, she saw him.

A Yankee infantryman, down against the bark of one tree, the gunfire-severed limb of another tree down upon him. She rushed across the copse.

"Oh, sweet Jesus!" he cried, seeing her. He was young. As young as some of the Rebel soldiers newly rushed into the ranks of the Florida militia. His hair was platinum-white, his whiskers nonexistent, his eyes powder-blue, making him appear even younger. His pale face was sooted and streaked with tears. "Please . . ." he said, reaching a hand to her.

She came to her knees at his side, aware of the ever-encroaching fire. "I've got to get the branch first," she told him, and she locked her arms around it, straining. Sweat broke out on her forehead. It had not looked so heavy. She changed position, trying to drag it from his thigh. He let out a horrible scream—and passed out. She saw that his leg was not just broken, but a bullet had probably lodged somewhere in his thigh. "God help me!" she whispered, tugging at the branch again. She wasn't going to make it. She could feel the heat of the flames beginning to lick at her now. "Miss Tia!"

She turned around. Corporal O'Malley had followed her. "Miss Tia, it's going to burn!"

"Help me."

"He's a Yankee."

"He's a boy."

"Big Yank, little Yank—"

"I'm not leaving him."

O'Malley sighed, anxiously coming to her side. He gripped the tree limb with his good arm. Gritted his teeth.

The boy's head began to wobble. His blue eyes opened. He quickly realized his situation and looked up at O'Malley. "Shoot me, sir, please shoot me before the fire . . ."

"Both of us at once," Tia said. "For the love of God, O'Malley! Come, man, please, you're a good Irish Catholic, aren't you? You should have heard him saying his Rosary just now. God could be watching this very minute—"

"Miss Tia, you know where to strike a man as the Yanks do not. On the count of three!" O'Malley told her. They both gripped the tree limb. O'Malley counted. The limb moved. They leapt quickly to their feet. "I can't lift him; my arm's broken," O'Malley said.

"Soldier, you'll have to limp with me."

They got the boy to his feet. Aware of the flames close behind, they hurried toward the road. Suddenly, before them, a tree fell, sending sparks flying everywhere. "Turn!" O'Malley commanded. "Run!"

They did so, the young Yankee screaming at the agony in his leg. They burst upon the road. The wagon had already started moving. "Help him!" Tia called to a number of the men. They did so without question, reaching for the boy. She didn't know if they were so weary and hurt that they didn't care that they reached their hands out to the enemy—or if they just simply couldn't tell what he was anymore. The boy was covered in dirt and soot and ash, making his uniform appear to be made of gray, Confederate-issue cloth. Now, the sounds of men coughing were almost loud enough to cover up the terrible crackling that continued to fill the air.

"Get O'Malley!" she cried loudly when the boy was up. "He can't use his arm!" Despite their own wounds, the injured soldiers responded. When O'Malley was boarded, the shattering sounds of trees exploding came from behind them.

Tia gasped. The crash had come from the site of the hospital. And Brent was still back there. The mules, pulling the wagon, bolted.

She heard the driver shouting, "Whoa!" The wagon was taking flight as if suddenly airborne.

"Miss Tia!"

She heard O'Malley's cry. And she ignored it. Her cousin was back in the flames. She was not leaving without him.

The wagon continued its wild race from the inferno.

Tia started to run back.

The continual twists and turns in the path of the fire had left many men lost, with no perception of the locations of the poor trails through the woods. Taylor Douglas had been ordered into the Wilderness, to find the various officers and commanders caught in scattered pockets in the woods and escort them out.

Moving into the smoke and fire, Taylor thanked God for Friar; his warhorse was an experienced animal as seasoned as any soldier. Instinct must have warned the horse to steer clear of the flames, but he stalwartly followed the course Taylor commanded.

At first, his mission seemed somewhat feasible. And he was glad of it. His orders coincided with the direction in which he had anxiously longed to ride—toward what had been the Rebel line.

He found able-bodied men caught in copses who were able to carry some of the wounded to the roads, and toward safety. Naturally, he had been ordered to salvage what he could of the Union fighting force. But no one had ordered that he should leave any Rebels in danger of burning, and he was more determined than ever to find Brent McKenzie and his field hospital—and Tia. With the fires raging so furiously, he knew that he was on a course that would take him far beyond his basic orders.

He meant either to find Brent and Tia, or at least locate someone who could tell them that the hospital had been moved, and that his wife and kin were safe.

Yet as time went on, the danger grew ever greater, and although he was aware that there were still men caught and trapped, soon, looking for anyone alive in the wildfire of the Wilderness would be madness. By now, every breath of air was filled with smoke.

And worse.

He could not inhale without breathing in the horrible scent of charred and burning human flesh. What devil had thought up this day's outcome to the battle? He could not believe that any man living would have wished such a fate on his enemy. And despite the horrible losses in the burning woods, neither side had gained a real advantage.

Hearing screams ahead, Taylor left the road, moving into the thicket. The smoke was so thick he could barely see. Friar began fidgeting at last. "Just a bit forward, boy, just a bit."

But a wall of flame suddenly rose before him. Beyond it, he could hear shouts. "To the south, see there, a clearing!"

"Take it, men, take it—"

"Try there east—"

"No, see the flames rising?"

"Friar, which way, boy?" he said to the horse. "And I don't mean hightailing it out of the woods."

Friar inched forward, reared back. Finally, the horse turned southward. Taylor allowed him to keep the lead, finally coming around to where he found a space in the wall of flames. "Hello! This way—if you're trapped, there's a space through here . . ."

He broke off, surveying the area. There were no flames there now because the scrub had burned itself out. He gritted his teeth, seeing that what had appeared to be a log were the remnants of a man, blackened beyond recognition.

And beyond North and South. What color he had worn in life, no one would ever know.

He nudged Friar through the slender trail. Coming around into the copse, he found the pocket of men. They had stopped speaking because they were coughing and choking. One had fallen. "This way, through the trail here!" he called out. Dismounting from Friar, he took his canteen, soaked the scarf of one of the men with water, pressed it to the man's face, then offered the canteen around. "Soak your kerchiefs! Head that way, quickly. It looks like a wall of flame but there's a trail through. Go! I'll get the sergeant!"

While the others obeyed him, soaking cloths and turning desperately toward the trail, one of the men came back to him. "Colonel, sir, I'll help with the old timer there!"

Taylor realized suddenly that this man, remaining in the inferno, ready to help the old sergeant who had fallen, was a Rebel captain. The smoke, ash, and constant soot had blinded him to this strange grouping at first.

"You're a Reb," Taylor said.

"Two of us, sir, are Rebs. Three Yanks." He shrugged. "We were busy killing one another in a crossfire when a tree went down. Fellow screamed so that we all dropped our weapons. Then the whole place was burning."

Caught in the flames together, they had looked for a way to live, rather than die.

Taylor studied the man and nodded slowly, looking back at the sergeant. The old, winded man probably didn't have a chance of surviving much more smoke.

"Let me take him, sir. I'll follow your orders; you can lead on!"

"Fine, Captain!" Taylor said, allowing the captain to take the sergeant. He headed toward Friar, took his horse's reins, and pointed out their route of escape. He looked at the young Rebel. "I won't be leading you anywhere. I'm going on a bit farther, looking for—others. You, sir, will give me your word that you'll be leading yourself toward Union forces," he said quietly.

The captain grinned. "Sir, you can lead me straight into prison camp, if you send me from this inferno. I will go, and gladly. Sergeant Foster, we're going to make it. Hang on, old man, hang on!"

Friar was beginning to react badly to the flames, and still, Taylor thought that the horse might be the sergeant's only salvation. He called out to the captain. "Get the sergeant up on my horse. I'll lead the way out and you go on. And so help me, Captain, come hell or high water, you take care of my horse!"

"Aye, sir!" the captain called.

With the sergeant up on Friar, Taylor led his horse out of the forest trail onto the road. Flames were shooting all around them, all but making an archway over the remaining passable road.

He should have gotten out. Gone with the captain and old Sergeant foster. He could not. He felt a strange restlessness in his spirit, as if he knew he could find Tia. And that she would be in trouble.

He heard more cries of anguish, terror, pain. He hesitated on the road, looking back.

"Sir, you should lead your horse out. I'll go back there for you."

"No, Captain, that won't be necessary. You take the sergeant out, sir. But tell me, do you know what troops were back there, and who was leading them?"

"Infantry troops . . . and there was a Rebel field hospital back in a copse. I know, because I was in at first when my calf was hit."

Looking down, Taylor saw that the man had been wounded. Blood seeped from a bandage around his calf.

Despite his wound, the young captain had apparently come back into the fighting.

"Why the hell did you leave?" he asked harshly.

"They were busy. Colonel, we haven't time to debate. I can't just leave, I have to find what men I can. You can shoot me in the back, or let me go do what I can."

"Sir, you can get up on my horse, and get your bleeding leg and this man to some help—I'll go back for your Rebs."

"They might shoot you on sight."

"I'll take my chances. Look after my horse!"

"Aye, sir."

A field hospital.

There were bound to be scores of physicians on the field today, Taylor thought, but his heart was pounding. This was where the Reb prisoner had said he would find Brent.

"Captain, do you know, by any chance, was a Dr. McKenzie at that site?"

"Dr. McKenzie was in charge of the site, sir. He ordered me not to move," the captain said with a shrug. "But then . . . well, there were so many men who were really badly injured. I think the ball passed right through my leg."

"And you may still bleed to death if you don't get help. Go."

The captain saluted him. "On my honor, sir. "I'll bring the sergeant to the Yanks, and turn myself in—and take damned good care of the horse."

Taylor nodded, turned, and started down the road. He was a fool. All around him now, the woods were burning. The sky itself seemed like a sheet of flame. Even if he could avoid the blaze, he'd soon die of smoke inhalation, no matter how he'd soaked his neckpiece.

His lungs were already burning. Brent had surely had the sense to get out by now.

He kept walking.

Finally, ahead of him, he could see the remains of the field hospital, in a copse. At first, it appeared, the hospital hadn't caught fire because it was enough in a clearing to be away from the dry shrubbery that filled the woods. But now, flame had leaped to canvas, the whole of the place had collapsed, and a huge, ancient tree from the forest flank had fallen. Smoke rose everywhere. A team of mules, caught when the tree had covered their wagon, whinnied and neighed with a vengeance, fighting their restraints. From the stalled wagon, wounded men, near death, groaned, their signs of life pale against the onslaught and fury of the fire.

"McKenzie!" Taylor called out. "Brent McKenzie!"

He headed first toward the wagon, saw the charred oak limb that trapped it, and the men lying in the rear of the conveyance.

Some were dead already. He looked away from their faces, from the eyes left wide open in death, and strained to move the fallen tree. Too heavy. Burned wood crumpled in his hands. He tried for better leverage, saw a downed pole from the canvas tenting, and worked it under the limb. Throwing his weight against the pole, he shifted the limb. It fell to the ground in a hail of ash. The heat around him was growing intense. He returned to the wagon, searching the bodies in it. No sign of Brent McKenzie.

Taylor heard the sounds of movement. One of the men in the rear of the wagon had stirred. Taylor shifted to the man's position. "Soldier, can you hear me?"

The man's eyes opened. His face was nearly black from the ash.

"The doctor, soldier, Dr. McKenzie. What happened to him?"

The wounded man tried to respond. His mouth moved. Taylor reached for his canteen, praying he had water enough let after soaking the scarves of the other men. Yes. He moistened the fellow's lips. The man drank then, slowly, carefully. "The . . . tent . . . collapsed," the man said. His eyes closed again.

"Hang on," Taylor said. "We're going to get out of here. I'm going to find McKenzie. We'll make it out."

He didn't know if he was believed or not; the soldier's eyes closed. But then the man spoke again. "Three of them. The boy the doc went back for . . . and the woman. The nurse . . . she went after him when the pole snapped and the canvas fell."

The woman.

Tia.

Who else would have gone after a McKenzie when threatened with certain death, trapped under canvas in the wake of a roaring inferno?

A shudder ripped through him and he turned, looking at the field of charred canvas. He raced for the fallen field hospital roofing, grabbed it firmly with both hands, and started pulling it, managing to move it no more than a few inches. *Naturally, fool,* he charged himself. *It took a dozen men to set it up!*

The woods were burning hotter, closer. He raged against the impotency of his own strength, then he gritted his teeth, his anger calming with the realization that he would lose this battle for sure if he didn't gain control of his fear and fight with logic.

Again, he saw the fallen pole, picked it up, searched until he found another, then slid both under the canvas. He could feel the heat around him continually intensifying as he worked, but he forced himself to take each step, securing the canvas to the poles with rope, then tying the poles to the wagon like a giant travois, and urging the mules farther and farther forward as the great canopy began to move, foot by foot, rather than inch by inch. The mule power gave him the strength he needed to move the fallen tent.

Then he saw her.

She lay on her back, rolled toward him by the shifting canvas, face white beneath the soot, black hair spread out in a giant fan beneath her. He hurried to her, kneeling at her side, brushing a strand of stray hair from her face and seeking a pulse at her throat. She shifted where she lay, groaned. Her eyes opened, and she stared up at him with disbelief.

"Taylor?" she said incredulously.

"Yes, it's me."

She shook her head. "Taylor, you can't be here, you

can't. It's a Rebel field hospital, the canvas collapsed, it's all burning . . ."

"Tia, I am here, you little fool, and it's no strange quirk of fate. I'm here because I was looking for you. *You're* not supposed to be here; you're supposed to be in St Augustine."

"I had to be here. There was no choice."

"There's always a choice. But we can't argue now. Can you move?"

The words came out harshly, spoken with a mixture of fear and relief. Perhaps it was good that he sounded so blunt and angry—his words brought a spark to her dark eyes. "I can move, yes, and I have to—oh, God! Brent . . . Brent!" She struggled up, using him to grab on to, then pushing him away to rise. "Brent, where in God's name is Brent? I saw him, I was trying to help him with the last man when . . ."

Taylor rose to his feet behind her. He realized that he was shaking; he was so very grateful that Tia was alive. She was racing toward a pile of rubble—cots, surgery tables that had fallen when the tent collapsed. Brent was facedown in the debris.

Taylor reached Brent right behind Tia. She fell down beside him, trying to move him carefully, calling his name.

"Brent, Brent . . ."

Something nearby exploded, perhaps a discarded powder bag, a rifle gripped in a dead hand. Flames seemed to shoot all around them.

Taylor reached down for Brent. "Taylor, we don't know his injury—"

"It's death if we don't move now, Tia!" He collected Brent swiftly in his arms, maneuvering through the rubble to get him to the wagon.

It was heavy laden with the dead.

The soldier who had spoken to him earlier had opened his eyes. He saw Taylor grit his teeth in a fleeting dilemma as he tried to find a place in the wagon for Brent.

"Colonel, roll young Ted Larkin there off the wagon. A funeral pyre here is as good as any. You'll have to leave some of the dead, if we're to get through with the living."

The man was right, and finding the spirit and will to live now that there seemed to be hope, he rose as best he could with his newly amputated leg and shoved the body of the dead man off the wagon, making room for Brent. Not even sure that Brent was still breathing, Taylor turned back for Tia, knowing they were truly running out of time. The air was barely breathable at all; the oxygen was being surely sucked from it.

"Tia!"

She was in the rubble. He ran to her. She was trying to lift the shattered pieces of a camp cot from the body of a soldier. Taylor started to help her, then saw that the man's eyes were open, staring heavenward. He was dead.

"He's gone, Tia."

"No, he just had a wound to his foot."

"His lungs were crushed, Tia."

"No—"

"Tia!"

She started struggling wildly against him. Desperate, he slapped her, hard. Stunned, she reeled back. He stepped forward, caught her arms, and threw her over his shoulder. He ran from the canvas and rubble toward the wagon. A large tree, the trunk ablaze, suddenly fell ahead of him. Tia screamed, and he jerked back just in time to avoid it.

"Colonel, move it, move it, move it, move it, sir!" the soldier from the wagon shouted above the renewed roar of the flame. He had dragged himself to the driver's seat.

Taylor didn't need any more encouragement. He ignored the instinctive fear of fire, made a running leap over the tree, and catapulted toward the wagon. He nearly threw Tia atop it, then crawled aboard himself, even as the soldier cracked the whip high over the mules' heads. They leapt forward—spurred by panic and fear. In a matter of seconds, they were tearing down the trail like a pair of racehorses. Someone within the wagon screamed. Taylor, flat on his back at Tia's side, gasped for air, glad at least that a few of the men were alive. He rose quickly then, but Tia had already staggered to a kneeling position in the wildly jolting wagon. She was seeking a pulse from Brent. She looked Taylor's way. "He's breathing!" she said.

"Good. Damned good."

The woods were still on fire, but the intense heat seemed to be fading with the breeze. They were recklessly racing from the worst of it. Explosions from behind them signified the ignition of the trees as the fire spread, but they were leaving the worst of it.

Then, the wagon wheels hit a pothole. The mules kept shooting forward. The wagon began to break up. The injured screamed as they were flung far and wide from the crushing boards. Taylor halfway rose, throwing his body in a brace over Tia and Brent, burrowing against them as they flew through the smoky air.

They landed hard in the dirt. For a second Taylor couldn't move. He heard the groans and cries around him. They had escaped certain death at the hospital site, but as he looked up, the tall oaks in front of them burst into flame. He swore, staggering to his feet, then he bent down and secured the unconscious Brent in his arms. "Stay with me!" he commanded Tia as she rose up, and he started to run, carrying his human burden around the blazing oaks. Miraculously, they had come upon a little pond in the midst of a copse. The damp earth by the pond kept the fire at bay. There were riders arriving there, shouting. Someone met Taylor as he staggered forward with Brent. "I'll take him, Colonel."

He handed Brent to the man. "There are more in there, just beyond the trees."

He turned. Tia had started back. "Tia! Damn you!" She was past the flame. He chased after her. She was wasting no time, reaching for the arms of a fallen amputee, ready simply to drag him around the flames. With others behind him, he wanted only to stop Tia. "I've got him!" he shouted, lifting the man. "Go!"

She ran. He heard a terrible crackling sound. He looked up. A huge branch was coming down.

He looked at Tia. Her eyes met his.

He heard her shrieking . . .

Then the branch fell. With barely an instant to spare, he leapt back. The fire roared and blazed high before his face. He ducked around it quickly. She started racing toward him. "Tia, no, the other way!"

A weakened tree limb snapped and fell. It struck her on the shoulder. She collapsed to her knees. She rose, fell again . . .

Soldiers were coming, finding the injured, sorting them from the dead.

Someone picked Tia up. Another came to Taylor and relieved him of the man he carried. He raced forward with renewed energy, caught up with the man carrying Tia.

"She's my wife!"

The soldier paused, letting him take Tia. Her eyes opened, caught his. Closed again. He kept moving forward until they came to the water. He went down, ripping her skirt, soaking it, cleaning her face. Her eyes opened again. She stared at him.

"Brent?"

"Safe."

"You can't be here!" she whispered.

"But I am here," he told her.

Behind him, a throat was cleared. "I don't mean to interrupt this reunion but . . . you *shouldn't* be here, sir."

Taylor frowned and turned. Behind him stood an officer. Beyond him, the injured had been taken from the wreckage and the flames. There were many soldiers surrounding them now, efficiently moving men into conveyances to bring them farther back from the flames. The night remained filled with the sounds of the dry trees catching and burning, but the sounds were becoming background noise, and even some of the shouts of the men seemed to be fading into the distance.

He noted what he hadn't taken time to realize before.

Like the officer who had just spoken to him, the soldiers here were all Rebels.

"I'm Colonel Josh Morgan, sir," said the Reb addressing him. The man was too young to be a colonel, Taylor thought. He was too young to be out of a military academy. "Your courage, sir, has been extraordinary. I'm sorry to offer you harm or discomfort in any way, but . . . well, sir, we're still at war. And no matter how it grieves me, I must inform you—you are now a prisoner of the Confederate States of America."

He had a chance, and he knew it. He rose, slowly, carefully, assessing the man. The colonel stood by his mount, a bay mare. It was unlikely that any of the men here were going to shoot him in the back. All he had to do was steal the horse, and ride back into the flames.

He saw the colonel's eyes—and knew that young Josh Morgan was trying to give him just that chance.

"Thank you, sir," he said, and he reached past the man, gripping the horse's reins and meeting the young man's stare. Then he burst into action, leaping on the horse.

And desperately—perhaps ridiculously—racing back toward the inferno. There had to be another way out.

But Tia didn't understand. Or she did. He heard her scream his name. "Taylor!" She was racing after him, coughing, choking, stumbling . . . but coming after him. He spun around on the horse. "Tia, go back!"

"Taylor, damn you!"

The fire lit the night. Smoke was everywhere, blinding him. She nearly reached him, then doubled over, coughing, gagging. She fell.

He reined in, came to her, dismounted. Her eyes remained closed as he lifted her into his arms. He didn't know if she was really unconscious, or if it had been a ploy to bring him back.

Whichever, it didn't matter.

He would not risk her life. He might dare the fires again himself, but he would not risk bringing her through the inferno again.

She lay limply in his arms. Perhaps it was just as well; the trail behind him now blazed with such a fury that it would be pure suicide to risk it. He carried Tia, aware that the good warhorse followed him as closely as a well-trained dog. The Rebels watched him return, the red of the blaze painting the night behind him.

He handed Tia over to one of the Rebel medics who had raced toward him. She was one of theirs; they would see to it that she was taken far behind the lines, and given all possible medical attention. Still, he watched the medic walk away, hearing the grate of his own teeth, feeling tense enough to snap.

He walked wearily to the far-too-young Colonel Morgan.

"Sir, it appears I am your prisoner."

Chapter 21

When Tia opened her eyes again, it was to daylight. She had no idea where she was, though she quickly remembered the terrors of the day gone by. She bolted up, and was startled to realize that she was in a house, in a pleasant room with cheerful blue and white wallpaper, polished paneling, and handsome furniture. Her charred, torn clothing was gone. She could smell a faint reminder of the fires—the scent was in her hair, she realized. But she was dressed in a blue-flowered cotton nightgown. It still hurt a little to breathe.

"At last. You're awake!"

Startled, she turned, and found Mary, Brent's wife, smiling at her from a rocker. She had not kept vigil in an idle manner, but was busy winding bandages from cotton reels.

"Mary!" Tia said, sitting up.

"Well, you were out long enough."

"I was? How long? Taylor . . . Brent . . ."

"Um . . . you've been out about a day and a half. Brent is fine; he's already back working."

"But he was unconscious—"

"Not for long. I reached you all soon after Morgan did. Brent was already coming around then—you were the one we worried about."

"And what about . . . Taylor? Taylor . . . he was there, after the canvas fell, and we made it out of the woods, and then he grabbed a horse and ran back into the fire."

"And you ran after him, you were hurt, and he brought you back."

Tia closed her eyes; she could see the flames again,

feel the awful heat. See his eyes as he sat on the horse. The way he looked at her, across the fire. She shouldn't have followed him. Why had she done so?

Because he was riding back into the flames. It was as if he had lost his mind, the road was becoming an inferno.

"Then . . . if he brought me back . . ." She hesitated, and looked at Mary. "What did they do with him?"

"They had little choice. He was taken prisoner. He's with a group of men who will probably be escorted to Andersonville. He's at a farmhouse now. Brent will know more later."

"He's—all right?"

"He's fine, Brent was told. The soldiers who took him were very respectful. He dragged Confederate injured out of those woods, you realize."

Tia nodded. "Yes, of course, I know."

"I'm sure when Brent returns tonight, he'll know more. Of course, you'll want to see Taylor. I'm sure Brent can arrange it."

"Mary, where are we now?" Tia asked, looking around.

Mary smiled suddenly. "My father's house. I haven't been back here in two years. But I have a wonderful, wonderful maid. We grew up together. She's just two years older than I am, and my father saw to it that we were taught up in the classroom in the attic. She writes to me, always assuring me that she's kept the house up. When my father died, I didn't care much. But now . . . well, it's good to be home, except that . . ."

"Except that?"

"Well . . . we're not really far behind the confederate lines, and the lines are shifting all the time now. And, well, some of the neighbors have reported that it doesn't much matter which army robs you blind when the soldiers are hungry."

"How close are the lines?"

"Sometimes," Mary said softly, "you can hear the shelling."

"My God, that close? Then more soldiers are dying— near us! We should probably be with Brent."

"He'll come to the house tonight. He said that you were not to leave here under any circumstances."

"Wonderful! Now *Brent* is telling me what to do!"

"Tia, Brent wants you to stay alive. You must take time to heal yourself."

"*I* must take time? What about Brent? He was out cold for hours, but *he's* back to work!"

Mary shook her head, smiling. "You're forgetting—it's Brent's surgery."

"I suppose you're right," Tia said, unconvinced.

"We'll be back with him soon enough." Mary shuddered. "Last night, I died a thousand deaths in my heart, seeing the fires, not being able to reach you, waiting, wondering, praying . . . it is the waiting that is the hardest job of all in this war."

Mary was right.

Waiting was the hardest job of all.

But Tia waited, and wondered, and she was afraid, dying to see Taylor, not wanting to see Taylor, and not understanding herself at all.

Taylor's imprisonment was not too grim; he was treated decently by the Rebs. He'd even heard that his old teacher and friend, Master Robert E. Lee, knew he'd been captured, and had ordered that he be treated with the utmost respect.

Owing either to Lee's intervention or to the reports that he had risked his own life to save Rebel soldiers, he had been sent southward toward Richmond to be held at an old farmhouse with other officers until he could be transported to a prison camp. The farmhouse had apparently stood empty for some time—or housed the headquarters of one army or the other on some previous date. It had a strange feeling of emptiness. Torn curtains, once white and beautiful, drifted in a gray dance when the breeze blew. Dust covered the finely carved mantle. Windows had broken and fallen.

It was said that the men being taken now were to go to Andersonville—reputed to be something of a death sentence. The overcrowding was beyond imagination;

disease ran rampant. The death ratio was horrendously high.

For the moment, however, his prison was not too grim. Days were spent in the fields—the fields had been mowed down at some earlier battle or skirmish, but there were still a few large oak trees offering shade. The Rebs had little but musty, maggot-ridden hardtack to eat, but what his captors had, they shared. Different men came, and shared the information of the war.

Most of the Confederates had thought that Grant would strike and sidle away—as the Army of Potomac usually did.

Grant sidled, but not away. He moved on to Spotsylvania Court House. The fighting continued, fast and furious. Union losses, they reckoned, were over fifteen thousand. Who could really count? The South . . . well, she wasn't losing so many, but then, she could ill afford any losses.

On May 12, the soldiers guarding them went into mourning; Taylor found out that Jeb Stuart, "Beauty," as they'd called him in class, had died on the eleventh, mortally wounded at a place called Yellow Tavern. He'd been the nemesis of the Union cavalry; he'd also been a friend, a good, bold man, cocky, wild, fun to be with, yet loyal to the core. It was a hard loss. The Rebels, he thought, were fighting a bitter battle, indeed. Stuart was lost now—hit not far from where Stonewall had received his mortal blow. Longstreet had been wounded in the conflict, Hill was ill, and Lee himself had gotten very ill.

Grant wasn't going home. He had decided that the army was staying in Virginia. He refused to accept defeat.

The battle at the Wilderness flowed into the battle at Spotsylvania, and when those battles were over, neither side could claim victory. The Union suffered tremendous casualties. The South lost fewer men, but they could afford far fewer men.

And, Grant refused to give up and go home. He wouldn't even leave the area to lick his wounds, so the soldiers complained. He shifted; Lee shifted. Grant was trying for Richmond. Somehow, Lee kept getting his army between the Union army and the Confederate capital.

At the farm, Taylor watched and bided his time. He was not under heavy guard. He listened while some of the other Union officers considered escape routes— tempting, naturally, since their own army was close. Exactly where, no one was certain. Pockets of fighting continually occurred.

He wasn't quite ready to escape himself. He wanted to know where Tia was, and just what she was doing.

His captors, though congenial enough, were pleased to tell the prisoners about the Rebel victories. On the fifteenth of May, a Union force was defeated at New Market. Major General John C. Breckinridge attacked Federal forces under Sigel, at the last minute unwillingly committing the two hundred and forty-seven cadets from the Virginia Military Academy.

It had truly become a war of children, Taylor thought. Ten of the cadets were killed, and forty-seven were wounded.

Toward the end of May, Brent McKenzie arrived to see him. Taylor had been down by the small pond in what had once been a large horse paddock—the horses had been gone for years now. The large oaks offered shade. By twilight, the area was beautiful. It helped him to go there, helped to still his restless spirit—and his self-recriminations. He shouldn't have been idle in a Confederate camp. He should have been out there, scouting positions, reporting on strengths. Every veteran of the war was needed, every experienced soldier. The war needed to end.

So thinking, he leaned against an oak, watching the late-day sun play upon the water.

"Taylor!"

Hearing himself hailed, he turned quickly. Brent was striding toward him. The fact that he wore gray and was among the captors seemed to mean little to him. He walked up to Taylor, embracing him quickly, drawing away. "You look well enough."

"I am, thank you."

"No—thank *you*. I would be cinders now if it weren't for you. I should have come sooner. I haven't been able to."

"Where is Tia, and what is she doing?"

"And why isn't she here with me?" Brent added softly.

"Yes, that is an interesting question."

"She will come soon. We are staying with a family that lives near here, and she is on her way."

Brent was uncomfortable. He felt as if he should apologize for Tia.

"She is anxious to see you, of course."

"Is she?"

"And to convey her deepest gratitude. She knows that you saved our lives."

Taylor was quiet. "I've killed men in battle, more men than I want to remember. But there are few men who would willingly be witness to others—even enemies— being burned to death. And," he added quietly, "I lost one wife in this tempest, a needless tragedy. God help me, if at all in my power, I would not let Tia pay the price for this bloodshed as well."

"Your wife—yes. But your compassion for your enemies has not gone unnoticed or unappreciated," Brent told him. "There were times when the North meant to refuse exchanges—to your side, all men are expendable; to ours, unfortunately, they are not—but still, there is word that certain men will be traded. You are among them. There has been a tremendous demand from those Yanks you saved from the fire—before plucking so many Rebels from the inferno. If I've heard correctly, though, we're getting back two colonels and a lieutenant for you."

"I'm flattered. Do you know when any of this is to take place?"

"No, I'm afraid not. There are pools of blood now being shed at Cold Harbor. The Union army is eight miles from Richmond, but Lee has entrenched, and you know how good our entrenchments are. Perhaps—"

Brent broke off, seeing that Tia had come at last. She stood a distance away, on the little hill that sloped down to the pond. She was slim, and stood very still. Seeing her, Taylor felt a sharp agony as his muscles constricted, and something inside him seemed to rip and tear as well. She knew that he saw her. She started quickly down the hill.

Brent waved to her. "Well," he said. "She has come, more quickly than I expected. I will leave the two of you alone."

But Tia had nearly reached them. She tried to offer a rueful smile. "Brent, you needn't leave us so quickly."

"Cousin, I am already gone," he assured her. "I will await you at the house."

He walked away. Tia stood some distance from Taylor still. He clamped down hard on his teeth and jaw, suddenly tempted to reach out and shake her. She was his wife. Granted he was a Yankee prisoner, but they were all but alone in the copse; his Rebel guards kept watch at the fences, and were pleasant and discreet enough to be looking elsewhere. When he'd last come upon her, they had faced death. Here . . . there was nothing between them but cooling night air. She should have rushed to him, thrown her arms around him. They were both alive. Seeing one another after so much time apart.

He held his distance for the moment, as she held hers. She looked far graver, saddened—even calmer than the wild spirit he had come to know. Very beautiful; appearing slim and sleek in a simple cotton day dress, the length of her hair wound in a twist at her nape. Her eyes were as dark and hypnotic as the promise of night; her features were pale.

"Taylor!" she said softly, then fell awkwardly silent again before she found speech once more. "I'm so sorry; honestly. You saved our lives, and I caused you to be here. Except, of course, that perhaps I should be glad you are a prisoner—there's such terrible fighting going on. Thousands of men are dead. Thousands . . ." She broke off, waiting for him to speak. "Thousands," she repeated. "Not just men—but boys. Real boys." She looked away for a moment. "Taylor, I'm so grateful to you. I want you to understand that, believe me, please."

Her manner was very strange. The tension in him seemed to be increasing. Of course, with his guards at the fences, with others surrounding—with him a prisoner—it would be difficult at best to follow pure instinct and sweep her into his arms and do to her everything that he longed to do. But he did, at the least, want her in his arms.

"Come here," he said.

"Taylor, it's a camp," she murmured. "There are guards."

"The guards won't care." It wasn't the guards. There was another reason she wouldn't come near him.

"Taylor, I—"

He didn't intend to hear it. She wouldn't come to him; he would come to her. He stepped forward, catching her shoulders, drawing her forcefully into his arms. She was soft, smelling more sweetly than he might have dared imagine, clean, feminine. Her hair teased his nose; his senses came to life. He lifted his chin, touching her lips.

She stiffened at first to his embrace, fought the intimacy of his kiss. Yet time made him strong, persistent, and persuasive, and in a few moments it seemed that she thawed, and melted in his hold. Soon his intimate invasion of her mouth was met with a wicked, searing passion that all but matched his own. He held her tightly, felt the supple fever of her form. And for that moment, he felt that, yes, there was something, she was wild and unique, and she was his, and when the war ended . . .

Yet she retreated again, pressing away from him. She didn't even pause to look at the guards, but stared into his eyes.

"Taylor, I've come to tell you that . . . I mean, of course, I came to say thank you, with my whole heart. I know that you came purposely to save me, that you felt it your duty to come for your wife, that you've paid a terrible price for what you did. I know all that, Taylor. My God, for Brent as well! Brent—"

"Brent is my relation, too, Tia. You owe nothing on

his behalf," he said, studying her eyes and feeling again as if a spring were winding within him.

"Taylor, what I'm trying to say is that I know that . . . I know that I do, just for myself, owe you so very much . . . and because of it, well, partially because of it . . . Taylor, it's all been my fault, I see that, I know that, but . . ."

"Tia, what the hell are you trying to say?" he grated out. He was aware, more than ever, that guards surrounded him. That he was a prisoner.

"I . . . plan to give you a divorce. I've decided that I very definitely don't want to have children."

"What? What does this sudden revelation have to do with now, with the war—"

"I want you to know that I don't hold you to anything. You're a hero, Taylor, to both sides, a rather difficult role in this wretched, bloody war. I know . . . I know how you felt about Abby, which was why you did marry me, feeling that . . . that it didn't matter, because you still loved her so much. But I suppose every man wants children, most men want children, and if not children, well . . ." She paused, her face flooding with color, her eyes falling from his. "Well, I mean, I don't want . . ."

"You don't want what?"

"I have to go, Taylor."

"No, you don't."

"Yes, I do. There are injured children—"

"That's what this is all about? You came to Richmond to see Varina, and she lost her little boy anyway."

"Taylor, I just don't want—"

"People lose children, Tia, yes. Every little life is very vulnerable. But where there is pain and tragedy, there is joy as well. Yes, you will lose in life! But Tia, you will not deny it while you live it!"

"I have to go!" she said, pulling away from him.

He might be a prisoner, but he'd be damned if he'd let her go. Not like that. He forced her closer again, tilted her chin, forced her lips, her hunger, with his passion. Again, she resisted, yet again, after a moment . . .

She fought so hard to deny it. Yet she was on fire,

the passion that had led her to war lived in her spirit, her heart, her soul. She could try to deny anything about herself, or the two of them. She could be his enemy, but she was also his wife, and he could make her realize that she wanted the role, desired his touch . . .

Her arms curled around, fingers wove into his air. She returned his kiss with hunger and yearning . . . then suddenly, she broke away.

"I have to go."

"Tia—"

"I have to go. I'll find a way to get a divorce."

"Tia, damn you—"

"Stop!" She screamed the word. Guards started to turn. She stared at him, seeing the outrage in his eyes. But she slapped him, with speed and with vigor. And she turned and ran.

Naturally, he started after her. She was swift and fleet, but he would have caught her.

Except that he suddenly had two men down upon him, and when he would have fought like a jungle cat, throwing them off, he felt the muzzle of a gun against his temple.

"Colonel! Colonel, please, oh, for the love of God, please!"

One of the guards who had brought him down was almost in tears, looking at him. "Sir, please, oh, please, don't make me shoot you."

He drew in a deep breath and went dead still.

"Sir, I will not put that burden upon you!" he declared.

The guard rose, stretched a hand down to him. Taylor accepted the hand and rose. Tia was just stepping into a covered wagon at the front of the farmhouse.

Taylor closed his eyes, lowered his head, and damned her a thousand times over.

Chapter 22

Tia was tired, yet determined that what she was doing was right. If she didn't take the time to think about the tragedy of it all, and just worked as hard as she could, all the awful sights she saw were bearable. Making a difference was what mattered.

From the third to the twelfth of June, battle waged at Cold Harbor, Virginia. Grant had brought his troops to within eight miles of Richmond. But the Southerners had dug in, and Lee's army remained between him and his objective.

Tia wasn't just glad to stay busy herself; she was glad to know that Taylor was being kept from the action. Now, each time she saw a Union uniform come into surgery, she had only to hope and pray that the man was not her brother. She knew that Brent feared finding Ian now more than ever, with the armies so constantly at one another, and she realized that he watched for Jesse Halston as well, the man Sydney had married. But either both Ian and Jesse were surviving the carnage intact—or their destroyed bodies remained on the field, or the Union surgeons were looking after their own with the same speed and efficiency the Rebels attempted. Brent worked at a frenetic pace, since men who could be saved far too often perished if left too long upon the bloody fields where the fighting took place.

It was as Mary had said. Waiting was hard. Working was much better. Much, much better for Tia, because she didn't want time to think about Taylor. She didn't want to remember either the way that he had held her, touched her, kissed her—or the way he had looked at her when she told him that she didn't want children and would give him a divorce.

And then, she had slapped him and run, and the Rebels had jumped on top of him, and she had looked back, seen his golden eyes upon her . . .

Much better to work, than to think.

And the work was continuous. From Cold Harbor, Grant began to shift again. The Rebels were praying that he'd decide he had taken his quota of blood for the time being and turn back. He did not.

Lee began to withdraw from Richmond, believing that Grant was heading straight toward the capital. But Grant was not, they discovered, heading toward Richmond. He was after Petersburg, considering it the back door to the Confederate capital.

With the tremendous fighting and the casualties sustained, Tia spent much of her time on the field with her cousin and his wife, using Mary's beautiful old home as a base.

But on the twentieth of June, a messenger arrived, stating they should abandon the house. It might well be in the way of the circling Union army.

Brent and Mary had packed and just finished with the house by late afternoon when Tia returned. She had remained at the Lutheran church turned makeshift hospital in the town center until the last of their young patients had been removed.

"Tia, hurry, we've got wounded waiting at the new facilities," Brent told her, anxiously throwing the last of his supplies on the larger of the two carriages they were taking from the stables.

"You two go on; I'll follow right behind."

"I'm not leaving you," Brent insisted. "There's no one else here."

"And there could be deserters," Mary added. "Yankee scouting parties."

"I just have a few things to take. I can manage the small carriage alone."

Brent looked around. There wasn't a soul in sight on the pretty, residential street. It had become a ghost town.

Dust swirled in the streets, caught by the breeze. The houses around them had been closed down in the hopes that the enemy would find them locked—and go away. The windows that gazed upon them from the street seemed like soulless eyes.

"Brent, go!" She kissed his cheek, then hugged Mary.

"All right, but when we go, you stay in the house. I'll send a soldier back to escort you to us."

"I promise. I'll stay in the house."

Even as she urged him, a rider suddenly burst onto the street, coming hard. "We have a general down, sir, begging we bring you in and quickly!" he said, saluting Brent.

"There you have it, get moving!" Tia said.

"Soldier, I'll go to the general; you stay with my cousin, bring her along the minute she's finished packing."

"Aye, sir!" He dismounted from his horse.

Tia smiled, waved as Brent and Mary departed, and thanked the soldier for staying.

"It's my duty, ma'am. I'll be at the fence, waiting."

"I won't be long."

She opened the gate to the white picket fence, and closed it behind her. The small buggy remained in the stately drive. Hitched to it was the best of their available horses, a tough little mare. "One minute, Suzie, and we'll be out of here as well!"

She should have come back from the hospital sooner, she thought. She suddenly felt a chill, as if the place really had become a ghost town, peopled with soldiers who had perished, who walked the streets wondering what might have come of their lives.

She was glad that Brent had left her an escort.

In the house she rushed into the room she had been using. It seemed so clean and neat and *normal.* She looked from the dressing screen to the hip tub and the bed with its soft, welcoming mattress. So much for luxury. Though she had spent her fair share of nights on the field, she'd had this place to come to as well. A haven for rest, for real baths with hot water, a place for clean clothes and the scent of rose soap, far from the smell of battle—and death.

She opened a brocade carpetbag on the bed and looked around quickly for the things she needed and wanted most. The soap, most definitely. Candles, matches, clean pantalettes, hose, and her freshly laundered blouses, tended by Mary's servants, all gone now as well. How many had gone with Mary and Brent? she wondered.

And how many had fled to the coming Yanks?

She folded her stockings into the bag, then paused, feeling a strange sensation that she was being watched.

Turning toward the bedroom door, she froze. Taylor was there, blocking the doorway. As she stared at him, her mouth dry and a sense of fear invading her limbs, he tossed off his hat and walked into the room. He helped himself to the nearly empty brandy decanter on the occasional table, and walked over to the mantle.

"Hello, Mrs. Douglas. Were you leaving?"

She didn't answer; she didn't move. "What are you doing here?" she cross-queried him. "You were a prisoner at the farmhouse."

"I felt I'd overstayed my welcome," he said with a grin. "Apparently, my captors agreed and were shipping me out—to Andersonville. The place has acquired a nasty reputation, so I decided not to go. The prisoner exchange that Brent was promised never took place."

"Did you escape from the farmhouse?"

"No. We were already en route. Ian and Jesse Halston—you know, he married Sydney—were coming to rescue me, but I'd already freed myself before they met up with me. Afterward, I had a chance to fill Jesse in on his wife's foolhardy exploits."

"How convenient," Tia said flippantly, not wanting to accept the sudden acceleration of her heartbeat. *Taylor was back.*

But what had happened to the Rebel soldier waiting for her at the fence? Was he watching the house, waiting to recapture Taylor?

"I missed you, Tia."

"Well . . ." she murmured, and she realized that what voice she had was husky and faint. "I was just leaving."

"But now you're staying," he said flatly.

She shook her head, moistening her lips. "No, I'm leaving. I didn't mean to be so rude and ungrateful when I saw you at the farmhouse, Taylor. I was trying to make you understand, I'm not what you want."

"Oddly enough, at the moment, you're exactly what I want."

"Taylor, I've told you—"

"And I've told you. You made a commitment. You want out of it? Sorry, already done."

"But I forced you into this. You can get a divorce."

"Come here, Tia." With purpose, he set his empty brandy glass on the mantle.

"Taylor . . ."

She backed away from him uneasily, feeling his eyes. A fluttering began in her stomach. Just the way he looked at her . . . she closed her eyes, gritting her teeth. Was she afraid of Taylor? She knew exactly what he intended. She didn't think he cared at the moment whether she was particularly willing or not. She'd slapped him, ignored him—and had him brought down by an enemy with a gun at his head. And still . . .

It wasn't Taylor she feared. It was the way she felt inside, just when he looked at her like that. It was the hunger he awakened when she gazed at his hands, at the bronze of his long fingers. The yearning that swept through her like a storm when he came closer and closer, when she felt his warmth, breathed his scent . . .

"Taylor, you haven't paid the least bit of attention to me. I don't want children. I'm sick of seeing them die. I won't go through what I've watched parents go through."

He caught her by the shoulders, forcing her to break off her words as he gave her a violent shake. "Shut up, Tia. We all play with what we're dealt. Life is the game, and we play it out. Yes, there is loss, and yes, we endure. Can I tell you that you'll never have a child die? That you won't face more tragedy, even when the war is over?

No, my love, there are no guarantees in life, none at all. But I'll be damned if I'll watch you risk your own fool life over and over again, and then turn into the worst kind of coward there is."

"Taylor, don't—"

"You'll deal with life, Tia, and that's the way it is."

"But I don't want this!" she cried, wrenching free from his hold, backing away again. "I don't want you, I don't want this! It was sheer accident, sheer stupidity, and I have said that I am deeply sorry, and deeply grateful, and I have given you your freedom."

"But I have not given you yours!" he snapped angrily.

She turned, trying to escape him around the bed. His hand snaked out, caught her by the arm with a vengeance. He pulled her back, and she fell on the bed. She lay winded. He crawled over her—staring down at her—and shoved her carpetbag off the bed. "Want to slap me? Call for the Rebs?"

She didn't answer him, but stared up at him hard.

He smiled. "Sorry—your Rebel escort isn't coming for you."

"What did you do to that poor soldier?"

"He's alive, Tia, but he won't be escorting you anywhere. There's no one to call, my love. I believe the tables are turned."

"Taylor, I . . ."

He leaned low against her. "You what?"

"I . . ." she began. "I don't love you!" But as she said the words, she knew they were a lie. She had started falling in love with him when she'd first met him. He was different from anyone else in the world. His voice captivated her, his eyes compelled her, his touch, his whisper, aroused her. He was her enemy, but a man who would die for her. An enemy who fought for what he believed was right, who would give his life for his convictions, never back down, never falter. And she did want him, but she was so afraid of pain now . . .

"Then we're even," he said softly. "Because I don't love you. But damn you, Tia, I married you, and you are my wife, and you are not free. I *will* have you."

That simply, he spoke the words. And that simply, he meant to have his way.

And she . . .

He kissed her.

Again, a kiss filled with force, with hunger, with passion. As relentless as a tempest, his tongue forced entry, drank, demanded, delved, and seduced. She tried to twist against the surge of his force, but could not. Tried to fight the rage of feelings that surged within her breast, her blood, her limbs, but could not. Dusk turned to dark red, red to night, and all that remained were the shadows of the moon. He didn't notice the bloodred coming of darkness. He kissed her, seized her lips again and again. Found the pulse point at her throat, touched her, stroked her cheek, her hair. Found the buttons on her bodice and swiftly unfastened them, chipping one delicate little piece of ivory in his haste to disrobe her.

Then he was everywhere . . .

Her shoes were cast aside, skirt all but torn away, pantalettes nearly shredded, stockings—precious stockings—seized like autumn leaves in the winter wind. And surely she should be pushing him away, struggling against this onslaught, but it seemed that she was tugging off his clothing as well. His shirt was open, slipping from his shoulders. Her hands were on his bare flesh as his lips pressed against her shoulders, her throat, and then her breast. She could feel the fever of his body heat against her naked belly as he captured her breast with his kiss, tongue laving her nipple, teeth capturing the pebbled bud, mouth forming fully upon it, suckling, taunting, arousing, creating sensations that caused her to strain against him, protesting, arching, crying out. She was tearing at his hair, cradling his head as he moved against her. His body on hers, between hers, the force of his movement thrusting her thighs apart, his lips running wild and rampant over the bare expanse of her abdomen, lower, upon her upper thighs, between them, touching, demanding, arousing, allowing no quarter in the quest for pure seduction. And he did seduce. At last she realized that she didn't fight, but clung. She didn't struggle, but reached. And she wanted him. Wanted this. Hunger so sweet and erotic it was anguish. What he could do with his touch. His kiss, the brush of his whisper, the sweep of his tongue. And then . . . the force of his body within her. A feeling of completeness, wholeness, part of him, still climbing—no, *soaring*—reaching to a sun that didn't exist, a panoply of stars in the velvet of the night that had come. His eyes on her in the night, gold eyes, cat's eyes, panther eyes, pinning her with the same surge of power as his touch, demanding, more so than the force of her touch, complete and unconditional surrender. She could not win the war.

She could hardly join in the battle, for it had been lost from the beginning, and it had never been the violence she had feared, but the knowledge that she hadn't the will to fight. He had stripped her of her clothing, and her defenses, and she had not just accepted his greater strength, she had embraced her own weakness, wanting him.

Loving him, no matter what her words . . .

Absence, anger, fear, tempest, perhaps they all added in as well. He moved against her with a strength that left her breathless, which seduced anew with every surge and eddy, which brought her flying ever higher, into the darkness, into the realm of lovers, where the world receded and only hunger and need existed. Then the darkness burst into white, blazing light; she closed her eyes and saw it still, and she shook and shuddered as sheer pleasure seized her in its sweet grip, and climax ripped into her with a searing ecstasy that defied the war, the day, the night, and all sanity and reason. His body heat melded into her own, and she was swept with the fire of his ejaculation, enwrapped in the warmth that encapsulated them both for the long, sweet moments as they flew, and drifted, and wound within one another, then came back to the reality of the earth and bed and their sweat-dampened bodies.

Tia lay silent, her heart pounding, in torment. It was frightening to want him this way, so frightening to realize how much she did care about him, what he meant to

her, and who and what he was. She had straightened
her world out—the best she possibly could in the
melee her country had become—and he had come and
twisted her inside out all over again. It had been so
much easier when she had thought him safely locked
away, when she had been able to turn to long hours with
the injured who needed her so much that she wouldn't
have to think about the tempest of her own emotions.
When she had convinced herself that she couldn't want
him, couldn't have him, because she couldn't bear the
consequences. If only he had stayed away . . .

"What now?" she asked him quietly after a long moment. "You are burdened with a Rebel bride you don't
love, who . . . doesn't love you, who costs you way too
dear a price in everything you do. What now?" she challenged. She was going to cry. It was so ridiculous. She
had to be stronger than this, not give way at every turn!

"Perhaps I should be grateful you don't love me.
Heaven help the man you do love; he would probably
die from the ecstasy of your touch."

"Taylor—" she began angrily, trying to roll away from
him and rise.

But he caught her, firmly placing an arm around her.
"What is the scale of your emotion? If I recall, you don't
dislike me. But then, that was what you said when you
had promised to stay in St. Augustine."

She was disturbed to hear her voice faltering. "I came
to Richmond because my sister-in-law begged me to do
so. I was trying to save a child. You can't begin to understand—"

"But I did understand."

"No, you really don't. There was a little girl in St.
Augustine, a carriage accident . . ."

"And because she died, you refuse to have children."

"Exactly," she said harshly. "So . . . what now?"

"What now?" he repeated, his voice soft and deep.
"Well, now, as I said, the tables are turned."

Her eyes widened.

"Are you having me arrested?"

"It's a thought," he said with a shrug. "However, I didn't say that."

"So I'm not to be your prisoner?"

"I didn't say that either."

"Then what—"

"I said I'm not having you arrested. But neither will I let you out of my sight for sometime to come."

"I'm to stay with you?"

"We'll arrange something. Here, I'm definitely not in charge, as I was in Florida. Still, my rank is high enough."

"Meaning?"

"I'll be close at all times. Damned close."

She felt his fingers on her shoulders, knuckles running down her bare flesh.

"So . . . you do not want children. They may die. And you do not love me, but lucky me, you do not dislike me. Who was it you might have loved? Our old friend from the blessed Florida militia, Colonel Weir? Do you believe you would have wanted children with him?"

"Weir . . ." she murmured. *Weir?* She hadn't even thought of the man in months.

"Yes, the good Rebel Raymond Weir. Well, if you think you wanted him, you really are a fool."

"Oh, am I?"

He met her eyes, his fingers curling into the strands of her hair. "Yes, you are. He is the type of man who would have admired Godiva—and he would have wanted to sleep with her. But he never would have married her."

"He is constantly asking me to marry him," she replied defiantly.

"Because he doesn't know you're Godiva. He is a man who would think nothing of having a wife and a mistress, and the mistress should be a wild and decadent woman to serve his sexual fancies, while his wife must behave with complete dignity and modesty. Maybe he'd even allow you to wear volumes of clothing in bed. He would tell you what to do all the time—"

"Ah! And you don't?"

"Do you think that he would marry you and allow you to work with Julian? I think not."

"I don't remember you allowing me to work with Julian."

"You were with Brent."

"And now, you say, I am with you."

"My concern isn't that you work with wounded men— North or South. My concern remains that you are reckless, and take far too many chances."

She felt a sudden shiver race down her back. The fact that she could have burned to death in the Wilderness was still a sobering thought. He must have thought that she was cold; though the days were hot, the night still brought in a cooling wind.

His arm came around her, and he turned her toward him. She saw that his hazel eyes were gleaming, and that he was tense, muscles taut, teeth jarring. "You didn't answer me. What if you had married your Rebel beau? Would you want children with him?"

"I didn't marry Ray, so this conversation can go nowhere."

"Would you want children with him?"

"I told you, I simply don't want children," she said, clenching her teeth, steadily meeting his gaze.

He looked at her as seconds ticked by, then abruptly he pushed away from her, rising. She was amazed at how cold she suddenly felt.

She hugged her knees to her chest, dismayed that she felt tempted to cry again, bereft, and as if she had lost more than the warmth of his body beside her own.

"Taylor . . . I don't expect you to understand, to tolerate—a distant arrangement as a marriage. I mean, the war causes *distances*. I mean—"

"I know exactly what you mean," he told her, dressing.

She felt colder, but she had started this, and she felt compelled to press forward. "So you understand, you agree—"

"Get dressed."

"Of course, quickly."

She jumped out of bed. Before she could swing around, he caught her arm. "I don't agree with anything. Your brother and Jesse will be here soon. That's all."

She wrenched her arm free from his grip, turning away, finding her clothing, and dragging her carpet bag back on the bed to repack the clothing which had fallen when he'd so rudely shoved the valise from the bed.

"It's good to see you're packed," he told her, walking to the window.

She realized, moments later, that he had heard hoof-beats long before she became aware that riders were nearing the house. He left the room, walking out front. She heard him call out greetings and she bit her lip, standing very still. Ian was out there.

She allowed herself to forget the Confederacy, dropping the blouse she had been folding, and she ran through the house and out the front door. "Ian!" she cried, seeing her brother dismounting from his horse. She raced to him, throwing her arms around him.

"Tia!"

He picked her up, enclosing his arms around her. She drew away, looking him over carefully, her eyes roaming up and down his length. "You've been well? You're not hurt?"

"Not a scratch," he told her, stepping back. She saw the second horseman who had ridden in with him. A tall cavalryman with brown hair and warm hazel eyes, dashing and good-looking. "Tia, this is Jesse Halston. Sydney's—"

"Husband. Yes, I know," Tia said, extending a hand. "It's good to meet you, Jesse."

He took her hand. His smile deepened. He had dimples, and he was charming. She knew why Sydney had fallen for this enemy.

"Tia. I've heard so much about you. How do you do?"

"I'm not at all sure. You'll have to ask Taylor," she said flippantly.

"She's not pleased to be joining our ranks, I'm afraid," Taylor said.

"Perhaps you'll feel a little differently, Tia, when I tell you that we don't have to go anywhere."

"What?" Taylor said sharply.

"We reported back to Magee already and found out that we're extending the Union line. This house is as good as any for an officers' barracks," Jesse said.

"This is Mary's house," Tia said protectively.

"The Union is moving into town. With any luck, we won't be outranked. Mary's house will fare much better with us using it than others," Ian told his sister. "Tia, is there any food left at all? Did our erstwhile cousin pack it all? Probably, if I know Brent, he didn't allow for much waste. We just shared most of our rations with some other fellows, and it would definitely be nice to have something hot and home-cooked."

"I don't know what's left in here," Tia said, smiling at Taylor with false sweetness. "I was on my way out when Taylor arrived."

"How fortunate he arrived in time!" Ian exclaimed.

"Well, we'll go see what's in the kitchen," Jesse said cheerfully. He smiled again. A very warm, kind, gentle smile. *Sydney must be very happy and love him very much,* Tia thought. She was glad. She loved her cousin, who was almost exactly her own age. They had been best friends throughout their lives.

"How is Sydney?" she asked Jesse.

"Fine!"

She was surprised that Taylor was the one to give her the curt answer. "Looks like there is a stable out back," he continued, talking to Jesse. "We can unhitch that mare of Tia's as well. By the way, did that Reb captain I fished out of the woods keep his word and watch out for my horse?"

"Magee has been keeping Friar, so your man was honorable. He's treated him like his own child," Jesse told Taylor. "I'll take the horses around back."

Taylor was hesitating. Hands on his hips, he stared at the road. "I should report to Magee tonight."

"He'll expect you in the morning," Ian said. "He knew you were working directly for Grant before the

Wilderness, and he's anxious to see you now, glad to have you back—though he doesn't know how long he'll get to keep you. I imagine that he'll move our companies into the field by tomorrow, and stage our reconnaissance from here."

"Well, good. Tia is unhappy enough in Federal company. I wouldn't want her to have to be uncomfortable as well," Taylor said pleasantly. "Shall we all go make this our new home?" He smiled at Tia.

A smile that gave her shivers all over again.

Hours later, they had finished an extremely palatable meal, under the circumstances. Jesse had found a ham left in the smokehouse, and there had been a few cans of fruit left in the larder. There had been some corn bread left over from the day before, and Tia had found a few dandelion greens to pull from the small vegetable garden. She was a rich man's daughter, but as capable in a kitchen as she was in a hospital, Taylor thought, and he realized that Jarrett McKenzie had raised his children to live in the world, not believe that they ruled it.

Tia might not have been happy in Federal company, but she loved her brother and she had no difficulty liking Jesse Halston. She was interested in Jesse, naturally— he had married her cousin. She didn't hide her curiosity, or her assessment, and Jesse seemed to like her in return. Ian had received letters from home in the last few weeks, which Tia had not, and she was anxious to hear about her family. Seeing the way her eyes lit up when she talked about her family to Ian made Taylor feel like the odd man out.

Leaving them to their conversation, Taylor came out to the porch with a good cigar he had found in Mary's father's desk. It had aged well, he mused, leaning against one of the posts to smoke it. He blew smoke rings, watching them on the air. *So she wanted a divorce!*
Like hell.

But what was he to do? This was a war. He couldn't have her arrested, even if he wanted to. He wouldn't give away her secret. But what recourse did that leave him? He couldn't be with her constantly; he couldn't force her to stay. When he'd left her the last time, she had even promised to be there when he returned. Now, she wasn't making any promises; she was telling him that she didn't want children and that she wanted a divorce.

The door opened. He saw that Ian was joining him. "Have you ever seen anything as quiet as this night?" Ian asked.

"It will change tomorrow."

"It will. Every house will be taken over. Troops will be camped all over those grasslands. And it will be for a long time, I think."

Taylor looked at him. "We're in for a siege. Petersburg is under attack, and don't think that Grant is going to leave until the city surrenders—no matter what the cost."

"What else have I missed?" Taylor asked. "I heard about the boys from the Virginia Military Institute going to war at New Market. What else?"

"Sherman is marching hard on Georgia—destroying everything in sight, I might add. We probably had a chance to capture Petersburg without a siege, but old Beauregard pushed Meade back too hard."

"Anything from home?"

"Skirmishes, a few naval bombardments. A couple of babies come the fall. Alaina is expecting, and so is Risa."

"So Jerome managed to make it home last Christmas!" Taylor said, grinning, as he leaned back and savored his cigar. But his smile didn't seem to touch his soul. It was a sore subject. He did want children. He hadn't thought about it much since Abby had died. Not even when he'd found himself marrying again in a strange fury.

"So this will be three for you," he murmured casually.

"Jerome's second. Prophesied by my brother's wife."

"Who sees too much, and not enough," Taylor murmured.

"She sees the end of this, but she says it doesn't matter. The Rebs will never believe her until they're beaten into the ground. My brother pays her no heed."

"Maybe he pays more attention than we know. What can he do—quit the army, walk away? He's a doctor. It doesn't work that way, and we both know it."

"But people do change," Ian said suddenly, looking at him. "Like Sydney."

"She claims she hasn't changed."

"But that isn't the truth, is it?"

Taylor shrugged, stubbing out the cigar. "No. She met a really remarkable black woman who opened her eyes to slavery—although Sydney still won't accept it as the major cause of the war."

"Lincoln has fought to preserve the Union, not to free the slaves," Ian reminded him. "As good a man as he may be, he's a politician. He used his Emancipation Proclamation just as much as any politician might."

"He does believe that slavery is an abomination."

"He does, but . . ."

"But what?"

Taylor stared at Ian. "Your father has always, openly and honestly, been against slavery. I can understand the hatred of this uniform where James is concerned, and how Jerome and Brent might have naturally been ready to fight the Union. God knows, there were times when I was young that even I thought all white men were murdering demons—because of this uniform. Why can't your sister realize that the South's fight is wrong, that it would be all but sacrilege to destroy the Union, and slavery is one of the cruelest and most unjust institutions ever twisted into being by man."

"She sees it. She's just fought too long and hard now to admit she's wrong."

"Well, then it's onward to battle I go, Ian. It's been one hell of a long day. Good night."

"Good night, Taylor. Go easy on the South, eh? We really are winning the war."

The house was quiet. Jesse had evidently picked a bed and gone to it. Tia had cleaned the dining room and kitchen, and she had disappeared as well. Taylor walked up the steps wearily. It was past midnight now. God knew what morning would bring.

He entered Tia's bedroom, feeling as if liquid fire coursed through his veins. What if she wasn't there, what if she'd locked the door, what if . . .

He closed the door behind him. The room was cloaked in shadow, but he could see her form on the bed.

He walked slowly over to her. She was on one side of the bed, curled away from him. A sliver of moonlight fell across her back. She only feigned sleep. The pulse at her throat gave her away.

He silently stripped his boots and clothing, crawled onto the bed, and reached for her.

She turned toward him, dark eyes wide, catching a spark of the moonlight. "Taylor, I—"

"I don't give a damn what you want," he told her, taking her into his arms.

She didn't protest. And in a matter of minutes, she was everything he knew, and everything he wanted. She teased and seduced and sated his senses, and in the end, she lay curled in his arms as sweetly as a kitten, seduced and sated and exhausted as well. He held her, suddenly grateful for the night just to sleep beside her, trying not to tremble in a manner that would give away the extent of his pleasure just to be with her. To feel the way she breathed, slept, moved in the night . . .

Later, he awoke, and he wondered why for a moment. He had always awakened to the slightest noise, but . . .

There was nothing. The night was quiet, the breeze was slight. And then he knew.

She still lay beside him, entangled in his limbs.

But softly, almost silently . . . so that he would not hear her . . .

She was crying.

Chapter 23

When Tia awoke the following morning, Taylor was gone.

Rising and dressing, she found that he had left the house altogether, as had Jesse.

What had been a ghost town, however, was suddenly filled with people again. Soldiers, servants, wives, laundresses—the inevitable camp followers. The field across from Mary's house was filled with tents; the sound of troop commanders could be heard, along with bugles, harnesses, hoofbeats, and shouts.

The Union had come in full force.

Ian was still at the house, receiving despatches. He'd be leaving soon as well, but he had wanted Tia to know that there was a Private Shelby on the porch, that the house had been designated as their quarters by the proper authorities, and that General Magee had chosen the large Colonial across the street for his own headquarters. The kitchen was being stocked, Molly was the maid and cook who would be looking after them, and Horace was the handyman who would watch the chickens, stock the smokehouse, and do any general handy work they might need around the place.

They had settled in for a long siege at Petersburg.

"Where is Taylor?" Tia asked her brother after she had come down for breakfast.

"Riding," Ian said briefly.

She was about to ask where, but she knew her brother wouldn't tell her. She remained a Rebel, and God alone knew just what she might be capable of doing.

Taylor did not return that night, or the next day, or

the next. At first, Tia remained in the vicinity of the house. When she left, she found that Private Shelby followed her. She felt like telling her brother, who returned to the house at odd hours, that if she chose to escape from Shelby, she could do so easily. However, she managed not to make such a confession.

On the fifth day of Taylor's absence, she could no longer bear the idleness of sitting in the house. The Lutheran church had again been turned into a hospital, so with Shelby at her heels, she walked down to the hospital to offer her services. There were two women in the main body of the church. Pews had been stripped; beds had been brought in. Tia made her way to the side chapel, where the doctor in command was quickly looking through the papers that had come with some newly arrived men. As she passed, the women—Yankee wives, she was certain—paused from their duties to whisper.

About her.

She ignored them.

She walked to the doctor's desk. "Excuse me, but I'm an experienced nurse and I'd like to work here if I may."

The doctor looked up. He was a tall man of about fifty, sturdy, gray-haired, and with a calm, steady manner that inspired trust. His gaze fixed on her despite the confusion and noise around them as another load of injured men arrived.

"And you are . . . ?"

"My name is Tia McKenzie."

"McKenzie Douglas, isn't it?" he inquired, smiling. He rose, offering her a hand. "Reginald Flowers, and I know who you are. You have dark eyes, and you're much, much lovelier, but you do bear a resemblance to your brothers."

"You know both my brothers?"

"Julian was with me after Gettysburg. I wish he were with me still. And Ian is legendary with the cavalry—as is your husband, Mrs. Douglas."

"Of course," she murmured.

The two women had followed her and were staring at

her from the entrance to the small chapel. She turned, staring back.

"They think you're a Rebel who will probably poison the injured men in the middle of the night!" Dr. Flowers said.

"And what do you think, sir?" Tia asked.

"I think they're a pair of plump old biddies!" he said conspiratorially, and she had to smile. "What took you so long in coming?" he asked her.

"Pardon?"

"Colonel Douglas was by several days ago, said your sympathies were Southern but your inclination was to heal. If you're Julian's sister, I haven't a doubt in the world that you'll be a tremendous asset to me. If you'll begin with the fellows who have just come in . . ." he suggested.

And so she did. She bathed wounds, sewed them, bandaged them, and found herself quickly taken in as Dr. Flower's surgical assistant.

The other wives, she was certain, continued to talk about her through the day. She didn't care. Several of the orderlies with Dr. Flowers knew Ian as well—and Rhiannon. The admiration and warmth with which they regarded both her brother and her sister-in-law quickly made them her friends, and by the end of the day, she didn't think at all about it being an enemy hospital.

She was back at the hospital at first light the next morning. Her routine became a twelve-hour day. Private Shelby remained her constant tail, and thereby found himself working at the hospital as well. He was a bit green at first, but was a pleasant enough young man, uncertain but ready to plunge in. Tia was surprised to find him quite bearable.

He seldom came in the house, though. He'd fashioned a hammock on the porch and slept there.

General Magee had set up his headquarters right across the street. Even though he was the enemy, he was Risa's father, and twice, having seen him ride home late, Tia sent messages, asking him to dinner.

One evening, he came. He was polite, charming, and

steady, and she knew why Risa was as assured and confident a young woman as she always managed to be, why she was full of warmth—and also, shrewdly intelligent. He had commanded her brother, Jesse Halston—and her husband. But he didn't talk to her much about Taylor's work in the cavalry, other than to say once that he was such a dead-on shot that it was chilling. Magee talked about the housing plans he had seen Taylor draw, how his real love was architecture—and his home. "He wants to build houses that catch summer breezes, that stand up to fierce storms, that capture the essence of the grass and trees, sea and sand."

"Maybe one day," she told him. And in turn, she talked about Jamie, his grandson, and how well Risa was doing—and that there would be a new baby.

"Ah, now, there's hope, isn't there? Thank God for the little ones. How would we endure the war if it weren't for the hope of the children?"

She didn't answer him. She would have told him that children all seemed to die too.

By the end of her first week at the hospital, she returned home to find that Ian was there before her, working on despatches at the parlor desk.

She watched him write for several minutes before she spoke.

"Ian, where is Taylor?"

He hesitated, watching her. "He was at the front at Petersburg for a while. He's cavalry, but because of his engineering background, he was working with some coal miners planning . . . planning some works at the line."

"He was?"

"He's also been running despatches between Grant, Sherman, and Sheridan."

"Is he coming back here?"

"Yes."

"Is he in danger?"

Ian hesitated. "Tia, it's a war. Everyone is in danger." He sighed. "Tia, he's an extraordinary horseman and a crack shot."

She sighed. "So I've been told."

"How was the hospital?"

"Filled with bleeding and dying men."

"But you'll be working there."

"Until I can go home."

"And what you want is to go home?" Ian said, then he smiled. "You don't actually mean *home,* do you? You want to go back and work in the woods with Julian."

"It's where I belong," she agreed.

"Has it occurred to you that you *belong* with your husband?"

"But he isn't here, is he?" Tia asked.

"He will be soon. You know, Tia, I only want what's best for you. I am your brother, and I love you."

She smiled. "And I love you, Ian—even if you are a sadly misguided individual."

"Ah. That means a Yank, doesn't it?"

"Like I said, big brother, I love you dearly, but you're not a doctor. And this isn't my state. Excuse me, Ian, Molly said that she'd fix me some bath water before dinner."

Thank God for Molly, and thank God for baths. Tia wanted to work with the soldiers; she needed to work with the soldiers. But when she came home, she couldn't get over the feeling of being drenched not just in sweat and blood, but in the anguish of the men. She could stay on her feet forever, help in the direst situation, deal with sick soldiers, gangrene, gut wounds, and the most horrible amputations—but she did dearly love to lie in a hot bath when the day was over. It was July, the summer heat could be stifling, and she loved to sit in the water until it turned cooler than the night air.

That night, she lay in the tub for a very long time. She was especially tired. Molly was a wonderful cook, but Tia hadn't been hungry. Though Ian was there with her that night, and she was glad of her brother's company, she went to bed early. However, she lay there awake, unable to calm her mind.

Around midnight, she heard the door to her room open. By the moonlight trickling through the thin curtains, she saw a tall figure there, heard the door close quietly. *Taylor*. Her heart began to thunder.

He moved about the room like a wraith, discarding his clothing then walking to the window. He stared out at the night for a very long time. Then he came to bed.

He didn't say a word to her, but lay on his back. She thought that his eyes remained open, that he stared up at the ceiling. She tried to keep her own eyes closed, to pretend that she hadn't heard him, that she lay asleep. But he knew, he always knew, when she really lay awake. And suddenly he turned on her. "What was that you said, Mrs. Douglas? How am I? Yes, alive, certainly. Well? I believe so, physically, I'm in excellent shape— no bullets lodged in me anywhere. I mean, that is the least you'd ask out of a man you don't actually *dislike,* isn't it?"

"Taylor, I—"

"Never mind, Tia. Never mind."

Startled by the tears his deep, sarcastic words brought to her eyes, she started to turn away. He drew her back. "I'm sorry, Tia. I don't want you to turn away."

He made love to her that night as if a demon rode his soul. He was still drinking coffee in the kitchen when she woke the next morning, but the way his gold eyes touched hers over his cup, she thought that he had never disliked her more intensely. Her eyes downcast, she strode past him, thanking Molly as she accepted coffee from her. The coffee churned in her stomach. She sipped it anyway.

"Find any good Rebels to save yet at the hospital?"

"No."

"Well, you may today. Goodbye, my dear," he told her. "Molly, thank you!" he called to their servant, then he started out of the house.

"Taylor!" she shouted, startled to find that she was following him. He stopped out on the lawn, turning to wait for her question. Friar, she noted, was at the gate. Good old Friar. He had his horse back. That had to make him happy—if having her didn't.

Private Shelby was leaning against one of the porch

columns, waiting for her. She felt awkward, smiling a good morning to him but not wanting an audience at this moment.

"Are you leaving again for . . . for a long time? Or will you be back soon?"

She felt the sweep of his distant, gold gaze. A slight smile curved his lips. "Did you want me back?" he inquired politely.

Shelby was behind them. She felt her cheeks burn. "Of . . . of course."

He walked back to her. Kissed her cheek. Whispered "Liar!" in her ear. And without giving her an answer, he strode to Friar, mounted up, and rode away.

At the hospital, she learned what demons tormented him. The soldiers, doctors, patients, wives, nurses—everyone—talked about the horrible events at the crater. Union engineers had dug a tunnel to reach Confederate lines. Black troops had been trained to go in—but at the last minute they'd been pulled out. The generals were afraid that it would look as if they were willing to sacrifice their black soldiers.

As it happened, explosives that had been set didn't fire properly. Then the replacement men, too hastily trained, faltered. The Rebels counterattacked. It had been a disaster. One of the injured men, learning that Tia was Taylor's wife, talked to her about what happened.

"Colonel Douglas kept trying to tell them there could be a fault with men being trapped, but somebody said he was cavalry, and even if he'd had training in engineering and architecture, he wanted to build mansions, not military works.

"Colonel Douglas was angry then, saying they shouldn't ask him for information if they didn't want his opinion. He was angry that they changed the troops at the last minute, and angrier still, I think, when so many men were blown to bits. He didn't want to be right. But he was there, ma'am, right there, racing into the action, trying to get men out when it all blew up in our faces.

He later asked to be sent back to General Magee and left alone as cavalry, since that was what he was.

"They say about twenty thousand men were involved and that we flat out lost a full four thousand of them. It was one of the most horrible things I've seen in the war, and I've been in the Army of the Potomac since the beginning. You'll see . . . when the fellows start coming in today. Some of them are in pretty bad shape."

They were. Men came in from the siege line throughout the day.

Rebel soldiers came as well, many of them dying, bodies maimed, limbs blown to bits in the explosion that had rocked the crater.

Tia stayed at the hospital through the night. The next day, she almost passed out at one point; she was nearly sick at another. She ignored her weariness. At dusk, Dr. Flowers made her go home, telling her that she was suffering from exhaustion.

When she reached the house, Taylor was there. She had been bone tired, but the news that he had preceded her home seemed like a stimulant. She was immediately awake and wary. Molly told her he was in her room— in the bathtub. She entered quietly, saw that he was indeed there, leaning back, a washcloth over his face. She started to walk back out. He didn't move the washcloth, but he had heard her, and he knew it was her. "Don't leave on my account."

Awkwardly, she moved into the room. She hesitated near the wooden hip tub. "I heard how many men were lost at the crater. I'm very sorry."

He pulled the washcloth from his face, studying her. "Well, I don't know how many, but I'm afraid a number of Rebs were blown to bits as well. Unfortunately, that's the idea with war. We kill one another. The last man standing wins."

"I heard that you had argued against it."

"I did, but I wish I'd been wrong."

"You were resting. I didn't mean to disturb you," Tia said.

"You disturb me, my love, on a daily basis."

She turned around, determined to leave the room. But before she could reach the door, he was up and out of the tub, water sluicing from his naked body. And when he caught her and swung her around, she was amazed at the way that just the touch of his sleek, bare flesh aroused her, at how she wanted him. "I have just come from the hospital," she told him, feeling that she was obliged to offer some manner of protest.

"Then you should share my bath." He spun her around, working on buttons and ties and closures. Her shoes flew, stockings followed, cloth lay on the ground in a pool of pastel color. He picked her up, plunked her into the tub with him, and when they tried to sit, their knees knocked. They stood again, facing one another in the water, and to her amazement, she found herself laughing. "We don't fit at all . . ."

"We don't, do we?" he inquired, but he cupped her chin, kissed her, and then she felt the soap in his hands against her flesh, and the sleek feel of it moving against her, over her breasts, between her thighs . . . she was shaking, still feeling his kiss. The soap was suddenly in her hands. She bathed his shoulders, his chest, back . . . buttocks, sex. The soap slipped from her hands, splashed into the water. Droplets cascaded around them. They both ducked for more water to rinse out, crashed together, laughed. Then her eyes met his, and she saw the fire, felt as if it touched her inside. He lifted her from the tub, fell instantly upon the bed, and within seconds he was inside her. Tia wondered how she had ever lived without him.

"You really don't ever listen to me, do you?" she murmured.

"I listen, but I simply refuse to agree. You're my wife, and I will be with you. Whether or not I am a Rebel countryman, as you would have liked."

"I told you, I don't *dislike* you."

"You'll have to quit saying so with such passion. I might start thinking you actually do *like* me."

"I just wish that . . . I were home."

"In Florida, you mean. Away from me."

"In Florida," she agreed. "And I told you . . . I just don't want . . ."

"Don't want what?"

"Children."

Exhaustion then seemed to be overwhelming her. If he said something more, she didn't hear it. Perhaps he was just as exhausted. He remained beside her. Sometime in the night, she awoke, feeling him at her back. The length of him against the length of her. Then he must have known that she had awakened, because he was touching her. His arms were around her, upon her breasts, and he was inside her, and she was soaring into the sweet warm rain of ecstasy, bursting into a field of light and stars, and drifting down into a night of velvet and blackness. "You'll simply have to forgive me," he whispered against her earlobe.

"I'll try," she murmured.

Yet, the next thing she knew, she was shaking. It was summer, it was hot, but she was freezing. She couldn't get warm enough. At first, she was against him, trying to gain his body heat. It wasn't enough. His arms were around her, she soon realized, then he was cradling her in blankets, but she couldn't seem to open her eyes.

Cold, cold, cold . . .

So cold . . . and she was dreaming. She was at Cimarron, by the pool. The sun was shining, but she was shaking.

Someone was calling her. Urgently. The sound was coming from the house. But she could see Taylor. He was standing on the other side of the pool. He seemed very far away. She wanted to go to him. But she was so cold, and they were calling her from the house, and if she could only reach Cimarron, she would be warm again. She would see the sun shine on the river, the way the lawn swept down to the embankment, the way the grass grew so very green, and even the way the white puffs of clouds moved across the heavens.

"I want to go home . . . I have to go home . . ."

"*Sh* . . . it's all right."

Then he wasn't across the freshwater spring from her

anymore. He was holding her again. She was glad; she was where she wanted to be. Except that she was slipping away. She needed to say something, hold on to him. She couldn't. She was falling . . . into darkness.

She couldn't seem to remember, or to feel, until she realized that she hadn't fallen; his arms were around her again. He was urging her to drink; she tasted bitter quinine. She opened her eyes, and she wondered what had happened. She was in a nightgown, and she wasn't alone with Taylor. He was there, in full uniform, but Ian was there, too, and so was Dr. Flowers. The doctor had his hand on her forehead, and he looked grave. "Can you hear me?"

"Yes." Her voice seemed thick. Her throat hurt; it was hard to talk.

"Drink more of this."

She did so, then closed her eyes. She wasn't quite so cold anymore, but she was very, very tired. "You picked up a fever at the hospital, Tia," Dr. Flowers told her gently. "But I think we're through the worst of it. You need to sleep, to rest. Do you understand?"

She nodded. She thought she heard them talking again—all of them. She tried to reach out. She had seen something strange in Taylor's eyes. "Taylor . . ." She managed to murmur his name. And she knew that he was beside her again, holding her hand. Then she felt blackness slipping over her once more.

When she next awoke Taylor was gone. Ian was in the room with her, sitting in a chair by the bed, his sharp blue eyes watching her. She managed a smile and a weak "Hi."

"Hi, little sister. How are you doing?"

"Better, I think."

He reached over, touched her forehead. He seemed satisfied. Rising, he brought her a glass of water. She took it from him, realizing she was tremendously thirsty. "Thanks."

"I'm going to tell Molly you're awake. She has some tea for you to start with, then you're to go to soup and toast, I believe."

"Sounds good. I'm famished."

He started out of the room. She called him back. "Ian? Where's Taylor? I'm not asking for the secret movements of the Union army or anything, just . . . where is he?"

"He had to leave. Jesse was ordered back to Washington. Taylor is down in Georgia."

"Georgia! When did he leave? When is he coming back?"

"I don't know. But he's arranged passage home for you."

"What?" she murmured.

"He said you wanted to be in Florida. When you're better, General Magee will arrange an escort to the nearest safe port, and you can return to St. Augustine by ship. I'll try to follow, since Alaina's baby is due in September and I'd like to be there."

"He's not coming back?" Tia said. "And I'm just to go?"

"Isn't that what you want?" Ian asked. "It's what you told me."

"Of course," she murmured. Her brother's eyes were on her. Her own lowered.

"Taylor stayed until he knew you were out of danger, but he said that even in your fever, all you talked about was going home." He hesitated. "He was carrying despatches down to Sherman. Once you were on the mend, he couldn't wait any longer."

She nodded. "I see."

Ian started out of the room again.

"Ian?" she said, again calling him back.

He paused. "I'd . . . wait for him," she whispered.

"Tia, I don't know when he's coming back. Sherman is trying to take Atlanta. Taylor could be gone a very long time. I thought you'd be happy about going home."

"I *am* happy about going home," she told him. And she was. But she was dismayed to realize that she was desolate about leaving Taylor. *But I'm not leaving him; he's already gone!* she thought.

"There's a note for you in the desk."

Tia started to rise but fell back, dizzy. She looked at her brother ruefully, seeing that he was hurrying to her side. "I'm all right, just not quite back to normal. Would you . . . ?"

Ian opened the desk drawer, brought her back a folded piece of note paper, and left her alone to read Taylor's words.

They weren't what she had hoped for.

> Tia,
> You've said you want to be in Florida. Under the circumstances, it seems that you should go. A Union ship will bring you to St. Augustine. I know that you can be with family members and find useful occupation there. Don't even think about a hair-cloaked romp about the state. Take care of yourself, stay well—and stay out of trouble. How's that for fair warning? Is this a threat? Yes, my love, it is.
> Taylor

She wouldn't cry—it would be so stupid! He had always made her stay with him. Now, suddenly, he was gone—indefinitely. And though he had left a threat . . .

Did he really care what she did?

This was what she'd wanted. No matter what she was feeling, he remained the enemy. A staunch enemy. And now, a threatening, unforgiving enemy.

So she was going home. Back to where she'd started. She couldn't stay in St. Augustine. She would go back with her brother. And at home, she would find the strength to begin again.

Tia burst into tears.

And then, only then, did she admit to herself that it all hurt so, so badly because she was in love with Taylor Douglas.

It was the middle of the night.

The door burst open.

Sydney bolted upright in a wild panic. What had happened? Had the Rebs stormed the capital? No! She hadn't heard a cannon or even the firing of a single gun.

She leapt from the bed and rushed out to the parlor. In the firelight burning low at the hearth, she saw him. Jesse. In full uniform, his plumed hat upon his head, frockcoat over his snow-white shirt and doublet. Her hand flew to her throat. It had been so long since she'd seen him.

Did he know that she had slipped her guard, left the city, defied his order? Was he here in anger, or . . .

Had he seen Taylor?

"Jesse?" she murmured.

He strode across the room to her. She felt his eyes, saw the lines about his handsome face. She backed away.

"Sydney, damn you, Sydney . . ."

He reached her. She met his gaze, mouth dry, heart hammering. He was alive. Just that seemed a miracle. She was so glad to see him, wanted so much to touch him . . .

"Sydney."

To her amazement, he went down upon a knee, drawing her to him. His arms encircled her waist; he held her like porcelain. She hesitated, her fingers falling on the brown waves of his hair. He stood, arms around her, holding her. His eyes met hers again. He kissed her, and kissed her . . .

"Sydney . . . you're a Yankee."

"I am not!"

He drew away, his smile gentle, beautiful, the smile with which she had fallen in love, from the very first.

"You were sneaking out to smuggle slaves."

"You saw Taylor."

"Yes."

"Did he . . . did he tell you . . ."

"Particulars? No. Don't look so relieved—*you're* going to tell me what happened. Everything. Then, I'm going to throttle you, of course, you little fool. It's every bit as dangerous as what you were doing, it's more dangerous . . . it's . . ."

"Jesse?"

"What?"

"I love you."

"Oh, God!"

He swept her up. She buried her head against his chest. Slipped her arms around his neck. He carried her back to the bedroom and they lay down together. He smoothed her hair back. "I love you, Sydney, I love you, I love you, I love you . . ."

It was many hours later when he warned her again that he was going to throttle her, and by then she simply didn't care. She knew he didn't mean a word of it.

Chapter 24

When Tia arrived in Florida, she returned immediately to Cimarron to spend some precious time with her parents. Her father was pleased that she had married Taylor Douglas, which she told herself was natural because her father was, at heart, a Yankee. But she knew it was more than that. Her father liked Taylor, and respected him, and for that, he was glad for his daughter. Her mother was sorry that they would never plan an elaborate wedding, but she was also pragmatic—they were living in wartime, and what was important was that they survived it. Neither of her parents seemed surprised about the marriage. "You were different with him from the beginning, my dear," Tara said. "There was something there . . . you just had to discover it. I'm so glad you did. I don't think that Ray Weir knows you've married, though. He was here just last week, asking for you. You should never have played him along so, dear."

"I never played him along! Did you tell him that I had married?"

"Actually, no. I never had the chance."

"Well, I assume he'll find out soon enough."

"Yes, I imagine." Her mother seemed unhappy then, as if she was hiding something.

"Mother, what is it?"

"He and your father got into another row."

"What happened? Oh, Mother, I wish Father would be careful with his convictions and his temper. We are a Confederate state."

"Tia, it was not your father's fault."

"Ray came in here demanding to know where you were. Your father said that you were with Ian in Virginia, and Ray exploded, saying he had no right to send you up with the Yankees."

"But he didn't *send* me anywhere. Ray is the most infuriating man. And to think that I did fancy I could be in love with him at one time. I've tried several times to make him understand that I am independent, that I *try* to make my own decisions, go my own way—despite Father and two older brothers and bossy cousins to boot and now Taylor. But—"

"Tia, don't worry about it. He came, and he left. Eventually, someone will tell him that you have married, and he will let it all go."

Later that day, she sat with her father by the river, and eventually she asked him, "Was I really such a horrible flirt?"

He looked at her, arching a brow. "Horrible? You were an excellent flirt, my darling daughter."

He was grinning, but she flushed. "Seriously, Father. I mean, I know that I liked to have a good time, and I did tease, but . . . life used to be so different."

"Tia, I'm afraid that Ray is somewhat obsessed. You did nothing wrong. You are beautiful, polite, friendly, you considered his suit . . . but you fell in love elsewhere."

She leaned back against her father's broad shoulder.

"We think so differently," she murmured.

"You and Ray—or you and Taylor?"

She laughed. "Taylor and I don't think the same at all, except . . ."

"Except that you do. You value life, and your belief in what is right and wrong, and the honor in a family, no matter what someone else's opinion may be."

"Perhaps."

"You did fall in love, right?" he asked gruffly.

"Yes, I did," she admitted. "Father . . ." she asked, but her voice faded away.

Jarrett turned to her, lifting her chin. He always seemed so wise to her. He saw so much, and understood so much, even when he tried to let her think out her own life.

"Do I think he loves you?" he asked.

"He sent me away," Tia admitted.

"He sent you where you wanted to be."

She bit her lip. Not really. She wanted to be with him. "The fighting has been fast and furious, Tia," her father said.

"You've heard from him?"

"From Ian. Taylor has been racing around, from Sherman to Sheridan to Grant. He's been in very hostile territory, seldom sleeping in the same place twice. He knew what his orders were going to be. And if he couldn't be with you, he apparently figured you should be with your family."

She smiled. "Thanks, Father."

"I know a little bit about rocky marital relations."

"You?" she inquired incredulously.

"Your mother. She can keep a secret until a man is nearly insane!"

Tara was coming across the lawn. He drew a finger to his lips, and Tia laughed, and she was suddenly very happy to be where she was, and who she was. She was glad to be with her father; she loved him so very much. And it was wonderful, new and fresh, to see him with her mother. They had been very lucky. The world around them had never been easy, but they had weathered it together.

Being home was almost like old times. Except that, sitting with her parents, she could see the man in the lookout tower at the docks, and she knew that Jarrett's men patrolled the ground constantly.

She didn't stay as long as she wanted—only a few weeks—but returned eastward to find Julian and Rhiannon and keep busy with them in the company of the militia. She wanted to help out when the babies were born, and from Julian's position along the river, she knew she'd hear when the time drew near. She did; Alaina sent them a message via a tobacco and coffee trade between the soldiers.

As it turned out, both babies came early. Katie Kyle McKenzie was born on the nineteenth of September. She had a headful of platinum curls, her mother's legacy, and huge blue eyes. Tia thought she was the most beautiful child she had ever seen. But then, Allen Angus McKenzie was born on the twenty-first of September, and he was as handsome as Katie was beautiful, with a touch of red in the thick thatch of dark hair on his head, and eyes already hinting of his mother's green. Tia was glad to be with her sisters-in-law and cousin-in-law and the whole little brood of McKenzies. She was able to fawn over the infants—and be helpful with the toddlers, who were proving to be quite wild under the circumstances.

Sean had taken it to heart that he was the eldest of this brood, a leader who was supposed to be responsible. Still, he had his moments when he wanted his mother's full attention. Ian was due; he had written that he'd received leave to come, but the war was becoming more and more demanding as the Union determined to end it—and the Confederacy fought on to the bitter end. Atlanta had finally fallen at the end of August. Although Tia still hadn't heard a word from Taylor herself, she learned from Risa that he had spent several weeks riding for General Sherman, maintaining tight communications between himself and other commanders in the field, and keeping a sharp eye on Rebel movements.

It wasn't long after she'd left Virginia that Tia began wondering if she herself was going to have a baby. The possibility was just as frightening as she'd feared it would be. She didn't want to lose a child—if she was definitely carrying one. She definitely didn't want to lose Taylor's child. She wanted a baby, as perfect as Alaina's little Katie, as sturdy and charming as Risa's young master Allen Angus McKenzie.

Tia spent most of October in St. Augustine, enjoying the newborns and her toddling little nephews and nieces. At the end of the month, she gave up waiting to hear from Taylor and returned inland with Rhiannon. Alaina told her that Taylor might have written several times— getting letters through was growing harder and harder.

That might have been true, but Alaina continued to hear from Ian.

There seemed to be a general feeling of despair that hung like a swamp miasma over the troops. Julian's hospital camp held three soldiers with gunshot wounds from skirmishing just south of Jacksonville, two sailors with cutlass wounds from a sea battle, and another three soldiers who had been hit with shrapnel during a Yankee bombardment of a salt mine. Although all were doing well, it seemed that they were listless, and waiting. There was hope in the South that Lincoln would be defeated by McClellan in the presidential election, but soon after the election on November 7, the news came that Lincoln had been reelected. The North would not be offering terms of reconciliation and allowing the South to go. President Davis kept making optimistic speeches, some of which filtered south. He believed that Lee's Army of Northern Virginia was invincible, but Tia could see that the fighting men thought otherwise.

In the middle of November, Julian was summoned northward to take care of several members of Dixie's band of militia. Nearly ten men had come down with the chicken pox. With most of the men doing well and Liam there, almost as familiar now with the treating of wounds as a trained surgeon, Tia thought that she would accompany Julian and Rhiannon, but as it happened, her sister-in-law wasn't going, and she also told Tia in no uncertain way that she wasn't going either.

"Tia, we're not going because it is chicken pox. And although I don't believe that I'm expecting another babe yet, I wouldn't want to discover later that I was wrong and that I'd exposed myself to an illness that would affect it. But if I'm not mistaken . . ." Rhiannon smiled knowingly at her sister-in-law.

"Can you tell?" Tia asked.

"Only because I know you."

Tia was quiet.

"Well?"

"I guess we'll stay here together. With Liam, of course."

Rhiannon was pleased. "Julian will understand; he'll manage alone."

Several days after Julian had left, two men who'd caught Yankee fire from the coast were brought in. It was very late at night when they arrived. Rhiannon was sleeping, and Tia decided not to wake her.

She recognized one of the men; he'd been her escort seemingly ages ago when Dixie's men had accompanied her to Cimarron for Christmas. His name was David Huntington and he was a very thin, charming young man who had just managed to grow his first mustache. He had been a brand new recruit with Dixie when she'd first met him; now he had nearly a year of service under his belt. She smiled at him reassuringly. "Bullet in his calf; shrapnel in his thigh. No bones and no blood vessels involved," she told Liam.

"Can you cut them out? Your brother is a day's ride from here. I can go for him," Liam told her.

"I can manage. Don't worry, I would never chance it if I couldn't. Soldier, I have some really fine whiskey for you to imbibe while I cut away! First—a little for the flesh—and then a little for the soul!"

The bullet came out easily; the shrapnel was harder. She winced each time she had to dig, and wondered if she shouldn't have waited for Julian. But then, she fished out the last piece, put in the stitches that were necessary, and bid her tipsy patient good night. Early the next morning, as she looked over her handiwork, she felt his large, anguished gray eyes upon her.

"Miss Tia . . ."

"Yes?"

"Lord love me, ma'am, I ain't no traitor."

"Of course you're not."

"But . . ."

"But what?"

He moistened his lips. Beckoned her closer. "I heard that you've done more than just patch up us boys, Miss Tia. I know your brother has saved hundreds of men. And I've even heard that your father has done nothing more than let officers from both sides meet on his lands.''

"That's true," she said, smiling at the soldier to encourage him to continue.

He started talking in a rush then. "Colonel Weir is going to attack Cimarron. He met up with our camp just a few days ago. I don't think that Captain Dixie believed him, I mean, you know what a fine man Dixie is, ma'am.''

"I do," she said gravely. "So how do you know—''

"Weir's got some other militia officer all fired up . . . he—he thinks that your father is a traitor, and that he has to be executed for what he's done to Florida.''

"What?" Tia gasped incredulously. "Executed! He can't execute my father; he's done nothing wrong—''

"*Sh* . . . *sh* . . . don't want no one calling me a traitor, saying I called the whistle on the colonel. Weir thinks he can prove charges that your father is a traitor, and if he thinks he can do it, he'll find a way. He hasn't got any real permission from the Reb army; he's just taking it all into his own hands.''

Weir is going to attack Cimarron? How dare he? Where does he get the nerve, the authority?

Then Tia knew. And she shouldn't have been surprised. Weir hated her father. Hated his confidence. Hated the fact that Jarrett was so deeply dedicated to his beliefs. Her father's courage was so strong and unfaltering. He had stood tall against the sea of difference all around him, never agreeing to what he thought was wrong just because others thought it was right.

"You're sure about this?" she asked quietly.

"Yes, ma'am, I am." He moistened his lips again. "He's gathering his troops at the old Ellington place. The Ellingtons have all been gone for some time now, you know.''

"Yes, I know. They were friends; the house is close to Cimarron.''

"Yes, ma'am. Very close. A good place to meet. He's going to attack . . . let's see . . . four days from now. At dusk. The timing is really important, 'cause he's going to coordinate an attack. Some other fellows will come down from the north while he moves up from the south in a pincer movement. Then he'll seize the property. And . . ."

"And what?"

"He intends to hang your father right there. Make him an example, he says, of what happens to Florida traitors."

"He's planning on hanging my father?" she said, outraged. "And my mother?" she asked sharply.

He didn't answer at first. His eyes were shamed, downcast. "She's . . . fair game for the soldiers. I'm not sure what will happen . . . when they're done . . ."

She stood back, horrified. She had to stop Weir. How? Get to him, buy time. Then what? She had to leave word right away; Liam had to get to Julian. Someone else had to get to St. Augustine right away, find Ian. Was Ian even there? Had he reached the city yet? If not, surely he had friends there, friends enough to raise a force against Weir's men. Friends who could get to Cimarron fast and stop what was happening.

"I have four days?" she whispered. Just enough time to get across the state.

"Well, three and a half, I reckon."

"How many men does Weir have?"

"Five companies, if I heard right. But there's maybe only ten to twenty men left alive in each of those companies. Miss Tia, Dixie would never have just let it go if he believed what Weir was planning. Still . . . he is Florida militia. And they're getting bitter, and hanging spies lots of places."

"Thank you, Private. Thank you so much." Impulsively, Tia kissed his cheek, then left him. She started to run to Rhiannon, but hesitated. No, she couldn't tell Rhiannon that she was going to Cimarron herself, that she had to. She would write Rhiannon a note. And she would write to Julian, and to Ian—oh, please, God, make it be that he had gotten to St. Augustine by now! Cimarron was his inheritance, his birthright. He would come, he would fight for it to his dying breath. Save . . .

Save their father. And their mother. Oh, Lord! She had to get to Cimarron; she couldn't risk anyone trying to stop her. She was going to have to race across the state . . .

She had Blaze with her. She knew the way, knew what she was doing. She could make it. She had to reach Weir. Stall him. What then? She didn't know. She just knew that she had to stop him somehow. And if she couldn't stop him, she had to buy time.

She hurried to her tent, wrote her letters. When she came out, she was ready. She went for Blaze, saddled her, bridled her, and started to mount her. Liam came hurriedly limping over to her on his prosthetic leg.

"Miss Tia—"

"Get these letters out for me, Liam."

"Now wait! What do you think that you're doing?"

"Make sure Rhiannon sees this right away. And get to Julian for me. It's a matter of life and death."

"Oh, God, Miss Tia, please tell me you're not going to run and do something dangerous or decadent—"

She was already on Blaze. "Liam! For the love of God! Do as I say."

She turned her horse and started riding hard from the camp.

No man in the whole of Grant's army had moved harder, or faster, Taylor thought, taking the time at last to dismount from Friar, empty his canteen—and look out across the devastated landscape. Damn yes, he was moving hard—and fast. Running. As if it could keep him from thinking, worrying . . . *being afraid.*

He should have made her stay. Strange, but he couldn't get over the longing. The passion they'd had. They'd almost been friends again. *And he had let her go. Like a fool. Why?*

Because, fool, idiot! he charged himself. Because you're in love with her, and it was happening from the first time you saw her. But you're a coward. You don't want to face pain again . . .

Well, that was it, of course. He had known how she'd

felt about watching the children die, had understood her fear. And scoffed at it, and told her that she was just going to have to live, and accept the tragedy as well as the happiness in life. But when she'd been so sick, tossing and turning, whispering that she just wanted to go home . . .

He hadn't been able to deny her wish. He'd decided that he'd fight harder and harder—as if he, one man, could make the war be over any more quickly.

So . . .

So now he was doing his damned best to follow the wily Confederate General Hood, who, in Sherman's own words, could twist an army around at will.

The problem was, pretty soon Hood wouldn't have much of anyplace left to twist it.

Sherman was destroying everything as he marched. It was said that a crow would have to pack a lunch to fly over Georgia. It was sickening, of course, what war had done there. God had seldom created such devastation with hurricanes, blizzards, tornadoes, floods, or other natural disasters. When Sherman's troops stripped the land, they stripped it good.

Taylor had just reported to the general and, to his surprise, received a personal letter from the general's headquarters. Chewing on a piece of hardtack, he hunkered down by Friar and perused the letter. It was from Jarrett McKenzie, a friendly missive, like one that any man might receive from his father-in-law. Jarrett congratulated him on his marriage and said that he had seen Tia. She had come straight there from Virginia. She must not have told her parents she had been ill, because Jarrett made no mention of the fact. He did, however, mention that Raymond Weir had been to Cimarron, anxiously asking about Tia. They'd argued. Weir had gone on, but Jarrett expected there would be trouble in the future.

Taylor folded the letter and slid it back into his pocket. Though there was nothing in the letter about Weir meaning anything to Tia, Weir was trouble—a fanatic dedicated to his goal.

He shouldn't have sent Tia home.

Then what should he have done? He could still remember the gripping fear he'd felt when he awakened
and discovered she was burning up. She was a fighter,
had been a fighter from the start, and Dr. Flowers had
never thought once that he was going to lose her. But
two men had died from the same fever at the hospital,
and that had scared him worse than he'd ever been
scared since . . .

Since the blood on his hands when he'd reached for
Abby.

Tia had pulled through, but watching her, day after
day, the beauty of her pale features, the silky sweeping
length of her "Godiva" hair, he realized just how much
he wanted and needed and *loved* his wife. He could remember telling her that only a fool would love her. He
was that fool. And although he admired her passion and
conviction and her fighting spirit, he was afraid for her.
Afraid that he wouldn't be there to protect her against
fanatics like Weir.

"Colonel Douglas!"

Hearing himself called, he stood and turned, frowning.
He didn't know the young infantry lieutenant striding
toward his position on the little hill.

"Yes, I'm Douglas."

"Hello, sir. Lieutenant Nathan Riley."

"Lieutenant," he acknowledged. "What can I do for
you?"

"Sir, I'm hoping I can do something for you."

"Oh?"

"My unit was a bit south of here the other day, down
closer to the border. We took some wounded militia
boys from North Florida prison. I was hoping to find a
way to reach Colonel McKenzie, but then I heard you
were kin to him, sir, that his sister is your wife."

"What's this about?"

"The McKenzie property is down by Tampa Bay. Jarrett McKenzie is a Union sympathizer, so I understand."

"Yes, he is."

"One of the Florida boys died just a few hours ago. I took this off him."

Lieutenant Riley passed him a creased sheet of paper. He looked at Riley curiously, then unfolded the paper and studied it. It was a map, he realized, crudely drawn. He saw Tampa Bay, the river, Cimarron. A plantation just south of Cimarron, and another one just north of it. There was a notation of "Major Hawkins" with an arrow coming from the north, and another notation, "Colonel Weir," with an arrow sweeping up from the south. The arrows met at Cimarron. There, a hangman's noose had been crudely drawn, and next to it, a date in November, just four days away. "Coordinated assault, must be timed to coincide from both fronts," was written in the corner.

He looked up. "Lieutenant, have we a working telegraph? I do need to get this information to Colonel Ian McKenzie, in Petersburg."

"As I said, I thought of Colonel McKenzie right away, sir. But he left Petersburg for St. Augustine several days ago."

"Then I need the information to reach him there. I know that lines are down, but Ian may be the only hope."

"I'll get it through somehow, sir."

"And send a message that when he gets this, he should go straight to Cimarron. I'll try to deal with Weir at the Ellington place before he can muster his men together for the attack."

"Aye, sir!" Riley said, saluting.

"Thank you, Riley."

"You're going to stop it, sir, right?" Riley asked. "My home is Tennessee. Some people didn't agree with Pa's dedication to the Union Jack, so they burned him out. I'd hate like hell to see it again. Thought Southerners were supposed to be gentlemanly folk, the last of the cavaliers."

"Many of them are, Riley. But some of them aren't. Hell, yes, if I can stop this, I will. I'm going to get leave from Sheridan, and ask for a number of troops. You want to come along, Lieutenant?"

Riley grinned. "Hell, yes, sir! I can round you up one of the finest companies of scouts and skirmishers in the whole Union army, assuming you can get Sheridan to agree."

He knew he could get Sheridan to agree. He was still carrying the leave papers that Lincoln himself had signed. Sheridan couldn't hold him, and knowing the fierce little man as he did, he was certain the cause would appeal to him—despite the fact that many men had lost their homes in the devastation of the war. Jarrett was a man who had never failed the Union. And securing Florida always remained an intriguing challenge to the Union commanders.

If he couldn't bring troops, he would go himself. But he believed that his own passion would be enough to convince Sheridan.

"Get those messages out for me by telegraph, Riley—and if the lines are down, get a runner. But make sure we get the information through to Ian. Meet me back at the general's headquarters. We haven't much time to travel a hell of a lot of miles."

Riley saluted. "Yes, sir! I'll be mighty proud to ride with you!"

On Friar, Taylor rode hard back toward headquarters, hoping that no recent development in the fighting would prevent him from an immediate audience with Sheridan.

He had to leave, now. As soon as Riley could muster his company together.

When the hell had militia been given the right to become judge and jury in the state? Was Weir going mad, seizing far too much power, thinking himself the law?

His heart pounded in his chest like a drumbeat. *Could he make it in time?* Where was Tia? Did she know about any of this?

She would never let men go against Cimarron without doing something.

How in hell was he going to endure the time it would take to get there?

Chapter 25

A House United

Fall, 1864
The West Florida Coast, Near Tampa Bay

The sky was strange that night. Though dark, the lingering effects of a storm at dusk had left crimson streaks across the shadowy gray of the sky. A cloud passed over the moon, which seemed to glow with that strange red light. Reaching Ellington Manor, Taylor lifted a hand to signify a silent halt to the men behind him. They could hear the clamor of other men, disbursing supplies, but they were around the back of the property. One lone soldier, leaning against a once-majestic column, guarded the house in front.

Taylor made a sign to Riley, indicating that he would take the fellow on the porch and that they would then move around the rear at his signal. Riley nodded. Dismounting from Friar, Taylor slunk low and approached the house from the northwest side. The guard never looked up. Taylor leaped over the porch banister, came behind the guard, and set the muzzle of a Colt against his neck. "Quiet, soldier. You may find conditions in a Northern prison better than what you'll have with the militia soon, and certainly better than the alternative you face if you so much as whimper now." The soldier lifted his hands in a gesture of surrender.

"Is Weir in there alone?" Taylor asked the guard softly.

"No, sir."

"Who is with him?"

"Miss McKenzie."

Taylor nearly dropped his weapon. "What?"

"Miss McKenzie, sir, Miss Tia McKenzie. A local girl, an old friend." The guard sounded terrified. Taylor realized that he had pressed the muzzle of his gun deeper into the man's neck.

Miraculously, he managed to ease his grip on the gun and let the man talk. "What's she doing here?"

"I don't—"

Taylor pressed the gun more tightly to his flesh. "What's she doing here?"

"She came to marry the colonel."

"Marry him?"

"Except that he couldn't marry her. We have no minister."

"But she's still in there?"

The man surely thought he was going to die. "Yes!" he gulped.

"Doing what?"

"Well, sir, I think she's trying to seduce him."

Taylor felt as if his flesh burned, as if his soul had exploded into a white light of fury. He forced himself to regain control. He gave the man a firm thump on the head. The Rebel fell without a whimper. Taylor hoped he hadn't hit him too hard. He didn't want to kill the fellow just for being the messenger of such tidings. He bent down, put a finger to the soldier's throat, and felt his pulse. He was alive.

Taylor wanted to rush into the house, but he couldn't, not yet, no matter how he longed to do so. This was his mission. He was responsible for these men, and he'd be damned if he'd be surprised by a few Rebels who slipped their cordon once he was in the house—and accosting Weir.

He rose, waving to indicate that Riley and the troops should come around. Again, as prearranged, they split up, coming around the back of the house. As they fanned out, they could hear conversation.

"I still say this ain't right!" a private, tightening the girth on his saddle, complained. "I mean, there's real Yankees in the state—why are we attacking a home?"

"Because there's no Yankee like a Southern traitor!" another man answered, shoving his rifle into the holster on his saddle. "Colonel Weir says this may be the most important work we do this whole war, bringing down McKenzie. McKenzie has been like a knife sticking right in the back of the state, admitting that he thinks secession is wrong and saying that it's immoral to own slaves. When we hang him, we send out a message to all other would-be traitors, to folks who think and feel like him but who have the sense to shut up—they'll know better than to ever become traitors to the South."

"Is he being a traitor to state his mind?" the first man asked.

"He's a traitor to everything we're fighting for!" the second thundered.

"Right! Like freedom of speech, eh, Louis?"

Taylor had heard enough. He didn't have any more time—Tia was in the house with Weir. The men were in position at the sides of the house. Some had crept around the barn, making sure they knew where their enemy lay. He estimated there were about sixty-five men. More than his own company of thirty—all that Sheridan would allow him. But his troops were seasoned scouts who had been following the likes of Jeb Stuart throughout the war. They'd already surrounded their enemy in silence. Time to take them down, and quickly.

He lifted his arm, then dropped it. His men suddenly appeared in a semicircle around the unwary soldiers, repeating rifles raised. Taylor spoke quickly and quietly. "Stay where you are, gentlemen. Don't make a move. Every man with me is armed with a Spencer repeating rifle, and every man is a crack shot. Now, I know you boys are good, and that you can load and fire those Enfields pretty darned fast—but you know that even at top speed, you'll be dead before you get to fire. Lieutenant Riley here will take your weapons. Form a nice line and deposit those Enfields, swords, knives—whatever else you boys might have." He saw that the man who'd called Jarrett McKenzie a traitor was sliding his hand toward the holster on his saddle. "You!" Taylor said sharply, raising a Colt to eye level. "I wouldn't mind shooting you down in an instant!"

The man dropped his arm. The line began to form. "Riley, I'll need some men in a few minutes. Two, to come for Weir. Then two more—yourself and one other."

"My wife is in there," he said flatly, trying to keep the fury and emotion out of his voice.

Yes, she was in there. *Seducing* Weir.

God help them both!

"Tia can't keep herself out of danger. Time the North does it for her."

"Yes, sir," Riley said unhappily. As Taylor started for the house, the lieutenant called out, "A word, sir!"

Taylor paused impatiently. Time, time, time . . . he had to stop time.

"*She* is the one being attacked, sir. They are after her home, her father."

"I know that, Lieutenant Riley," he said.

Taylor slipped through the back door of the house. He could hear movement upstairs. He followed the back stairs up, careful not to let a single board creak.

He heard them in the hallway.

Heard them enter one of the bedrooms. Thankfully, the only light in the room was moonlight—strange red-glowing moonlight. He saw her standing there, near the window. He clenched down his jaw, trying not to let out a sound. She had shed her bodice. The moonlight played upon the sleek lines of her back. Her hair, that wretched wealth of hair that had created a legend, fell about her in a lustrous sheen, like a raven's wings.

"The bed is clean, the sheets are fresh, tended by my men," Weir was saying.

Taylor ached to stop them right then. To pull a Colt, shoot Weir through the head. What if Weir shifted in the shadows at the last second? What if he heard Taylor, and drew his sword?

Against Tia . . .

He had to wait, let Weir drop his weapon.

He stood in the shadow by the door, neither of them noting him.

"So you said," she whispered.

"My love . . ." Weir walked up behind her, drawing her against him. He shifted the fall of her hair, pressed his mouth to her shoulder. His fingers were on her skirt; it fell away. Then her pantalettes, and she was naked.

"Come, my love . . ." he said.

"Look at the moon!" she entreated, walking way from him, toward the window.

His chance! Taylor's hand itched to draw the Colt. No! he wouldn't shoot a man in the back, even if the bastard had the bloody nerve to be touching his wife . . .

"Tia, the moon, like the war, will come again."

"It's a beautiful moon, yet shaded in red—"

"There's no time for talk."

His scabbard and sword were, at last, cast aside. Taylor prepared to strike.

Weir's cavalry jacket and shirt were shed.

"I need another drink, Raymond," Tia said. "This is new to me."

New to her? At least she was making some attempt to slow things down.

Weir wasn't having any of it. "Madam," he said curtly, running his fingers through his hair. "I remind you—you invited me to this room. Shall I leave?"

"No! You mustn't leave!" Tia cried out.

He lifted her, bore her down on the bed.

"My love!" Weir said again. He kissed her fingertips.

"My—love," she whispered in return.

"Oh, good God!" Taylor's voice, shaking with rage, suddenly filled the room. He approached the bed, his body on fire, shaking, fighting desperately to control his murderous impulses. "That's it—I've had it with this charade!" he lashed out.

"What in the name of the Almighty?" Raymond grated, twisting around to see who'd had the gall to interrupt him. "Taylor! You!" he spat out.

Taylor drew his sword, pressed it against Weir's throat.

Somehow, Taylor kept himself from slitting the man's jugular vein. "Stop. Stop right now." It still sounded to Taylor as if his very voice shook. He kept the sword point resting just at Weir's vein. He stared at Tia; she stared back, her eyes glistening like ebony orbs.

"Ah, good, I have your attention!" he told her. And at last, he had managed to speak softly, mockingly, controlling the shuddering that had seized him and nearly ruled him. "I'm sorry," he continued, "but this charming little domestic adventure has gone quite far enough. Colonel Weir, if you will please rise carefully."

"Damn you, Taylor Douglas!" Weir swore furiously. "You'll die for this. I swear it! How did you get in?"

"I entered by the door, Captain."

He felt Tia's eyes on him. Still huge, so dark, containing so many secrets, lies, truths. He swung the point of his sword around. Laid it between her breasts. She was so beautiful, so still, staring at him. He couldn't endure her lying there, where she had been—if briefly— with Weir.

"Tia, get up. And for the love of God, get some clothing on. I grow weary of finding you naked everywhere I go—other than in our marital bed, of course."

"Marital bed!" Weir exclaimed, stunned.

"Ah, poor fellow, you are indeed surprised. A fact that might spare your life, though I had thought of you before as something of an honorable man, just a fanatic. But yes, I did say marital bed. You hadn't heard? Though it grieves me deeply to admit it, the lady is a liar and a fraud. She can marry no one for she is already married. She is wily, indeed, a vixen from the day we met. All for the Southern Cause, of course. She will play her games! But what of that great cause now, Tia?"

Her eyes seemed to crackle with a dark fire. She was never a coward. She caught the tip of his blade and cast the sword aside as she leapt from the bed. Her eyes touched his—with an amazing pride and hauteur. She searched about in the shadows for her clothing, then dressed very quickly.

"Tia?" Weir asked suddenly. There was a sad crack

to his voice. Weir had loved her, really loved her, Taylor thought. It didn't ease the tempest inside him. "You are *married* to him," Weir said.

"Yes," she said.

"But you came to me . . . tonight!" he cried, his ego demanding that she had come to him because she had always wanted him, no matter what she had said or done before.

Tia lifted her chin. "You were going to attack Cimarron," she told him, her tone cold and brittle. "And kill my father."

Raymond shook his head, trying to appear very earnest to her. "Your father . . . no, Tia. I meant to seize the property, nothing more."

"That's not true!" she said. How she had learned about this, Taylor had no idea. But Weir wasn't fooling her in the least. "My father was to be killed—executed," she said.

"I would have spared his life—for you!" Weir told her.

Taylor had definitely had enough.

"How touching," he interrupted, his voice a drawl that didn't hide his fury. "Tell me, Tia, was that explanation for him—or me?"

"Taylor, you're being a truly wretched bastard. You don't understand anything!" she lashed out at him.

Raymond suddenly made a dive for the sword where it lay on the floor. Taylor was itching to slash it out of his hands.

He forced himself to refrain from cutting flesh. He hit Weir's sword with a vengeance. The blade flew across the room. He pressed the tip of his own sword to Weir's throat once again.

"Taylor!" Tia cried out. "Don't . . . murder him. Please!"

He stared at her, fighting for control.

"Please, don't . . ." she said simply.

He returned her gaze. Remembered that he had come to prevent murder, not to do the deed himself.

He turned his attention to Weir. "I've no intention of

doing murder, sir. We are all forced to kill in battle, but I'll not be a cold-blooded murderer." A bitterness he couldn't control welled up in his throat. "I've yet to kill any man over a harlot, even if that harlot be my own wife."

"Call me what you will," Tia cried to him, suddenly passionate and vital, "but your life is in danger here, and, you fool, there is much more at stake! There are nearly a hundred men outside preparing to march on my father's house."

"No, Tia, no longer," Taylor said. "The men below have been seized. Taken entirely by surprise. Quite a feat, if I do say so myself. Not a life lost, Colonel," he informed Raymond. Weir stared back at him.

"So you'll not murder me. What then?" Weir asked him.

"I believe my men are coming for you now, if you would like to don your shirt and coat," he informed Weir.

Raymond nodded, as if grateful for the courtesy. He reached for his shirt and frockcoat. The latter was barely slipped over his shoulders before Riley and another of Taylor's men, Virgil Gray, appeared in the doorway.

"To the ship, Colonel?" Riley asked him.

"Aye, Lieutenant Riley. Have Captain Maxwell take the lot of them north. Meet me with the horses below when the prisoners have been secured."

"Sir?" the lieutenant said politely to Weir.

Weir looked at Tia and bowed elegantly to her. She stared at him, and kept staring at him as Virgil slipped restraints around his wrists. Then he turned with Riley and Gray, and departed the room.

Then they were alone. Taylor and his wife. After so much time.

After this!

She was so still, not facing him now. But again, asking no pardon, no quarter, giving no excuses, saying nothing at all . . .

He came to her suddenly, because he couldn't help himself anymore. He gripped her shoulders, his fingers biting into her flesh. She met his eyes. He felt as if he had been seized by every demon in hell, and he wanted to strike her to her knees. *No!* He pushed her away. There was more to the night.

It seemed that he stood there forever, wanting to do some violence to her, wanting to stop the rage that warred inside him, wanting just to hold her. And finally, he managed to walk away. The time had finally come when he didn't dare trust her, himself, or the future.

Walk away! he told himself. *Let your men come and escort her to prison. Get to Cimarron, while there is still a Cimarron to get to!*

But now, she had suddenly found movement, and a voice. She came flying after him, catching him on the stairs. She pushed past him, turning around to face him. He saw the grief in her eyes, heard the pain in her voice. "Taylor, I—I—they said he meant to kill my father."

"Step aside, Tia," he said.

"Taylor, damn you! I had to come her, I had to do what I could to stop him. Can't you see that, don't you understand?"

He lashed out, sarcastic and cruel, striking her with the anguish that ripped through him.

"I understand, *my love,* that you were ready, willing, and able to sleep with another man. But then, Weir is a good Southern soldier, is he not? A proper planter, a fitting beau for the belle of Cimarron, indeed, someone you have loved just a little for a very long time. How convenient."

"No, I—"

"No?" he challenged. How many times had she defended Weir to him?

"Yes, you know that—*once* we were friends. But I . . . please!" she whispered. His heart constricted, fingers plucked at it, tightened, squeezed. There was so much in that simple word. And the way she looked at him.

He reached out, lightly stroking her cheek. "Please? Please what? Are you sorry, afraid? Or would you seduce me, too? Perhaps I'm not such easy prey for you, for I am, at least, familiar with the treasure offered, and

I have played the game to a great price already. When I saw you tonight . . . do you know what I first intended to do? Throttle you, you may be thinking! Beat you black and blue. Well that, yes. Where pride and emotions are involved, men do think of violence. But I thought to do more. Clip your feathers, my love. Cut off those ebony locks and leave you shorn and costumeless, as it were—*naked* would not be the right word. What if I were to sheer away these lustrous tresses? Would you still be about seducing men—friend and foe—to save your precious family and state? Not again, for until this war of ours is finished, I will have you hobbled—until your fate can be decided."

"I—have seduced no one else. I . . ." she said. Tears glistened in the darkness of her eyes. "I'm not a harlot, Taylor!" she managed to whisper. There was a wealth of hurt and sorrow and reproach in her words, and he found himself trembling, shaking, glad to find that she was safe, glad that she wanted him to believe her.

He reached for her, drawing her into his arms. He kissed her too hard, with too much violence in his soul. Felt her hair, her flesh, tasted the sweetness, tempest, and passion in her lips. He was in love with her, did love her so much, had sworn that he would not. He wanted nothing more than to be with her. Hold her, forget. Make love then and there, and let the world crash down around them.

No, good God, he could not be seduced now, couldn't forget his anger, didn't dare. He pulled away from her, speaking hoarsely. "Ah, Tia, what a pity! I'm not at all sure of your motives at the moment, but for once, when you are apparently ready to become a willing wife with no argument to give me, there remains too much at stake for me to take advantage of your remorse. There's a battle still to be waged."

"A battle?" Either she hadn't known about the pincer movement planned against her father, or she had forgotten. "But you've stopped Weir from the war he would wage against my father."

"Tia, you little fool! Weir was only a half of it! There's

a Major Hawkins with militia from the panhandle who will bear down upon Cimarron at any moment now. I don't know if Ian ever received word of this, or if Julian knows somehow. You apparently learned about it. But I may be the only help your father will have."

She stared at him, stunned. And terrified, he thought. "Dear God! I'd forgotten there would be more troops. I've got to get home!" she cried, and she turned, running frantically down the remaining steps.

"No! Tia!"

He wasn't going to allow it. She was willing to risk far too much. He ran after her, caught her first by the length of her raven dark hair. She cried out; he ignored the sound, winding her back into his arms, meeting her eyes. "You're going nowhere," he told her firmly.

"My father—my home—"

Yes, they were everything to her. And once, she had probably thought that Weir would be the one to fight for them. "Your enemy will save them for you," he said.

"No, please, you have to let me ride with you. I beg of you, Taylor, in this, I swear, I—"

"Make me no more promises, Tia, for I am weary of you breaking them."

"But I swear—"

"This fight will be deadly, and I'll not have you seized by either side as a pawn in the battles to be waged."

"Please!" she begged.

No, no . . . no. He could not let her be there. She would die to save her family, or Cimarron. He almost explained that to her, but he heard footsteps at the landing. His men had come for her.

"Gentlemen, take my wife to the ship, please. They'll not be surprised to find another McKenzie prisoner at Old Capitol."

One of the soldiers cleared his throat politely. "Mrs. Douglas, if you will . . ."

She lowered her head, stepping away from Taylor's hold.

Now she really hated him, he thought. And again, the

longing was there to pull her to him, to forget everything else.

No!

He released her.

She stared at him again. "No!" she said softly. Then
she cried out, "No!"

He had forgotten who she was, how fast, sleek, supple,
and determined. She spun around with such a swift fury
that she tore past him, and the soldiers who would have
taken her.

She raced down those steps. As she did so, he swore,
thinking that Blaze was probably out there; he hadn't
thought to seize her horse when they'd arrived.

"Colonel, sir, sorry! We'll catch her!" one of the men
swore quickly.

"No, you will not. I barely have a chance myself," he
said without rancor. "Tell Riley to leave all the prisoners
with the captain, and to ride hard for Cimarron behind
me."

He burst outside just as Tia leapt up on Blaze. Her
eyes met his.

"Home, girl, home!" she told Blaze, nudging the
animal.

Taylor whistled for Friar, mounted him in a flying
leap. Tia had already filled the air with her dust.

The pounding of the earth beneath him seemed to fill
him. He rode hard a good ten minutes before nearly
catching her. He shouted; she didn't hear him, or
wouldn't stop. He rode abreast from her and leapt from
Friar to Blaze, catching her in his embrace. She resisted
him, twisting in the saddle and bringing them both flying
down from the horse. He pinned her. She fought him
like a wildcat. "Please, Taylor, please, for the love of
God . . . Please, please!" she whispered. "Bring me
home! Let me be there. Bring me home tonight. I'll stay
by your side, obey your every command! I'll surrender,
I'll cease to ride, I'll turn myself in to Old Capitol, I'll
put a noose around my own neck, I swear it, Taylor,
please, I'll—"

Her eyes were, for once, so honest. She loved her

family. If only she felt half that for him. "Love, honor, and obey?" he asked wryly. And it wasn't even that he had chosen to forgive her; it was that they were closer to Cimarron than they were to going back.

He stood, drawing her along with him. "You'll ride with me!" he told her harshly. "And go where I command, stay away from all fire! Blaze can follow on her own—she knows the way."

"Yes!" she promised.

He whistled again. Friar, good old warhorse that he was, had stopped his flight with Taylor gone from his back. He returned. Taylor set Tia upon his horse, mounted swiftly behind her. He kneed Friar. The horse began a hard flight once again.

The night sky remained bathed in blood. Indeed, when they neared Cimarron, coming from the south below the river that would be one line of defense, the white plantation house itself was steeped in the blood.

Before they reached the property, he could hear shouts. Commands being given, responses, men moving quickly. Defenses had been erected against the river, and men were already busy at the work of battle, taking places behind newly erected earthworks.

Ian had arrived with troops; they were positioned behind the earthworks.

But there were Rebels on Cimarron's side as well. And he saw Julian in the midst of them, calling out, giving orders, receiving responses.

They might not have known, might not have made it. But they had. Now that Taylor was there, they had the superior numbers. And for once in the war, the color of the uniform meant nothing.

He was accosted by a guard at the rear of the property. "Halt, or be shot!"

"It's Colonel Douglas, here to defend with the McKenzies!" Taylor shouted, sliding down from Friar.

There was a gunboat out on the river. Men were loading rifles, manning the single cannon.

Behind him, he suddenly heard Tia leap down from

Friar. "Mother!" she shrieked, and she was gone, racing across the lawn.

"Tia!" He thundered in warning, just as he saw Tara McKenzie hurrying across the lawn to her husband's side, ready to duck beneath the earthworks. But the Rebel soldiers had learned to use their Enfields swiftly in this war. The fire could come too fast.

"Tia!" He shouted her name again. She had reached her mother. Throwing herself against her, Tia meant to bring them both down to the ground.

Taylor heard the volley of fire.

And they were both down.

He raced to her like the wind. The Rebs on the river were getting ready for a second volley of fire.

He drew his guns, sliding to his knees beside his wife and her mother. He started to fire rapidly, buying time to move the women. He felt her eyes. She was looking at him. He bent over her, trying to assess the damage. She reached up, touching his cheek. Her eyes closed. "Tia!"

There was blood on her shoulder. He didn't know where the bullet had ripped through her, only that at least it hadn't struck too close to her heart. Tara groaned, trying to rise.

"Down!" he warned. By then, Jarrett McKenzie, his face a mask of fury and concern, was down beside him. And Julian followed.

Jarrett was lifting Tara. "We've got to get them back to the house," he said gruffly.

Taylor started to lift Tia. Julian reached for his sister; he met Taylor's eyes. "Taylor, let me take her. You might know something about bullet wounds, but not as much as I do. And I'm a damned good shot, but you're better. You can cover us."

He wanted to be with her; more than anything he had ever wanted in his life, he wanted to be with her. But Julian was right. Julian was a doctor. He was not. He was a crack shot.

If she died, he didn't want to live!

The thought passed through him. No, he wasn't going

out there to kill himself. He was going out there to end
this thing.

So that he could go back to her.

He heard his men arriving behind him. Reinforcements. This could be over quickly; they even had Rebel
forces on their side. Sometimes, even in the middle of
war, men knew the difference between right and wrong.
"Taylor!" Julian gave him a shake. "Keep those bloody
bastards out of my house so I can tend to my mother
and sister!"

He nodded to Julian, rose, and running along the
earthworks, started to fire. The cannon suddenly exploded, shattering the dock. Dirt and dust blew everywhere. Running along the dirt, he found Ian's position.
Ian didn't know what had happened to his mother and
sister. Taylor decided it wasn't the time to tell them.

"Barrage them!" Taylor exclaimed. "I'm going for
the cannon!"

Despite the earth and powder that filled the air
around them, Ian saw his intent. If he could get to the
gunboat and disable the one cannon, the main threat
was over. He nodded. He called out orders to his men.
"You'll have to watch out for friendly fire."

Guns fired in a continual fury from the shore line,
striking the gunners in the boats and the foot soldiers in
the fields beyond. Taylor shed his boots and jacket and
slipped down by the ruined dock. He dived into the
water, keeping low. He could hear the spitting, soaring
sounds as bullets whipped by him in the river. He dived
more deeply. When he came up behind the gunboat, he
saw that the defenders had done their work well.

The boat held numerous corpses. He walked low and
silently across the deck to the single gun. When the
Rebel cannoneer went to load the weapon, he drew his
fist back and caught the man with a deadly right hook.
The man fell. A second gunner was drawing a pistol to
shoot him. Taylor caught the man's arm, twisted it, and
the gun fired into the fellow's gut. Another man flew
across the deck at him, bearing a naval cutlass. Taylor
dodged the flight, allowing the man to pin himself into

the wooden body of the vessel. Then he threw the man overboard, still using the impetus of the man's flight. He heard something behind him and turned. Sweat beaded on his forehead. He would have been run through by a man with a rapier, but the Rebel merely stared at him, then fell, shot from the shoreline.

Taylor quickly overstuffed the cannon and lit the wick. With only seconds, he dived into the water and swam as hard as he could. He was still beneath the water when he heard the explosion. It rocked him toward the shoreline with a massive catapulting action, then sucked him back. For a minute, he thought that, after all this, he was going to drown. Then he found the surface, broke it, and stumbled on to the embankment.

He lay there in the night, feeling the damp earth beneath him. He gasped for breath. He opened his eyes and looked up. An unknown Rebel soldier stood above him. The man grinned, reaching a hand down to him.

"Colonel, sir, that was one of the most remarkable acts I've ever seen! And they say that we're better soldiers and better strategists!"

Taylor just stared at him for a moment. Then he grinned with relief as well. "Unfortunately, sir, most of the time you are. If you weren't so damned good, this wretched war could have been over long ago."

"Let me help you to the house, sir," the soldier said. Taylor saw that he had one good leg and one wooden leg. "Name's Liam, sir. At your service."

He was up, facing the man. The boat on the river continued to burn, adding to the red haze of the night. Men were racing around, stopping by the injured, assessing the damage and the situation.

"It's over?" Taylor queried.

"It's over."

Taylor nodded, and turned instantly for the house. He ran across the lawn, up the porch steps, and into the entry. Still dripping and muddied, he burst into the parlor.

He saw Tia first. Pale as a ghost, laid out on the Victorian sofa. Sheets covered her; she didn't move. A black woman was at her side.

He walked across the room, his heart in his throat. He looked at the black woman, and sat down by his wife.

"Tia . . ."

Her eyes opened. "Taylor?" she whispered.

"I'm here." He took her hand. "It's over Tia, it's over. Your father is safe. Cimarron is safe."

She squeezed his hand back. *"You're safe!"* she whispered.

Her eyes closed again.

"Tia!"

"She's all right!" he heard from the doorway. Julian was back. "Flesh wound, Taylor. She caught it in the upper arm. If she hadn't deflected the bullet, though, my mother might have died. Tia will probably have a nasty scar, but then, when this is all over, we're all going to have some nasty scars, inside and out."

"But she's unconscious," Taylor said.

"A touch of laudanum. It must have hurt like a bitch when I was sewing her up. And she was making me crazy, insisting she had to see Mother. You know your wife."

Yes, he knew his wife.

And she would make him insane forever with her spirit and courage and determination.

But then, that was partly why he loved her so very much.

Chapter 26

Three days later, Taylor walked down to the spring pool that was just through the woods on the McKenzie property. Julian had told him that Tia had gone there. It was the family reflecting pond, he said, glancing toward his older brother. "In fact, Ian looked in the water there once, and found Alaina."

"Very amusing, little brother," Ian said.

"Little! I think I have half an inch on you, Ian!" Julian told him.

Taylor grinned, leaving the two on the porch. The bullet that had grazed Tia's arm had lost its impetus and had stopped short of doing any serious damage to Tara, breaking her skin and lodging in the flesh just below her collarbone. Julian had dug it out quickly and easily. Tara had lost a lot of blood, but today, for the first time, she was feeling strong. She knew she couldn't hold her family at home much longer, so she wanted to be with her sons while she could. Most of the Union soldiers had already returned to their posts, Ian's men traveling back across the peninsula, Taylor's recruits taking the prisoners who had survived the attack at Cimarron on the ship north. Julian's band of orderlies and injured remained, while Ian had added men to his own operations, just in case the war should come home again. Taylor doubted that it would; only a personal vendetta had brought Weir's troops here. The South didn't have enough men left anymore to waste on a private war.

He still had days left himself, days given to him by President Lincoln.

He had wasted a few of those precious days dealing

with military matters, cleaning up the dead at Cimarron, sending men and prisoners on. And though he had sat with Tia, he hadn't gone to her room at night yet, and they hadn't really talked. Once she was up herself, she spent her time with her mother. And he hadn't dared get too close to her until Julian had assured him that her arm was healing very nicely.

Once he had felt that he couldn't afford to take time from the battlefield, even when time had been offered to him; the war effort needed him. Now, he needed the time, and the war effort would go on without him.

As he walked to the pool, he paused for a minute to close his eyes. Home. This was home to him, this warmth. A touch, just a touch, of a winter's chill in the air. The whisper of a palm, bending in the breeze. The cry of a heron.

Yes, it was nearly winter, but still the days were warm and beautiful, the sun brilliant. The pines, oaks, and palms offered a gentle relief from the heat of the sun as he headed toward the pool. When he had reached the copse, he saw Tia there. She sat on a log, dangling her bare feet into the cool spring water. She wore a soft blue-flowered cotton gown, with the full length of her hair untied and sweeping around her. She appeared very young, like a little nymph, a water sprite. But when she turned toward him, her dark eyes were far older, and the tension in her beautiful features betrayed the strain she had been under.

He walked to the log and sat down beside her.

"So this is the McKenzie reflecting pool," he said after a moment, aware that she was watching him.

"It is. It's my favorite place here," she said, and he heard her voice tightening. "I love it. I love the birds, and the water—the fresh water, and the river and the sea beyond. I love the heat, and the breezes, and the days and the nights and . . . Taylor, thank you. I . . ." She turned and looked at him. "Cimarron means a lot to me. But . . . but it wasn't the property that made me do what I did. My father has always taught us that there is no *thing,* no object in the world that is worth a man's

life. I went to Weir thinking I could stall him. I didn't
have anything planned. I . . ."

She didn't finish. She looked away.

"Taylor, why did you send me away?" she asked him.

His heart shuddered and squeezed. "Because you
wanted to go home."

"I wanted to be home," she whispered. "But not away
from you."

"Every time I made love to you," he said harshly, "it
was as if I forced a burden on you. You told me you
didn't want children."

"I was afraid! But I—I was glad that you were impatient with my fears. My God, Taylor! You must have
known how I felt!"

"I know that you cried!"

"Because . . . because I needed you so much, and
you . . ." Her voice trailed. She stared at him. "Well,
when you came to the Ellington place, and then let me
ride with you—"

"I was an idiot! See what happened."

She smiled. "I'm all right, and my mother is all right.
I had to be here, Taylor. That was fate maybe. But
you—you could have stopped me. And I said that I'd
do whatever you wished—afterward. And I'll keep my
word to you, Taylor. I'll go wherever you want—lock
myself into prison, if that's your wish."

He stared at her a long time. Then he grimaced in
return. "Tempting!" he said softly.

"You mean . . . you . . ." She hesitated, looking away
again. "Taylor, another man might have cut my throat
that night. I assume that, at the very least, you must
want a divorce now."

"True, another man might have been really tempted
to skewer you!" he reflected, picking up and throwing a
pebble, then watching it skip across the surface of the
water. He turned to her again. "But a wife without a
throat does not do a man much good."

She looked at him again. "Wife . . . but Taylor . . ."

"We both made a commitment, Tia. I said I wouldn't
let you out of it. And I won't."

"And as for prison?" she whispered softly.

"I think your mother is going to need you here for a while," he said.

He felt her eyes, felt the heat and amazement in the way she looked at him. Then, suddenly, he was pitching off the log, totally unprepared as she threw herself at him. "Taylor, oh, my God, Taylor . . ."

He would have to learn never to underestimate her. She straddled him this time, her hair falling all over him, teasing his nose, making him sneeze. Then her lips were on his, sweet with passion, salty with tears. She kissed him, and kissed him, and then he heard her whisper, "Taylor, thank God, thank God. I didn't want our baby born in a prison."

Baby.

He still had the strength. He rose swiftly, pinning her beneath him. "What?"

"Sometime in April, I believe," she said. Then her eyes watered again. "Oh, Taylor, I swear that it's ours . . . yours. I . . . love you. I think I started loving you when I met you, you aggravated me so badly, being so damned certain that you were right, being a . . ."

"Yankee?" he supplied.

"But you just wouldn't act badly, you were always so . . . well, determined, but honorable. Passionate . . . but honorable."

"You didn't want children!" he said hoarsely.

"I was afraid, so afraid!" she whispered. "I'm still afraid. So much bad happens, but then, you should see the new little McKenzies, they're so wonderful . . . so beautiful . . . I do want our baby, Taylor. So very much. And I was afraid again, afraid that taking the bullet the way I did might cost us our child, but then again, I couldn't have watched my mother die . . . and I've been thinking, Taylor, and I was so wrong, but if I had to go back . . . I couldn't have let my father die either."

He smoothed her hair from her face. And he understood, and he should have understood her so long ago. No. He couldn't have done anything other than fight for the Union. And she never could have allowed either of her parents to be harmed.

"We just have to be grateful that it's over; that it ended as it did," he said softly, brushing her lips with a kiss.

Her eyes, so huge and dark against her delicate features, locked with his. "Can you really forgive me?"

"Can you forgive *me?*" he asked.

"I never betrayed you!" she whispered.

"You're right. I was just a horse's ass!"

She smiled slowly. Her arms wrapped around him. She drew his head down to hers. She pressed her lips to his, kissing him, slowly at first, sweetly. Then her lips formed to his, her tongue snaked along his, pressing entry, and her kiss became amazingly provocative. He kissed her back, parting her lips further, penetrating her mouth deeply with his tongue in return. Amazing what a kiss could do. He felt it straight to his groin, felt the hunger, the need, the time between them, the sudden desperation to touch more of her. He found the hem of her gown, slid his hand up the length of her bare legs, heard her soft gasp against his lips as his touch teased along her upper thigh . . .

Then, abruptly, he pulled away from her, aware—too late—that they were not alone.

Weir hadn't quite come up to them. He stood five feet away, a pistol in his hand. He had meant to reach them, Taylor realized, and press the gun straight to his temple. His uniform looked torn, ragged, slept in. Weir's cheeks were dusky with a few days' growth of beard. His eyes were wild. Red-rimmed, nervous, darting.

He had escaped, Taylor realized, *by diving into the sea. He had come straight to them.*

He had watched and waited until they were alone and absorbed with one another. He had meant to walk right up to the two of them—then pull the trigger. Then, so that Taylor's blood and bone would shatter over Tia . . .

Taylor leapt to his feet, dragging Tia up with him, pressing her behind him.

Weir had the advantage. Taylor had come here unarmed.

"Hello, there—Colonel!" he said contemptuously. "And Miss McKenzie—oh, excuse me, Mrs. Douglas. That's right, you married him, but came to me. Well, well."

"How did you get here, Weir?" Taylor demanded.

"Oh, Douglas! You do seem to think that you're the only man who knows the woods, the streams, the oceans . . . I grew up here, too, you red bastard. No, I don't have the savage blood in me that makes a swamp rat, but I sure as hell can escape a knot, dive into the ocean, make the shore—and then find my way back here."

"You escaped the ship," Tia said.

"My love!" he exclaimed. "Nothing would keep me from you. Having a taste of all that is offered . . . well, I simply hunger and pine for more."

"Raymond Weir, you meant to kill my father. I loathe and despise you."

"And you, Tia, are nothing but a strumpet and a whore," Weir said. "Don't fear. I don't love you anymore, Tia. When I finish with you, there are armies out there who are welcome to you!"

"Call my wife a whore again, Weir, and I'll kill you," Taylor told him. He sounded confident. Fool. What the hell was he going to do? Weir held the cocked gun.

"Douglas!" Weir said. "By God, but I do despise you. Do you want her to die, too? Get away from her. I won't kill you, Tia. I'll just make you wish you were dead. You think you could make a fool out of me? Take down my men, and I would meekly go to prison and forget? Oh, no, my love. You want to be part of this war? You can pay the price of it as well."

"This war is lost!" Taylor said. "Give it up, Weir. The South that you knew is dead and gone, never to come again."

"Never!" Weir said. "The South is a taste and a feel, and it is honor—"

"Yes! The South can be a taste and feel of what is beauty and honor and graciousness. But you would take all that from her. You call yourself honorable?" Taylor demanded harshly.

"You don't understand. The courage to kill McKenzie when others hadn't the strength or power to pluck a viper from our nest is honor, sir! Now . . . Tia! Ah, Tia! You beautiful, beautiful little *whore,* come to me."

Taylor had only one chance. Maybe a stupid chance. But it was all he had.

He drew Tia from around him—astounded to hear her cry out and throw a thick handful of dirt into Weir's eyes. Weir swore, reaching for his eyes.

Taylor catapulted hard against the man. His flying assault threw them both against the earth.

They struggled for the gun. He had Weir's wrist, fighting for control.

There was a sudden explosion of sound. Raymond Weir went deadly still. Taylor looked into the man's eyes as they glazed over.

The gun had gone off. The bullet had barely missed Taylor. It had lodged deep inside Weir's head, taking Weir just as he had intended to take Taylor.

"Taylor!"

Tia screamed his name. She was at his side, and in his arms. He cradled her to him, and held her, and held her, and held her . . .

It was some time later before they could get up and go back to the house, and have someone else go to the pool for Weir's body. It would be some time, Taylor thought, before he would enjoy the pool again.

But not before he would love his wife.

The war had taught him the lesson that life was precious.

He had never learned it so thoroughly as that day.

That night, she touched him with a tenderness greater than any he had ever known. He made love to her with an equal, heartfelt fervor, passionate, forceful, and humbled.

For all the time that they could be together, he held her. Each night he made love to her.

Every moment, he thanked God for her.

Someday, they would have a real future, but . . .

Time, like life, was precious. It slipped away far too quickly.

They both knew it. They cherished the moments they shared. They touched, they talked earnestly, they were passionate, they were tender . . .

It wasn't over.

Soon, he would have to leave.

There was one more skirmish in Florida, occurring in January of 1865. The Florida troops were victorious. Julian wrote Taylor that there had been little of a victory celebration then. The war was lost. To many, many men, it was far too obvious. Many wished they could walk away. Some deserted. Others could not walk away. They had to see it through to the bitter end.

Lincoln's speech at his second inauguration spoke well of the man. He wanted peace, not punishment. He wanted to welcome the South back to the Union. "With malice toward none, and justice for all," he said in his heartfelt, country manner of eloquence.

Grant was finally the man to win the war. He hammered at Petersburg, never giving up until the desperate city was forced to surrender.

The way to Richmond was open. The Southern capital was abandoned. The government ran.

Taylor was at Appomattox Courthouse the day Lee surrendered. He was able to salute his weary old friend as he gave up the battle, and the death. All around him, North and South, soldiers hailed him as one of the greatest generals ever to rise in America. *America.* They had been North and South. And now, again, they were Americans.

On the day that it ended, Taylor, Jesse, and Ian were able to meet up. In the next few days, they were able to find Brent and Mary. It was another few days before they were able to receive leave together and ride home.

At that moment, home meant Cimarron. To all of them. Sydney had gone there soon after Christmas, knowing that she had done all she could for the Underground Railroad, and that her mother and father would be there.

James and his extended family had traveled north after the events at Cimarron. It had seemed a time to be with family.

It was nearly the middle of April when they heard the news that Lincoln had been assassinated. It was a bitter blow. President Johnson might be a good man who would try, but the Congress would stand up against him. They would enter into a bitter struggle. Taylor was bitter himself, but not surprised; President Lincoln had seen his own death coming. He was legend now, a man greater than he had ever imagined himself to be.

A few days later, their long journey home was almost over. They had tried to find Julian in north Florida, since the last of the Florida troops had yet to surrender.

They learned he was at Cimarron.

When they arrived at the property, Julian was waiting in the parlor, having heard they were coming. "I have something for you," he told Taylor.

And the bundle Julian carried was suddenly in Taylor's arms.

"A daughter. If she's anything like her mother, you're in serious trouble. She was born the day we heard about the surrender. Tia named her Hope."

He held his child, shaking. He found the strength to hold her more tightly, afraid that he would drop her. She had a head of dark, curly hair already, and huge, huge dark but multicolored eyes with just a touch of gold.

Taylor cradled his child to his heart, and took the stairs two at a time.

In his wife's room, he fell to his knees at the bedside, and Tia touched his hair, threading her fingers through it, drawing his head to hers. She kissed him with tears, with love, with tenderness, with passion . . .

And at last, with all the promise of a real future stretching before them . . .

The land was torn. Beaten, scarred.

But peace had been declared.

And the healing could come at last.

"Hope?" Tia questioned softly.

"Hope," he agreed. And kissed his wife again.

Epilogue

September, 1876
Cimarron

Jarrett McKenzie stood in the graveyard, one booted foot upon an old, weather-worn border stone. The sudden sound of a screech made him wince, but he smiled and shook his head as he did so. There had been a lot of screeches thus far—and there would be many more to follow. Tara had warned him it would be so when he had determined to invite the entire family for a post-Centennial Fourth of July celebration. That's what happened when you had that many children about. Lord, how many of them were there now? They seemed to be all over the place, a new race of being, totally populating the lawn.

"Father!"

It was Tia coming toward him. Still delicate and tiny, despite the five little Douglases she and Taylor had contributed to the family tree.

All these years gone by . . . and he still felt a special warmth in his heart when he saw his daughter. A daughter was definitely a man's jewel, so he had determined with his son-in-law at the birth of Jessica Lyn—a girl after four boys. He adored his sons, he always would; he respected them now as men. But his daughter. . . .

She was flushed, a bit breathless. He had watched her running with the younger children below on the lawn. She was delighted to be back, and with the children, having just returned from a long-planned trip to Egypt with Taylor. They had come home by way of New York and stopped at the Centennial Exposition in Philadelphia on their way home.

Tia's excitement over the exposition was encouraging. War wounds were beginning to heal. More than a decade after the conflict, there were still huge slashes and scars from the bitter divide to mar the country. But most men wanted to look to the future—and peace.

"Father! Why are you standing up here in the cemetery? Mother wants to have birthday cake for the children."

"Which children?" he teased.

"The September children," she said with a laugh. Her dark eyes flashed with humor. She lifted on her toes, hugged him, and kissed his cheek. He slipped an arm around her. They looked down on the lawn together.

Young Anthony Malloy, the oldest of all the McKenzie third generation, was nineteen, and had just returned from classes in Tallahassee. Like his cousin Taylor Douglas, he wanted to be an architect, and he was seated at one of the picnic tables now with Taylor, who was making a point, building with the picnic ware.

Taylor had come home from the war to build many of the houses he had dreamed of creating. He claimed that his wife still loved her family home, Cimarron, above any mansion he had ever tried to build for her—and his brood.

Anthony seemed oblivious to the nearby teasing of his half-siblings, twins Ana and Ashley Long. Good-naturedly, he ruffled the girls' hair as he listened to Taylor. Young master Sean McKenzie was not being so tolerant—when his sisters Ariana and Kelly sprayed him with water from the gardening hose, he turned on them with what might have been a vengeance, but helped by cousins Conar, Allen, and Tia's oldest boy, Robert, they turned the tables on the girls, and the laughter and shrieking rose again, especially after they showered Risa, who was walking across the lawn with fresh lemonade.

Jerome had gone back into shipbuilding, he and Risa owned a marina—and even allowed Yankee tourists down to stay at one of the houses they kept on the beach. Ian had gone into politics, determined to see the state completely repatriated with all due dignity.

Julian and Brent continued to practice medicine. Sydney and Jesse remained in Washington most of the time. Jesse worked with the Pinkerton Agency, while Sydney pursued equal rights for all—men and women. But even Sydney and her brood had come south for this occasion. She sat with her father now, loathe to let go of James's arm, even to show her baby sister, Mary, the correct way to hold yarn.

"There were times when I never thought that I would see such a day as this," Jarrett said softly to his daughter.

"I know," she said. "But we did survive it all, we survived it so well as a family! Thanks to you, and Uncle James, of course."

"We were at odds throughout the war."

"We were all at odds. But you taught us all something we never forgot."

"Oh? And what is that?" he asked, turning to his daughter.

"Love," she said, smiling, and her dimples showed, and he thought again that she was, indeed, his treasure.

"Love, hm. Well."

She laughed. "Courage . . . perseverance! And we made it and oh, Father! You can't begin to imagine the things we saw at the exposition! Dual telegraphs, telephones! New steam engines, new ideas, air-conditioning, motor-vehicles . . . oh, some of them we won't really see for years, of course, but the prototypes are out there."

"Your children will see it all," he told her.

She smiled. "Maybe I'll see it, and maybe it will all come more quickly than you imagine, maybe we'll all see it."

"Maybe, and if I don't, well . . ."

"Father—"

He shushed her. "I've lived to see peace. I've lived to see my family grow, and my children and nephews and nieces become thoughtful, intelligent, and caring adults. I know that whatever the future brings, you will soar along with it, bringing dignity to men and women of different races and colors and creeds."

"Thank you," she told him, smiling at him. She smoothed back a stray strand of dark hair. "The state is booming, Father. But it isn't all peace, yet. Real peace may take many more decades."

"It may. But we're entering a new era. Of invention, of posterity." Another screech rose from the lawn. "Oh, Lord! An era of McKenzies!" he said with a groan.

"You love it all, and you don't even pretend to be an old grouch well!" she teased. "Shall we have cake?" Tia asked.

Jarrett looked at his daughter, and at the lawn of Cimarron, where his family played.

He glanced at his father's grave.

If you could only see this wild land of yours now, Father! Peopled with those who will love it, who will see it into the future . . .

"Father?" Tia said, as he still hesitated.

"I was just thinking that my father would be very proud," he said. Then he drew her arm through his and started down the lawn.

"I hope so," Tia said as they walked. "He really believed in people. I think he might be proudest of Sydney. You know, she's working very hard toward women getting the vote."

"What?" he demanded, stopping.

"Father! You know that women are equally intelligent and—"

She broke off, aware that he was laughing. She flushed.

"Well, it's probably a long way off."

"Well, the future waits for no man," he said. "Come, let's go have cake with the children."

"How many of them are there now?"

"You can't count my grandchildren?"

"Well, there are nephews and nieces down there, too—"

"And another one with us now, I think."

He stopped, arching a brow. "Tia . . ."

"Father, it was a very romantic trip down the Nile."

"But . . . six? I had thought there was a time when you didn't want children."

She smiled. "I didn't want death, war, or pain. We're at peace."

"Death and pain still come."

"I know. But we've met so much together . . . I'm not afraid anymore, maybe that's it." She hesitated, glancing to the lawn, smiling at her father again. "I share all that's good with a very special man; he'll stand behind me whatever pain or sorrow we meet in life as well."

"You have everything," Jarrett told her.

"And six little people to share it all with!" she laughed.

He cradled her chin gently. "Your husband must be very happy."

"He is."

"*My* wife and my children have been everything in life," he told her. "Everything. And it's my greatest happiness that you have known the same. But, you're right. Let's head down for cake before those children eat it all, eh?"

And so they did.

War and peace.

Time . . .

Time always went on.

And so it would.

Florida Chronology

(And Events Which Influenced Her People)

1492   Christopher Columbus discovers the "New World."

1513   Florida discovered by Ponce de Leon. Juan Ponce de Leon sights Florida from his ship on March 27th, steps on shore near present day St. Augustine in early April.

1539   Hernando de Soto lands on west coast of the peninsula, near present day Tampa.

1564   The French arrive and establish Fort Caroline on the St. Johns River. Immediately following the establishment of the French fort, Spain dispatches Pedro de Menendez to get rid of the French invaders, "pirates and perturbers of the public peace." Menendez dutifully captures the French stronghold and slays or enslaves the inhabitants.

1565   Pedro de Menendez founds St. Augustine, the first permanent European settlement in what is now the United States.

1586   Sir Francis Drake attacks St. Augustine, burning and plundering the settlement.

1698   Pensacola is founded.

1740   British General James Oglethorpe invades Florida from Georgia.

1763   At the end of the Seven Year's War, or the French and Indian War, both the East and West Florida Territories are ceded to Britain.

1762–1783   British Rule in East and West Florida.

1774   The "shot heard round the world" is fired in Concord, Massachusetts Colony.

1776   The War of Independence begins; many of the British Loyalists flee to Florida.

1783   By the Treaty of Paris, Florida is returned to the Spanish.

1812–1815   The War of 1812.

1813–1814   The Creek Wars ("Red-Stick" land is decimated. Numerous Indians seek new lands south with the "Seminoles.").

1814   General Andrew Jackson captures Pensacola.

1815   The Battle of New Orleans.

1817–1818   The First Seminole War—Americans accuse the Spanish of aiding the Indians in their raids across the border. Hungry for more territory, settlers seek to force Spain into ceding the Floridas to the United States by their claims against the Spanish government for its inability to properly handle the situation within the territories.

1819   Don Luis de Onis, Spanish minister to the United States, and Secretary of State John Quincy Adams sign a treaty by which the Floridas will become part of the United States.

1821   The Onis–Adams Treaty is ratified. An act of congress makes the two Floridas one territory. Jackson becomes the military governor, but relinquishes the post after a few months.

1822   The first legislative council meets at Pensacola. Members from St. Augustine travel fifty-nine days by water to attend.

1823   The second legislative council meets at St. Augustine: the western delegates are shipwrecked and barely escape death.

1824   The third session meets at Tallahassee, a halfway point selected as a main order of business and approved at the second session. Tallahassee becomes the first territorial capital.

1823   The Treaty of Moultrie Creek is ratified by major Seminole chiefs and the federal government. The ink is barely dry before Indians are complaining that the lands are too small and white settlers are petitioning the government for a policy of Indian removal.

1832   Payne's Landing: Numerous chiefs sign a treaty agreeing to move west to Arkansas as long as seven of their number are able to see and approve the lands. The treaty is ratified at Fort Gibson, Arkansas.

Many chiefs also protest the agreement.

1835   Summer: Wiley Thompson claims that Osceola has repeatedly reviled him in his own office with foul language and orders his arrest. Osceola is handcuffed and incarcerated.

1835   November: Charlie Emathla, after agreeing to removal to the west, is murdered. Most scholars agree Osceola led the party that carried out the execution. Some consider the murder a personal vengeance, others believe it was ordered by numerous chiefs since an Indian who would leave his people to aid the whites should forfeit his own life.

1835   December 28th: Major Francis Dade and his troops are massacred as they travel from Fort Brooke to Fort King.

Also on December 28th—Wiley Thompson and a companion are killed outside the walls of Fort King. The sutler Erastus Rogers and his two clerks are also murdered by members of the same raiding party, led by Osceola.

1835   December 31st: The First Battle of the Withlacoochee—Osceola leads the Seminoles.

1836   January: Major General Winfield Scott is ordered by the secretary of war to take command in Florida.

February 4th: Dade County established in South Florida in memory of Francis Langhorne Dade.

March 16th: The senate confirms Richard Keith Call governor of the Florida Territory.

June 21st: Call, a civilian governor, is given command of the Florida forces after the failure of Scott's strategies and the military disputes between Scott and General Gaines.

Call attempts a "summer campaign," and is as frustrated in his efforts as his predecessor.

December 9th: Major Sidney Jesup takes charge.

1837   June 2nd: Osceola and Sam Jones release or "abduct" nearly 700 Indians awaiting deportation to the west from Tampa.

October 27th: Osceola is taken under a white flag of truce; Jesup is denounced by whites and Indians alike for the action.

November 29th: Coacoochee, Cowaya, sixteen warriors and two women escape Ft. Marion.

Christmas Day: Jesup has the largest fighting force assembled in Florida during the conflict, nearly 9,000 men. Under his command, Colonel Zachary Taylor leads the Battle of Okeechobee. The Seminoles choose to stand their ground and fight, inflicting greater losses to whites despite the fact that they were severely outnumbered.

1838   January 31st: Osceola dies at Ft. Marion, South Carolina—A strange side note to a sad tale: Dr. Wheedon, presiding white physician for Osceola, cut off and preserved Osceola's head. Wheedon's heirs reported that the good doctor would hang the head on the bedstead of one of his three children should they misbehave. The head passed to his son-in-law, Dr. Daniel Whitehurst, who gave it to Dr. Valentine Mott. Dr. Mott had a medical and pathological museum, and it is believed that the head was lost when his museum burned in 1866.

May: Zachary Taylor takes command when Jesup's plea to be relieved is answered at last on April 29th.

The Florida legislature debates statehood.

1839 December: Because of his arguments with federal authorities regarding the Seminole War, Richard Keith Call is removed as governor.

Robert Raymond Reid is appointed in his stead.

1840 April 24th: Zachary Taylor is given permission to leave command of what is considered to be the harshest military position in the country.

Walker Keith Armistead takes command.

December 1840–January 1841: John T. MacLaughlin leads a flotilla of men in dugouts across the Everglades from east to west; his party become the first white men to do so.

September: William Henry Harrison is elected president of the United States; the Florida War is considered to have cost Martin Van Buren reelection.

John Bell replaces Joel Poinsett as secretary of war. Robert Reid is ousted as territorial governor, and Richard Keith Call is reinstated.

1841 April 4th: President William Henry Harrison dies in office: John Tyler becomes president of the U.S.

May 1st: Coacoochee determines to turn himself in. He is escorted by a man who will later become extremely well known— Lieutenant William Tecumseh Sherman. Sherman writes to his future wife that the Florida war is a good one for a soldier; he will get to know the Indian who may become the "chief enemy" in time.

May 31st: Walker Keith Armistead is relieved. Colonel William Jenkins Worth takes command.

1842　　May 10th: Winfield Scott is informed that the administration has decided there must be an end to hostilities as soon as possible. August 14th: Aware that he cannot end hostilities and send all the Indians West, Colonel Worth makes offers to the remaining Indians to leave, or accept boundaries. The war, he declares, is over.

It has cost a fledgling nation thirty to forty million dollars and the lives of seventy-four commissioned officers. The Seminoles have been reduced from tens of thousands to hundreds scattered about in pockets. The Seminoles (inclusive here, as they were seen during the war, as all Florida Indians) have, however, kept their place in the peninsula; those remaining are the undefeated. The army, too, has learned new tactics, mostly regarding partisan and guerilla warfare. Men who will soon take part in the greatest conflict to tear apart the nation have practiced the art of battle here: William T. Sherman, Braxton Bragg, George Gordon Meade, Joseph E. Johnston, and more, including soon-to-be President Zachary Taylor.

1845　　March 3rd: President John Tyler signs the bill that makes Florida the 27th state of the United States of America.

1855–58　The conflict known as the Third Seminole War takes place with a similar outcome to the earlier confrontations—money spent, lives lost, and the Indians entrenched more deeply into the Everglades.

1859　　Robert E. Lee is sent in to arrest John Brown after his attempt to initiate a slave rebellion with an assault on Harpers Ferry, Virginia (later West Virginia). The incident escalates ill will between the North and the South. Brown is executed on December 2nd.

1860   The first Florida cross-state railroad goes into service.

November 6th: Abraham Lincoln is elected to the presidency and many Southern states begin to call for special legislative sessions. Although there are many passionate Unionists in the state, most Florida politicians are ardent in lobbying for secession. Towns, cities, and counties rush to form or enlarge militia companies. Even before the state is able to meet for its special session, civil and military leaders plan to demand the turnover of federal military installations.

1861   January 10th: Florida votes to secede from the Union, the third Southern state to do so.

February: Florida joins the Confederate States of America.

Through late winter and early spring, the Confederacy struggles to form a government and organize the armed forces while the states recruit fighting men. Jefferson Davis is president of the newly formed country. Stephan Mallory, of Florida, becomes C.S.A. secretary of the navy.

April 12th–14th: Confederate forces fire on Ft. Sumter, S.C., and the first blood is shed when an accidental explosion kills Private Hough, who then has the distinction of being the first federal casualty.

Federal forces fear a similar action at Ft. Pickens, Pensacola Bay, Florida. Three forts guarded the bay, McRee and Barrancas on the land side, and Pickens on the tip of forty-mile long Santa Rosa Island. Federal

Lieutenant Adam J. Slemmer spiked the
guns at Barrancas, blew up the ammunition
at McRee, and moved his meager troops to
Pickens, where he was eventually reinforced
by 500 men. Though Florida troops took
the navy yard, retention of the fort by the
Federals nullified the usefulness to the Rebs
of what was considered the most important
navy yard south of Norfolk.

July 18th: First Manassas, or the First Battle
of Bull Run, Virginia—both sides get their
first real taste of battle. Southern troops are
drawn from throughout the states, including
Florida. Already, the state, which had been
so eager to secede, sees her sons being
shipped northward to fight, and her coast
being left to its own defenses by a government with different priorities.

November: Robert E. Lee inspects coastal
defenses as far south as Fernandina and de-
cides the major ports of Charleston, Savannah, and Brunswick are to be defended,
adding later that the small force posted at
St. Augustine was like an invitation to
attack.

1862   February: Florida's Governor Milton publicly states his despair for Florida citizens as
more of the state's troops are ordered north
after Grant captures two major confederate
strongholds in Tennessee.

February 28th: A fleet of 26 Federal ships
sets sail to occupy Fenrandina, Jacksonville,
and St. Augustine. March 8th: St. Augustine
surrenders, and though Jacksonville and
other points north and south along the coast
will change hands several times during the
war, St. Augustine will remain in Union
hands. The St. Johns River becomes a rib-
bon of guerilla troop movement for both
sides. Many Floridians begin to despair of

"East Florida," fearing that the fickle populace has all turned Unionist.

March 8th: Under the command of Franklin Buchanan, the *C.S.S. Virginia,* formerly the scuttled Union ship *Merrimac,* sailed into Hampton Roads to battle the Union ships blockading the channel. She devastates Federal ships until the arrival of the poorly prepared and leaking Federal entry into the "ironclad" fray, the *U.S.S. Monitor.* The historic battle of the ironclads ensues. Neither ship emerged a clear victor; the long-term advantage went to the Union since the Confederacy was then unable to break the blockade when it had appeared, at first, that the *Virginia* might have sailed all the way to attack Washington, D.C.

April 2nd: Apalachicola is attacked by a Federal landing force. The town remains a no-man's-land throughout the war.

April 6th–8th: Union and Confederate forces engage in the battle of Shiloh. Both claim victories; both suffer horrible loses with over twenty thousand killed, wounded, or missing.

April 25th: New Orleans falls, and the Federal grip on the South becomes more of a vise.

Spring: The Federal blockade begins to tighten and much of the state becomes unlivable. Despite its rugged terrain, the length of the peninsula, and the simple difficulty of logistics, blockade runners know that they can dare Florida waterways simply because the Union can't possibly guard the extensive coastline of the state. Florida's contribution becomes more and more that of a breadbasket as she strips herself and provides salt, beef, smuggled supplies, and manpower to the Confederacy.

May 9th: Pensacola is evacuated by the Rebs and occupied by Federal forces.

May 20th: Union landing party is successfully attacked by Confederates near St. Marks.

May 22nd: Union Flag Officer DuPont writes to his superiors, with quotes, that had the Union not abandoned Jacksonville, the state would have split, and East Florida would have entered the war on the Union side.

Into summer: Fierce action continues in Virginia: battle of Fair Oaks, or Seven Pines, May 31st, the Seven Days Battles, May 25th–7th, the battle of Mechanicsville, June 26th, Gaines Mill, or Cold Harbor, June 27th. More Florida troops leave the state to replace the men killed in action in these battles, and in other engagements in Alabama, Louisiana, and along the Mississippi.

Salt becomes even more necessary: Florida has numerous saltworks along the Gulf side of the state. Union ships try to find them, confiscate what they can, and destroy the works.

August 30th: Second Battle of Manassas, or Bull Run.

September 16th and 17th: The battle of Antietam, or Sharpsburg, takes place in Maryland, where the "single bloodiest day of fighting" occurs.

September 23rd: The preliminary text of the Emancipation Proclamation is published. It will take effect on January 1st, 1863. Lincoln previously drafted the document, but waited for a Union victory to publish it; both sides claimed Antietam, but the Rebels were forced to withdraw back to Virginia.

October 5th: Federals recapture Jacksonville.

December 11th–15th: The Battle of Fredericksburg.

December 31st: The Battle of Murfreesborough or Stones River, Tennessee.

1863   March 20th: A Union landing party at St. Andrew's Bay, Florida, is attacked and most Federals are captured or killed.

March 31st: Jacksonville is evacuated by the Union forces again.

May 1st–4th: The Battle of Chancellorsville. Lee soundly beats Hooker, but on the 2nd, General Stonewall Jackson is accidentally shot and mortally wounded by his own men. He dies on the 10th.

June: Southern commanders determine anew to bring the war to the Northern front. A campaign begins that will march the Army of Northern Virginia through Virginia, Maryland, and on to Pennsylvania. In the west, the campaign along the Mississippi continues with Vicksburg under siege. In Florida, there is little action other than skirmishing and harrying attacks along the coast. More Florida boys are conscripted into the regular army. The state continues to produce cattle and salt for the Confederacy.

July 1st: Confederates move towards Gettysburg along the Chambersburg Pike. Four miles west of town, they meet John Buford's Union cavalry.

July 2nd: At Gettysburg, places like the Peach Orchard and Devil's Den become names that live in history.

July 3rd: Pickett's disastrous charge.

July 4th: Lee determines to retreat to Virginia.

July 4th: Vicksburg surrenders.

July continues: The Union soldiers take a very long time to chase Lee. What might have been an opportunity to end the war is lost.

July 13th: Draft riots in New York.

August 8th: Lee attempts to resign. President Jefferson Davis rejects his resignation.

August continues into fall: Renewed Union interest in Florida begins to develop as assaults against Charleston and forts in South Carolina bring recognition by the North that Florida is a hotbed for blockade runners, salt, and cattle. Union commanders in the South begin to plan a Florida campaign.

September 20th: the South is victorious in the Western field of battle when General Bragg routes General Rosecrans at Chickamauga.

November: The Union army is besieged at Chattanooga. On the 24th, Sherman crosses the river and, the next day, the Confederates are forced to flee the field.

1864   February 7th: Union General Seymour comes ashore in Jacksonville, Florida, preparing for an offensive.

February 20th: The battle of Olustee, Florida, takes place. The Southern forces win the battle when the South is weakly faring elsewhere.

April 9th: Union General Grant tells Meade that "Wherever Lee goes, there you will head also."

April 12th: Bedford Forrest's Confederate cavalry storm Ft. Pillow, Tennessee. Many of the soldiers at the fort are black, causing the North to claim that the battle was a massacre. Later, the Confederates involved will be accused of committing horrible atrocities.

April 30th: Joseph Emory Davis, son of Jefferson Davis, dies in a fall from the balcony of the White House of the Confederacy.

May 5th and 6th: The Battle of the Wilderness takes place. The terrible fires that break out make battle even more horrible for the men wounded and left to die in the tangled brush.

The Union does not retreat.

May 8th: Anderson, commanding Longstreet's forces, gets between the Yanks and Richmond. The Confederates entrench, and the Battle of Spotsylvania Courthouse begins.

May 10th: Skirmish at Beaver Dam Station.

May 11th: At Yellow Tavern, the great cavalier Dixie, J.E.B. Stuart is mortally wounded. The South loses another of its most able commanders.

May 15th: The Battle of New Market. Desperate, Confederate General Breckinridge commits the 247 cadets of the Virginia Military Academy to the battle. There are ten dead and forty-seven wounded cadets.

Through the end of May, the Northern and Southern troops clash in their race south.

June 1st: Grant begins to batter Cold Harbor. The heavy fighting lasts from June 3rd through June 12th. The cannon fire can be heard in Richmond. No matter what Grant's losses, Lee holds. Grant heads south to try to get to Richmond through Petersburg. By the end of June, both armies are entrenched.

July 12th: President Lincoln is on a parapet at Ft. Stevens where Early's Confederates are sending sniper fire. "Get down, you damned fool, or you'll be killed," he is told. The messenger is a young officer named Oliver Wendell Holmes, Jr. The president takes no offense. Ducking down, Lincoln comments that Holmes knows how to talk to a civilian.

July 30th: The Crater. A Union decision to mine a crater beneath the Southern lines at

Petersburg goes horribly awry. Hundreds of Rebels are instantly killed, but the attacking Union soldiers become trapped in the crater and are slaughtered by the defenders. Four thousand Federal troops are killed or wounded within three hours of fighting. Confederate losses are about 1500.

August 31st: Hood desperately telegraphs Lee to come to Atlanta—he must abandon the city.

September 2nd: Federal troops occupy Atlanta.

September 5th: Declared a day of celebration by President Lincoln as Atlanta has fallen and Admiral Farragut has taken Mobile Bay.

October 1st: A Confederate soldier finds the body of a woman on the beach. She is Rose Greenhow, the Confederate spy, drowned while escaping her ship from Europe after it was accosted by the Union blockade. The soldier had taken some of the gold she carried; discovering her identity, he gave it back.

November 8th: Lincoln defeats George B. McClellan to win a second presidential term.

November 11th: Union troops in Atlanta begin the systematic destruction of food supplies and arms, anything that might be left behind, for the South. Sherman's "scorched earth" policy is given full measure. November 16th: he begins marching through the heart of Georgia, heading for the sea.

December 22nd: Sherman sends Lincoln the message, "I beg to present you, as a Christmas gift, the city of Savannah."

1865   January 15th: Fort Fisher, at the port of Wilmington, North Carolina, the Confederates last real point of contact with the outside world, surrenders.

February 17th: Columbia is occupied and destroyed. Ft. Sumter, held by the South from the first action, falls back to the Union. Charleston is abandoned.

March 4th: The Battle of Natural Bridge, Leon County, Florida. The "Baby Corps," troops under General William Miller and troops that included boys from the Seminary West of the Suwannee (now known as Florida State University) repel three strong assaults by Union General Newton and save Tallahassee. It is the only Southern capital not taken by Union troops before Lee's surrender. Also on March 4th, President Lincoln is inaugurated for his second term.

March 24th: Lee makes plans to remove his army from Petersburg, knowing all is lost if he does not. On the 25th, a plan to break through the Federal line has a handful of "deserters" appearing to remove Federal defenses while Gordon makes an assault. There are 4,000 Rebel losses—many of whom surrendered rather than face the slaughtering fury of fire set upon them.

March 28th, The Army of the Potomac prepares for its final assault. 125,000 Union troops are gathered to face fewer than 50,000 remaining Confederates. Lee hopes to join Johnston and make a last stand in North Carolina, the "Tar Heel" state.

April 1st: Florida's Governor, John Miton, foreseeing the fall of the Confederacy, commits suicide.

April 2nd: The Confederates abandon Petersburg. A. P. Hill is killed in the fighting. The Confederate capital is lost; Richmond, too, abandoned.

April 9th: The Army of Northern Virginia fights its last battle. Knowing all is lost, Lee, the great commander, surrenders to Grant. He tells his men to go home and be "as good citizens as you were soldiers." On April 10th, the hungry Rebels receive rations from the Union army. The Confederate government receives word of the surrender, and heads deeper into North Carolina. On the 12th, General Gordon leads the official surrender, accepted by Joshua Chamberlain of Gettysburg fame.

April 14th: Lincoln is shot by John Wilkes Booth at Ford's Theater. He survives through the night, and dies on the 15th.

April 16th: Confederate General Johnston surrenders 31,000 Rebel troops.

June 2nd: General E. Kirby Smith surrenders his troops. The most ardent of Southern generals, he is the last to surrender such troops in the field. His mother has remained in St. Augustine throughout the war. One of his officers, General Shelby, will not surrender, but takes his troops south to fight in Mexico.

July 7th: Four of the Lincoln conspirators are hanged; four are imprisoned at Ft. Jefferson on the Dry Tortugas off the Florida Keys. Dr. Mudd, who treated Booth's leg, is later pardoned for his work in the yellow fever epidemic of 1867.

President Johnson tries hard to follow Lincoln's resolves for peace and forgiveness; he cannot help the bitterness that will divide the country for decades to come. Only one man will die a "war criminal," Henry Wirz, who commanded Andersonville, notorious for being a prison where death was prevalent and sometimes preferable to life. He was hanged—slowly. It took him seven minutes to die. President Johnson will see most of the Southern cabinet paroled; Jefferson Davis will suffer imprisonment for several years after the war.

Lee will go on to teach, and, as he had instructed his men, he will look to peace with the same determination with which he fought in the war.

Florida will face Reconstruction as do the other Southern states, but she will be partially saved by those factors that still make men and women love her and hate her—the sun, the heat, and the humidity! Carpetbaggers will come, but not nearly so many as arrive in other areas of the deep South. In the years ahead, Florida will reach her golden age with the rich purchasing their "winter" homes, inventors coming in droves along with the one true saving grace of the state—air-conditioning!

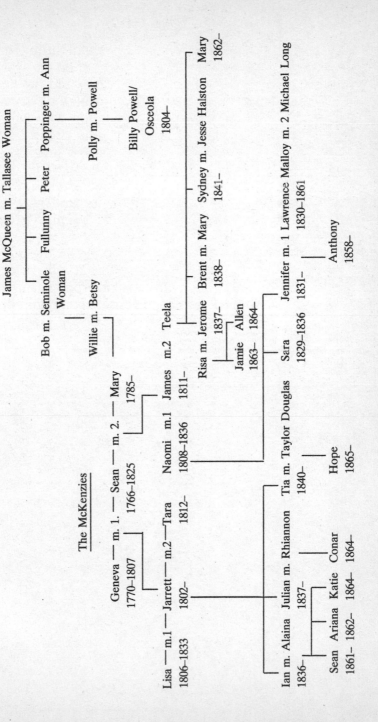

The Seminole Connection

James McQueen m. Tallasee Woman

Bob m. Seminole Woman   Fullunny   Peter   Poppinger m. Ann

Willie m. Betsy   Polly m. Powell

Billy Powell/Osceola
1804–

The McKenzies

Geneva — m. 1. — Sean — m. 2. — Mary
1770–1807   1766–1825   1785–

Lisa — m.1 — Jarrett — m.2 — Tara   Naomi m.1   James   m.2 Teela
1806–1833   1802–   1812–   1808–1836   1811–

Brent m. Mary   Sydney m. Jesse Halston   Mary
1838–   1841–   1862–

Risa m. Jerome
1837–

Jamie   Allen
1863–   1864–

Jennifer m. 1 Lawrence Malloy m. 2 Michael Long
1831–   1830–1861

Sara
1829–1836

Anthony
1858–

Ian m. Alaina   Julian m. Rhiannon   Tia m. Taylor Douglas
1836–   1837–   1840–

Sean   Ariana   Katie   Conar
1861–   1862–   1864–   1864–

Hope
1865–